"AS OF THIS DAY, I AM NO LONGER A SON OF PANSHINEA.

I relinquish all claims to the throne of Cho. And, on this day, I declare myself no longer a son of the House of Star. I am a *tezar,* and my heritage comes from the lost House of Flame."

The watching crowd reacted with a roar of startlement. Palaton put his hands up, let his *bahdur* free, let it shine. He stepped before the crowd to give his farewell—and Panshinea's first blow hit him. It knocked him off his feet.

"Remand yourself into my custody!"

Hoarsely, determined, Palaton got out, "No."

He staggered to right himself, gasping for breath, feeling the immense power of the emperor. He managed to turn around, and he saw Panshinea standing with his palms upraised, his red-gold hair streaming about his horn crown. All pretense of civilization had been stripped away, and before Palaton could shield himself, Panshinea struck again—with the *bahdur* of legend which only emperors could use. . . .

CHARLES INGRID'S
Magnificent DAW
Science Fiction Novels:

***THE PATTERNS OF CHAOS** Series:*
RADIUS OF DOUBT (Book One)
PATH OF FIRE (Book Two)
THE DOWNFALL MATRIX (Book Three)
SOULFIRE (Book Four)

***THE MARKED MAN** Series:*
THE MARKED MAN (Book One)
THE LAST RECALL (Book Two)

***THE SAND WARS** Series:*
SOLAR KILL (Book One)
LASERTOWN BLUES (Book Two)
CELESTIAL HIT LIST (Book Three)
ALIEN SALUTE (Book Four)
RETURN FIRE (Book Five)
CHALLENGE MET (Book Six)

SOULFIRE

Patterns of Chaos #4

Charles Ingrid

DAW BOOKS, INC.

DONALD A. WOLLHEIM, FOUNDER

375 Hudson Street, New York, NY 10014

ELIZABETH R. WOLLHEIM
SHEILA E. GILBERT
PUBLISHERS

First Printing, October 1995

1   2   3   4   5   6   7   8   9

DAW TRADEMARK REGISTERED
U.S. PAT. OFF. AND FOREIGN COUNTRIES
—MARCA REGISTRADA
HECHO EN U.S.A.

PRINTED IN THE U.S.A.

Chapter 1

Palaton received two summons the day after Blue Ridge flight school burned down. Both were imperative, and he was disinclined to answer either.

The first came from his emperor, so timely on the heels of disaster that it seemed Panshinea had been prescient considering the time lag of subspace bulletin boards. But Pan had not foreseen the destruction of the pilot's training grounds. He sent an ETA from Sorrow and the Halls of the Compact, demanding the return of his throne, ordering Palaton to relinquish the heirship formally, setting a time and place for their meeting. If Palaton had once thought he could dissuade his emperor from this action, that thought had gone up in smoke with Blue Ridge. As soon as Panshinea learned of that, as well, the heirship would definitely be taken from him.

Most likely over his dead body. The emperor would not want any disputes later. The Choyan line of ascension must remain unmuddied.

Even more distasteful was the summons from the Prophet.

The biotox crew came in the next day, late, almost as though they did not wish to acknowledge what had happened. By the time they arrived, the ashes had cooled, a temporary morgue had already been set up in the only building which still stood, and Hathord, as master of the flight school, was scanning the bodies and matching the dental records with his on-line files. His square, stolid body stood at the screen impassively while the scans did most of the job.

Palaton worked outside, with the main task force of the biotox crew, for the reek of spilled fuel and flame-fighting foam lay spewed over acres. He had done what he could to put the wreckage of the planes to one side, though he received no thanks from the crew for his efforts.

They were his people, Choyan, but the majority of them were the Godless, the God-blind, those Choyan not gifted with the extrasensory perception and talents which made them sensitive to the life which lay with their surroundings. They could not hear the ground soil moan under the scorch of fire and chemicals. They could not feel the tremble of the organic world about them, the silent screams of the ecosystem so damaged and disrupted. They had no senses to detect the vibrancy of God which ran through all things in creation, and it was just as well, for if they had, they would not have been suited for their work.

But that did not mean that the stench of fire and spilled fuel and death did not bother them. He could read it in the lines of their faces as they jumped from their cruisers and readied their shoulder tanks, preparing to lay down detox foam. He could see it in their wiry bodies as they bent their double-elbowed arms to the task of spraying, then plowing, then seeding the damaged earth. The biotechs gave him scarcely a glance as they went out on survey to determine the environmental impact.

Thanks did not lie in their Choyan eyes. Instead, if anyone met his face, it was only for a brief, flinching moment and then they looked away. He set his jaw and worked harder at his task despite the injuries he'd taken in the disaster, despite having lost his Companion to the enemy, despite knowing that the emperor was about to return home and rip the throne away from him, despite everything.

He deserved the condemnation. He'd brought civil war to Cho. Pilot had turned on pilot, destroying Blue Ridge, one of the finest of the flight schools. He had brought aliens here. He had failed to discharge his duties as heir. He had given status to those who were God-blind, and then he'd barged ahead as though he, too, were blind to the patterns of life which the God-in-all had woven through every fabric of Choyan being.

He had been the most blind Choya ever born.

And Palaton was still uncertain if the veil had been lifted from his eyes. In the last few months, much had been revealed, but even more had been clouded. *A wise man knows that he knows very little,* the *tezar* thought as he leaned upon his hand-plow and let the biotox crew part around him like a tidal wave and pass him upon the fields. They sprayed down their enzyme cleaner with an efficiency that was almost lulling in its rhythmic motions.

There was a movement behind him. A tall, chestnut-haired Choya watched him, sprayer held across his chest in a dormant position.

"*Tezar* Palaton."

Tezar. Said grudgingly, as if Palaton had not sacrificed all that he had been to gain the title of pilot. But after this, after all this, how could he blame the other for the bile in his tone?

"Yes." He straightened. The hand-plow vibrated down to idle in his hands, purring quietly.

"I have a message for you." The Choya's face was already soot-streaked, muddying the fine jewelry accents tattooing his cheekbones. "The Prophet says you must come to her."

His lips peeled back from his teeth before he caught himself, smoothed his mouth, and considered the matter. "No," he answered quietly, after a long moment of thought.

The faintly green eyes of the other lit up, as though already knowing what the answer would be.

"She says to tell you that you *will* come to her. Only that you must ensure it is not too late."

"I have no business with the Prophet." He thumbed the plow back up to speed, and its mechanical voice grew loud.

The Choya dared to lay a hand on him, callused fingers gripping him tightly on the lower wrist. A tiny spark of blue arced between them, like a zap of static electricity, *bahdur.* Power calling to power. Palaton looked down at the crewman's hand and then up to his face.

"I was *Changed,*" the Choya confirmed. "By Rand. You must return him to us. He is the Bringer of Change. He is the catalyst which gives us all the power, which brings sight to the God-blind, faith to the Godless."

Palaton felt as though he'd been gut-kicked. He shook the Choya's hand off roughly. "The humankind has been taken from me! Tell your Prophet that. Tell her that if word travels throughout Cho who and what the Bringer is, his life will be worth no more than a piece of yesterday's garbage. Tell her that! Without her silence, I have no hope of finding and restoring him."

Disbelieving, the crewman rocked back. "No. . . ."

"Do you think Blue Ridge was destroyed over nothing? Do

you think I brought civil war to my home because I was
bored? Or because of petty jealousy against another pilot?
They came after us because they wanted to devastate us, and
from the ashes they took Rand to ensure my silence, my com-
plicity. But they don't know exactly what they have in him.
They don't know what he's capable of, and if your mistress
and her crusade endanger his life further, not only will I meet
with her, but she will regret every moment of that meeting!"

His voices roared over that of the hand-plow and other
Choyan nearby looked up from their task.

The messenger stood with thinning lips, then gave a
brusque nod and turned away. Palaton, unblinking, watched
him work through his sector, before turning off the hand-plow
altogether.

He decided that his presence was superfluous and turned
his equipment over to one of the crew so he could go check
on Hat, who was still trying to get control of his emotions.
The Choya'i who wore the bars of crew supervisor met him
beside the equipment pallets.

"You in charge inside?"

"One of them."

"Good." Her nostrils flared slightly as she handed him a
notepad. "Sign for supplies. I need a tally of how many
you're sending out, so I can arrange for transport."

"You're not hauling them?"

"No."

It was strange, but he did not remark on it. He didn't have
to; he saw the flicker of awareness deep in her eyes. He
looked over the supply roster. They were being given field
packs, not the usual crisis supplies. He did not like the impli-
cations, but he made his sweeping signature across the
lightscreen anyway. "I'll get back to you on departees."

She turned away, leaving him facing the burned-out hulk of
the school.

Duty leaned heavily on him. He still had not decided his
course of action, but it seemed best to take one step at a time.
The first step began here.

The dining hall smelled, not of death, but of disinfectant.
Palaton came to a halt, felt his nose wrinkling with its pun-
gency. Even if that had not been offensive to him, his *bahdur*
reacted strongly. The aura of death and destruction permeated

this building. It pooled in the sooty shadows, scraped along the splintering floor, hung from the massive overhead beams. The psychic vibrations of the disaster which had descended upon them resounded so strongly that even those Choyan who had no ability, the God-blind, could feel them.

Palaton swung his head about as Rufeen's booming voice resounded from the galley area. As soon as he tuned in to her, he began mentally reciting almost word for word her lecture—they had rounded up the cadets who were waiting for transport out and reassignment and she was teaching, returning the flight school to as much normalcy as was possible. A whispery scribbling on the scribe boards followed her bombastic speech as the cadets raced to keep up with her. A smile tugged briefly at the corner of Palaton's mouth. Even though these were no longer Blue Ridge students, even though some would flee reassignment and join with the House of Tezars, she was giving it her all and would see that they did, too.

At the far end of the dining hall, plastisheet rippled in the tent structure erected there, catching Palaton's eye as Hat moved in and around the tables within, scanning and identifying the dead.

If he noticed the stench of burned flesh, he did not reflect it. It was as though he were carved from the Earthan matter which represented the sign of his House. Palaton alone knew what an effort it was for him to identify the bodies of the dead cadets. These were his children, in a way, taken in and taught and groomed to be star pilots, *tezars,* masters of the Patterns of Chaos. Each and every death diminished Hat in a way he could probably not have expressed with mere words, but he felt it keenly and Palaton knew it because he felt every death twice as sharply.

Palaton strode across the immense and now far too empty room, a room which had always evoked in him memories of hot fry bread on cold winter days, and mugs of steaming *bren,* dark and fierce as poet's ink, just the way he liked it. The tables and chairs had been previously shoved aside for barricading. What was left when the front doors had been blasted open by Qativar's entrance still lay tossed over. His boots crunched on dirt and ash. By the time he reached the medical tent, the smell of disinfectant had grown disagreeably strong. He paused again, head up, his horn crown aching.

Hat made a note on his scribe board and ordered out a chip. When it was produced, he took the end neatly on his scalpel-implant and punched the chip under the dermaline, just below the horn crown of the corpse. Their skulls being what they were, hard and thick to protect the dual brainpan, and the scalloped edge of the horns which arose from that, were nearly indestructible. The scans of the horn growth, coupled with dental records, made identification incredibly accurate. And the chip containing the medical information, ID, student records and the official report of the disaster, once implanted into the beginning of the horny outgrowth, would stay firmly with the body for whatever official need until interment or cremation when the chip would be removed and stored. Hat worked with a brisk detachment as he made sure the implant was secure, then closed up the coffin bag before he looked across the table at Palaton.

His dark brunet mop, shaggy about his own low scalloped horns and showing a touch of gray at the temples, hung into his eyes. He shook his head impatiently. "How's it going?"

"I came by to ask that of you." Palaton found himself somewhat amazed by Hathord's resilience. He had expected his friend to collapse in dismay, though perhaps this frenzy of activity was itself a denial of all that had happened. "The enzyme foam is down. I don't think the contamination was too bad. You'd have gotten more if a raw recruit had panicked while taking off from the plateau and dumped a planeload of fuel. The crew chief told me they'd be out of here before sunset." He hesitated.

Hat had been reaching for another gurney. He stopped and looked up sharply. "What is it?"

"I'm not sure. It's their attitude, I think. They were not happy to be here."

"Our cleanup contract is current. We're in their sector. I don't think Blue Ridge, given the circumstances, has been too demanding of their time."

"It's not that, Hat." Palaton looked out of the dark plasti-sheet tent rigging, away from the gurneys with their still, silent bags. "They responded a day late to the alarm, as it was. Maybe it's me, maybe it's what I perceive—they didn't want to run into our enemies, then or now. They're not taking us out, although they'll arrange flights for the cadets."

Hat blinked. "Not taking us out?"

"No." Palaton watched his statement sink in. As neatly as the biotox crew could have said it without saying it, the three of them were on their own. "They left us a pallet of journeypack rations and water filters."

"We're on our own," responded Hat slowly.

"Yes."

There was another pause, then Hathord drew a long, shivery breath. He held it a second, then sighed it back. "Well," he said. "We thought this would happen once the emperor got back."

"We wouldn't be standing here talking if he were," Palaton answered dryly. Their emperor was not one to mince words or actions. The treatment by the biotox crew went beyond that.

"Then I've got time to finish this." Hat hooked a thumb, pulling a gurney into scanning position. "Rufeen's got the wings under control until the biotox crew takes them out. I guess you've got to find us sanctuary."

"Leave me the easy job, will you?"

Hat flashed him a quick grin. "Always." His expression became somber. "This is the last of the idents. The humankind's body was not in the wreckage."

Palaton felt a twinge, as though Hathord had been speaking of Rand, but he had not. He had been speaking of the other, the female who had been a Companion to the traitorous pilot Nedar. She should have been among the dead.

"No? Do we need to sift the ashes?"

"No. It didn't burn hot enough to cremate remains. She should have been there."

Alexa gone. Palaton pondered the meaning of that. Had Qativar taken the corpse for some reason, as well as taking Rand from him? Of what good would a dead humankind avail a living one? If Rand were still alive.

He had to be. Palaton would have felt his death, and he had to go on believing that Rand survived. That Qativar and Vihtirne had a use for their hostage or he wouldn't have been taken.

"Palaton."

"I'm thinking." He looked back to Hathord. "The ambassador was notified of his daughter's death. All we can do is send additional notification that we cannot turn over the remains. We're going underground anyway. I can't do anything more for him."

"But why do you think—"

"I don't know! I can't possibly know what Qativar intends to do. He has his House of Tezars now. Allied with Vihtirne, I can only guess that they intend to use the water patent for leverage if they need it. They have Rand to keep me from their throats—" Palaton bared his teeth slightly as he thought aloud, as if tearing their throats out sounded appealing.

Silent tears began to course down Hat's face. He staggered back a step, bolstered unintentionally by a wall of gurneys, their bagged remains already processed. "I'm sorry, Palaton. So very, very sorry." His voices dropped to a husky whisper. "I let Nedar and Alexa use me. I didn't know! I couldn't see what they were doing. . . ."

Palaton reached out to take his friend by the sleeve and draw him close, embracing him in a warm hug. Hat, square and bulky in the way of all who descended from the House of Earth line, stood quietly for a moment in his arms and then hugged back. Palaton, whose genetic qualities came from the Houses of Star and Flame, stood taller and much thinner. He braced himself to support his friend. He could feel Hat's shoulders shake as the Earthan began to cry in earnest for all that he had lost.

His job as flightmaster for Blue Ridge.

Blue Ridge itself, with its hundreds-of-years-old buildings and traditions, refitted for the age of star-faring.

His students, some dead, most alive but taken from him.

Nedar, flamboyant *tezar,* who'd schooled with both of them, Hat's friend and Palaton's enemy. It was Nedar who had led several wings of cadets into the sky to slug it out with Palaton and Rufeen, an ambush whose jaws should have closed irretrievably about them but had failed. Palaton would not miss Nedar. Though the Sky had been an excellent pilot, he had never been admirable, but he knew Hat would miss him. The bond between the two of them had been strong, though it was something Palaton could not understand any more than any fellow Choya could understand the bond between himself and the humankind Rand.

All of this, and more, Palaton's actions had taken from Hat and from Rufeen and from himself. He patted Hat's thick shoulder. "It is I who should apologize to you," he said, and held his friend close while he cried.

Hat had lightly suggested that he had the easy job of finding sanctuary for them, but both of them knew what lay ahead of them immediately. Theirs was a psychic race, secrets were difficult to maintain.

With the emperor returning, there was no room on the throne for the heir. And Panshinea would not brook his living to provide a focal point for dissidence. His life was now forfeit.

With a House of Tezars formed, breaking all precedents, and Palaton alone to stand against it, his life was now forfeit.

Among the Housed, his life was forfeit for the effort he had spent elevating the second-class citizens of the Godless.

Among the Godless, whose psychic abilities were genetically less or blocked or totally nonexistent and who had spent generations waiting to be delivered, for taking Rand away from them, Rand who seemed to be the catalyst and the messiah predicted to them, his life was now forfeit.

They had no place to go, and no one would suffer them to live.

Not an auspicious beginning for a rebirth.

Chapter 2

A hand gripped Palaton's shoulder from behind. As he felt its warmth and aura, he realized that Rufeen's lectures had ceased.

The pilot said, as he turned, "What's left of Red wing is ready to be pulled out."

"They've eaten?"

"Rations have been distributed. No one's eaten yet—nothing looks too appetizing. The biotox crew is packing up. How many are they taking with them?"

"None." Palaton caught the flash in her eyes. His rough-hewn friend had come to the same conclusions he had, only she did not voice them. "They're calling in transports."

Hat paused in his examination of the remains on the gurney. "I'm almost done here. There's nothing either of you can do at this point."

A muscle worked in Palaton's jaw before he answered, "Except get the cadets out of here. Come on. I think I have some heads to bust."

"Oh, goody," Rufeen said at his side. "It's about time."

Palaton went outside for a long moment. Clouds had begun to gather on the horizon and a lowering sun tinted them a fiery orange which would, like burning embers, turn to crimson and then darken to ash with the night. The biotox crews had nearly finished packing up their cruisers. He scanned the silvery planes.

With an expert eye born of his years of piloting, he knew for a certainty that they could take out two dozen of his cadets. They had brought in pallets of equipment which, now used, would be broken down into scrap, and the pallets of supplies now sat at the airfield's edge, meaning the cruiser bellies were even emptier. He said to Rufeen, a bare second before she spoke to him, and her voices were an echo of his, "Two dozen."

Rufeen grinned then, adding, "Easy."

He nodded.

"That would cut our responsibilities in half."

"Umm." Palaton was already back in full stride and Rufeen had to double-quick to keep up with him.

He caught the crew supervisor by surprise outside the freight doors of the first cruiser.

"We're done here."

"Not quite," Palaton said. "You're taking some of the students with you."

"We told you we were only prepared to call in transport. It's been ordered for you. You shouldn't have to wait more than five or six hours."

"Any wait is too long. You know what transpired here. Lives were lost. *Tezarian* lives."

The Choya'i looked him steadily in the face. She'd cleaned the soot away, though she was still a bit sweaty and begrimed along the forehead and temple. "Any loss of life is regrettable," she responded.

"And we are still in peril from further attack. I want these students out as soon as possible."

"That is your problem." She handed her notepad to an adjutant who came quietly up behind and shadowed her, eyes on Palaton and Rufeen, one hand resting comfortably close to a hip holster.

"It's going to be your problem. Rufeen, call out Red wing. We should be able to get all but one or two senior cadets aboard."

"Yessir." Rufeen turned, put her fingers to her lips, and let out a skull-splitting whistle that lanced through the dusk.

Red wing came on the run, packs on their backs, eyes wide and expectant.

Palaton said to the biotox supervisor, as the cadets ran toward them, "You explain to them why you intend to keep them in jeopardy. You explain to them that you haven't the guts to do what they pledged to do the moment they left behind their Households and entered a flight school. You explain why they left behind homes and family and property in order to expend their lives and their *bahdur* for fellow

Choyan who don't give a damn that some of them died yesterday and many of them will die in some tomorrow, off-
planet, alone, piloting. You explain to them why you don't
care that they are *tezars,* the only beings who can navigate
Chaos, and bring home honor, trade, and glory to Cho. You
explain to them why the very soulfire which gives them life,
which burns in their veins as brightly as blood, why it isn't
good enough for you that they have pledged to drain every
drop of it *in your service?*"

He kept his voices low, pitched so that none but the three
of them might hear, and he used his vocal cords well, under-
scoring one timbre with the other. Rindalan, of the stentorian
priestly voices, would have approved. He missed Rindy, could
have used the elder Choya here and now, but it appeared his
voices had hit home. The biotox crew chief trembled slightly
beside him as the Red wing fell into place, eyes intent on
Rufeen and Palaton.

Rufeen had done her job well. The horror of yesterday's air
strike, *tezar* against *tezar,* had faded from their fresh, young
faces. She had reminded them of their calling, their destiny,
and they were once again ready and eager to fulfill it. If not
at Blue Ridge, then perhaps at the Commons if there were
room enough.

Palaton could not predict the status at either Salt Towers or
the Commons. If they had realigned their traditional neutral
positions which had been intended to prevent the Houses and
branch Householdings from using the *tezars* as leverage during various wars and political strategies, Palaton might simply
be sending the youths off to the enemy camp. He strongly
suspected the Salt Towers, long an elitist flight school, would
probably play right into the hands of Vihtirne of Sky.

If he thought Vihtirne was holding Rand hostage at Salt
Towers, he'd commandeer a cruiser on the spot. It was ridiculous to think that Qativar and Vihtirne would hold his Brethren at such an obvious site, however. But the commandeering
might just have merit. . . .

Sotto voce, he nudged the biotox crew chief. "I know how
much room you have. You can split this wing into two and
take them, or perhaps you would rather I took one of the
cruisers and let you make do with the other?"

"My ship!" started the chief. She composed herself. "You have aircraft."

"Not for passenger transport. Take it either way, Chief, but my cadets are getting out of here. You can assimilate them among your crew, or I can take the cruiser we need."

He felt another tremble run through the body of the Choya'i, but the chief swallowed tightly before snapping out, pointing, "You dozen go this way, you dozen that. Quarters will be cramped. If you need to sleep, do it sitting up. When we get back to dispatch, I'll arrange for further flights."

Palaton murmured a thank you, but the supervisor had thrown herself into action, and he was not entirely sure he'd even been heard.

Rufeen watched the cadets load. She slapped Palaton lightly. "I'll stay," she added, "until takeoff. Just to see them off."

"Whatever it takes," he responded before heading back to the mess hall.

Inside, Hat was sealing the last of the temporary coffin bags and shutting down the morgue. They would be sent out on more appropriate craft. The Earthan looked up, fatigue and sorrow deeply etched into his square face. "Everything all right?"

"It took a little persuasion."

Hat pulled up a stool and perched on it. His barrel chest heaved a sigh. "What do you think will happen?"

"If we had comlines open, we'd have a better idea, but since we don't—" Palaton paused. "I imagine Salt Towers is probably the new base of operations for the House of Tezars."

Hat rubbed his brow wearily, just below the bulge of his horn crown. "That would make sense," he agreed. "Not that I want to see Vihtirne firmly entrenched anywhere. When it was just Nedar, one of us, I could see it. I should have known that wherever Nedar stood, Vihtirne hid in his shadow. I should have known that."

"He could scarcely help it. He was the foremost of his line, and she the head of the House. He was never her puppet, but I doubt that any move he made was unknown to her."

"Alexa was."

Palaton drew up another stool. "The humankind?"

Hat nodded. "I heard her arguing with Nedar after they

came here. Vihtirne wanted him to be rid of the alien. He would not have it. There was a bond between them—it makes me cold to think it, but I think she was his *durah*."

"They were lovers?" said Palaton in shock.

Another weary nod. "I think so. I don't mean to speak ill of the dead—but I can't overlook that possibility."

Memory played out an awful scene in Palaton's mind. Yesterday's crash, Nedar's broken body thrown from the wreckage, and his pleading for a fellow *tezar* to end his agony. It no longer mattered that only moments before they'd engaged in armed combat, that Nedar had led a wing of raw recruits into the air to bring Palaton down. In that time, there had only been the two of them, Palaton shadowed by Rand, his humankind link, and Nedar broken upon the burning ground.

He'd ended his classmate/nemesis' life as Nedar had begged, only to have the disheveled human girl burst out of the aircraft wreckage, screaming in hatred and distress. Rand had saved his life and Alexa had died when the fuselage exploded. Palaton had not understood her actions fully then. If what Hat mused about now were true, though unthinkable, it explained much.

"I didn't know," Hat concluded, "that such things could happen." He looked up then, and met Palaton's gaze. "You and Rand—"

"No," answered Palaton firmly. "Though what it is that binds us, I cannot quite explain."

"Oh," Hat mumbled and lapsed into silence.

Palaton could explain, but he chose not to. That Rand had taken his *bahdur* and borne it, and cleansed it was beyond Choyan understanding. How could their soulfire be transferred in its entirety? How could an alien race with practically no extrasensory abilities whatsoever be involved in such a procedure? Did it mean that the inevitable burnout of the power and the awful neuropathy which accompanied it could be postponed indefinitely? Did it mean that *tezars* no longer had a future of disease and emptiness facing them? Palaton wasn't sure. He only knew that retrieving his *bahdur* from Rand had left the humankind crippled and bereft, nearly as mindlessly numb as suddenly losing the soulfire would do to a Choya. Palaton would not choose to benefit at the risk of another, nor would he let anyone else do so.

However, it made the mission to recover Rand, who was hurt and vulnerable, that much more desperate.

Rufeen interrupted their companionable silence, bearing a tray of mugs. The steaming odor of *bren* filled the air. "We've still got work to do."

Hat shook himself as though stepping out of a cold shower. His dark eyes were bloodshot as he snagged a mug and rolled a glance at her.

"Supper," she suggested. "Then we need to bed the other wings down."

Palaton lurched to his feet. "I'll see the pallets get unloaded. Maybe something hot can be made out of those ration packets." It felt welcome to target his thoughts on the immediacy of the action needed. He would worry about Rand later. This had to be done now.

The ordered-in ships touched down around midnight. Their beams lit the one airstrip and pad which had not been destroyed by the combat. Palaton stood in the night which had rapidly grown chill, and he greeted the pilots who stepped down.

"There's a storm front moving in," the graying Choya, a son of the House of Star, like Palaton himself, said. He removed his helmet. "I'm Jago." His hair of bronze and red flowed back from his forehead, streaks of age lightening it. There was a slight weariness in his aquamarine eyes. "I can take two dozen. Maybe a few less, if they're carrying full packs."

"They're carrying everything they can salvage," Palaton told him.

The first pilot indicated the second, a slender Choya'i, of the House of Sky, ebony-haired and light-eyed, so much like Nedar that she might have been the late *tezar's* sister . . . or she could have been his child, Palaton thought, reminding himself of the years which had passed.

"I can take nearly three dozen," she said.

"Coffin bags?"

"I have room in the cargo hold. Two dozen, then, if you have bags and equipment to go. *Tezar* Palaton," she began and hesitated.

"Yes?"

Her lips pursed, then she finished, "We would advise you strongly not to travel with us."

"We have no intention of doing so."

Tension fled abruptly from the carriages of the two. Palaton had swung around to signal Rufeen to start the remaining cadets boarding, when Jago asked, "Should we call in more cruisers?"

"No. I'm afraid that's all we need taken out."

Their faces went bleak. Blue Ridge, the first and greatest of the flight schools, had had its ranks decimated. Dwindling due to the ever growing scarcity of enough talented recruits, now their ranks were being thinned even more by civil war. The elder Choya nodded brusquely and replaced his helmet.

"I'm ready when you are."

Palaton returned to the mess hall where Hat and Rufeen were rousing the sleeping students. He made himself useful checking packs and accepting salutes from the cadets as they formed a line by the makeshift doorway, their faces crusted with sleep and dreams.

A clatter came from the galley. Pans went rolling and a young, panicked Choya cried, "*Tezar* Rufeen! Help!"

He entered the galley from one end, Rufeen from the other. The brawny Choya'i knelt down as one of the Blue wing lay on the floor, frothing from the mouth, body writhing in convulsions. His classmate knelt at his flanks, trying vainly to capture his flailing hands.

"What is it?"

"He just—he just collapsed."

Rufeen frowned heavily at Palaton, then muttered, "No one just collapses." She tried to cradle the cadet's head on her knee, keeping him from bashing the floor repeatedly in his agony. "Head injury?"

"N–oo."

Palaton thought he recognized both cadets as pilots whom Nedar had foolishly taken into the air with him, the only two survivors of the opposition who'd ambushed him. If they had been flying combat, then this one on the floor could not have been an epileptic. He would never have passed the physicals and training to this point.

Foam spattered the Choya's light blue flight suit as he

writhed in their arms. His agony cut to the quick to even watch. Hat leaned in past Palaton.

Palaton pushed him back. "Get the others loaded."

"What is it?"

"Convulsions. We'll take care of it."

"My student—"

"Hat. We'll take care of it." Palaton stood to block his view.

Hat's dark-shadowed eyes deepened a second, then he gave way. He left the galley without another word.

Rufeen met Palaton's gaze as he knelt back down. Wordless agreement passed between them: Hat did not need to handle the death of yet another of his charges.

Rufeen had her fingers lightly pressed on the major pulse point of the Choya's neck. She said softly, "I'm losing him."

Palaton swung on the sobbing wingmate and grabbed him up by the neckline of his flight suit. "Tell me what's happening!"

Chapter 3

Even with his wingmate's life at stake, Palaton could feel deceit throbbing through the cadet's aura. He shook the youth. "His life for your lies!" he warned. "Tell me what you know."

"It—it won't help him."

"Are you so sure of that? Are you ready for the weight of his death? It's a heavy burden." As if accenting Palaton's words, the dying pilot's heels drummed on the galley flooring. "What brought this about?"

The cadet twisted slightly, trying to see his friend's body, then looked back to Palaton. "He took the . . . he took the drugs Nedar brought back." He clawed a hand at the front of his flight suit, trying to loosen Palaton's grip a little.

"Drugs? What drugs?"

"Nedar said—Nedar said they would be the foundation of the House of Tezars. No more burnout. No more layovers waiting for the *bahdur* to freshen. No more borderline talent hoping to fulfill lesser piloting jobs."

Palaton relinquished his grasp on the youth's neck enough to set him back on his feet and let him take a gulping breath. Rufeen rebutted what he could not.

"There is no such thing."

"Nedar brought them from off-world. He took them. One or two of the elder *tezars* tried them as well. They work! And when Kano heard we were shipping out, he wanted to make sure his *bahdur* tested high, that it burned as brightly as it could. I told him not to . . . that Nedar said the drug was only to be taken if the soulfire was dormant. But he didn't listen. He was desperate! He's been on the edge all year. Hat warned him he could wash out. He wanted to be a *tezar!*" The cadet's eyes filled with tears that began to slide down his pale face.

Rufeen said quietly, "Palaton. Look."

The cadet in her hands had ceased to convulse. Now he lay sprawled and still, his heaving chest the only proof he still lived . . . that and a network of *bahdur*-laced fire that seemed to play over him. It sparkled from head to toe, lacy cobalt blue lines that danced and hissed as energy burned freely.

It brutally mimicked the Patterns of Chaos that all *tezars* must one day learn to master if they wished to be space pilots. It tangled and untangled in the swirls of random matter motion, yet Palaton could look into the net and see the signposts by which he navigated FTL flight. The soulfire twisted and formed, then re-formed the Butterfly, the Singing Choya'i, even the treacherous Arachnae. With each coil that broke and re-formed, the dying student let out a gasping moan.

The *bahdur* network grew darker and darker, as the cadet's face grew paler and paler, the soulfire leeching the very life from his body. It glowed midnight dark and then, with a hiss, it was gone, leaving a shell of a body behind.

Palaton let the other youth go, and with a wail, he fell to his knees beside his friend's hulk.

Rufeen's jaw had dropped. She worked a moment to form words. She looked up at Palaton.

"What in hell has Nedar done to us?"

"I don't know," he answered, and an icy finger of foreboding brushed the back of his neck.

Off-world. Nedar partnered with a humankind woman, a woman who had been known to have been allied with the Abdreliks. Off-world and intergalactic. He rocked back on his heels. Had the Abdreliks hoped to instigate civil war here, seeking to conquer from within what they had spent hundreds of years trying to conquer from without?

He could only hope that, with Alexa and Nedar dead, the House of Tezars had no destiny, no miraculous if deadly panacea, that the link to this drug had been severed. He could hope that, but he knew he could not count on it.

"What are we going to do?"

He gave Rufeen a hand up. "Hat's equipment isn't sophisticated enough to do an autopsy here. Besides, I wouldn't put him through that. But we need to know what really killed him, and why."

She nodded, a stunned expression still on her wide face.

"I'll get a coffin bag." She started to push past him, then stopped.

"What if—"

"If what?"

"It works. It kills some of us, but it works on others. What if it works on a lot of us?"

"That's our soul, Rufeen. No one can chemically create what doesn't exist in us."

"But what if it can restore . . .?"

Palaton looked back to the sobbing youth and his dead friend. "Then they'll own us," he answered briefly. "Choyan will do anything for soulfire."

Rufeen gave a shudder. She stopped. "I know that look. What can you possibly hope to do?"

"For one thing, I'll have to change my travel plans."

"You can't stay here."

"No. But I won't be going on with you and Hat, either. I've got to meet with Pan. This issue gives me no choice. The emperor has to know what's been sown here, what's at stake."

"He intends to kill you, Palaton."

"I know that. But first, he'll damn well have to listen to me."

Rufeen looked at him silently, and he could read her thoughts as clearly as if she had sent them to him. The emperor was the emperor. Panshinea did not have to do anything he did not wish to do. Anything she might have decided to say was interrupted by Hathord, who paused at the door to the galley, and finally said in a broken voice, "By God-in-all, I hope this is the last of my dead."

He took his student by the shoulders. "Go and get me another bag."

The Choya looked at him with a stunned and pale face. Hat gave him a rough shake. "Go. Then get your kit. The last transport is waiting for you."

Finally, after the weeping cadet had recovered enough to bring a sheet and coffin bag for his friend, and they had tucked the body in, she said, "You have three days, four at the most, before he arrives. You should be in place before then—"

"In place?"

Her face averted now, as her hands busily prepared the

body, she continued, "In place. Arrange that whatever confrontation Pan wishes is in public. Use the broadcasters to keep him honest. If he attempts to bring you down, let it be in full view of everyone. Unless he has branded you as traitor and is prepared to offer incontrovertible truth, he won't dare lay a hand on you. Find whatever allies you can—"

"With Jorana out of the palace, I can't count on anybody."

Her gaze leveled on him then. "You can count on a good many more than you think. The only problem you might have is that Vihtirne and Qativar will strike, making it look as though Panshinea has done it." She finished with the seal on the coffin bag and stood. He drew up with her. "You'll have to be in place with the Choyan you can trust."

A glimmer of what she was saying touched him. He shook his head. "No. You and Hat are not going with me."

"You *can* count on us."

"No. No, I won't risk the two of you. If Qativar is using drugs to build the House of Tezars, there won't be anybody left to train true *bahdur*. He's going to leave Cho in shambles. The two of you need to be able to rebuild, pick up the pieces. If I have only one legacy to leave behind me, it's going to be that. Do you understand me? You and Hat have to take the jet sleds and get as far away from here and the capital as possible. Don't look back."

From behind him, Hathord said, "Don't do this, Palaton. Don't go."

"I have to. I have to relinquish the heirship, and I have to let Pan know what's happening. There can't be two emperors of Cho. Our world can't survive that—it's already fracturing under the strain. Pan can have his throne, but he'll keep it only if he's strong enough to face Qativar and Vihtirne. I'll do anything I can to give him that strength, but I'll have to do it alone."

Rufeen commented quietly, "That's why they took Rand. You know that. As soon as they suspect you're moving against them in any way, he will become expendable."

He didn't know that, but he also had no doubt that was why Qativar had taken his Brethren, his humankind . . . his friend. "I know. Which is why I have to go alone. I have to send you two on as decoys and attract as little attention as I can. As much as I need your help, as much as I want it—I can't afford to have it."

His friends fell silent. The three of them bent to grab the corners of the coffin bag and transported it to the storage room where the other dead lay. They stood for a moment, aware that they were the only beings left alive in the ruins of the flight school. Palaton could hear the faint afterburn of the last transport as it circled once, took its bearing, and disappeared into the midnight sky. He realized belatedly that it had been doing a flyover in mourning for Blue Ridge.

He encircled his hand about Hat's wrist. "I pledged to you once before, and I do it again: Blue Ridge will be rebuilt."

Hat looked at him, eyes shining with emotion. He nodded wordlessly in understanding.

The Choya'i who, in her former life, had been a Commons and had had beautiful blue eyes, eyes the color of the sky after a refreshing rain, sat quietly in a straight-backed chair, head tilted to one side as if listening, a cerulean band of cloth covering scarred eye sockets. She raised a hand, a crackle of *bahdur* accompanying the gesture. The Choya who had been approaching her paused as she halted him in his tracks.

Her name had been Dorea. She was young, barely out of her teens, and she should have been flirting with other Choyan, dancing and laughing, her life stretching ahead of her. Instead she sat as still as if life had already used her, filled her with wisdom and care and strife and memory, her skirts demurely about her ankles, her back pressed to the chair as if seeking solace against some unseen burdens weighing upon her shoulders.

Or so it seemed to Malahki—lately wrenched from his destiny as one time mayor-luminary of Danbe, head of the underground which sought to free the common people from their second-citizen status—as he felt his own *bahdur* answer to hers. Power to power. It was no wonder the Housed felt superior to the God-blind. They *were* superior, in many ways. No wonder they feared the religion and revolution which had driven Malahki's people into hiding. *Bahdur* unleashed was a fearsome thing. When the humankind known as Rand had touched Dorea, Changing her, opening up and unsealing her bands of power, she had become the Prophet. Dorea no longer, young and carefree no more, unable to understand or bear her new foresight, she had gouged her eyes from her face.

Yet she still *saw,* and was *seeing* even now, as she waited for Malahki to join her.

He did not stir until she dropped her hand to her lap and straightened, turning her blind face toward him, nostrils flaring slightly.

"He will not come," she said.

"Palaton? Why do you say that?"

"Rand is no longer with him," Her voices were flat. Like most born of common blood, she had not had the auditory sensibility or *bahdur* to teach her to use the dual pitches of her double larynxes to full ability. Her voices twinned one another. Malahki was keenly aware that another Choya'i, one born into her power, would have used one voice to convey one emotion, the other to underscore it, or seduce or even scold, at the same time.

Of foremost importance, however, was the whereabouts of Rand. "He has him secured somewhere. Gone to ground, where we cannot sniff him out."

The Prophet considered that before shaking her head slightly. "No. I cannot sense Rand. He is lost to me, and Palaton refuses to respond to my plea. He will not come to me, will not listen to what I have to say."

Malahki hesitated, thinking to offer to be a messenger, but he knew better; the Prophet did not yet have a message for Palaton. She would, and knew she would, but more than that . . . his presence must be needed to stimulate the full import of her foresight. He could not think that Palaton would knowingly ignore her, despite all that had happened between them. He might have been wounded in the attack on Blue Ridge. He must surely be caught up in the events which would precede Panshinea's return to Cho.

"Prophet. Let me carry another summons."

One hand went up. Her fingertips gently touched the cloth which bound her empty eyes. Patted the cloth as if reassuring herself. Then Dorea dropped her chin slightly, and her forehead wrinkled.

"All right," she said finally. "But do not go to Blue Ridge.

He won't be there. Look for him at Charolon. Look for him in the eye of disaster."

Malahki did not like the sound of that. He'd turned and left the tiny room when her voices caught him at the door.

"And Malahki."

He turned.

"See if you can bring him to me alive."

His blood chilled. "Yes, Prophet," he promised, and left.

Chapter 4

The day on Sorrow was pleasant enough for GNask to lower the frequency of his bodyshielding as he strolled along the quartz river path to his ambassadorial wing. His bodyguards lumbered along behind, grumbling quietly to one another, unable to understand his predilection for this walkway, his fascination with the sentient life frozen forever inside the rivers and lakeways of the planet. He did not take the time today to meditate, as he would have liked to have done, to philosophize about these people and what they had done to attract such a powerful enemy. He did not pause to watch and stalk as a predator would, imagining the skillful prey one of them would be, bipedal, upright, lithely mobile as they must once have been.

Nor did he indulge himself in cataloging the various facial expressions preserved for eternity on their slender, oval faces. There was a certain serenity as well as fear to be found, giving any observer pause.

It was those expressions, those bodies, which had wrought a truce between the Abdreliks, the Ronins, the Choyan, and the other quibbling races of the Compact. Here a civilization had died and been entombed by a technology which none of them could yet match. Somewhere, out there, was an enemy more vastly powerful than any of them.

It had been a sobering thought centuries ago. It still was today.

Who had these people been, and who had been so almighty as to bring them down? The crystals of Sorrow did not tell them. They could only hint and warn.

Truth to tell, GNask had to admire a predator who could accomplish such a massive kill, with no need to take any sustenance or reward for the effort. The planet of Sorrow was

nearly pristine with the exception of its network of frozen waterways. They were not an amphibian people, yet they had
stepped into this liquid and died nearly instantly. Nearly,
GNask thought, because his minute observations over the
years had revealed a few bodies, here and there, showing ab-
ject pain and terror. Not quite instantaneous enough for some,
it appeared.

GNask always took the lesson of Sorrow personally. He
had an enemy to meet, one that would demand the very best
he could offer, and he had a fine line of compromise to walk
in the meantime while he grew strong enough to meet the
challenge. He did not allow himself the luxury or compla-
cency of thinking that Sorrow's history was in the distant
past. It would forever be as fresh to him as the moment in
which their lives had been snuffed out.

His bodyguards uttered a grunt of relief as he turned away
from the walkway and jogged up the steps to the ambassadorial wing. He lowered his bodyshield as he entered and one of
his aides darted out to meet him.

GNask came to a halt, his massive bulk settling into a sudden stealthiness, all his instincts directed momentarily on the
preylike movements of the aide.

The youngling, not far from the egg or initiation with his
tursh blushed, turning his dark hide even darker. His sluglike
symbiont turned color as well and hugged close to the nape of
his neck, eye stalks pulled in and quivering. The *tursh* had
more sense than the aide did, though the youngling finally
seemed to catch wind of his predicament and stammered. "I
b–beg your pardon, Ambassador."

In their wild days, this one would not have lived to leave
the nest. GNask made a noise at the back of his throat, non-
committal as to whether pardon had been granted or not.

"That damage report you wanted just came in. Class Zed
cruiser, currently being leased and operated by Ambassador
John Taylor Thomas is anchored at bay station 17 for repairs.
A report detailing a minor skirmish with a Ronin privateer is
on file."

GNask could feel the warmth bubbling inside of him. As
he'd thought, Thomas had not had the guts to report a direct
attack by them. It had been a warning shot only. If GNask had
commanded rrRusk to take them out, there would be no one

to make reports. The point had been made, and understood, that Thomas was not to play lightly with the alliance they had made. The Terran ambassador had stolen two agents from him. GNask had vented his anger. Now they were even again, though their little alliance was somewhat in doubt. Thomas would have to convince him that there was still an advantage in their association. Meanwhile, his aide waited.

"Good. Is that all?"

"No, Your Eminence. You have a call waiting, of high priority."

GNask nodded and rolled past his aide, leaving him trembling in his wake, making even more preylike movements to attract the attention of the bodyguards following.

GNask saw the scramble link when he sat before the screen and knew that no one higher among the Abdreliks could be waiting for him to pick up. He licked his lips, jowls rattling, as he settled down and powered the screen.

The Abdrelik president sat hunched and glowering. GNask recognized the deep meditation of a classic stalk as a flicker of light came into the other's eyes as Frnark launched into words. "With the human girl gone, we have lost our link into Cho."

GNask grimaced, his lips skinning back from his tusks, and he made an effort to keep from revealing more ivory than he should. It would be an egregious breach of etiquette to do so. And, furthermore, it could cost him the ambassadorship which he had won so dearly four decades ago and had no desire to give up until he was ready to place himself even higher. Damn John Taylor Thomas for tampering with his agents, even if the girl had been the manling's own daughter. "That is so. But not all is lost. What I have gained in information was worth the time, the risk. . . ."

Frnark glared at him, small piggish eyes in a face of purplish hide, a lean face like and yet unlike GNask's. He had fought for his position and would fight to keep it. Neither had any doubt that they looked into the face of their most probable next opponent. However, neither was ready for the inevitable battle. Not yet.

GNask felt a string of spittle cascade from the corner of his lips. He mopped it away delicately on the back of one large, well-muscled wrist. He was easily twice the bulk of Frnark, and aware that he gave away in agility what he'd built in strength. He did not blink voluntarily, but rather let his eyelids drop ever so slightly, in a subservient manner, breaking his stare so that the president would not think himself challenged. Not yet, not at this time or place.

He lowered his rumbling voice a notch. "I am not so new from the egg that I cannot see this unfortunate death as a setback, but neither am I so hidebound that I cannot accept the loss and move on. The consequences of the girl's death to the Choyan far outweigh any inconvenience to me. Panshinea has been moved to leave the safety of the Halls of the Compact. Leadership on both Sorrow and Cho are now in jeopardy."

"Do not lecture me."

"I did not seek to do so. Only to encourage you."

"I do not need encouragement! I need results! Any upheaval on Cho that disrupts the availability of pilots is disastrous to us. The Ivrians are the only ones who can make do for any time at all without piloting—do you want to leave us open for an Ivrian invasion?" The Abdrelik across from GNask paused for a moment, then began to laugh at the notion. The reedy, avian aliens could scarcely conceive of an attack on Abdrelikan holdings and the thought of one was so ridiculous that both GNask and the president lapsed into deep, rumbling laughter.

The speaker waved away his humor finally, saying, "Be that as it may, they're the only ones who can even come close to fulfilling Choyan contracts. They may not come at us militarily, but they'll sure as hell be in our pockets."

"I can arrange a deterrent."

"I'm sure you can." Frnark dipped a hand down into a gurgling pot by the side of his chair, plunged a talon into the turgid waters, and pulled out a struggling *scriff* which he stuffed into his cheek and began to chew with great enjoyment. He swallowed, aware of the avid attention his actions drew. When his throat was clear, he said, "Do not think, GNask, that we are unaware of your actions of the past few days. We fully expect the humankind ambassador to file a protest with the Compact in a matter of hours."

GNask had thought that that action might have gone unnoticed. He should have known better. No matter how he had weeded out his crew and command, there were always spies. Always. "He can prove nothing. There were Ronin privateers in the sector. His ship was a casualty of friendly fire."

"Mayhap. How badly damaged was he?"

"Enough to remove him from the sector. Not so badly he would have suffered casualties of any degree. If he is alive, squawking, perhaps not badly enough."

"Perhaps you would care to explain to me your course of action. I would like to share in the rationality of such an attack."

GNask got to his feet. His bulk, in motion, was a majestic achievement of which he was well aware. He would, when the time came, quash his foe as easily as the president had eaten the *scriff*. "I think not. You have granted me certain autonomy of movement and action. I would like to hold onto that independence a little longer, but I assure you that you will be pleased with the final results."

He was gazed at darkly. The president's lips thinned, his ivory glistened whitely. "Tell me some some particle of your ultimate objective."

It was a request which he, for the moment, dare not refuse. GNask leaned close to the viewing screen. "Nothing less," he said, "than the *tezarian* drive itself."

"A goal which has been in our sights for centuries."

"A difference," GNask returned. "I know what it is. I quest now to learn how to control it."

The president sat back with a hiss.

GNask waved a palm over the controls, closing off the view screen and ending transmission. He stood by the chair, watching the blank screen for a long moment, pondering his boldness. The president did not renew the signal.

He had either succeeded in his statement, or he had just cut off the last of his ties. Either way, it would not matter, if he succeeded in this final mission. He had almost had the secret of the drive when he had Nedar in his hands. The implantation and imprinting of his symbiont in the pilot had been as successful as it had been in the human girl. He knew it, though Thomas had taken the two out of his grasp before he could complete the experiment on the Choya. His *tursh* was strong and resilient. It could withstand another segmentation for implantation.

All he needed was another pilot.

He headed out of the communication deck, bellowing for rrRusk as he lumbered along.

Chapter 5

It seemed the cruiser had barely stopped vibrating from the bay station launch when his commander called him to the con deck. Thomas stood wearily, feeling the buzz in the soles of his boots, the sway of the ship disorienting him ever so slightly, the weight of his years and his loss upon his shoulders. A dull thrum continued to sound through the vessel from repairs being made internally while in flight. Major hull repairs had been completed before disembarking from the Compact bay station. They'd already had trouble. Frankly, John Taylor Thomas had not expected to draw any more.

"We're being approached," the commander told him.

Surely not the Ronin and Abdreliks again. Thomas felt himself twitch defensively, away from the screen projection of their deep space position. They were beginning acceleration for the FTL run even as they continued making repairs, but were still hours, perhaps even days, from being able to make the jump. The laser dot of light which indicated their position shone strongly. Pulsating ever closer on the 3-D screen came another pin of illumination.

"Any ID?"

"Not at this point in time, although our pilot doesn't seem particularly worried. But whoever they are, they deceled, looking for us, or someone. I'd say it was us as they've set an intersect course."

Out of Chaos, looking for them. They'd have the speed advantage, decelerating as they were. His vessel's own engines were laboring to pick up the acceleration they needed to gain FTL. Thomas stood, musing, thinking so deeply that he must have missed something, for his commander put his hand on his shoulder, saying, "Ambassador?"

"Yes?" Thomas looked up. He'd been thinking of Alexa,

dead, lost to him finally, lost to him in more ways than he could ever imagine, even more forsaken than when the Abdreliks had taken her. He was wondering who could possibly threaten him with anything more devastating than that.

"What do you want us to do?"

"ID and hail them as soon as you can. I'll be in my quarters. Wake me if necessary."

His commander nodded. "Very good, sir."

Thomas shrugged wearily and left the con deck. Sleep beckoned, but he would not get much. He could not, thinking of Alexa's legacy. He found it ironic that on this voyage of endless night there would be little, if any, rest for him. *I regret that I have but one life to give for my country. . . .* Would that it had been his own instead of his daughter's. Would that he had had anything to give which could have spared her the course she had taken. Would that anything but power would have pleased her.

He must have slept the deep, unconscious sleep he had hoped for, because the clang and jolt of a hard-docking woke him. The hammock bed swung uneasily as the ship moved and echoed with the metallic hammering. Boarded. They were being boarded. Forcibly? Surely not, or his commander would have woken him. But then, his pilot was a *tezar* and there were bounds there which crossed the contracts of commanding a vessel.

Had his commander betrayed him?

Thomas had gotten to his feet, hammock still swaying violently behind him as he went to the sink and scrubbed his face. The cold sting of the water woke him a little. He stared at himself through red-rimmed eyes. Had he cried in his sleep, dreamless ease giving vent to emotions he had not been able to allow himself otherwise? He washed his face again, more carefully, then dragged a comb through thinning hair. The downtime light in the cabin made him grayer than he remembered. Distinguished. More like the experienced ambassador he portrayed. Less like the grieving father.

He had finished straightening his jacket when the commander called for him.

"Ambassador. We have guests from Cho who respectfully request audience with you."

His heart squeezed a painful beat. From Cho. No wonder his pilot had allowed boarding. The Choyan were not in the habit of initiating warfare. They did not need to. Their mastery over Chaos was enough in itself. So what Choyan came to treat with him? Not Panshinea, or his commander would have announced the emperor. "Where?"

"Bay deck D, sir."

Just beyond the docking deck. Why not come into the vessel, into the belly of the beast? Why hover near the exit? Thomas put his shoulders back and chin up, and went to meet his guests, wondering.

"I don't like this, Qativar." Vihtirne paced just beyond the bulkhead, looking back frequently as if she wished to leave, with or without him. Her sable tresses swung with the agitated movement of her graceful form and her long, midnight blue dress swept the deck with every step, She was beautiful, elegantly so, and used to being obeyed. It was etched as much into her movements as her race and her sex.

Qativar straightened the line of his trouser. "This act would seal the bond between us."

"We have no bond with humankind! You would deal away the only bargaining chip we have—"

"No. Need I remind you that we could not keep him if we wished, that Palaton would go to the ends of Cho to find him eventually, no matter what blackmail we hoped would stop him. We must use him while we have him—if we wish for the House of Tezars to succeed. We do wish that, don't we, dear Vihtirne?"

She'd pivoted neatly and now leveled a sapphire gaze into his eyes. Cold as any gemstone. Vibrant but icy. Multifaceted but unliving. She had had a House at her beck and call, and had forsaken it to build a new House with him. She had known what she was doing, he thought. Known that with him she'd have but one person to deal with as she plied her strategy to change the fate of Cho and Choyan instead of the tradition-bound infrastructure of a long established genetic bloodline. He would have to remember to be terribly careful in the days ahead.

"Yes," she said icily. "We do wish that. But you leave us scant protection."

"Boost will be our protection. They'll do anything for it, for a steady supply. *Anything.*"

Her lips thinned. She swung away from him, a tiny movement underlying the major one . . . had it been a shudder? A grimace of distaste?

No matter. Qativar heard footfalls nearing. The ambassador must be coming to meet them. He checked the lines of his suit, especially tailored for moments like this. He was Choyan, that bespoke his lineage in itself. And now he was the establishing head of a new House, a feat which had not been accomplished successfully in hundreds of years. His robes of priesthood in the House of Star had been thrown aside. He was newborn, he was the foundation of the House of Tezars. It did not matter that he had never been a *tezar,* that he had not the soulfire to pilot. Without him, none of them would pilot. That would suffice.

He stood. As the two figures drew near down the dimly lit corridor beyond the docking area's bulkhead, he could easily distinguish between the tall, loping form of the commanding pilot and the awkward straight-armed stick figure of the humankind. The manling walked with all the gawky attitude of a child hoping to become an adult. The only graceful feature about him, when they drew near, would be the eyes. Like Choyan eyes, large and luminous and expressive. Among all the races, none had eyes quite like Choyan did—with the possible exception of the humankind. The Ronins were full of slit-eyed guile, the Ivrians double-lidded like the birds they so resembled, and the Quinonans had eyes of tar that dominated their skull-like heads though little intelligence or compassion lit the depths of the hive-consciousness aliens.

The ambassador stumbled crossing the bulkhead, then caught himself, and Qativar clenched his jaw to squelch any possible derision at the action. He could read an aura of fatigue from the manling, fatigue and sorrow. Vihtirne caught his eye as she joined him and he knew she'd read the same emotional psyche. He'd planned correctly, he thought triumphantly.

As the pilot and the ambassador came to a halt in front of them, Qativar thought he recognized the *tezar,* a Sky from his sable hair and silvery eyes, an older commander, one

Dilarabe, if he recalled correctly. Not wanting to be in error, he let Vihtirne greet them first.

"Ambassador Thomas, *Tezar* Dilarabe," she said warmly in Trade. "Thank you for allowing us to dock."

Pleasure spiked in Qativar's chest. He'd been right again. It augured well for the meeting they were about to conduct. As Vihtirne presented him, the humankind ambassador turned to face him, weary expression sparked by a momentary curiosity. Fleeting, yet it had been there. He bowed fluidly in greeting.

"Forgive us for intruding, Ambassador. I know that you are in mourning, and we join you in your inconsolable loss."

Thomas' eyelids fluttered slightly. "Thank you, Mistress Vihtirne, Your Eminence Qativar. However, I hardly think you have flown this distance to sit with me in my grief. Forgive my brusqueness, but I have little patience left. What do you want here?"

This was a being, Qativar thought, who was plumbing the depths of his soul and found he had little left to lose. He would take careful handling in the future, if he ever reached these depths again. The manling might decide that he had nothing to lose.

Qativar inclined his head, and tried to project understanding. "I trust you are somewhat familiar with the history of my home world?"

"I have a working knowledge of it."

"Then you must know, and sympathize with from your own history, the strife and difficulty concerning the raising of a House. Our people came to terms with aggression long ago. We do not colonize; therefore, it behooves us to keep the peace so that our planet, as well as our people, do not suffer. Yet incidences do happen from time to time. It is most regrettable to us, Vihtirne and myself, that your daughter Alexa was caught in the midst of our actions. Although we are not personally responsible, we bear the onus of her death." He paused, allowing the weight of his words and the pitch of his voices to sink in.

One of the manling's hands twitched a little, as if urging him to say what he had to say, and finish.

"To that end," and he moved, gesturing to a crewman who stood silent guard at the far bulkhead, "we have done the only thing we could, and brought you her remains."

The air lock door opened like a giant metal maw, and issued forth an honor guard of Choyan bearing a coffin between them. They paced slowly and with great dignity, their boot soles scarcely drumming on the metal plate of the deck. The coffin moved between them as if borne by nothing but air. It was draped with a silken ebony cloth, simple but effective. Though both he and Vihtirne had moved to face the guard, Qativar slipped a glance to the side to see the look on the ambassador's face. It was all he hoped for. He had brought a father's child home.

Thomas took a furtive step toward the casket with a smothered cry, but Dilarabe caught him, saying, "Sir. The coffin is sealed. You cannot see her." He held the manling still for a moment, looking over Thomas' shoulder at Qativar and Vihtirne, his face stony, then he released his employer. "You cannot see her," he repeated.

Thomas took another halting step, then seemed to recover his composure as the pacing guard reached him, did a step in place and came to a stop. With their voices echoing one another, the Choyan counted off and lowered the casket to the deck. It settled without a sound, yet with its lowering, an atmosphere of gravity fell too, an oppression so dense that for a moment Qativar believed a sending or curse had come with it, though humankind had no such abilities.

John Taylor Thomas stretched out a hand and laid it gently atop the ebony drape. A moment of silence, then, "Open it."

"We cannot, sir." The honor guards looked imploringly at Qativar. He stepped forward.

"The coffin is sealed both for quarantine and aesthetic purposes, Ambassador. What is inside does not resemble the daughter you bore and raised. We have," and Qativar beckoned forward one of the crewmen at the air lock bulkhead. He offered a small package which Qativar took. "We have samples for DNA testing which should allay any questions you have about the identity of the remains."

Thomas had gone pale, so pale he seemed translucent. "I want it opened," he repeated.

"You would not want to see her," Vihtirne said. Her overvoice was silken, compassionate, but her underlying pitch was one of stern command which Qativar heard well. He wondered if the humankind could hear it so well, or if he would just find it compelling.

Thomas stared at them now, his eyes like burning coals in his face, dark and searing. "Who are you," he said, "to question what I want."

It was a moment which went beyond diplomacy or even the alienness of their races. He was a father. He had a murdered child in the casket in front of him. He had a need to know the truth of her death.

Qativar swallowed. "Very well," he said. He reached inside his jacket for the key.

Vihtirne moved, her dress of darkest blue swirling about her, as she placed her hand across the ambassador's. She was barely taller than the manling, and they looked into one another's face. "You can do this if you wish," she said, "but I would advise you not to. You have memories of her now which will be changed forever by what you see within. Trust me. We have nothing to gain by bringing you another's remains. I ask you not to do this for your sake, and your sake alone."

"I want to see her."

"As any father would. But it is not her you will see."

"I cannot believe . . . ."

"You do not want to believe, and we understand that. But we have made the identification and have brought samples so that your staff can confirm it. Besides," Vihtirne added firmly, "we were there. We saw her heroic death, trying to defend Nedar, who was the foremost *tezar* in my House of Sky. There is no doubt." She took her hand away from Thomas. "Qativar."

He held out the key which would open the hermetically sealed box.

Thomas looked at it for a long moment, then took a quavering breath. "No," he refused it. But he did take the package of testing samples.

"Believe me," Vihtirne breathed. "This is for the best."

Dilarabe called out for crew to take the coffin and stow it away. Thomas watched it go with extreme longing etched into his face. Qativar recognized the expression with satisfaction. He had high hopes for what would follow. He waited until the bulkhead doors had closed again before speaking.

"Our commiserations, Ambassador. We extend our sincerest apologies for the actions of our colleagues and hope that what we offer next will help begin healing the breach between our governments."

Thomas seemed to be standing on his feet with a power that had gone beyond his own meager strength. Color had begun coming back to his face, however, though new lines etched into his cheeks did not appear to be smoothing. "What action?"

Qativar said, "As you know, Nedar and Alexa had begun an alliance, an alliance with us which would allow the birthing of a new House, the House of Tezars. No longer would pilots be slave to or subject to the whims of the Houses and Householdings of their birth."

Dilarabe seemed to draw himself close behind Ambassador Thomas, though he remained silent. The humankind closed his eyes a momemt, swayed, and then pulled himself tall again. "For the return of my daughter's body, I owe you thanks. But I don't owe you anything else, Qativar. I know what Alexa wanted from you and what you probably sought from her, but I do know that if I return to the Halls of the Compact and announce to the worlds in general that the *tezarian* drive, the mechanical discovery of the millennia is nothing more than paranormal drivel, space flight will be ruined. So you have my silence. For the moment. I cannot give you anything more."

Dilarabe jerked in surprise and looked down on the man he shadowed.

Vihtirne began, "You rave—"

Qativar interrupted her. "The truth is not quite what you perceive it to be."

"Oh? It isn't You don't navigate Chaos by esper perception? You don't get from jump-off to decel by merely having a hunch that you're where you want to be? Explain to me, if you can, just where I've gone wrong."

Qativar opened his mouth to respond, but it was Dilarabe who answered, "We do not guess, we *know.*"

Thomas took a step back, as if suddenly aware that his humankind crewmen had all left the docking bay and he was surrounded by Choyan. He looked at his commander.

"We *know* because we are masters at reading the Patterns

of Chaos. There are random patterns, fractals, attractors which are loci for us. We can read them, though they are never the same, readable even though normal space has collapsed, contracted into an unnavigable miasma. We can read them because it's in our bloodlines to do so. We can guide a ship through FTL because the *bahdur* burns in us. There is no doubt in what we do, and when the power leaves us, when the soulfire is gone, it's as though the very heart is cut from us. But until it leaves me or is torn from me, when I tell you that I know where we go, no matter how we're to get there, I *know*."

Thomas moved back yet again, his voice defensive. "I know what I know," he repeated, though his tone, already thin sounding to Choyan listeners, was barely audible.

"You may know," Dilarabe answered sadly. "But you do not understand."

"It doesn't matter what I understand." The flush which had come back into his cheeks now began to blaze. "It matters that I have the means to produce a drug which can revitalize your *soul*."

Dilarabe's jaw dropped. "What?"

Qativar said smoothly into the sudden silence, "You grieve, Ambassador, but I have misjudged your head for the business at hand."

"We have no business."

"You are a Class Zed planet. You have difficulty obtaining piloting contracts. You've been permitted to remain a part of the Compact temporarily, by the grace of your Abdrelikan status, but that probationary status is soon to come before review. We can help one another greatly."

Qativar was not sure what he read in the depth of the other's eyes, but he stood his ground confidently. He had leverage yet to reveal.

Thomas started to respond, then laughed without humor and shook his head. Then he managed, "You don't get it. If word about the *tezarian* drive gets out, your piloting contracts won't be worth the material they're recorded on."

Qativar shrugged. "You don't seem to get it, either, Ambassador. Without us, there is no intersystem trade. Colonies will wither and blow away like so much chaff in the galactic wind. You can't get off-planet without us."

"It would perhaps be better than being lost in space."

"Not with boost," Vihtirne put in hurriedly. "Ambassador, we can help each other greatly. Hundreds of years of the *tezarian* drive can't be overlooked, not even by one so new to FTL as you are. You may not fully comprehend what we do, but it is undeniable we are successful until fatigue or permanent burnout affects our abilities, and even those vagaries are offset by boost."

"You've even named it."

"Our pilots have. You must understand that it does not give soulfire to those who do not have it, or to the untrained who cannot use it. You are only augmenting a skill, not grafting one."

"I want nothing to do with it. It's a drug, untested, and its effects are unknown."

Qativar said softly, "We know what it can do."

They looked steadily at one another and then Qativar added, "We need the drug. We need a provider. And I think you will want to give it to us, for reasons even other than the advantages we have just pointed out."

"Why?"

"Because," said Qativar even more softly, leaning forward so that only Vihtirne and the ambassador could hear him. "I have come to gift you with the humankind who murdered your daughter. Want him? He is yours, if we can come to an understanding."

Chapter 6

Thomas leaned over the cryo chamber. He had not answered Qativar's question, but neither had he turned the Choyan crew away when they brought in the medical equipment. The honor guard had wheeled it in with considerably less ceremony than they had his daughter's coffin. It was bigger, built for the needs of a Choya, and it dominated the small bay. Its slate gray sides radiated an unemotional frost. Its observation window drew him now, closer, a fatal attraction. He felt as though he were standing on the edge of a tall bridge, unable to fight the gravity which would pull him over and down, down into an uncertain but surely deadly fate.

The chamber sank a chill through Thomas' clothing as he brushed its surface. Its drone was nearly out of his register of hearing, but hung there, an irritating noise that made him clench his teeth as he leaned against the side and bent closer to look into the observation port. He should not look, knew he should not, but he could not help himself. Like a moth nearing a flame, he bent close enough to position himself over the window.

Cold flesh. Even the recent bruising had dulled to purplish charcoal streaks along an alabaster complexion. He had been in a fight or a battle, and had been put down still disheveled, streaks of soot and grit across the backs of his hands, across one brow like a chevron or badge. The dark hair lay unruly, the eyes were closed, the flight suit was torn open along the neckline revealing only a few fine hairs lying curled on the upper torso. He was—he had been—a good-looking young man, Thomas thought. It was no wonder Alexa had taken him for a lover, once. What had Randall thought of her then? Had he been grateful for the gift of passion, of life? Had he loved her back? Had he known and understood her in the ways a father never could . . . duplicitous Alexa, Alexa with a dark side she kept well-hidden from all but the most intimate. What had he thought when he'd murdered her? Did he, in a sleep beyond dreaming, have the slightest idea of who watched him now, who hated him beyond even the boundaries of time and space?

"Do we have an understanding? Do you want him?"

The ambassador found himself standing with his hands clenched on either side of the observation port window, clenched until the skin across his knuckles went livid. With a slow deliberation, he took his hands away, breathed deep, and stepped away. But it was too late to back away from the brink. He had fallen and knew he would never hit bottom.

"Yes," he answered. "And yes."

* * * *

The Halls of the Compact bustled with life, teemed with sentient races which were, for the most part, at the top of their respective food chains. Rindalan thought that that made them more or less secure about their position in the galactic scheme of things as he watched them file into the subassembly room where a good many things would be decided concerning their fate, and he could not tell them the truth.

The horns upon his head seemed to bear the brunt of the burden he felt, sending a dull throb through him. Perhaps he had not convalesced enough before taking up this position. Perhaps he was not diplomat enough to be here at all, he thought, once more scanning the hall's interior. Sharp eyes met his glance and turned aside, some defiantly, most resentfully, a few curiously. He had claimed what few favors Panshinea had left in his wake to call this vote, and now that he had it, he was not at all sure he could sway it in his favor.

He watched the Abdrelik contigent enter, the heavy amphibious bulk of GNask and rrRusk swaying with each ponderous step, but he was no more fooled by their size than any other member of the Compact. The Abdreliks were quick, rapacious predators, swift as lightning, and as vicious as any primal race still struggling to escape the gravitational ooze of their world. No, the Abdreliks could not be escaped easily, except in the long run, where stamina and strategy could be brought into play. Thus the Choyan had survived their first encounters with the Abdreliks, and stayed ahead of them, though the long chase had begun to wear on them.

Rindalan reminded himself that he was not in the Halls for Cho alone, but for all races, for any who chose to face the Chaos created by FTL flight. Without *tezars* to pilot the nether regions, no race could spread its wings wide enough to span the galaxies, all the galaxies, known and unknown. Without the *tezarian* drive, there was no destiny for any race beyond the mundane, and without *bahdur,* there was no safety. But after the centuries of Cho's monopoly, even the lowliest of Compact members had come to chafe under the secrecy of the *tezars* maintained.

What would these fools do if they even guessed that the Choyan piloted, not by superior navigational devices and drives, but by the psychic skin of their teeth, Rindalan thought with a grim satisfaction. And he was here to save them once more from the disaster such a revelation would bring. His head continued to throb, and he wondered again, if it was worth it, all the subterfuge, the manipulation.

The Ivrian ambassador fluttered in, all atwitter. With a swirl of color and down, he settled at his voting pod.

"Order," stated the Ronin chairperson. His empty quills rattled at the back of his neck as he looked upon the assembly. This committee had once been Panshinea's to chair—he had lost it to the Ronin. Rindalan turned jaundiced eyes on the former assassin who now occupied a podium of power as if born to it. Faln narrowed his gaze back, his pointed nails ripping at the notes in front of him, then looked away as Rindalan met his stare squarely.

The elder wondered what the worlds were coming to. He stifled a sigh and folded his hands across his lap. Below him, the Ivrian caught his attention and stared, boldly, for a split second.

That was a vote he had, Rindalan thought. He gave a tiny nod in acknowledgment. Immediately in front of him, the voting pod activated.

"I wish to state my objections," the Ronin said, his voice vibrating with the strain of reproducing Trade, his tones rusty as though he had not spoken the language for a long while. He always sounded like that, the result of a throat wound he'd taken, the wound which had ended his career as an assassin. "This vote has been taken once, and settled, and I do not feel an appeal is necessary in this committee."

Rindalan braced himself for a reply, but GNask took issue instead, interrupting, "Not all of us feel this way, Faln, or the appeal would not have been allowed. Step down and let the process evolve."

The Choyan did not look across at the Abdrelik, lest he show his surprise at the unexpected support.

GNask sat back in the booth, rumbling quietly in his pleasure. rrRusk said, "The old relic is pointedly not looking at us."

"He would not. The prey knows better than to let the predator see the whites of his eyes." GNask put up a hand, caressed the symbiont life which was curled behind his ear. The slug warmed to his touch, stirred, and shifted its footing upon the amphibian's purplish hide. "Nonetheless, he wonders what we are up to."

rrRusk, whose career in the diplomatic pits of Sorrow was nonexistent, said, "What are we up to?"

"We are observing the Choyan ambassador in crisis." GNask took his hand from the *tursh,* which pulsed in a kind of contented purr, and tucked his hands under his heavy jowls. "Do not you, my general, be like these shortsighted fools and ignore the real purpose of this vote. Cho teeters in an uneasy balance, and if she falls, her mystery will crack and perhaps even the *tezarian* drive will be revealed to us."

"I will listen closely, then." The Abdrelik war general grunted and shifted his weight upon the massive bench which held them. Unlike the ambassador's, his symbiont had been left at home. He depended on the various moisturizing and exfoliant creamicides to keep his skin comfortable in space. They did not, nor did the distance from his *tursh* improve his temper any. He looked forward to a mud bath and a cool bottle of beer, one of the few contributions of Terra that he had any use for.

GNask panned the gallery. Though Faln protested the appeal and considered the matter done, the subcommittee had drawn nearly its full roster. There might be some major shifts among the diplomatic blocs this session ... or there might not. Rindalan, revered though he was on his home planet, hardly held the charismatic abilities of the emperor himself or even of Panshinea's ill-fated predecessor. In the months of his appointment, he had not yet proved to be the torch which illuminated them nor the glue which bound them together.

All of which did not mean that Rindalan did not have the support he needed to sway this vote. He must have, or he would not have called the appeal. Still, GNask thought to himself as he surveyed the hall, there might be some good to be had by adding his own sway. It would be a reversal of his earlier position, but he thought he could explain it if it gained the advantage he needed. If not, well, his career and rrRusk's were already on the line. The only thing that could save him now was the *tezarian* drive.

Cho was undergoing a massive upheaval in its internal politics and alignments. The dearth of eligible pilots had suddenly changed and become, almost overnight, a flood. But the sudden availability of pilots for Compact contracts made GNask as suspicious as it did hopeful. He knew the rigid Choyan standards, and realized that many of those coming into the job were not as qualified as they had been in the past. They had what they wished—more pilots to use the *tezarian* drive—but they did not have what they needed: safety crossing the chaotic zone of warped space. He hoped to be able to press the point over the next session, lobbying for the secret of the drive itself to be made available to all, arguing that piloting was a difficult skill which even the Choyan could not always guarantee, and that it was a burden which should be shared for the good of all.

He perceived the situation like a cracked seal on an air lock, enough pressure and the whole thing would blow sky-high. The Choyan had begun to fracture along what was once a seamless society. He, among others, could apply the pressure.

GNask rolled back onto a haunch and watched the sharp-faced Ronin ambassador. Faln betrayed little emotion except the bright-eyed attention which typified all of his ilk. He still watched with a hunter's eyes. GNask did not flinch when the Ronin examined him and moved on. Faln had once tried to assassinate GNask within these very halls, and if it had not been for the quick reactions of a Choyan patrolman, GNask would not be alive today. It was the second time in his life a

Choyan had saved him. He did not hold it to their account. The patrolman had done it because it was his job within the Compact. Palaton had done it because a Norton assassin had come after the two of them, and it was necessary to save both to save the one. GNask had no illusions. The personal amplifications mattered little to him. He allied with Choyan rarely, and Faln had his uses.

"Order," called the Ronin for the second, and last time. He signaled for the assembly doors to be shut and locked, and the room became muffled and oppressive as the members were sealed in. As the silence shrouded them, Faln pointed his chin at Rindalan.

"I trust the ambassador from Cho has gathered the support he needs to call this assembly."

"I have, your honor," the Choyan said, as he got to his feet. "Or we would not be here."

Faln scarcely acknowledged the formality, eyeing the electronic roleboard in the podium. "Sign in accordingly," he ordered the delegates.

GNask watched Rindalan closely, from a three-quarter angle, searching what he could see of the aged ambassador's face for signs of worry or hesitation, and saw none. He could read nothing in the Choya's body language either, beyond Rindalan's advancing years. The naturally wiry musculature had given way to gauntness, the fringe of hair steadily losing its red-gold luster, the horn crown, bold and impressive even by Choyan standards, seeming somehow diminished. By the egg, Rindalan was old enough to be GNask's grandfather, for the ancient enemy was incredibly long-lived, outside of a pilot's span, and that made Rindalan old indeed. Old but not infirm, never infirm, and GNask could not count on any weakness there.

The Abdrelik leaned forward and punched his own signature on the board. He wiped the corner of his mouth with the fleshy back of one hand, catching a tiny string of spittle from his tusk as he did so. Sitting back, he stared overhead at the screen, waiting for results. Nothing would be projected until all votes were in, so as not to influence those still undecided on the question.

Out of the corner of his eye, GNask saw the first undeniable reaction as Rindalan jerked in surprise as the totals flashed into visibility. The vote was close, extremely close, near enough so that GNask might have been the deciding vote which meant that Rindalan had lost support he'd been led to count upon. The Choya looked as though he fought with himself to not turn and survey the assembly, to see who had defected.

As the ID came up on the voters, however, the Choya's body jerked again, then swung about stiffly as if unlocked, and Rindalan leveled his gaze at GNask. The Abdrelik peeled his lips back in a half-smile. The other knew how he had voted, and that his unexpected support had given the Choya the appeal he asked for, though the question of why the Abdrelik should support Rindalan surely gave the Choya reason to pause.

Faln called for attention and stated, "The vote goes in favor of Rindalan's request, and we are now prepared to hear the appeal."

"I am prepared to give it at this time." Rindalan swayed a bit, then settled back in his chair. The neck which had been slightly bowed, now straightened with determination.

"State your position."

"Ambassadors and delegates of the committee, I would like, first, to thank you for this opportunity," Rindalan began, his voices dry but commanding. The richness of the Choya's throat, with two vocal cords resounding and two voices, subtly underlying one another, filled the small assembly room.

"It was approved by this committee, several days ago, to negotiate with a second pilot contracting group from my world, a group which exists outside the framework of the three schools which have trained *tezars* since the beginning of flight. This was a decision which, I know, was not undertaken lightly, but which I must respectfully request you to rescind. Although the sudden influx of available pilots for contracting must seem a boon to many of you, I must stress that these are not necessarily qualified pilots, and that crossing the void does not leave room for error."

From a dark swirled corner of the assembly, a being stirred, a lithe, sinuous beast which unslitted green eyes, and leaned forward from the shadow. Its Trade was accented with a sibilant hiss. "Does the ambassador suggest that any Choyan pilot is inferior to the challenge of the *tezarian* drive?"

Rindalan looked toward the Norton delegate which, with feline grace, had resettled into the inky backdrop of its area.

"I suggest," the Choya returned, "that you do not know who you're dealing with, and that the current state of internal politics on my world makes normal negotiations considerably riskier."

"Are we to understand that the Vihtirne group is unreliable?" asked the Ronin ambassador sharply.

"I do not have enough facts to prove so, Your Honor, but it is not facts I seek. Those facts, each and every one of them, would mean an unmitigated disaster. I wish to prevent such statistics before they can occur."

The Norton gave a lash of its whiplike tail, but subsided into silence and said nothing further. However, Faln was not finished.

"If we made laws or negotiated by innuendo," the Ronin said, "we would never be done with the process. This appeal was granted on what should have been more concrete offerings. The Compact is aware of a power struggle on Cho, and that the Vihtirne group is but one of several contending against the emperor for control. The Compact intends to stay neutral with regard to your internal politics, but we have been offered what seems to be a good faith opportunity to hire pilots. Unless you provide me with incontrovertible proof that hiring those pilots would be reckless endangerment and downright stupid, I would hesitate to even call this appeal for a vote." Faln cleared his raspy throat after he ground to a halt.

"The proof," Rindalan said, "is that we cannot cross space without the *tezarian* drive and qualified pilots to use it. Those of you who have, over the centuries, tried to discern our navigating process know the truth of what I'm saying. Few can use the drive. Even amongst ourselves, there are those who are borderline in ability, which is not good enough when lives and valuable cargo are on the line. Chaos is an unforgiving phenomenon. It does not give up its dead, or our mistakes, easily."

"You contend that the Vihtirne group offers up ill-qualified pilots."

"I do."

Faln brought up a reading on the podium screen. He looked

at it for a moment, then said, "Is Birgnan of Sky an unreliable pilot?"

Rindalan hesitated only a second, but even that hesitation made GNask grow alert. "Your Honor, he graduated from the Salt Towers, but suffered a severe bout of what we call burn-out fever and, yes, I would call him unreliable."

"Dangerous?"

Rindalan's spine went stubbornly rigid. The Choya paused before nodding his head once. "Yes."

"What about Lilen of Star?"

"From Blue Ridge. She quit the school voluntarily and returned to run her Householding. She never finished her training."

"And Paes?"

"A stellar pilot. Too old, however, for the job."

"One might say that of you, Rindalan." And Faln glowered down at him.

Rindalan looked back with pale blue eyes. "One might. The difference between the two of us is that this assembly is not going to disappear forever from space norm simply because I requested the hearing."

"Yet, based on the reports I'm bringing up, there have been no complaints from their current contractors."

Rindalan said patiently, "As I've stated, Your Honor, when there is a complaint, it will be because there has been a disaster, perhaps an irreversible one. Shall we sit and wait for it to happen, or should I take action and prevent it?"

GNask listened to the Choya fence with comments from others in the assembly hall, but his attention had become internal now. Rindalan was not telling the truth, entirely, and GNask knew evasiveness when he heard it. But there was a kernel of truth in his statements which had brought the Abdrelik fully awake.

It was not the *tezarian* drive. Perhaps it never had been. The issue here was clearly not the availability of the drive, but of those interpreting and using it. All those centuries, all those lost decades of research, knowingly misguided. *It was the pilots themselves.* And Rindalan had been handcuffed by his own people's secrecy. He could not say what it was that had gone wrong, only that it had and even his own people were no longer to be trusted. It was not in what he had said, in whatever it was he was going to say, the truth lay in what he could not say, not matter how this council went.

And GNask had had a pilot in his hands and let him slip through. The Abdrelik clenched his fists. John Taylor Thomas had wrenched both his human daughter and the Choya pilot Nedar right out of his grip. As his pulse surged, his *tursh* made a slight murmur of awareness, and its antennae came out, stalk eyes peering about in alarm. GNask reined in his anger and put a soothing finger out to stroke the symbiont's chin. He told himself that if he had done it once, he could do it again, and what better timing than amid the confusion of Cho's own civil war? A great many crimes could be committed in such a climate.

He closed his eyes and prayed to the bogs which birthed him that he had not grown soft in his years as an ambassador, that he would be able to seize this truth and make of it such a victory that his people would never be able to forget it.

When he opened his eyes, to the sound of vigorous piping and arguing by the Ivrian delegate, the vote of the appeal had been postponed. The doors to the assembly hall opened, and the delegates began to leave. Rindalan sat in his booth, unmoving. GNask waved rrRusk off and waited until the Choya finally got to his feet. He stood as the other passed.

Rindalan halted. "Don't think I did not notice your vote," the Choya said, his voices deep, if somewhat thin.

"I knew that you would have," GNask returned.

"And do not think you will gain an advantage by it."

GNask let his lips curl back against his tusks. "I do not," he said. "None that you will give me, anyway."

Rindalan's expression changed, as if he would answer that back. Instead he clamped his lips shut and leaned into motion, moving past the Abdrelik. GNask felt the satisfaction that comes with successfully tracking and cornering a prey. The kill might be postponed, he might toy with the other a bit, but the end was inevitable. Any good hunter knew that.

Chapter 7

"Two things." Panshinea entered his palace, with the bent elderly minister scurrying to keep pace with him, and he paused long enough to let Gathon catch up. "Rindalan was to call a vote. I want to know from him immediately what the outcome was. Secondly, I want to know if you or anyone in security has heard from Palaton." He had just arrived, and the smell of burn off from the landing pads was still on him.

The palace at Charolon was vast, built and rebuilt over the centuries from its early years as a fortress, to a high tech center, and now retrofitted into its past glory, though it would not be inaccurate to say that it was probably a hundred times bigger than its predecessors. Yet, Gathon reflected, Pan filled it. He always had, and even in death, probably would still.

The ruling head of the House of Star cast an aura of charisma and vigor that went beyond finite limits. When he was gone from Charolon, the palace was bereft. When he was home, it seemed bursting with Panshinea's presence. Although, Gathon reflected with a small bit of irony, it did not necessarily indicate Pan's fitness for the throne he occupied.

He took a deep breath, for keeping up with the emperor had winded him somewhat. He was well aware of what he looked like next to the other: spindly, hair thinning from black to yellow-white strands of age, his shoulders bent from the burdens of his job and his scallop-edged crown beginning to grow brittle. Another looking on him might think of retiring him, but Gathon found comfort knowing that Pan did not. Gathon had long ago crossed the threshold of his House. He was not a Sky, he was a Choya in the service of Cho and the emperor of Cho, and if the job were a harness, he wished only to be allowed to die in it. He did not wish it because there would be no retirement for him, no returning to the fold of his

Householding because they had forsaken him as he had forsaken them. No, he desired it because it was fitting for him to
die as he had lived, in dedication to his office.

He became aware, as Pan's forest green and jade eyes
sparked a little, that the emperor had tired of waiting for him.

He cleared his throat. "I have an open line to Rindy, but
have not had any word yet on the vote, although he did trans-
mit that a vote had been called."

"Success in that, then, if limited. Hopefully, more news
will bring greater success."

Gathon nodded, looking down his notepad, scarcely paying
attention to Panshinea's words. "No word from Palaton yet,
and I have to replace the head of security. I've taken the liberty of hard-copying some résumés and putting them on your
desk for your earliest review."

"What's wrong with Jorana?"

"Nothing that I'm aware of. She left her resignation when
you announced your return." Gathon lifted his chin, watching
Pan.

The emperor's jaw moved. He looked through the massive
marble lobby of the entrance hall. His bronze hair curled back
thickly from his forehead, a typical Star, gold cast with auburn highlights, face delicately pale, eyes of green or blue,
square jaw, tall and wiry of strength. There was aging apparent in his neckline, to be sure, for he was no longer young,
but neither was he old. And, even if he were, Panshinea
would never have admitted it. Losing Jorana, though, had
been a blow. Gathon could see it in his aspect. Though the
emperor had not yet taken a wife because his throne took his
time and devotion, at one time, he and Jorana had been lovers. He had never admitted it to be more than a dalliance, but
Gathon knew that Panshinea's mixed feelings toward Palaton
had as much to do with Jorana as they did with the undeniable fact that Palaton represented the future beyond Pan's
time as emperor, a future which Pan was trying as hard as he
could to delay.

"Is she . . . all right?"

"I could not say, sire. I have not heard from her, or of her,
since she left."

"Did she give an explanation for her resignation?"

"Only that it was a personal reason, and that she could not serve with divided loyalty."

Pan's jaw ticked. He stared into the palace lobby as if seeking an answer written on air, before looking down at Gathon. "I'll look over the files. I take it you recommend promoting from within rather than searching outside the ranks?"

"Jorana left you an excellent security force. There are half a dozen candidates who ought to do well in her position."

"All right, then." Panshinea paused, then gathered himself. "The rest of the business we should conduct in my music room."

The music room, along with a small and intimate library, were the only rooms in the palace guaranteed to be secure against all manner of eavesdropping, both high tech and psychic, although Gathon sometimes wondered to himself how such a thing could be guaranteed. It mattered to him because if the security of those two rooms could be breached, then his own life would be worth very little in the emperor's eyes. Still, for all the conversations they had had in those two rooms over the decades, no word had ever been repeated. Perhaps Panshinea's faith was not misplaced, after all.

Pan sat at the self-standing *lindar.* He splayed his right hand over the keyboard, barely touching it, and producing a plaintive strain. He stared at the keys a moment as if contemplating another stroking, then put his shoulders back and lifted his head to gaze across the room at Gathon.

"No word from Palaton."

"Not yet."

"It would not be well advised if he were to hold his peace."

"I agree with you," Gathon remarked, though both knew well it did not matter if Gathon agreed or not.

"But he does not respond."

"I have had no word of him since he left Blue Ridge five days ago."

Panshinea flinched. His verdant gaze moved past Gathon to stare out the music room window, at a garden few if any even knew existed within the palace walls. Because of its secrecy, even the landscapers did not tend it. Only Pan, in sporadic moods of floral creativity, or Gathon if the drought withered it too badly. It was feral and somewhat seedy, and altogether beautiful because it had not been so carefully sculpted. It simply *was,* and that in itself was quite an accomplishment. "Blue Ridge in ruins," he murmured.

"Yes, sire."

"How could that have happened?"

"Not by Palaton's design."

"No. No, I think he would sooner have cut off his right hand than destroyed a flight school. Although neither Qativar nor Vihtirne have proved any more agreeable to an interview than Palaton, I will lay the blame in their laps. They will feel no guilt, of course, using the martyrdom of Blue Ridge to help build the foundation for their new House." Panshinea's thick neck muscles rippled as he looked back to the keyboard. This time, he deliberately stroked the *lindar,* evoking a sinister chord. "What about the drug?"

"It's called boost on the streets."

"Does it work?"

"Only if one has *bahdur.* The commons have no real use for it."

The *lindar* quieted. Panshinea met his eyes. "Do you think it will help me?"

This was a conversation Gathon suddenly knew he wished to have no part of. He shifted weight. "I . . . don't know."

"I understand it banishes the fatigue which blocks *bahdur.* That would seem to be something quite desirable."

"It's an off-world drug. Supplies, now, are limited. I have not been able to obtain any for analysis, but even if I could, we don't know that we could duplicate it. Pan, it is like wondering if sleight of hand and illusion can substitute for *bahdur.* It may seem adequate on the first flash, but its substance is entirely different and transient."

"But you don't know that."

"No. I don't."

Panshinea became very quiet, and Gathon knew he was pondering what the drug might mean to him if it were genuine. His gift of *bahdur* had been prodigal, but his days as emperor had steadily drained it, and now his body felt the creeping agony of neuropathy, the death of the nerve field which created and fed soulfire. As surely as a *tezar,* he was burning dry, and as surely as any pilot who'd lost it, he felt the edge of the madness and the emptiness which accompanied the condition. But while there were Householdings which would take back their sons and daughters who'd mastered Chaos and been fortunate enough to return, there was no niche for failed emperors. Cho never had more than one emperor at a time. Death was Panshinea's only future, if the soulfire guttered out completely. His enemies, and perhaps even his successors, would tear him to shreds.

They would do so even sooner if they knew that he perpetuated what little *bahdur* he had left by stealing it from others. Gathon did not approve of Panshinea's actions, but he was an accomplice in them nonetheless, and had been for twenty years, because until this juncture in time, Pan had been the emperor for Cho. Now, he was beginning to have his doubts. Now, he did not know how far he was willing to continue to go to keep the throne occupied. He stood, with a face as blankly solemn as possible, knowing that if Pan could read his thoughts, he would be dead before he crossed the threshold of the music room.

But theirs had been a long association. Gathon had never had any indication that Panshinea, though rumored to, had ever possessed that particular Choyan ability. Few did. Perhaps it had been eradicated when the House of Flame had been destroyed centuries ago, a talent erased along with others, good and bad, out of fear and jealousy. "I have to do something, Gathon," Panshinea said softly, his voices shot through with desperation and longing.

"I know, sire," Gathon responded with compassion. "I know you do." His communicator let out a low buzz and he clapped a hand to his belt. Stepping to the desk near him, he picked up the comline and found that the transmission from Sorrow they'd been waiting for was now coming in.

Pan let out a sigh. "I'll wait," he said, and beckoned for Gathon to go retrieve a printout from decoding. He looked back to the garden and the walls which harbored it. "I'm not going anywhere."

Malahki found Father Chirek in the second bolt-hole he searched, a squalid, odoriferous excuse for a home in the undersection of the commons' quarter in Charolon. He had not thought to find Dorea's priest anywhere in the capital, but his objective had been to find a place from which he could operate business of his own, and the priest had been there, sleeping on a low-slung cot which had seen better decades.

The boat trip from the harbor city where Dorea quartered had left him stiff and tired. City security in Charolon had been alert and he'd taken back streets, wending his way into the inner quarters. He'd thought for a brief moment that he was too old for this, that he was nearing the age of being a grandfather, that he ought to be sitting in a solarium watching his grandchildren romp, but he had no family left. Jorana had been his fosterling and he'd thought perhaps to share her family, but once she had gained the talent necessary to become Housed, he'd been forced to carve a new destiny for her. His work with her had its successes and failures, but it had changed the relationship between them forever.

As a security agent, she had been his contact as well as his enemy. He could not fault Jorana. She had managed to walk a fine line, serving both her emperor and her foster father well. But how did she now serve herself? Malahki had no delusions that he had followed Dorea's instructions as much to find Jorana as to find Palaton.

And all he had done so far was to find another strife-worn revolutionary. Malahki smiled gently and leaned forward to awaken his old friend.

A spark of *bahdur* jumped from Malahki's hand to the other's brown-clothed shoulder as he touched him into waking. Power calling to power. The phenomenon never ceased to amaze Malahki, though it could be something as simple as static electricity being released. He had never been aware of it in all the years of his life among the greetings of the Housed. Did they even notice it? He wondered if his newly awakened soulfire were perhaps stronger or greater than the average.

Father Chirek opened heavy eyelids and groaned when he saw Malahki leaning over him. He sat up, slumped against the rough adobe walls of the room, and rubbed his eyes clearer. "Took you long enough," he remarked.

"She sent you here as well?"

"Indeed. Said that we were a pair, useless at anything without the other." The renegade priest smiled wryly. He was at the crossroads between youth and age, his face just beginning to acquire character and wisdom, his eyes still clear and unlined, a face of earnestness and honesty, Malahki thought. Father Chirek had lived for years working for the future which blind Dorea saw so well, and he had been far from ineffective with or without Malahki. The room which held him now was quite different from the home which he had occupied formerly—before the Change had been wrought in him, and the prophecy for which he had trained his whole life had begun unfolding about him. That home had been abandoned, for he had left a life as a mere data clerk in the employ of the government and gone in search of a Prophet—and found her.

Malahki pulled up a stool and rested his weight upon it. "She chides you inappropriately."

"She chides all of us, the child suddenly become parent. As for the appropriateness—she has the Sight, I do not. Like a tapestry weaving, tomorrow is far more subtle and varied than I could guess." Chirek took a deep breath and then let it out. "I doubt that Palaton will contact us, but if he is here, thinking to respond to the emperor publicly, then he will need to have some sort of network in place. He won't come to us, not after taking Rand from us, and may well avoid all commons because of that. No allies there. Yet, despite all that happened at Blue Ridge, I think I may have found it."

"Who would he go to?"

"Who else would a pilot go to but other *tezars?*"

Chirek's statement took Malahki aback. "Surely not, after what Vihtirne has done. There is no refuge there."

"Not pilots who can work. There is too much chaos there, at the moment. I mean pilots who cannot. Retired *tezars.*"

"Ah." Malahki scratched his brow. "Few and far between. Reclusive. Embittered. Nor particularly sane, any that I ever met."

"All it takes is one or two. There was the *tezar* who worked as bodyguard for young Rand. . . ."

Malahki searched his memory frantically for a name that fit the image: *tezar* in his prime, cut away from service by an injury which even their medical technology could not reverse, fitted with an arm prosthesis he sometimes used and sometimes shunned. The name came to him in a flash.

"Traskar!"

Chirek nodded. "If we can find him."

Traskar had not suffered burnout, he had suffered amputation. He had *bahdur*, he had tolerated, even developed a friendship with Palaton's alien companion—yes, Palaton might well feel Traskar an ally to be sought out.

For the first time in days, Malahki felt as though Dorea had not assigned him an impossible task. He rubbed his hands as though anticipating the pulling together of the hidden reins of Chirek's network. "Oh, we'll find him. Let us hope that Palaton finds him as well."

Chapter 8

"Vihtirne of Sky awaits, Your Majesty," Gathon said.

The emperor of Cho looked up from his console, responding to his friend's tone. "Do I detect a note of disapproval in your voices, Minister?"

The aging Choya raised an eyebrow, adding another knife-like crease to the many in his face. The yellow-white streaks in his dark mane had increased, Panshinea realized, multifold during his absence. "You do, Panshinea," Gathon returned. "By asking her here, you lend her authority she does not need."

"You think this private council legitimizes the House of Tezars?"

"I think this meeting will confirm several of her suspicions, as well as lend weight to her usurpation. However," and Gathon bowed stiffly, "what's done is done."

"What would you suggest I do now?"

"I would suggest," the minister answered quietly, "that you not keep her waiting." He stood in the doorway, shoulders hunched slightly.

Panshinea took a deep breath. He did not like crossing the instincts of his minister, and bearing Gathon's disapproval now was like adding a heavier weight to the burden which already threatened to overwhelm him. Anger began to shove his regret aside. Where was Gathon when these momentous decisions had to be made? No, that was when he, Panshinea, stood alone. He always had. He always would. The emperor motioned with a hand. "All right. Show her in."

After a moment of silence, she filled the threshold. He would, Panshinea reflected, have to have been a dead Choya not to feel her presence charging the room. As a faint drift of perfume reached his nose, he turned and beheld her.

Vihtirne of Sky was still a Choya'i of great beauty, he thought. If the genetic imperative to stay within one's House were not so great, he, a Star, might even have considered her a potential mate and empress. He had flirted with that consideration many times during his long reign and association with her. She was, like him, no longer firmly in her prime, but it scarcely mattered to a Choya'i. If they wished, they could be fertile until far past their middle years. Fertility among the Choyan was not a gender issue. The female, as well as the male, had complete control over her ability to conceive and bear children.

Perhaps, Panshinea reflected, he should simply have asked Vihtirne to become his mistress. No untoward mingling of their Houses' genetic heritage would have been called for, though the arrangement would have been just as unconventional. The couplings of ambitions, as well as sexual drives, would have been spectacular. But he doubted that she then, as she certainly would not now, would have accepted such a proposal.

She wore a sheath of deep, shimmering blue that accentuated her eyes and the still jet-dark mane of hair that cascaded from her horn crown. Her shoulders remained as smooth as her neckline, her peach-toned skin firm and unblemished. As she stepped forward, there was something more to her regal and sophisticated carriage, an air of expectation, and Pan knew with a sinking heart that Gathon had been right, more than right. Vihtirne thought this meeting of greater import than he'd intended.

Another mistake, for a throne already mired in mistakes. He threw back his shoulders, then stood to take her hand, remembering all too well why he'd never asked her to be his mistress. She would never have been happy in the throne's shadow. She intended to have it for herself.

And she would have it yet, over his dead body, if she could contrive it.

"Emperor. It has been too long." She offered him a hand, which he took briefly.

"I agree. You look as lovely as ever."

Her deep-set eyes considered him. "I wish I could say the same for you," she returned finally. "But I do not think the burdens of the throne are good for a Choya of your temperament. The confinements of the position have worn on you."

He led her across the chambers and let her choose where she would sit, on a divan or the *lindar* bench or a high-backed chair upholstered to look as though it were the feathered tail fan of a *ferentar.* She chose the chair. The multihued splendor of the tail fan set off the dark sheen of her hair spectacularly, giving him pause and her an advantage which he was not willing to grant. As he caught his breath, he deliberately chose the *lindar* bench, sitting before the keyboard instrument as if the meeting were incredibly casual. The briefest of frowns creased her face and then was smoothed away.

"The position," he admitted, "has duties and obligations more wearing than most Choyan could imagine. Even without interference, it would be difficult to do one's best. Yet, if you or anyone else were to ask me if I wished to give it up, I would have to be frank and tell you that I am not yet ready. There is much I think I can still accomplish."

Vihtirne arranged a fold of her skirt about her ankle. "Perhaps I can be of assistance."

"No. I don't think so," Pan told her easily. He put an elbow on the *lindar.* A faint note tinkled from the keyboard.

"Then, please, Your Majesty, tell me why you've summoned me. I assure you I cannot possibly guess." The natural arrogance of the House of Sky rose in her face, intensifying her blush.

"To warn you, not once but twice."

The hard glitter in her eyes did not soften a speck. "Warn me? Pray tell, Emperor, am I in trouble?"

"I will not recognize the House of *Tezars,*" he told her. "Nor will the Congress."

She put out a hand, smooth, relatively unlined or freckled with age, and stroked her knee through the fabric of her skirt. She looked back up at him, unruffled. "Perhaps once," she said, "you could have known that, with whatever assurances and guarantees came to the emperor who sat the throne of Cho. Now, however, our world is upside down. You cannot threaten me with any great surety, just as I," and she smiled coldly, "cannot threaten you."

Panshinea let his face move in an unanswering smile of equal chill. "Do not make light of this, Vihtirne. I'm busy. I didn't summon you here to trivialize matters. I have word from my ambassador on Sorrow that the Compact there has agreed not to accept piloting charters with your House, pending investigation."

He expected her to show the blow he'd dealt her, perhaps even to surge to her feet, voices ringing as she declared, "You have done what?"

But Vihtirne of Sky did not even twitch an eyebrow. The moment of silence stretched between them. Finally, she stirred. "The Great Wheel, with only three Houses to turn upon it, is unbalanced. You can't be so much a fool as to ignore the *tezars*."

"I find it in the best interest of Cho to do so."

Vihtirne now moved her head, stretching her graceful neck, to look at him slightly askance. She turned her hand, palm up, on her knee as if she cupped something. "The courts have returned the water recycling patent to my House. More specifically, to me. Do not make me use something so vital as clean water as a tool to have the House of *Tezars* recognized."

Her declaration struck him to his core. She had him, if she chose to use her power. The recycling patent had been made public centuries ago, for the common good, but he knew she had been pursuing its return. Damn Gathon, who had not told him the decision had finally come through. And damn the courts, who normally could have kept this ball bouncing for a decade or so, if they'd wished. The House of Star was in its descendant. He knew it, they all knew it. The only question now was how long, how far, the fall.

Vihtirne returned his stare evenly. He felt something turn in him. She did not have him, or she would not be sitting here so meekly. He did not know what it was, but there was something holding her back. She had hoped, not demanded, that he would recognize the founding of the new House. There was something she had *not* said which was equally as important as what she had. There was danger here, but not necessarily defeat. Panshinea sucked in his stomach as well as his resolve.

"You cannot be of two Houses," Panshinea told her. "Either one or the other. If you leave Sky for the *tezars*, think very carefully on what it is you leave behind." He stood. "And that brings me to my second warning. You presume, because of our chaotic situation, that the Wheel must be balanced, but you've assumed there is room for your ambitions. There is not. The fourth House has returned to its rightful place on the Wheel, a House risen from out of the ashes of its downfall. What you Skies, we, and the Earthans feared most has come about, regardless of our past. The House of Flame has returned to Cho."

He heard, with satisfaction, the tiniest of gasps from Vihtirne. When he looked back at her, he saw she had paled.

"How is this possible?"

"A genetic selection which could not be denied, however destructive it may be." He shrugged. "Who knows? If any were left or hidden, there was bound to come a time when they would gain enough strength to be felt again. And if they were the tree from which we all branched, we would be fools to ignore them, my dear. We learned some difficult lessons in our past about genetic manipulation. It appears we are still students to the God and nature which carved us."

Vihtirne did stand then. She mouthed derision. "Don't spout platitudes at me, Panshinea. There could be no Flames today if someone had not hidden them during the scourging. What was destroyed once before can be destroyed again. They will not take my spot upon the Great Wheel! The *tezars* have made Cho—they will have a House, if I have to build it stone by stone. If there are Flames, they can't be in force, not yet, or they would have shown their hand. What do you know of them?"

"I know," said Panshinea heavily, "that they won't be put down again. We have, both of us, tried to deal with Palaton before."

"Palaton! A Flame!" Vihtirne spun about, her dress shimmering around her slender form. "That explains much," she commented softly. Her eyes met his squarely. "And you, fool, made him an heir to the throne."

"A warning," repeated Panshinea, as though what she said had not stung him, though it had. "Make of it what you will. Before you threaten the throne, and the fabric of life on Cho by rescinding your patent, I think you had better consider the enemy a little more closely."

Vihtirne's eyes narrowed, and her voices dropped into a faint purr. "Do you suggest an alliance, Emperor?"

Panshinea dared to turn his back on her, spreading his slender hands over the *lindar* keyboard, keeping his fingers suspended over the instrument. "I suggest only," he said, "that you have more options to consider than you believed." He then dropped his hands lightly down and began to play, drowning out whatever her response might have been with music, an imperial dismissal. He did not sit, but let the keyboard take his leaning weight.

Gathon came, in response to the *lindar,* and escorted Vihtirne out. She looked back once, eyes flashing, over her shoulder. Panshinea, swept up in the beauty of the song he was playing, tossed his head back and caught a glimpse of her look before she swept out the door. It sent a chill down his back, and he frowned in concentration to keep his playing from faltering.

It was as though he'd looked Death in the face and won only the barest of reprieves.

Still, he must have set her to thinking, and hesitating about weakening his position further. For the moment, she would be pondering what to do about Palaton and the possible rise of a House of Flame. The corner of his mouth quirked. Not that Palaton would do such a thing by design. Wherever the heir to the throne was, he must surely be focusing on more elemental matters—like staying alive.

If the imperial guards could not ferret out the pilot, perhaps Vihtirne's more numerous and less scrupulous contacts could do the job. Then Panshinea could throw him a lifeline, if Palaton acquiesced to his will and terms. And if Palaton destroyed Vihtirne instead, so much the better.

Gathon returned.

Sharply, Panshinea broke off playing. "Why didn't you tell me the decision had come in on the recycling patent?"

"Has it?" Gathon knotted his face tightly. "I was unaware. I knew it was pending. . . ."

"I don't think she was bluffing, entirely," Panshinea remarked. He sat down heavily on the bench. "She wants that House."

"Did you think she would renounce it for you?"

"'No,'" he answered to the minister's dry tone. "Not really. Do you think, old friend, there's room on the Great Wheel for five Houses?"

"I imagine," Gathon told him, "that the God-in-all would

have room for any number of Houses, if we had the strength to found them. It is we who are limited, not the Wheel of Life."

The minister's words hit him like a refreshing spring breeze, and he gave out a soft laugh in response. "Are you sure you wouldn't want to consult with Prelate Rindalan before you answer so quickly?"

"No," said the other solemnly. "We've traded philosophies before. I believe we would be of the same mind on this matter." Gathon did hesitate, however, before leaving. "Anything else you wish at the moment?"

Panshinea knew that the other was going to check his court reports, as well as attend to other duties. He sighed heavily as the moment of lightness inevitably fled. "Find her, Gathon, find her and bring her back."

"Who, Your Majesty?"

"Jorana."

"I'm afraid that's not prudent at the moment, but I will issue the orders, if that's what you wish."

Pan's eyebrow flew up. "You know where Jorana is?"

"No, sire. I can issue the order, but I'm afraid it won't do much good. Rindalan might be able to unearth her. He has resources we cannot count, as well as abilities. He seems to be doing quite well on Sorrow. Perhaps a prelate is not so different from a diplomat after all, eh?"

"No. No, I guess not. And from what sideline might the best emperors come?"

Gathon answered with scarcely a pause. "I always thought that those who wanted it most fiercely ought to be given the throne. You were a natural. Vihtirne, too, would have been, if she had been a Star instead of a Sky. The Houses should stay in order."

"And after the Stars, who do you look for?"

He scratched his chin quickly. "The Flames. The Earthans cannot compete within the Compact. If your House must give way, then it should go to the Flames. The Skies have had their turn."

"And what about blood?"

"I have never approved of a succession. Emperors ought to fight for what they want, like the rest of us. May the strongest one win."

"Only the strongest? What about the best?"

"It scarcely matters, Your Highness. We have a representative system in place. Checks and balances. No. The strength, the desire, that's what should win out. It's the only rock which will withstand the weight of the office." Finished, the minister began to walk out the door. He paused on the threshold. "Don't you agree, sir?"

"I'll let you know," Panshinea said dryly, "when I'm finished."

Gathon sketched a bow and left the study.

Chapter 9

Berthing at Sorrow with a crate big enough to handle both the coffin and the cryonic casket under the seal of a diplomatic pouch was difficult only in the actual physical transference. Deep space cruisers were not allowed dirtside on the Compact planet. Ambassador Thomas had to wait for a shuttle with a large enough cargo hold to give him transport down. He'd asked legal to meet him and Maeva was at the dock, a dash of a frown line marking her young face.

"You do know you're pushing ambassadorial rights bringing that in. The boundaries of our probation are being stretched very thin."

Thomas watched as robot arms unloaded the massive crate, their cables groaning in response to its weight and unwieldiness. "It's my daughter's remains," he answered slowly. "I do not feel like putting my life on display, at the moment."

His legal counsel shifted uneasily, then said, "Then that's the biggest damn coffin I've ever seen for . . ." She paused.

Thomas tore his gaze away from the crate and looked down at her. Young, he thought, as Alexa had been. And, in her way, equally ambitious. Her boss had sent her in his place to greet the ambassador. Thomas did not normally appreciate youth and inexperience, but felt it could work to his advantage in this instance. "Yes? For what?"

She blushed faintly. "For someone supposedly burned to death in the wreckage of a crash."

He could feel himself blink. Anger, such as he'd had, and tears, had been replaced by a core of iciness. Her statement hit home and found an emotional vacuum. The corners of his lips pulled. "Yes," he agreed. "It is. The biggest damn coffin I've ever seen. But I don't want the seal on that pouch broken."

"It won't be. That's why I'm along," Maeva said confidently. She took an extra half step to keep up with Thomas as he took the walkway out of the docks. Compact customs inspections looked up, scanned their notepads, matched the bar codes on the crate, and frowned almost in unison, but no one stopped the barge which carried the diplomatic pouch through the docks. A forklift took it from the hover barge as it emerged from the warehouse without incident.

Maeva let out her breath in a tiny puff. Thomas looked down, amused that she had been so confident and yet so tense. "Primed for a fight?"

"If necessary." She had her notebook open. As the forklift transferred the pouch to the embassy's own hover barge, she flipped the notebook closed and sealed it, and slung it from its strap over her shoulder. "I have a car, Ambassador."

"Good. Is the freight barge programmed as I requested?"

That intense little dash-line of worry reappeared. "Yes, sir, but it's highly irregular—"

"I'll take care of it. This is my business. I don't want Quinonan or Abdrelikan spies looking over my shoulder."

"Yes, sir."

The car door opened for them. Thomas offered her a hand in and then, ducking slightly, seated himself. The car was from their own embassy, nonetheless he ran a quick scan for bugs before he settled back into the upholstery, the attorney watching him closely.

"Ambassador."

"Maeva."

"How much interference are you expecting?"

"None, if the freight barge follows its delivery programming." The delivery programming took the crate to their warehouse where, ostensibly, it would be left. However, Maeva knew that cloaking had been ordered, and that the crate would be transferred later, in stealth, to the embassy. Uncomfortably, she wondered just what else was being brought in.

She shifted uneasily. "I must protest, Ambassador, if anything you're doing jeopardizes our diplomatic mission here on Sorrow."

"You must?" He looked down at her.

Maeva felt her lips going dry. His seniority was unquestionable, as had been his integrity and his service. That had been his reputation, but now, as he looked at her, she could see the years in him, and the death which his daughter had brought to him, and the emptiness in his eyes. She tried to swallow, and did not find it easy. "Yes. I must. If only to protect your own rights, as well. This procedure is highly irregular and—"

"Necessary."

"Necessary?"

"Yes. I brought not only a body back with me, but a life. The life of the man accused of my daughter's murder. But he's more than a murderer, he is the only one of us to have lived successfully among the Choyan. He is the only surviving eyewitness to the firestorming of Arizar, to the attempted invasion of Cho by Abdrelika, and to the current political turmoil surrounding the throne of the *tezarian* empire. Now tell me, Maeva—how far do you think this young man will get if we do not give him full embassy protection?"

Thoughts flashed by. "Not far," she answered briskly.

"Then are you reassured that there is a method to my madness?"

"Yes."

"Good." He sat back in the car again, eyes glittering. "This information is given in confidence, and I expect it to remain confidential. Even from your supervisors. When the crate has been delivered successfully, you and I have an interview to conduct."

Maeva nodded. She sat back as well, still and quiet, and wondered what she'd gotten herself into.

Palaton had thought to leave Charolon for sanctuary at Blue Ridge and the irony of returning to find haven, even if only temporarily, did not escape him. After sending Rufeen and Hat reluctantly away, he had worked his way cross-country by jet sled to the capital. He decided to hide among the crowds of workmen from the God-blind classes, construction crews who had been brought in to rebuild the quarters devastated by the rioting of months past. The regeneration of Charolon was in full swing, and he found it fairly easy to pass on the streets and in the lunchrooms among the workers even though the city teemed with security.

It was not only the commons who were blind, he thought, as he made his way through the crews. Security looked through him and his rugged coveralls and the ragged shag he'd cut his hair into, his shuffled steps and chin down walk, looked through him as though he did not exist. Perhaps it was his discipline as a *tezar,* but the inevitable calling of talent to talent was one which he could keep under tight control, and he thought perhaps it was one of the ways in which they'd hoped he'd betray himself. If that was what they wanted from him, Palaton determined, they would not get it. He was a master and when he came to Emperor Panshinea, he would do it in his own time and his own way. So their sharp-eyed sight looked straight through him, never identifying their prey. In the meantime, he walked the streets of the commons, ate with them, slept at the work camp sites, and searched the city.

At night, he slept fitfully, his dreams invaded by the countenance of the Prophet, her eye holes bound from sight by a rusty cloth, yet looking for him. The summonses she sent him remained the same when they reached him in his slumber and he kicked them off as fitfully as he did his meager flophouse covers. He awoke cold and shivering, his jaw clenched in determination not to answer her, not to reveal himself despite the inhospitable condition of his surroundings, as though her displeasure had visited it upon him in punishment.

He had little enough coin. Hat had pressed it upon him when they parted, dear stumpy Hat whose crust had dissolved when the last of his cadets had gone. It had been as though Hat had kept going only as long as there had been the least facade of his school. When the last pupil left, so had his competent exterior. Rufeen had clucked and taken him under her brawny wing, so to speak, and that was when Palaton knew he could never have brought them. Hat could not have managed, at least not at the moment, and Rufeen had to manage for Hathord, so he could not ask her to abandon their friend.

But Hat had torn up plaster at what had once been the doorway of his study and unearthed a stiff, leather bag of coin and split it two ways, tucking the major portion into Palaton's hands.

"You'll need it," he said.

Palaton had been unable to dispute that. He would need it, to live, at least until he faced Panshinea. After that it depended on how well he'd planned. He'd curled his fingers over the money. "Thank you."

Hat had nodded brusquely, as though his neck were stiff and disjointed, and turned roughly away. Rufeen's lips came together in tight sympathy, as her eyes met Palaton's for a last time, and she turned away also.

Now, awake in the early morning hours, aware of the workers beginning to stir in their rough cots around him, Palaton fished out a coin for *bren* and held it between his knuckles as he completed dressing. He took everything with him in a meager kit. He'd stayed there three nights in a row, one night too many for caution, but he'd been tired and lazy last night. He would not come back to this sleep-house this evening.

He rubbed sleep from his eyes as he passed the house's doorway. The sky was streaked charcoal and blue as dawn fingered its way into being through clouds. He could smell *bren* brewing from a sidewalk shop down the street, strong and substantial, just how he liked it. He made his way there and plunked his coin down on the counter.

The commons server did not look at him twice as he dipped out a huge mug and passed it over. He did not look at Palaton at all until their hands accidentally touched as Palaton reached for his drink.

A tiny spark shot through them. The server's chin jolted up and his eyes flew wide. He looked at his fingers and then at Palaton. He blinked.

"You," he said quietly, containing the word with difficulty, as though he'd wished to shout it.

Nearly as startled, Palaton had jerked his *bren* back across the counter, hugging it to his chest to keep it from spilling, shocked that a God-blind would have provoked such a reaction from his *bahdur*.

He swallowed. "You mistake me."

"Never. But that does not matter. I must talk with you. . . ." The server's gaze left Palaton's face as the door opened, and a crowd of eager workmen came in, calling loudly for their mugs to be filled.

Palaton stepped back, thinking of disappearing in the crowd, knowing that the server would never find him if he did. But something held him back, tugging at his curiosity and also his duty. He found a corner and sat, unfolded a plastisheet to look over the synopsis from the local broadcasters, and waited for a lull in the activity.

More than an hour passed before the servers finished with the demand, and dawn streamed fully in the windows as the crew stamped out of the *bren* house. The last dregs in Palaton's mug had gone cold and muddy, and the broadcasters' words had been tossed to another table when the server straightened his apron and came from behind the counter to sit with him. He left a Choya'i to fill the last few orders of stragglers and brought a fresh pot with him, filling Palaton's mug anew and then his own.

He tapped a packet of sweetener into the *bren* and even then drew back his lips after swallowing, as though its bitterness was not appreciated. Palaton reflected that perhaps only a pilot could fully appreciate *bren* for the subtlety and depth beyond its bitterness. He could see the other prepare to speak.

"Do not use names."

The commons answered, "I do not intend to. However, I know who you are."

"You might be mistaken."

"If you're a laborer, you've missed the opening of your shift."

"My skills allow for flexibility."

"You're lucky at that, then. I have a friend with skills similar to yours, but he's no longer in demand. With only one good hand—" The server shrugged.

"One hand." Palaton could only think of one *tezar* with whom he had a relationship, and that had been one-armed Traskar. He'd brought Traskar back into the palace to guard Rand temporarily. Did this commons claim to know both Palaton and Traskar?

"One arm," the server corrected congenially. "But even shortchanged as that, he does not have to work among the commons."

The hair prickled at the back of Palaton's neck. This one need drop no more hints. He knew Palaton for a pilot, even if he did not know him for the heir to the throne of Cho, although Palaton thought perhaps this one knew him for all that he could lay claim to.

"What," he returned, "can I do for you?"

"Meet with my friend. His skills might be to your advantage."

"Somewhere public. I am a bit shy, at the moment."

"The fountain at Cliburn Street," the server returned promptly.

"That will do. Noonish?"

The server looked out the bank of windows where the cloud-streaked sky looked as though it were trying unsuccessfully to warm. "I think," he answered carefully, "that could be arranged. But I would urge you to act with caution, shy or not, for public places can draw attention neither of you will wish."

"I'll keep that in mind." Palaton stood, set his empty mug down, and dropped a small denomination coin into it. "Thank you for the *bren*."

The God-blind server picked up the cup. "It is my job," he answered simply. "I was Housed once, but showed no talent for it. I have a great-uncle who was Housed as well, and left it to serve the throne of Cho. We agreed not to mention names, but I am proud of my uncle Gathon. He says that each of us should serve the destiny of Cho as best we can. He would be pleased to know we had this conversation."

Before Palaton could quite comprehend all that the Choya had said, the server had left the table and disappeared into his kitchens, where the rattling of pans indicated he had begun brewing *bren* again, for the next wave of morning workers.

Palaton left, musing. So canny old Gathon had thought to put him together with Traskar. A good thought. Probably one the minister had never hoped would come to fruition, but which he had scattered throughout his many networks, hoping that if anyone came in touch with Palaton, it would be passed along.

And it had.

Gathon, Palaton thought, would have been a far better emperor than Panshinea. He shrugged into his jacket, letting his mane slump shaggy and matted over his forehead, and shuffled against a brisk wind as he walked crowded sidewalks.

The server watched him go through his window banks, then walked to the rear of his shop and opened a comline. When Chirek answered, the server said only, "It is done." Without waiting for answer, the Choya hung up and then looked at his

fingertips where the talent had zapped him gently, as if
chiding him, reminding him. He stopped by his sink and
laved his hands thoroughly before going back out front where
late breakfasters would soon begin to clamor for *bren* and fry
bread.

Chapter 10

Even looking for him, Palaton did not find it easy to spot Traskar. He was wearing his prosthesis, which filled out his jacket naturally, and he walked through the lunchtime crowd with an easy swing of his arms that belied his artificial limb. It was the walk itself which gave him away as he approached the fountain, the walk of someone who had strolled cruiser corridors, who had dealt with artificial gravity and zero gravity, who carried his body with a different sense of symmetry than a Choya who had never left the dirt of his birthing. It was a swagger not unlike a sailor's swagger, as distinctive as the plowman's trudge of a farmer, or the balanced carriage of a dancer.

Palaton's senses knew it almost before he recognized it, knew it and alerted him. Then he recognized the horn crown and brow. It was Traskar and the former *tezar* was just as carefully looking for him as he crossed to a seat below the famed fountain of Cliburn and sat down to wait.

Palaton did not suspect treachery, but he allowed himself a quick sweep of the area. Because it was a little after noon, and because he had had only *bren* that morning, he bought himself a twist of vegetable stew and, cup in hand, joined Traskar at the fountain's base.

Traskar flinched as he sat down, then, eyes trailing over him, flicking away and coming idly back, the pilot gaped in astonishment.

Palaton smiled around a forkful of lunch. "Time doesn't change you much."

"Necessity warps the hell out of you." Traskar stuck his natural hand out. "Good to see you again. I heard you've lost the manling. Need some help trailing him?"

"Had him stolen, and no. No, whoever's got him is keeping

him for leverage, I fear." The falling water of the fountain kept their voices from carrying, but Palaton watched as they spoke, nonetheless. "He's gone and now is not the time for me to deal with it."

"Then what can I do?" Traskar sat back against the lime-stone, eyeing him somewhat warily. There were shadows under his eyes, faint bruises of sleeplessness, but for all the wear and tear caused as a result of his career, he looked fit.

"I want you to protect me against the emperor."

"What?" Traskar could not contain a sputter. Then he com-posed himself and shook his head, crossing his arms over his chest. It was a most un-Choyan gesture, but Rand had done it often and it startled Palaton to see the other had picked it up.

"I'm going to meet him, but on my terms."

"Ah." Warmth glowed in the depths of the other's eyes, kindled by interest. "You won't survive the meeting, not with-out help. My help, I presume."

"Yes, and don't you dare ask what a one-armed Choya can do."

Traskar showed his teeth in a smile. "If I asked, I would not have been much of a pilot, even when I was able."

"Can you stand by, then?"

"What did you have in mind?"

"I want a levitation, then a simple hook and snatch."

Traskar's well-tanned face blanched. With an effort, he asked, "Where?"

"The Emperor's Walk. I won't face Panshinea anyplace less public than that."

"There's nothing simple about that." Traskar scrubbed his hand over his face, as if he could wipe out the fear that way. "There will be crowds, security. We'll be drawing fire."

Palaton had not stopped eating; two days of very short ra-tions had sharpened his hunger, but he paused now, utensil in hand. "I can take care of security."

"How?"

He called for his *bahdur,* felt it answer him like the warmth of the meal which slowly began to fill his stomach with com-forting heat. He shaped an illusion and then moved quickly to Traskar's other side.

The former pilot never noticed, watching the shape which Palaton had left behind him.

"Traskar," murmured Palaton gently, as he placed a hand on his friend's shoulder.

Traskar exploded with a curse that Palaton had not heard since his days working on contract deep space freighting. Traskar ended his curse with a fit of coughing, doubling over, sending the curious glances of other Choyan past him. When he'd finished, he sat up sharply.

"What in the—"

"A talent," Palaton told him. "Not well known in my House."

"Nor any other." Illusionists could rarely solidify their projections, or make them look much different from holograms, projections out of time and space that inevitably gave themselves away. This image *was* Palaton, in every detail and way, paused as though listening intently to their conversation. Traskar looked from the illusion to him and back again. "How did you get behind me?"

"It's an echo of the original illusion. It's as though I'm simply there and nowhere else."

"How long can you hold it?"

"Not long." Palaton smiled grimly. "Let's hope long enough."

"Well," returned Traskar. "It ought to draw their fire." He stood up. "I know a place where we can plan a little better."

"No." Palaton tossed the remains of his lunch away and dusted his hands. "I've endangered you too much already. Listen to the broadcasters. They'll let you know when Pan and I intend to meet. Then, if you can do what we've discussed, you can. If not," Palaton tilted his head and shrugged, "we *tezars* have more lives than most Choyan."

"Aye," agreed Traskar sourly. "But ill spent." He stood in the misty shade of the fountain and watched Palaton walk away.

"Will it work?" asked Malahki intently.

"I don't know." Traskar had been pacing uneasily, difficult enough in the low-roofed hovel of their shelter, but he seemed to fill the place to bursting and now stood hump-shouldered as he paused. Malahki, who knew he was bigger than the pilot, had never felt that confined. He moved in the chair he straddled, and it creaked as though to confirm his presence in it.

"I can't tell you if it will work," Traskar repeated.

Chirek had been sitting quietly in the corner, his chin dropped to his chest, so quiet and small that his presence was nearly ignored. "We'll have a network spread all through the crowd at the Walk. I'll see to it." His voices dropped like a pebble into a still pond and rippled outward toward the two of them.

Malahki growled back, "I still don't like it."

"Nor do I, but he asked me for what help I can give and, by the God-in-all, I can still do this. *This,* I can do." Traskar fisted a hand and pounded it into the palm of his other hand. Synthetic flesh smacked into skin. "And it is daring enough that Panshinea would never anticipate it."

"At least," Father Chirek said as he stood, "it gives him a chance." His wrinkled robes smoothed about his form as he straightened. "That's all she asked of us."

Malahki closed his eyes for a second in thought. "When?"

"He would not tell me, but he said the broadcasters would carry it. I won't have much time for preparation, but I think that's what he intended. Less chance for anyone else to decipher what we're doing."

Chirek consulted his chronogram. "Then all we can do is wait. Prepare and wait."

Traskar went to the doorway. "After I've pulled him out, if I pull him out, then what do we do with him?"

Malahki let out a rumbling sigh. "That part is easy enough. *She* wants him."

Traskar's bulk shadowed the doorway to the small cottage like a thunderhead. "As long as she knows that once I've taken him from Panshinea, there will be no place on Cho safe enough for him—or anyone who knows him. One doesn't have to be a prophet to know that." He left the doorway, and bright sunlight slowly filtered in to replace him.

Malahki blinked once or twice, then scratched his jawline. "The truth," he said, "is hard to dispute."

Father Chirek crossed the room briskly to close the door. "As the Prophet would tell us, the truth is changing from moment to moment, decision to decision. The Emperor's Walk is both terribly open and terribly closed. You and I have some planning to do if we want agents in place there, in case Traskar cannot carry out his role."

Malahki watched the tabletop as Chirek called out a line diagram of that part of the capital. Infiltration would be difficult among the government buildings which dominated the north side of the Walk, but it could be done. He would have more confidence in the entire operation if he but knew where Jorana was.

He was almost certain she had fled to avoid this moment, hoping never to see the time when Panshinea would return to destroy Palaton. He'd had no word from her nor had the Prophet yielded to his pleas to look for her. But if anyone could sway Palaton from his suicidal course, it would be Jorana, his Jori.

Chirek looked up, caught his eyes. "Malahki, are you listening?"

"Listening," Malahki confirmed heavily. "And thinking."

"There is little margin for error."

If not Jorana herself, he still had the benefit of the years she'd spent at the palace. Malahki took the map pen from his friend's hand and began to sketch along the diagram. "There are secret ways, here and here and here. . . ."

* * * *

The chill of the cryo chamber seemed to permeate the entire lower level of the embassy. Maeva ran her card through the door locks, containing a shiver as she passed across the last threshold, and the smell of the level hit her fully. The ambassador was waiting for her. He looked better than he had before, rested, shaved, barbered, and wearing clean clothes, but he had lost a few more pounds, she saw, and his eyes were still and dead.

She resisted the impulse to hug herself for warmth, glad she'd worn red because it reflected its heat and passion inwardly back into her, and she needed that in this sterile environment. "Do you think this is such a good idea, sir? Keeping him down would be far easier."

Thomas turned about to face a viewing window into the medical lab. "I want," he said flatly, "to see the man responsible for my daughter's death. I want to *talk* to him. I want to—" Thomas swayed slightly.

She rushed to bolster him up, pushing him back gently against a wall and taking his arm.

He took a deep breath.

"Are you all right?"

"I will be." He shook her off.

Maeva stepped back, uneasily aware that she had crossed some kind of line which the ambassador had drawn. She turned away from him as he peered once more into the lab room as the automatic crèche prepared its occupant for waking. From the healthy color of the face, she could see that the procedure was nearly finished.

An attendant came into the room, an androgynous construct of a being, leaned over Randall's sleeping form and checked the vitals and shunts, preparing to disengage the crèche completely. She restrained a shiver at the sight of the medico. Neither human nor inhuman, it was one of half a dozen such beings who worked in the secured depths of the embassy.

Dead men tell no tales.

And what the construct did could hardly be called living. Maeva knew that every embassy here on Sorrow had its share of secret servants, beings who would ask no questions, tell no truths, hear no lies, speak no betrayals, formed out of whatever clay their particular race had chosen to shape them from. She did not like it and before she'd taken this assignment on Sorrow, she would have been hard-pressed to admit that any race could ever do such a thing.

In the absence of thoroughly reliable and independent robotics, such beings had become both necessary and indispensable. Still, it did not mean she had ever become used to their presence.

The medico turned about as if attracted by her thoughts of it. However, its blank, almost completely unformed face looked for the ambassador and, finding him framed in the portal, the creature gave a beckoning wave.

"He's awake," said Thomas. "Let's go down to the interviewing room." He strode off briskly down the corridor, his momentary lapse of strength forgotten.

Maeva pushed away reluctantly, catching in her peripheral vision the sight of Randall being sat up and groggily sliding down from the crèche to his feet, supported by the unyielding form of the medico. He might be awake, but she could tell he was not yet aware, and she felt a pang for him as she hurried away from the window to catch up with her employer.

The interviewing room was little more than a turn in the corridor, a bay, which opened up to the cell beyond. Its front had been structured with a beam latticework, hardly more subtle than old-fashioned metal bars. Thomas indicated a chair for her but stayed on his own feet, pacing in a tightly constricted circle, waiting for the prisoner to be brought out.

The erratic sound of their progress preceded them. When they finally came into view, she could see the medico stoically steering the weaving steps of his charge down the hallway and into the bay. The medico stepped back unobtrusively, face as unlined as that of the wall behind it. Rand came to a sudden halt and pivoted toward them, dark hair ruffled from his long sleep, face alert from some sense other than vision, for she had the sudden, piercing intuition that he saw them by other means than his newly awakened eyes.

"Who's there?" His voice was deep and clear, and she wondered if sleep had deepened it beyond his normal range. She moved as if to answer him, but the ambassador twitched a hand at her. She realized that there was a lightscreen between them, filtering them from view.

Rand extended a hand. "Holding me won't do you any good. He'll do what he has to do, you know that."

Maeva kept silent as indicated. The ambassador moved a step closer. The sound carried, for Rand reacted. He repeated sharply, "Who's there? Who's watching me? What do you want from me?" He stared at them without seeing them, his eyes so intensely aquamarine it was like watching the shore of a Caribbean sea. Maeva looked away.

Thomas paced across the barrier and back as though his silence bottled up more than words, more than mere emotion.

At first Rand followed the movement, head tilted, waiting, but then a momentary disorientation seemed to overcome him. Maeva had seen a few come out of cryo; the drift was normal. In fact, his lucidity had surprised her.

Without putting his hand down, he said, "Come to me if you want to. I can't do it anymore. Is it the Change you want?

I don't have it, I'm empty. Is that what you want to know? *I don't have it in me anymore.* I can't do it. Not for you, not for *her.*"

Thomas made a sound under his breath like an angry, spitting cat, a noise which Rand could not hear because of his rambling. Maeva heard it, though, and got to her feet quickly.

"Amb—"

He sliced her words off with a savage, hacking gesture. She came to a complete halt, afraid.

Rand stopped talking and stood, swaying. He blinked once or twice. "I'll prove it to you," he said, and he lurched forward. "Take my hand. I'd give you anything, but I can't. I'm empty. Take my hand and see."

He hit the barrier, hands outstretched. He dug his arms into it up to the elbow as if not feeling the surge, though his back arched and his hair stood on end from the contact. The energy sizzled once, twice, striking back. Flesh scorched. She could smell it burn. See it open up in black and crimson gashes, raw nerves exposed. She heard him scream in a pitch so high it went silent from a throat achingly contorted with his agony.

Thomas shouted at the medico. "Get him out of there!"

The construct hesitated, dumbfounded by the crackle and sizzle of the attacking levinfire. A smell of ozone and blackened skin and molten copper filled the bay.

Thomas stepped forward as though he might shake the other loose himself. Then Randall bounced back from the field, shaking, fingers curled in pain, and when he screamed a second time, it was in full voice.

He fell back into the cell, but the barrier wasn't done with him yet. It followed him, a crackling maw of gold and silver sparks. He rocked back on his heels when the phenomenon erupted.

Energy crawled over him, electric blue, spitting lightning, covering him from head to toe, wild static energy. It answered the attack of the first and swallowed it down, consuming it, then turned on Rand himself. Like a flame it devoured him until he stood cloaked in blue sparks. Maeva stared. She'd never seen anything like it. Her throat ached rawly in sympathy with his agony.

Rand thrust his hands above his head, reaching, and the

energy followed his gesture, twirling overhead, arcing as though he controlled it with his will. It swirled about his hands, and then she saw the livid angry welts bubble and begin to heal.

"Get out!"

"Ambassador—"

"We can't help him from here."

Thomas grabbed her shoulder and pushed her out of the interviewing room, stumbling after her. She turned her head, watching the bluefire consume Rand, imprisoning him, cocooning him, as his cries grew weaker and weaker.

She lost sight of him just as he collapsed and the construct medico gained enough confidence to come forward and collect him.

Her last view was of him lying on the floor, as the bluefire subsided and faded away, his scarred and throbbing hands and forearms akimbo, flesh healing more rapidly than was humanly possible.

In two or three days, the scars would be gone. She knew that instinctively.

If he lived two or three more days.

What had just happened to him? What had she seen?

Thomas escorted her through the tunnel of the secured level. She had to quick-step to stay with him, his hand roughly on her elbow.

"What was that?"

"I don't know."

"Ambassador, you can't just leave him here."

"I can and I will. The medico will see to him. You see that you're ready to depose him in two or three days—or whenever he's coherent."

"But—"

"We don't have any choice! Until we know what he's done, what's been done to him—we can't let him loose. You know that."

Not on Sorrow, at any rate. The Abdreliks or the Ronins would snatch him up and, from what she'd heard, they were not averse to vivisecting other races if they felt it was to their advantage. Maeva grew breathless keeping up with the ambassador, but it did not matter if she could not speak.

She didn't have words to express the emotions running through her.

What had she just seen happen? How much of Randall remained that was human? How could he have survived it otherwise?

Chapter 11

Rand did not wake for three days, and when he did, he was profoundly disoriented. Maeva stood at the observation window, something cold growing inside her, as the medico tried to cope with the flailing body and mind of its charge. While Rand wheeled about, fighting aimlessly and weakly, there seemed to be no evidence of any mind behind his actions. She watched until she could stand to watch no longer, made a note of the waking and feeding timetable posted by the medico, and resolved to return the next day.

And the next and the next until she found a subject whole enough to interrogate, to *understand.*

In the meantime, her trade law files were backing up, and she had to reapply for security to this sector of the embassy, as Thomas had only granted her a temporary pass. She realized as she made plans for the application that she could be becoming involved in something that might absorb her completely. It was as though she stood at the edge of an abyss and willingly contemplated the downward slope.

She had to know. She had to understand, and she had to resolve. If she had to jump to accomplish those goals, she would.

* * * *

Rain showers swept through the Charolon sky just after dusk, accompanied by occasional rumbles of thunder, muted, and quieting as though easily spent. Malahki and Father Chirek worked until the priest sat back with a sigh and said, "We've done all we can."

Unsaid was the worry that it would not be enough. Malahki watched his friend pad off to the sleeping nook where their crude pallets lay waiting. Sleep, however, did not seem to welcome him that night, not even after Chirek's gentle snoring filled the room.

Malahki sat with his hands resting on the table and played for a moment with the *bahdur* sparks that resulted if he pushed his palms close enough together. So he had talent. Foolish Choya, how often he had thought that having it would be all that mattered. He had all but moved the sky and Cho to get to Rand, to experience the Change for himself. Now, having it, he had no idea what to do with it. What his genealogical heritage for the soulfire was. Was he Earth, Sky, or Star? Or had he perhaps mutated from the lost House of Flame, destroyed so many centuries ago? Oh, yes, he had the talent, but no head for it, and he was like a child with an enforcer, dangerous and lethal but not particularly effective. He could beam death anywhere he wished, without knowing what he should wish. Jorana had warned him of such consequences.

And, realizing that, he was not so fanatical as Chirek and the Prophet Dorea to find Rand and return him to his role as the Bringer of Change. Change wasn't enough, it wasn't all, and if the streets were filled with Choyan brimming with untrained power, he could foresee anarchy. For once, he thought ironically, he shared a reaction with Palaton. The *tezar* had been horrified at what Rand could do, had been doing. The *tezar* had already looked down those roadways and seen the pitfalls awaiting them.

So, as necessary as it was to find Rand, it was even more necessary to prepare his own people. To find those among the Householdings who would be willing to train those newly empowered. Dorea would be disappointed in him, that his agenda was not hers or Chirek's. Malahki wondered if she suspected it or had *seen* it, and so sent the priest along to ensure her commands. Keeping Palaton safe was the key to finding Rand.

It was not necessarily, in Malahki's mind, the key to restoring Cho.

He needed to find Jorana as well. Brought out of the common stock, tested and rising to the status of the Housed, she more than any would know what he and all those who had been Changed faced. She would understand how his mission had evolved.

Thinking of Jorana drowsily, wondering where she was and how, he caught a sense of her. A wispy feeling of green growth and flowers and Cleansing prayers . . . she sat among a garden of rocks and blossoms and looked up sharply as if she sensed him watching her.

He caught himself spiraling downward into sleep, leaning on his elbows on the table, jerked back into awareness.

A dream, he told himself, a dream with his eyes half-closed and his own throat beginning to sag into stentorian breathing. The day was finally ending for him, too, and Malahki shrugged off the fancy that he had viewed the Choya'i. In his wanderings, he had nearly leaned over the computer board and wiped out the maps and placements they'd been working on.

He took a moment to store their efforts of the day and then cleared the screen. He pulled up the newsline and sat, waiting for it to come on-line, bouncing among the various networks he used for cover until it came to him, untraceable, broadcasters looking solemn.

"A public meeting tomorrow at noon in Charolon, where Emperor Panshinea is expected to strip the heirship to the throne from his once favored protege, *Tezar* Palaton. We will bring it to you live from Emperor's Walk. Once again, the rumors surrounding the forced abdication of *Tezar* Palaton from the heirship to the throne of Cho are evidently well-founded as Panshinea has demanded a meeting and Palaton has agreed. This meeting will take place tomorrow at noon, from the capitol grounds and war memorials on the Emperor's Walk. Stay tuned for coverage on your local weather."

Tomorrow. Malahki shook his head, felt the weight of his crown, and got up. He entered the sleeping nook quietly and stood over Chirek for a moment, debating, then leaned down and put his hand on the priest's shoulder.

Chirek came awake instantly. "What is it?"

"Tomorrow," Malahki told him. "At noon."

"We'll be ready." Chirek cleared his throat. "Coming to bed?"

He sounded like Malahki's deceased wife, and the burly Choya hid his amusement. "In a moment. I have one last thing to attend to." Malahki left the cubicle and closed the sound curtain behind him, muffling Chirek's quick return to snoring.

He put on his jacket, found it growing tight across the shoulders and around the arm joints, and grimaced uneasily. Not muscle, he thought wryly. Not at this point in his life. He shrugged into the garment to stretch it a little, then stepped into the damp night.

He did not believe in visions or dreams, but now he had power, and perhaps it had been the power in him calling to the *bahdur* in her. He could not discount it; he needed her assistance too much, and if she were where he'd seen her, then it was indeed a hiding place he would never have thought of looking for her. He would have to hurry.

Jorana sat among the slab boulders, listening to the silence, breathing the soft aroma of the flowers which had been strewn upon the temple grounds, and contemplating the cleansing of her soul. Although it had been years since Rindalan had presided here, his resonance could still be felt. If she were not newly with child, she would be tempted to go to Sorrow and spend her waiting days at Rindy's side, so keenly did she feel the need for the other's tempered wisdom.

Instead, she would abide here, seeking cleansing, doing the daily rituals, hiding, given sanctuary which not even the emperor's security forces could pierce, contemplating her own life and the one she had stolen from Palaton. She did not think there was enough forgiveness in all the temples on Cho to filter the black marks from her psyche. Jorana reconciled herself to the fact that she must seek mercy instead.

An uneasiness stole over her. Protectively, she curved the palm of her hand over her stomach where the life she anticipated did not even show. She peered up through the carved stone arches and saw nothing, heard nothing, but sensed . . . something.

As she continued to look up, it seemed to home in on her, focusing more intently, and hackles rose on the back of her neck. She shielded herself quickly, but knew she had not reacted soon enough.

Someone knew who she was, and possibly where.

Jorana rose from the stone couch where she had been

curled, and hurried down the temple corridors, out of the maze of meditation chambers, and toward the living quarters. She would have to leave and in a hurry, but not so much in a hurry as to arouse suspicion. The priests were circumspect, always, but they could be political, too.

She secured a comline and arranged to send herself a message summoning her, making sure its origin could not be traced back. She was resting in her room when the Prelate came, bowing, apologizing for the lateness of the hour, with news that she had been called away from her retreat. He had been awakened for his task and stood, sable hair rumpled, creases on his face imprinted from the embrace of his bedsheets, his robes knife-creased, fresh robes he'd laid out to wear in the morning.

Jorana got to her feet reluctantly, with the air of one both worried and loath, and reached for the small piece of luggage she had brought with her when she'd first come to the temple, opening its catch to pack it.

The Prelate caught her slim wrist. "There is no time," he said. "I'm sorry. Someone has come for you and waits in the outer garden."

Jorana froze. "Someone's here?"

"The matter must be most urgent. He asks that you attend him as soon as possible."

She glanced sharply about the room, deciding if she should flee now or take her chances and leave from the outer garden. She was still deep in the sanctum, trapped in the rock it had been carved from. In the garden, at least, she was only lengths away from freedom, even if closer to her pursuers. Her skin chilled as she made a decision.

"I'll send for my things."

He nodded. "We will keep them here for you. Do you . . . wish me to accompany you?"

"No. I . . . do you know what it is?"

He shook his head. "No, my dear, I have no details. Whatever you fear, God-in-all will give you strength." He blessed her as he followed her from the room and locked it behind them.

There were things in that room she did not want to leave behind, but nothing of personal consequence. Those items she had cached when she'd fled the palace. There was nothing which had been in her possession long enough to absorb a telltale aura or give her away. She would be inconvenienced, nothing more, though she did not know when or how she would be able to stop and replace the necessities.

She took a deep breath as she hurried down the corridors leading to the surface and the outer gardens and the ancient temple gates. The smell of night and dampness came to her. It must have rained since dusk when she'd first gone to meditate after a light supper. The footsteps behind her, the Prelate returning to his own chambers, faded. She could flee now, but she was in the throat of the temple grounds and all she could do would be to return the way she'd come, a dead end, or go on, past the teeth and hope she could get by whoever waited for her.

Expecting palace guards, she stepped into the grassy glen of the garden and saw but a single burly figure waiting, back to her, bent to examine a fruiting shrub near the wall. She thought she knew the body language of the hulking Choya. Her heart did a tiny flutter, and Jorana came to a halt, her breath catching momentarily in her throat.

He heard the sound, however, and turned. "Jori."

His face reassured her even more. "Quiet. No one here knows me by that name."

Malahki smiled widely. "I should have known." He spread his arms.

She walked into them, thinking of her childhood, as well as of her adulthood. One, he had fostered, the other manipulated for his own needs, but she could not help loving him or responding to him. He was the only father she had ever known. "Malahki," she whispered into his jaw.

He said softly, "Palaton meets Panshinea at noon tomorrow. Had you heard?"

She shivered. "No."

"We need you, Father Chirek and I. *He* needs you."

He kept his arms loosely about her, though she no longer surrendered to the reunion.

"I can't."

"We have no time, Jori, and you know the importance of this."

"I can't."

He bent back slightly. "Why?"

"I'm with child."

His eyes widened. Then, "His?"

"Yes."

"Does he know?"

"No." Her shame rose to her cheeks, flooding them with heat, despite the chill she felt elsewhere. Malahki would know then, that she had used the drug he'd given her and stolen Palaton's fertility from him, conceiving a child in a union not meant to bear fruit.

Malahki cleared his throat huskily. "Well," he said. "Your timing."

He had wanted this child as badly as she did, but even he knew now was not the time.

"If not now, when," she began, and he hushed her with a rough finger to her lips.

"I understand. But you must understand that I am reluctant to undertake any kind of rescue without your deft hand. Panshinea can't let Palaton leave their meeting alive."

Jorana stepped out of his hold, looking back toward the temple complex. She had to leave, not giving herself a choice, but did not know where she could go. Dorea had told her, foreseen for her, and she had not wanted to hear it then or now. *Cho cannot have two emperors. You must choose.* The Prophet had not meant for all of Cho to make the decision, but for her and her alone.

She didn't want this!

He reached for her hand, and there was a familiar tingle as their flesh met.

She looked down and then up, into his eyes. "Was it you who found me?"

"Earlier, in the caves. Yes. I don't know how—"

His newly awakened talent was untrained, unhoned. If he had found her, others would. For the moment, perhaps there would be safety among the numbers and chaos of Chirek's and Malahki's network. That might bypass any *bahdur*-augmented search as well as the usual methods security forces had at their disposal. She stopped his words. "It doesn't matter. I'll come, but I can't stay. You understand that, don't you?"

"No, but I'll accept it." Malahki stood back and opened the temple gate. "Don't you need to get your things?"

"There is nothing here," she said, passing him. Not even sanctuary, any longer.

Chapter 12

Shortly after the midnight hour, Traskar went in search of a miracle. He would have pledged his aid to Palaton regardless of whether or not Malahki had come to him, but it helped to know that future years would be soothed by Malahki and his network. Although he had medical coverage in perpetuity, he was not a Choya who wished to be a debit upon the system. He wanted nothing more than to work again, to pilot, to use the soulfire he had been born and trained to. Malahki had promised him work and usefulness. Palaton had always given him respect. Those three things, he had found in his years since forced retirement, he needed more than air. He made the arrangements he and Palaton had agreed upon the moment the meeting had been announced. Now, he decided upon additional measures.

He drew on a rough cloak against the weather, a cloak good not only against the inclemency, but also proof against the quarters which he would travel. It would hide the swing of his walk and give him passport to the areas he sought and, because of its looseness and flexibility, might even save his life if someone thought to knife him. He had other tricks which were more dependable and skills he'd learned while piloting for various trade ports, but even a humble cloak might have its purpose.

As he, himself, might.

Palaton had not asked much of him, only something that any second-year cadet in flight school would be able to do, but Traskar wanted to be certain he would not fail.

As he brushed through coarser elements in alleyways and substreet dives, where Choyan waited the tables and counters instead of servos, their faces heavily tattooed and jewelry-bedecked to hide the ravages of the lives they lived, he made inquiries and followed a trail of whispered clues. He had heard only rumor previously, but rumor was confirmed, and it led him to a shop in a section of the commons which had suffered most during the riots, a shop which was little more than a lean-to set up against a burned-out frame.

The shop, like the night, would be gone with the dawn. Possibly to set up at a new location with the next evening, or perhaps never to return again. Traskar shrugged deeper into his cloak with a grunt. Satisfaction would not be guaranteed with purchase. He examined his motives and needs before he stepped into the shop. The Choya who sat crossed-legged on a crude mat was gambling at sticks with another who looked enough like him to be his son. They were both beady eyed, with their manes roached and their horn crowns shaved so close to their skulls as to be nonexistent. *Family business,* thought Traskar to himself. There was not likely enough trust to bring in anyone else.

"Who are you?"

"It does not matter, any more than it matters who you are." He snugged his cloak at his throat. "I am looking for something, and I am told you have it."

The younger commons drew back on his haunches and sat warily, watching. The elder crossed his arms about his chest, at which action Traskar calmly requested, "Keep your hands where I can see them."

An unpleasant look crossed the seller's face, but he eased his position in response, flashing his palms. "What do you want?"

Traskar told him.

The seller rocked back a little. "Who told you I had it?"

"Does it matter?"

"It might. Describe him."

"*She* wears amber and onyx, highlighting her cheekbones in strata. Possibly a common, more probably a Housed who didn't have enough talent to stay there, even through marriage, black hair, bleached at the ends."

Recognition flickered in the other's muddy gaze. "All right. Perhaps I have what you want. How do I know you have enough buying power?"

Traskar felt his body react with an annoying flinch. The muscle movement was picked up by his prosthetic, which reacted as well, much more openly. The commons stared as he raised his arm and made a fist.

Traskar relaxed and the arm settled back. "I haven't time to waste," he said. "Name your price."

The seller named a price that was twice his monthly pension.

Traskar surprised them both by agreeing. He dipped his good hand into the pouch at his waist, punched in a credit amount on the disk and tossed it at the seller's feet. He had been uneasy carrying the disk around as a blank, anyone could have punched in any amount. He had his retirement online with that account, he could have been wiped out.

As it was, his capital took a hit.

The seller kicked the disk over to his son who picked it up and eyed it carefully. He pulled a crate off a hidden processor and ran it through, looked up and said, "It's real, and funds are verified."

The commons pulled a packet out of his waistband. "Two doses. All I've got. They're yours." He tossed it over.

Traskar neatly caught the packet in midair. Two tabs. He could feel them through the envelope. The elder watched him keenly, saying, "Too bad you're in such a hurry. Word says in a moon's time, they'll be as common as *bren*. They call it boost. The House of Tezars says it works miracles."

Traskar secured it in a shirt pocket. "Let's hope," he answered.

The storm had cleansed the air. Day bloomed brilliantly clear. Palaton rose from the private room he'd secured and stared into the reflective screen, then set about grooming himself as much back to normal as possible. He shook his dress uniform out of his duffel bag. Light, durable, made to be compressed into as little space as possible, it unfolded immaculately. He straightened the neckline, thinking of Blue Ridge's colors. *May they be worn again with pride long after me.* He did not think that anything he did this day would sully them. At least, he hoped not. He owed Hat that much, at least. Not to mention his promise to resurrect the school.

He bathed, in what little water he'd been allowed to decant for his usage. He fastened a utility belt around his right wrist, not much in the way of weaponry, but the rope it carried might come in handy. He dressed, reviewed himself, then pulled his bulky workman's coveralls over the uniform. It would do no one any good to plan if a patrol spotted him and picked him up on the way to the meet. Then, it was only a matter of finding some breakfast and waiting until it was time to cross town. There was no safe way to reach Traskar. He had either done what he'd agreed to do, or he had not been able to. Either way, Palaton was committed to his own course of action.

He bought breakfast and fetched it back to the loft room, where he sat and brought his journal up to date while he ate. Then, he posted the journal to a safe address that he knew of, and fished for the last crumbs of the sweet buns he'd been dunking into the *bren.* Thinking that he should have purchased one more bun, he sat back and watched the day blossom. There were Choyan he wished he could have by his side: Rufeen, Hat, Jorana. He thought of Jorana for some time, her luxuriant bronze hair, her fine-boned face with its strong jawline, her eyes. She had hoped for his understanding when she'd left. He did not understand, but Palaton took that as a fault of his own rather than hers. He *should* have understood. God-in-all, one day he would see her again, and she could explain.

Gathon, whose hand kept the throne steady despite all the turmoil within the one who sat on it, he would see when he met Panshinea. There were only two he had no hope of seeing again, to whom he had not said good-byes. Rindalan was beyond communication, the tall, spindly, proud priest who was now a reluctant diplomat. And then there was Rand, not Choyan at all, but without whom he was not really complete. Their bonding had gone beyond the sharing of his *bahdur* in a way he had not known until the manling had been taken from him.

He had brought Rand to Cho because he'd had no choice, Rand had been receptacle for his power, cleansing it, holding it until they could figure out a way to transfer it back. The humankind had been a survivor who had needed his guardianship, the pilot was an heir to the throne who desperately needed to hide his lack of *bahdur.* Their bonding of necessity had become one of respect and friendship—and more. Was it the *bahdur* which had tied them together? He didn't know. It was as though Rand had become the Brethren he had never had. Taking his power back, literally ripping it from the manling, had nearly destroyed them both. And then Qativar had stolen Rand before Palaton had had any chance to pick up the pieces of their lives, to make amends for what he'd done.

He was not ready to die. He had not made his peace with his friends and settled with his enemies. He would have to cheat Panshinea this day.

He was content when the time came.

He stood and stretched, then took his chronogram off its alarm, already knowing the time in his head, knowing he was ready to meet Panshinea. He'd taken a room near the quarter of the city which was ruled by the palace and governmental structures. A brisk walk would take him there.

Traskar settled into the single engine skimmer. He'd bulked out since he'd quit flying, the seat felt a little hampering, but on the panel in front of him everything responded as he stretched out his hands. He'd swallowed down one of the bitter pills just before climbing into the plane. It sat in the pit of his stomach like a glowing ember.

He set his view screen on the local news channel and saw a pan of the crowds growing below Emperor's Walk, waiting to see the emperor and his heir. Broadcasters stalked the area, on foot and in communications towers. Cams were everywhere, gobbling up the sights. Traskar turned the engine on to warm it, secured his harness, and watched, listening, waiting for the time.

It was just a little game of lancing, played by second-year cadets, a skill of flying, with a backup of *bahdur.* The skill he had. The power . . . it was difficult to explain what losing a limb did to the talent. He had used very little of it since waking in rehab, permanently altered, never to be the same again, unable to be restored to whole. The one time he had—

Traskar shuddered, and the burning in his stomach splashed up the back of his throat. He swallowed it down tightly. It had been like bleeding to death, having an open artery, out of which the *bahdur* flowed, taking everything, even life itself, with it, the soulfire determined to fill a phantom limb and draining into nothingness. A black void which had sucked eagerly at him. . . .

He was not so newly healed now. It had been decades. He'd managed to keep a thready use of soulfire going, off and on, to keep himself both sane and useful. What he had to do today would demand very little from him, just an edge to his senses and skills. He'd taken the boost just to ensure that nothing would go wrong.

He sat, keeping an eye on the fuel and energy cells, waiting for the emperor and Palaton to make their appearances.

Panshinea appeared, in full regalia, his gold-red hair flashing in the sun, bent Gathon a half-step behind. The emperor wore muted green robes, green and gold, which would accent his own coloring, and upon his shoulders lay a collar of gemstones which were worth the price of the entire capital. Gathon, moving stiffly after, wore a somber ebony robe and under that, shirt and trousers of charcoal and umber.

But it was Palaton who drew the eye of the cams, the *tezar* in his dress uniform, a glorified flight suit, nothing spectacular, simple and utilitarian in its lines, edged by gold thread, the fabric a rippling palette of blues. He wore no jewels, his horn crown and forehead bare of all but his mane of hair which a light breeze teased while the sun lent glints to its malt-brown depths. The cams brought his face into sharp focus. No ornaments, no tattoos, just a leanly handsome face dominated by clear, amber eyes. The stare from the eyes was steady. Traskar knew there was no way Palaton could see him through the cam, that Palaton was not looking at anybody or anything beyond the emperor, but he felt as though the pilot looked right into his depths, and he answered that look.

"I won't fail you," Traskar vowed, and put his hand to the throttle of the skimmer.

The instrument panel flashed a light, indicating the engine had warmed properly. He taxied out to the end of the strip and sat, waiting.

"We are not well met," Panshinea said, as Palaton drew close. He signaled the pilot to halt on the Emperor's Walk and although close to two hundred thousand watched and listened, they did so in utter silence.

"To my sorrow," Palaton answered, and truth rang in his voices, because he truly felt it. He caught a glimpse of Gathon, where he stood behind Panshinea. The minister looked pained. Age had sunken his cheeks, and the yellow-white streaks in his dark hair had nearly overwhelmed his brow.

The emperor, however, looked stunning. If the flight from Sorrow had tired him, it did not show in his face, his flamboyant mane of red-gold fire, or in his jade eyes. This was his stage, the only one he'd desired to hold or had trained for, the role which had consumed his entire life.

Palaton felt a tiny stretch of humor at the corner of his mouth. Though the emperor was playing to the crowd, he had not forgotten to take precautions. Panshinea's collar reflected brilliantly in the overhead sun. Palaton knew it, though he had only seen it once before. Its usage was more than ornamentation. When activated, it soundscreened the area around it. When the emperor let him come forward and kneel to be disinherited, the screen would be activated and whatever final words they exchanged would be private.

Panshinea lifted his chin arrogantly, as if tired of meeting Palaton's gaze, and lifted his hand. "On this day, let it be known that the heirship to the throne of Cho, held by myself for the House of Star and all Choyan, is rescinded from Palaton of Star. The heirship is surrendered, voluntarily resigned, to me by *Tezar* Palaton who admits no wrongdoing, but must now face inquiry. Do you resign your office and obligation and duties, Palaton?"

Pan glanced at him quickly. "I do," replied Palaton evenly.

"Then come forward and kneel, and relinquish your burden."

A murmur began through the crowd of watchers as he stepped forward, an underlying current of faint noise which was truncated when he stepped into the broadcasting influence of the soundscreen. He dropped to one knee.

"What have you done to me?" asked the emperor.

"Nothing. A house built on quicksand is doomed to sink, sooner or later."

"You call my work, my life, quicksand!"

Palaton looked up, though he knew he should not, but he had to know when Pan would strike at him, and he had to look him in the eyes to know that. "Not your work alone," he said. "But we cannot live as a people divided. The commons are as much a part of us as ourselves. If we do not unite, our powers will continue to fade, and we will find ourselves in a system of master and slave—and the masters too weak to survive inevitable insurrection."

"You think to lecture me?"

The tiny smile widened. "I think that, if you were ever to listen to me, now would be the time."

"I entrusted you with Cho's peace."

"You put me on the throne as a shock absorber or, if it came to that, a scapegoat. Let us be realistic about what you expected of me."

Pan tilted his head slightly and pursed his lips. He looked back to Gathon. "The child matures."

Gathon inclined his head. "That, too, is inevitable. With maturity comes wisdom. Even an emperor cannot afford to turn away wisdom."

Panshinea looked back at Palaton. "My minister counsels me to listen to you. But your words are like bitter poison to my hearing." A storm began to gather in his eyes, darkening them.

"I don't have much time," Palaton responded. "The House of Tezars is using a drug. There's already street slang for it: it's called boost. It affects *bahdur* in those who have talent. Supposedly, it rejuvenates the power."

Panshinea's green eyes glittered. "And that is crucial news to a *tezar?*"

"The hope of unlimited power is a false one. The drug can be fatal. It comes from off-world. There may be additional side effects which we cannot possibly anticipate. You have to know this. It wasn't manufactured for the purpose for which it is being used—the consequences could be catastrophic."

"Fatalities?"

"A cadet at Blue Ridge. He died in my arms in convulsions. Nedar brought the drug in; Vihtirne and Qativar have it now. Consider its off-world origins. Consider what can happen if we grow dependent on it, or if the Abdreliks learn about and take control of the supply."

"Only the one death."

"Is one death so insignificant?" He stared at Panshinea, knowing what the other had planned for him.

The emperor was the first to look away. "Perhaps not," he said quietly. "Consider yourself heard."

"Good." Palaton got to his feet and backed out of range of the jeweled collar. He raised his voices as Pan flinched in surprise.

"As of this day, I am no longer a son of Panshinea. I relinquish all claims to the throne of Cho. And, on this day, I declare myself no longer a son of the House of Star. I am a *tezar*, and my heritage comes from the lost House of Flame." Those last words dropped like a blazing comet into still water, exploding into the silence.

The expression on Panshinea's face in reaction to his declaration was thunderous.

The watching crowd reacted with a roar of startlement, a noise which threatened to wipe out all other noises, even Pan's shout of displeasure. Palaton put his hands up, let his *bahdur* free, let it shine. He stepped before the crowd to give his farewell—and Panshinea's first blow hit him. It knocked him off his feet.

"Remand yourself into my custody!"

Hoarsely, determined, he got out, "No."

He staggered to right himself, gasping for breath, feeling the immense power of the emperor. Measure for measure, if *bahdur* could be so weighed, Panshinea was, had been, incredibly powerful. Though his last decade or so of rule had drained him, had made his use of his talents erratic and desperate, Palaton hoped fervently he had not underestimated his opponent.

He turned around, facing Panshinea, and saw the emperor standing with his palms upraised, his red-gold hair streaming about his horn crown. All pretense of civilization had been stripped away, the imperial robes shrugged off in a heap at his feet. Gathon had been shoved away and struggled to right himself, his robes of office disheveled and imprisoning him in their twists.

Before he could shield himself, Panshinea struck again, with *bahdur*, a strike few could see. It hit Palaton like a juggernaut, driving him to his knees.

"You leave me no choice," Panshinea declared.

The very air in his lungs knifed through tissue. He saw red for a second, then his sight cleared. He looked up. Pan reared over him in triumph, and Palaton realized that the emperor would, indeed, kill him. He had thought it possible all along, but had not believed it, not in the core of him, that Panshinea would murder him in front of all these witnesses.

"I've done nothing wrong. I've brought you no treachery!" His voices, reedy and brittle, protested.

But he realized now that he had played into Panshinea's hands. He had declared himself son of an outlaw House, declared that he was a survivor of genetic manipulation, for how else could a fallen House be resurrected? His freedom would be taken from him, if not his life.

Pan was free to unleash his imperial powers, the *bahdur* of legend which only emperors could use.

Bahdur the sole use and purpose of which was to kill.

He had not seen it used in his lifetime, nor, he supposed, had it been used in the last several hundred years. As he fought for breath now, as he wheezed and flailed and resisted with his own soulfire, his head pounded in time with his heart.

Pan *would* kill him.

Palaton staggered to his feet. The crowds, limited on the capital side of the walkways, and thronging the other side, surged, held back like a floodtide by security troops. Through blurring vision, he sought help and saw no escape. He looked up, his hearing muted by his agony. *Where was Traskar?*

Panshinea gathered himself for another blow. Palaton could feel it in the atmosphere, like the dulling change of pressure just before a lightening strike. He braced himself with his own power. When it struck, he gave way, staggered back helplessly, and yet his shield held, and *bahdur* sprayed out, like wildfire, scorching the crowd about them.

He heard screams of panic and pain. The crowd turned away from them, away from the spectacle, and ran in fear, but there was no place to go. Bodies began to clamber and shove. He saw a Choya'i go down, her muffled screams cut short.

Pan blasted him again. He absorbed what he could, but he could not contain it, and wildfire sparked everywhere. Horrified watchers turned and stampeded from being destroyed themselves by the emperor's powers gone mad.

Their panic deafened Palaton. He looked up wildly and saw a glimmering of what he hoped to spy.

He took a deep, hurting breath and began to recreate himself. His heart fluttered wildly and his vision blurred again, head ringing. If he didn't get out now, if Traskar's ploy did not succeed, he would be too weak to resist Panshinea much longer.

He let out a throaty yell of defiance and, hands upheld, rose into the air. Stately levitation, not quick, but steady, above the Walk, above the tumultuous crowd, above the murderous emperor. Cries of surprise followed him.

Palaton took another stabbing breath and concentrated, his *bahdur* answering him with pain of its own, the soulfire telling him that he was nearly drained, finished, empty, burned out.

He continued to rise above the crowd. Twenty feet, thirty—Panshinea commanded the security forces to begin firing, but his bodyshielding took the brunt of that. Only *bahdur* could bring him down.

The droning roar of a single engine grew closer and Palaton could see it now, dipping low over the roof of the palace. Painfully, he threw a loop upward from the utility belt strapped around his wrist. It defied gravity just as his form did. The needle nose of the skimmer pointed for him, and it was clear it would thread that loop and draw him away, safely out of Panshinea's reach.

Panshinea let out another roar of pure rage and frustration. He unleashed a wave of *bahdur* that engulfed Palaton's form, the loop, and fogged the skimmer as it hit.

Palaton could feel Traskar's determination. The pilot answered with *bahdur* of his own, trying to break Palaton loose. There was a second when Palaton hung in the sky, caught in a tug-of-war between the two, his body like a bright shining star brought down from the heavens.

Panshinea's strength was unquestionable, but the pilot had fresh power, untapped, unused, uncalled for, and threw it into the fray.

Then, abruptly, Traskar began to bleed to death, his *bahdur* draining. It flooded out of him, a rushing torrent of power being lost. He was failing Palaton, himself, everything, the boost no good. His hand wobbled on the stick. He had the pickup, but he could not carry Palaton free.

He would die with Palaton, and when the skimmer went down, it would take out half a city block with it. A city block crammed with surging, stampeding, trapped Choyan.

As his life geysered from him, and his vision darkened, he *sent* his regrets to Palaton.

Caught between Traskar's dying power and Panshinea, Palaton felt his own heart slow to a thready beat. He looked up at the plane, knew he could not let Traskar fail, and sent what last *bahdur* he could summon.

He fell. His illusion soared at the rope's end, and Traskar broke free, his drain of power abruptly cauterized. The pilot could feel the emperor's hold on him snap. He grabbed the stick and brought up the plane's nose abruptly, taking it out of hover and accelerating as fast as he could. He had Palaton on the loop and bore him out of harm's way.

Or so he thought.

Palaton, body and illusion separated with a cold slice that seemed to tear life from death, plunged to the ground.

He hit the Emperor's Walk and lay, unable to move, hearing the crowd running below, stumbling and screaming as the plane flew off. His plan had failed, done the opposite of what they'd schemed . . . he was to have sent his illusion plunging to death at Panshinea's feet and himself flying to freedom. Now he lay in a crumpled heap, hurt, powerless, nearly senseless, invisible for a few moments as the illusion carried his semblance to freedom.

At least Panshinea could not hurt him any more.

He rolled onto his flank and saw Panshinea topple, wheezing for breath as though his heart had given out. Gathon bent over him in concern.

"Guards! Guards!" the minister called, to no purpose, as the crowds had carried them away.

"Panshinea," Gathon cried beseechingly. "Ah, God, what have you done, Pan?"

The emperor let out a broken noise that echoed what Palaton felt. Palaton tried to crawl toward the emperor, thinking that they had killed each other. But his senses reeled and then closed in on him. His last thought was of Rand. Palaton felt he was dying as but half a being, and if he had only kept Rand with him, he would have had the strength to save both himself and his emperor.

All went black.

Chapter 13

Jorana thought her heart would snap in two when the emperor collapsed and Palaton fell. She dropped linked arms with the riot guards around her and ran over to the walkway, staring at its surface. Then she looked up and saw what appeared to be Palaton, still holding to the loop which the skimmer had captured, being borne off safely, and she blinked.

The skimmer's flight stuttered and bucked in midair, and then it turned on one wing. It made a slow, downward turn and crashed into the free ground just beyond the Congress building. A resounding explosion followed and flames rocketed into the air.

Palaton, gone.

She shoved the visor off her riot helmet, jostled and pushed as Choyan around her reacted in sheer frenzy. She stood and swayed, eyes closed, thinking that he'd almost made it. He'd almost survived what Panshinea had planned for him—

"Oh, God, Pan, what have you done!"

Gathon's agonized voice brought her eyes open again, and she turned from the flaming crash as sirens began to sound and fire units dispatch automatically. The minister had gotten to Panshinea and the scene filled her with a dull shock. Everything was different now. Palaton, gone. Panshinea, perhaps dying himself. The throng around her coming and going in disorganized terror. But even as she stared, she thought she saw something nebulous on the walkway, some . . . cloud, or shadow . . . which was not right, which had not been cast there but which had plunged out of the skies.

She reached up and vaulted onto the walkway, her patrol uniform sensors reacting to the guards' devices which had been put up on the Emperor's Walk, allowing her access. As loath as she had been to put on this uniform, it let her move unnoticed into the thick of things. Pan had gone down, moaning and making a broken sound as though dying. No one on the walkway could read her face through her helmet. She snapped a hand out. Choyan faces stared at her, frozen. A handful of guards lay unconscious, their forms charred and maimed by the backlash of Panshinea's killing stroke.

"Get emergency teams landed here now!" No one moved. "I said NOW."

They unreeled from their stupor and ran for dispatch. She shot a look. Gathon cradled the emperor on his lap, crying in despair. He would recognize her if she went to him. She pulled her visor back into place.

"Who knows CPR?"

From below, one of the patrol raised a hand. She bent down off the walkway and gave him an arm up. "Go help the minister. Let's see if we can get Panshinea back into sinus rhythm."

The guard nodded and ran to the emperor's side. Jorana sidled along the walkway backward a foot or two until she reached the area which was wrong somehow. A distortion shimmered off it and she knelt down.

She could not see it, but she could feel it as she reached. A warm body, cooling rapidly. She pushed her hand deeper into the illusion and found a pulse, barely markable. More than a pulse, she touched an aura, a sense of being that she recognized almost as intimately as she knew herself.

Palaton. It had to be. She felt it with every fiber of her being, and as she thought of him, his image began to flicker into sight.

She took her hand away quickly. Let him be cloaked but a moment longer, so she could get him out of here.

Jorana stood, her throat closing with fear and love for him, her eyes and heart and mind searching. The crowd had thinned by nearly half, but there were bodies everywhere. Some were clearly dead, lifeless, trampled by others when fleeing Panshinea's power surge. Others flailed and cried out for help. The curious and the hardened had begun to push toward the Walkway again.

She knew Malahki and his network would reach her soon, if she signaled. But she was also aware that she would be giving Palaton into a custody which he would not thank her for.

Malahki had an agenda. He was not here to rescue Palaton for the altruism of it, and even though he worked for the Prophet now, there were shadowy underpinnings to everything he did. Malahki was her father, who knew him better?

She swallowed down her indecision. Palaton would die if she did nothing, and he would soon lose that last spark of *bahdur* which empowered the cloaking which hid him. When that happened, security would execute him the moment he was revealed.

Emergency techs landed on the walkway. They surrounded Gathon and Panshinea with all the fervor of their lifesaving activity. Jorana took a freight hover and dislodged their gear from it, setting it close at hand and making pretense of getting the hover out of the way while they worked.

She rolled a guard's body over and heaved it onto the freight hover. Then she pulled at the nebulous shadow which she knew to be Palaton. Without clear vision, it took her more precious moments than she had, but finally, she got it loaded. She kept a hand on his chest a second, felt the shallow and racked breathing.

She looked up, saw a guard watching her curiously. She jerked a thumb. "Get these bodies out of here, call in techs for the injured down below."

The Choya closed his jaw, then nodded. She kicked the hover into low and took it off the walkway. She paused to pull on another dead body, in case anyone questioned her actions later.

A burly form brushed past her as she paused for breath, bent over and head swimming with uncertainty, and she straightened. Recognition flooded her, and gratitude thickened her voices as she said, "Hey there!"

The Choya did not know her, but she reached out and caught his arm, and his partner swung in behind defensively. The Choya'i was bigger than her *tezar* friend and flexed her shoulders warningly.

Jorana put up her visor and gave a brittle smile.

"Take the hover and get as far out of Charolon as you can." The two stared at her.

"*Do* it," she said. "I know who you're looking for. Take the hover and get the hell out of here. It's the only way you can help him."

Rufeen moved while Hathord could only stare, entrapped by the horror they had just witnessed. The Choya'i sat down in the driver's seat. Jorana boosted the other onto a free area.

She kept her voices low and tense. "Don't look back. Do you understand?"

Rufeen nodded and kicked the freight hover into high gear. Jorana jumped back as it bucked out from under her. She watched them wend their way out of sight.

Hat hugged himself around the knees, inundated by more death than he had ever hoped to see in his life, keening to himself that, although they'd come to help Palaton, they had not succeeded. He stared at the charred guard, the second sprawled across him, his nostrils full of burned death and his stomach sickened.

He shoved a leg out to kick them over the side of the freight hover. The guard rolled off the edge and made a terrible noise when he hit the street below. The hover rocked a little under the change of weight.

"What are you doing?"

"Getting rid of the dead weight." Hat made a funny little giggle deep in his throat at that, and with a second nervous laugh thrust his foot toward the remaining body.

He hit something solid that he could not see. It groaned, and Hat realized that he was looking at a cloudy outline and the more he concentrated on it, the more it coalesced.

He grabbed at Rufeen's elbow. The freight hover skidded sideways across the air lane.

"We've got him!"

"Got who?"

"Palaton!"

Rufeen craned her head back, as the illusion shredded completely.

Hat crawled forward on his hands and knees, rolled the second dead body off the hover and then pulled Palaton's crumpled form onto his back. He slid a hand inside the flight suit.

"Heart rate's bad. Really bad. He's shocky . . . Rufeen, we've got him, but we could lose him."

"Will he make it?"

"The last few days . . ." Hathord rubbed his free hand over

his chunky face, wiping his eyes dry. "I've seen more death than life. I don't know, I can't tell. He's comatose. I won't know anything until he wakes, if he wakes." He met Rufeen's frown. "We can't keep him, Rufi."

"Where else is he going to go? Why else did we circle back and come here?"

"He needs medical attention."

"We can't risk it!"

Hat felt his eyes shift back and forth, unable to meet Rufeen's intensity. "He's from a House that was destroyed. Pan tried to—"

"Have you a spine? Or are you still full of the lies Nedar tried to feed you?"

He knew he ought to flare up, ought to feel insulted, but he didn't. He did have doubts, some of them planted by Nedar, some grown by himself. He thought he should know what to do, would know when he agreed to come back with Rufeen. But he didn't.

Rufeen let out an exasperated sigh. "Hat, quit backpedaling on me."

Hat bit his lip. "I'll try. At least they won't be looking for him. And we can't tell him about Jorana. She would have stayed with him if it had been safe. All we can give him is shelter and warmth. There isn't anything else we can do for him."

Rufeen set her jaw. "Not if I have any damn thing to say about it." She jammed the freight hover into overdrive.

Qativar turned away from his view screen in satisfaction. "One down, one to go." He relished the safety of the opulent suite they had chosen to watch the abdication. The broadcasters were still showing the EMT efforts to tend to those trampled in the panic.

Vihtirne had left the divan and gone to the window of the suite. She stood pensively, hugging herself, her face in shadows that showed her age. She turned painfully to face Qativar, keenly aware that the same sun which gave harshness to her features outlined his with vigor, youth, and a petulant handsomeness. He did not wear the robes of his office as a priest for the House of Star, he'd thrown them over long ago for the tight fitting trousers and silken shirts and jackets of the fashion-conscious. But for all his beauty, there was no light in his eyes. No soul. As for herself, the spectacle they had just witnessed left her riddled with doubts. Experience against youth, she thought wryly.

"Are you sure of that?"

"You saw the crash."

"I know that Palaton has more lives than anyone has a right to." She rubbed her temple gently as if suppressing a headache. "If he is gone, we can concentrate on the throne. With Panshinea down, we have opportunity we did not have before. . . ."

Qativar waved a hand. "Please enlighten me as to your logic. The emperor lies near death, recuperating from the expenditure of his imperial *bahdur*. We don't dare move openly now. Before, we might have had a chance, but he gave his all trying to destroy a traitor, a genetic aberration—his approval rating will go through the sky now. He's a hero, albeit a comatose one. Too bad. He's extremely vulnerable."

"Fool," she said icily.

He tilted his head, but there was no whimsy in his posture. "What do you mean?"

"Panshinea expended everything he had. If he survives . . . he will need us, Qativar."

His eyebrow quirked.

Vihtirne smiled thinly. "We have boost, and the emperor needs *bahdur*. He'll be ours for as long as we need him."

"Ah." Qativar sat back and put the heels of his boots up on the small table fronting the divan. "I shall have to think on it. Gathon is canny, he won't let us in easily. But once we are—" He smiled widely. "I suggest we not leave this to chance."

Her feet wearied. She drew up a small upholstered chair and perched upon it, spine straight, slender neck held just so to balance her head and horn crown. She knew how she must look, yet it fatigued her, this constant fight to maintain her looks, her poise. She smothered a sigh. Her companion must be coaxed. She wished for handsome, passionate young Asten instead of this self-absorbed cohort, but he was elsewhere, tending to her business. "Tell me."

"I have a supply of *ruhl* on hand. Let's assert your right to the water patent and visit the local pumping plant."

While boost had come from off-world, *ruhl* was strictly

Choyan, an aphrodisiac which disrupted *bahdur* and loosened inhibitions. Normally it was used for lovemaking, to unbind the fertility of either partner, since among Choyan both male and female controlled their fertility. It was dangerously easy to overdose to the point of death, but Qativar had been working with it to alter its effects. "Distribute the *ruhl* now?" It would be potent, she thought, and when soluble in the water, no Choya who drank would be free of its numbing effects. *Bahdur* would be masked almost beyond the endurance of its possessor. They had talked of this before, but she had just thought it talk. Other than surreptitiously distributing it among the *tezars* to keep them demanding the boost, she had not really put much stock in Qativar's grandiose plans.

"What better time? No one knows what the side effects of imperial *bahdur* are—but you and I both know he had to siphon that much energy off someone. Maybe the entire population of Charolon. We will be here during the emergency, of course. Available. With the medication which enables our *tezars* to recover so quickly and completely that their flight time is doubled—no, tripled. Of course, the ordinary Choya is scarcely a *tezar*. But," and he looked down his nose at her, "I can guarantee we will have them lining up in the streets for boost."

"And the emperor will scarcely ignore what is happening."

"Nor is Panshinea likely to accept a populace more powerful than he."

"That is a hook," she agreed, "upon which we might persuade him to hang himself."

* * * *

The call came late in the night when dawn first begins to tug weakly on its edges ... and on an old Choya's bladder, Rindalan thought wryly as he staggered up to answer the embassy alarm. The view screen lit up as he approached it, and Gathon faced him as soon as the scrambler decoded the incoming signal. Gathon, light-years and seasons away. His old friend did not look well, and Rindy's heart sank. There was no good news behind this urgent sending.

Gathon spoke. "Eminence Rindalan, Rindy, this is to inform you that Emperor Panshinea today met with the heir to the throne, Palaton, and took back the heirship, which Palaton voluntarily abdicated."

As the words trickled in slowly, synchronized with Gathon's face, yet unreal because Gathon did not speak slowly and deliberately—that was the decoder's fault—and because the nuances of the blended voices could not be transmitted well, Rindy's mind raced ahead. How could Palaton have so cut himself off from Panshinea, unless Pan left him no choice? And what then . . . civil unrest over which to follow, the head of a House in its descent on the Great Wheel, or the *tezar* who had proved himself time and again?

"Palaton then declared his true genetic heritage—the House of Flame—and Panshinea declared him outlaw and an abomination and attempted to use imperial *bahdur* to destroy him."

Gathon's words struck deeply into Rindy, shaking away the last of whatever drowsiness had been nestling in him. There would be no going back to sleep this night, or perhaps even the next. Imperial *bahdur!* Rindy had only heard of such things in the old texts, describing the wrath of the God-in-all or some of the old emperors, whose powers had been legendary. There were depths to Pan that Rindy had never guessed. And the use of terminology describing their esper powers was forbidden over subspace transmission, scrambled or not, for there was no knowing how clever the Ronins and Abdreliks had gotten in their spying. Gathon was desperate indeed if he discussed their soulfire . . . but perhaps there was hope somewhere in this message. The keyword was *attempted.* Rindy narrowed his eyes, the better to listen to what followed.

"The use of that ability has felled Panshinea temporarily. I am assuming his duties for the next span of days. He lives, but is weakened. Details to follow. Palaton escaped the wrath of the emperor, but his skimmer crashed and he and his accomplice are presumed dead. I am sorry, old friend."

There came a lengthening silence. It took a moment for Rindy to realize it was not the fault of the decoding program, that Gathon had stopped speaking.

He grabbed the edge of the desk before him, leaning forward intently into the view screen's focus. "I will assume that word of Pan's disability will be kept confidential before the Compact because of our opportunistic friends. However . . ." and he stopped, searching his heart as well as his mind for words. Palaton, dead. He rejected it. He had not saved the boy from his brutish grandfather and from his own blemished heritage, to have him inducted into flight school, and succeed from there, only to see him die before his time. No. "Palaton *cannot* be dead. Gathon, I know that I have not your cold logic, but I would know if he were dead. I would know it! I can only give you assurances that all is not lost. Do not despair."

He sat and waited for Gathon's reply, long, long minutes during which his feet grew cold upon the tile flooring, and a cramp came and went fitfully between his shoulder blades (heart, he thought, and knew he would have to take his medicine before he did anything else), and his bladder pressed with urgency upon him.

Finally, Gathon's image moved upon the screen. "I hope and pray you are correct, Rindy. Try to keep a vote on the pilot contracts from being called until Pan is recovered. I will let you know the minute I hear any further developments."

The screen went dark. Rindy sat back on his chair and flexed his shoulders.

He, too, hoped and prayed he was correct.

Chapter 14

He had offended the Prophet. She stared at him with her blindfolded face, in a long room with many doors, and he could hear trouble outside those doors, danger coming like thunder rumbling in a stormy summer sky. Palaton knew he could not face her or the looming menace, and he turned to run down the length of the hall. As if in a dream, his limbs obeyed, but the gravity was strange.

She pointed commandingly at a door. He knew he could not listen to her, for he had a destiny of his own, and she did not respect that. He ran the other way, while anger creased her face. The menace came closer, thunder booming louder. One of the walls exploded, splinters and debris flying everywhere. He dodged, grazed, but the Prophet stood implacable.

"Stop!" she cried and pointed again.

He could not bow to her wishes. His destiny was not written yet, he still had things he needed to do, obligations he had to fulfill, and he could not go the way she wanted to send him. Sometimes leaping, sometimes running, he fled.

Palaton threw open a door and great, yammering *things* surged after him. He slammed the door in their faces, and stood a moment, heart thudding, taking stock of which way to go.

The Prophet stood aloof in a whirlwind of storm. She raised her hand and pointed a third time.

He would not yield. Palaton took a deep breath, dashed across the hallway which grew longer and more dangerous with every footfall. The floor beneath him was dirt, and it heaved as though quake-ridden, breaking away from him as he raced over its surface. There was no safe passage anywhere.

The *things* chasing him down drew nearer with every stride.

They nipped at his heels, threw dirt clods and more dangerous weapons at his shoulders. They harried him as he took evasive action, their hot sulfurous breath roaring at him, their howls and yips of the hunt making his head ring. The hall stretched before him in a gentle curve, walls wavering and re-forming as he neared them until he had come full circle, winded, spent, wounded. He did not know when he had been gashed and stabbed, but he ached as he struggled to breathe, and he could feel hot blood trickling down his side, his shirt hanging in tatters.

Finally he threw open the door she had shown him. He had no other way to go. It opened into an immense, columned room with an empty throne, and the Prophet stood before it.

"Come to me," she said, beckoning.

Palaton ground his teeth. He could not turn back, the howling pack would be upon him in a moment. He could not go forward, because he knew what she wanted from him, and he did not have it to give. Rand was not his, and even if Rand were to be found, the manling was a free entity, not a commodity to be traded.

He halted and stood, torn, tormented, unable to go forward or back.

The pack of things' howling grew to a frenzy. He heard them as they gathered for a leap and came at him, barreling down on his shoulders with the weight of the world. He went down to his knees under the assault, eyes still upon the Prophet.

At last she turned away, whispering, "If you survive . . . come to me."

The pack bore him all the way to the ground. As he rolled, he put his hands up, wrestling and flailing with *them*, their hot, slavering breath all over him, fangs flashing, tusks slicing the air, closer, closer, closer. . . .

He woke with a shuddering gasp.

A hot compress sloughed away from his brow as he opened his eyes. Hat leaned over, looking closely into his face, his own visage blurred and wobbly.

"He's back," the Earthan announced over his shoulder to someone. "I told you."

"You weren't so confident yesterday. Or the day before."

Rufeen's melodious voices, deep for a Choya'i, filtered into Palaton's hearing, though he could not see her.

He lay back upon a hard pillow, his head throbbing. He knew the feeling which permeated his very bones. His *bahdur* had been expended almost to the point of permanent extinguishing. He put a hand to his horn crown, hoping to still the throbbing or at least make it bearable. Traskar had nearly killed both of them. What had happened?

"How—" the word stuck in his throat. He tried to clear it, choked and coughed harshly. Hat helped him to sit up, pounded his back until he coughed again and spat it out, then wiped his mouth and fed him an herbal tea. The tea went down comfortingly.

"How long?" Palaton said, when he felt he could talk.

"Ten days, and counting."

Ten days. He looked about the low-beamed room. Its modesty was readily apparent. "Where?"

"Semola. I was raised here." Rufeen leaned into his frame of view. She had an apron around her thick waist, looking incongruous over dungarees. "I doubt if anyone's looking for us here."

"Traskar. The plane." The *tezar* had been in distress. "Did he get clear?"

Hat was busy cleaning away compresses and a wooden bowl of scented water. He paused, then said apologetically, "He didn't make it. The plane crashed just past the Congressional dome."

"He should have done it," Rufeen added. "Just a simple lance and snatch. Any second-year recruit could have done it."

Palaton swung his legs out of the cot and sat up. The touch of his feet on the floor grounded him, but sent his equilibrium swinging for a second. He was weaker than he thought, as he gratefully took the hand Hat quickly put out. His own wrapped around larger, his fingers and palm slim, but Hat's were thick and callused and warm.

"Something went wrong," Palaton said. "He tried to shield me from Pan. The *bahdur*—it was like a dam burst. It all came rushing out of him at once. It was fatal. He knew it, I knew—I tried to cut it off. He couldn't control it. I thought I'd succeeded when I broke away. I could feel it seal off. It must have been too late. Why didn't he tell me he couldn't handle it? What was he thinking of?" Palaton closed his eyes, his head filled with the image of the very life flooding out of Traskar, out of the stump which had once been a part of him.

"He didn't want to fail you. You gave him purpose, I would guess. Not many ex-*tezars* have that."

Hat squeezed his hand gently. "You can't live our lives for us," he said.

Palaton looked at him. His friend's stocky face blurred a second, then focused sharply, as his senses weakened and then sharpened. "No. And I wouldn't want to. God knows, I have enough trouble with this one."

Rufeen thumped down on the end of the cot and thrust a steaming mug at him. "Traskar may have brought the skimmer down on purpose. No one knows you're alive."

That struck him as probable. Traskar would have thought the sacrifice fitting, after his initial failure. Palaton looked down into his *bren*. He would never have asked another to die for him, but it was too late to alter the event. "And where did you two come from?"

They exchanged looks as if there was something they weren't quite willing to tell him. "You didn't think we were going to let you face Pan alone. We followed you to Charolon."

"I thought we had agreed something to the effect that we would be stronger split apart."

Rufeen wrinkled her nose. "You agreed. We listened. I don't remember saying anything definite."

"It's a good thing you didn't. Tell me what happened." Palaton put his mug up to his lips, hiding his smile.

"Pan used imperial *bahdur*. He went out of control. The backlash killed a handful of the guards, sprayed across bystanders. There was a stampede to get out of harm's way, and more were trampled. It was pretty awful, but it looked as though Traskar pulled you out of there."

"He tried until I had to break loose to save him. I remember falling. Not much after that. How did you find me?"

Hat said quickly, "I stumbled over you. There wasn't anything there but a kind of . . . distortion. I reached down and your aura was plain. We commandeered a hover brought in to transport bodies and got out of there as quickly as possible."

"Poor Hat," Palaton murmured. "More bodies."

Hat shuddered and let go of Palaton's hand. "I'll never get used to it."

Palaton got to his feet, as the strength of the *bren* coursed through him. "You've nothing to be ashamed of. There are depths to you that I never suspected."

Rufeen echoed his words with a slap to Hat's shoulder, a blow that rocked the narrow pallet they sat on.

Palaton decided to stay on his feet. It seemed easier than negotiating the two or three steps back to the cot and sitting down. "What about Panshinea?"

"Collapsed, like you. The official word is that he's awake, resting, but has everything in hand. Unofficial buzz says he's still out, but Gathon is running everything." Rufeen added, reflectively, "What are you going to do about it?"

"I tried to tell him about boost. He would not hear of it. So we're going to have to take stock and see what happens."

The two Choyan exchanged uneasy looks again.

"What is it?" Palaton asked sharply.

"Boost. It's everywhere. Overnight."

"Side effects?"

"No one knows, yet. But from my own view—" Rufeen paused.

"What?"

"Anyone who's had the power, and felt it diminish, would do anything to get that old feeling back. It has to be highly addictive, Palaton, emotionally if not physiologically. It has to be."

As *tezars*, they had all seen the ravages of drug addiction in other societies. "Not here," Palaton said. "Not here."

Rufeen lifted her eyes to him. "Sooner or later," she answered back, "someone had to find our weak spot. Do you think we're beyond the same grievances everyone else has to struggle with?"

"I think, with our powers, that we have to be." He fought to stay upright, on his feet, and steady. "It's off-world. That gives Pan a chance to cut it off before we find a way to synthesize it. I have to find a way to convince him to do what he has to do."

"It will be difficult. I don't understand about imperial *bahdur*, I've never seen it used before—"

"None of us have," Hat put in.

Rufeen gave him a look before continuing. "It appears Panshinea was able to siphon off *bahdur* from unsuspecting donors all over Charolon. There was massive power loss all over the city."

"Havoc in the streets," Palaton said slowly. He knew what a Choya was like without his power, with the sudden loss of it. Mindless terror. They would turn to boost. Eagerly and desperately. "Any deaths?"

"None that are being reported. It doesn't seem to be an issue. They could be hiding side effects."

"It's a cycle," Palaton said. "One that needs to be broken. We have to find a way to do it. What about Rand? Any word at all?"

Rufeen looked at her knees. "If Qativar thinks you're dead," she responded, "he may think he has no use for the manling."

"No!"

"Without needing to control you, Rand's too big a liability for the two of them to hold onto him."

"Then my first order of business is to let them know I'm still around. And to let Pan know. We need to go after the pipeline bringing in the drug."

A silence fell, broken only by the loud gurgling of Hat's stomach. Rufeen snickered.

"First order of business would seem to be to eat that stew I've been simmering."

Hat got up with a grateful look, offered his shoulder to Palaton to lean on. "Food first. Planning later."

Palaton found himself agreeing. He put an arm around his friend's shoulder, leaning heavily as they traversed the small room to the kitchen. "Have I thanked you for coming after me?"

"No," they answered together. "But we're sure you'll get around to it," Rufeen added.

Chapter 15

They came and woke Rand, quietly, shadow-people with rough hands and voices, and told him to clean himself and dress, that he had an appointment later. Rand woke slowly during this process as he always did, as if he rose from the dead, so stiff and cold and weak did he find himself. His senses seemed to thaw slowest of all. His handlers would be gone before he could identify them, but he thought they were human. Sometimes.

Like himself.

It couldn't be, of course, because he knew he was still on Cho. Off-worlders were not allowed on Cho. He was being held, perhaps to bring pressure on Palaton, and without the *bahdur* the pilot had shared with him, he could no longer protect himself from the prodigious telepathic powers of the Choyan race.

He found the shower and used it, his mouth brackish-tasting and dry, even when he stood under the showerhead, mouth open, water running from his lips. He could never have used water like this on Earth, but he could here, and he let it pound him awake. He creamed his face for stubble, washed his hair, then stepped out. New clothing had been laid out for him, and a breakfast tray.

He looked at the food, scrambled eggs, bread, and fruit, and what smelled like coffee, real coffee. He did not remember ever having a breakfast like this on Cho. Someone evidently wanted him on their good side. Someone wanted him badly enough to import coffee.

The rich smells drifting toward him turned his stomach. He could have eaten but he was not ready to, yet. *Drugs,* Rand thought. He'd been kept out on drugs, as well. He toweled off briskly and dressed and then sat at the small table which had been put into his holding cell.

He could only remember having been up once before. He still had welt burns across one thigh and the palms of his hands from testing the barriers of the restraint center. The sonics had been only partially effective, but the laser bars still left pain lashing through him. He looked at his hands. They'd healed partially, and he knew that the incident had to have been a few days ago, or longer. Yet this was only the second morning he remembered awaking.

Was Palaton looking for him? He knew the other would never leave him vulnerable in enemy hands. Despite the upheaval of Panshinea's return, and the destruction of Blue Ridge, Hat's and Palaton's beloved flight school, Palaton must be searching for him. Having so crudely stripped Rand of the *bahdur* they had both shared, he must now feel tremendous guilt for letting the enemy take Rand. Theirs was a bond which went deeper than shared power, or common enemies. They had developed a deep friendship which went beyond all barriers. Palaton would leave no stone unturned.

If any good were to come out of this, it might be to drive the *tezar* into alliance with Malahki and the network of Chirek's underground religion although they had argued bitterly over it. Did the Prophet see him in her visions and help the search for him? What happened on Cho without, or because of, him?

Palaton would not involve himself in the metamorphosis of Change, but Rand could not turn his back on the plight of the millions of Choyan who could not access their hereditary powers. Now he had nothing, though he owed them everything. He owed them that right to live as equals. Emotion washed through him, leaving him feeling bereft in its wake. He was not what he had been, and he didn't know if he could deal with being less . . . and yet he would have been nothing at all, if it could have saved the Choyan the grief he'd seen.

Rand pushed his plate aside, barely touched, but drank the bitter coffee down, hoping to clear his head. He looked across the neutrally colored cell, beiges and taupes, the woven fibers of his bedding and furniture in pale blues, and watched where the wall intersected with what appeared to be an open corridor, though its bend went beyond his field of vision.

He sat and watched, saw an occasional flicker of the laser bars, a silver tracking, like the trail a snail left on walkways after passing, nothing more than a hint of the deadly force which kept him imprisoned. He sat and waited for the Choyan who held him to come, tall as they all were, even the squatty Earthans, tall and arrogant, handsome, with a sculptured crown of horn upon their brows to protect their dual brain-panned skull, aliens who held the only method to traverse space when warped, waited for those beings to come and tell him why he was being held.

His ears told him when they were coming. First, the slight change of pressurization in the chamber, and then the footsteps. Two, one long-striding and measured, the other hurrying to keep up. Male and female, probably. Rand watched the corridor intently to see who his captors were.

When they came into view, he sat dumbstruck, then got to his feet so hastily the small table overturned and the food tray clattered away sharply, bringing the young woman's eyes to his face in alarm.

Human. They were human. They were more than human, for the man who walked to the fore wore the black and gray, and white bars upon the shoulders of his jacket, and Rand had seen his face on view screens for most of his life: Ambassador John Taylor Thomas. It was that mature visage which held his attention, the slowly receding dark hairline, the eyes lined at the corners, the jaw tight. The chiseled resemblance to his daughter was uncanny.

Rand felt bowled over. Who had him, who could get permission to bring down outsiders to Cho? No one outside of the palace ever entertained aliens, and even those occasions were rare. Had he been bartered to Panshinea? If not . . . who else kept him prisoner?

Thomas stopped just outside the laser and sonic barriers, distaste flickering over his face quickly at the food scattered across the cell floor. He said to the young woman, "Get that cleaned up as soon as possible after we're done."

She nodded and jotted down the instruction on her notepad. She was also, Rand saw, fitted with a minicam and recorder. Her fair blonde beauty seemed more alien to him than human.

Ambassador Thomas looked at him. "Randall."

"Ambassador Thomas." Rand paused, his voice rusty in his throat, thinking oddly that if the ambassador had been Choyan, with his coloration, he would have known he was a Sky, and how to deal with him, knowing his inherited temperament from his genetic House, but he wasn't, he was human, and suddenly Rand felt adrift among his own kind. What was he to say? He had seen the man's daughter die. He reached desperately for that bridge. "I'm sorry about Alexa. Words aren't enough, but I—I'm so very sorry."

The ambassador blinked tightly. Rand wondered for a moment if he had even known, but as the man composed himself, he realized that Thomas knew. Perhaps not every detail of her death on Cho, but he knew. "She chose her own course."

"Does that make a difference? I would have changed it if I could have. I think you would have, too."

Thomas cleared his throat. "You have other concerns."

"Is that why you were brought to see me? Who holds me here?"

The ambassador answered shortly, "Your perception of 'here' is probably a bit skewed. You've been brought to Sorrow, and you're presently a guest in the holding cells of my embassy."

Sorrow? What was he doing in the Halls of the Compact? "I don't understand."

"Which is precisely why it's important you remain in protective custody."

The young woman had been watching Rand intently and her concentration distracted him. She was pretty enough, perhaps a little older than he was, her hair that golden-hued color which was neither blonde nor brunette, but both, depending on how much sun she'd been in, touched with honey tones. She wore a navy suit, a red scarf curled at her neckline, giving her a brief fountain of color. Her eyes, outlined in dark blue pencil, were a light sky blue, reminding him of Rindy's eyes. Like the elder statesman, she had the appearance of a seeker of truth. She listened to every word, every nuance with intensity. Rand found himself staring, and turned back to the ambassador.

"Who else knows I'm here?"

Rindalan had been appointed to Sorrow. He, at least, should

have been made aware. If Rindy knew, then Palaton would know. And if Palaton knew, then his release was imminent.

The ambassador took a slight step away from his assistant, giving Rand a view of his profile. Thomas cocked his head a little as though considering his answer. "No one," he said shortly.

Rand felt as though the floor under his feet had given way. He put a hand behind him, found the chair, and brought it up so he could sit down. "No one," he repeated.

"That's right. We thought it best, considering the charges against you, and the charges to which you could be witness, when the time comes."

He was witness to the fire-strike of the Abdreliks upon the renegade Choyan colony on Arizar. It was for that Palaton had taken him in, and protected him, and befriended him. It was because of that they had exchanged *bahdur* and the Abdreliks had later hunted him down and tried to strike against Cho itself. But Rand knew that the Abdreliks would not, could not, touch him here on Sorrow, cell or no cell. "Why am I being detained?"

"For your own safety," the young woman said, her voice melodious and low.

Rand did not look at her. He stared at Ambassador Thomas. "Why am I being detained?" he repeated.

The older man frowned. "For crimes against Cho," he said, "at their request, pending investigation." Thomas pulled himself up briskly. "I think, Maeva," he said to his assistant, "that we'll postpone deposition for a little while longer. Give him a chance to clear the cobwebs out, and think about his options."

"I want to speak with someone, let him know I'm here."

"I'm afraid that's not possible," Thomas answered. "Not for the present."

It began to dawn upon Rand that, his own people or not, he was not among friends. "Will it ever be possible?"

The young woman gave him a startled look, but the ambassador showed no emotion as he answered, "That depends upon the findings of our investigation."

"I have rights—"

The ambassador had begun to turn away, to leave. He now swung back and leaned dangerously close to the imprisoning barriers. "No," he said tightly. "That's where you're very much mistaken. You have no rights. For the murder of my daughter, for the inciting of riot upon Cho, for the attempted overthrow of a government sanctioned by the Compact, for meddling in the treaties of senior races of the Compact," and the ambassador took a deep breath, adding, "and for other crimes I haven't the time to delineate, you have no rights. You gave up your citizenship when you became a member of an outlaw colony. The only right you have now is the basic right to continue living until tried by your peers—and I wouldn't press that too hard if I were you."

Rand sat, bathed in the venom with which the man spoke, his heartbeat growing slow and steady as Thomas ground to a halt.

The ambassador shook and forcibly calmed himself. Rand stayed silent.

Thomas finished. "Have you nothing to say to that?"

Rand knew Maeva watched him closely with those Choyan-like eyes, those eyes which sought for truth. "I gave my life for my world," he said slowly. "I gave up my childhood, my family, because I wanted to be a pilot, and I thought I could bring that back to my people—the way through, safe and clear, the *tezarian* drive. I thought that, if I studied hard and learned swiftly and worked beyond endurance, I could bring it back and lay it in your hands and it would be worth it—worth all of it—to know what I'd made possible."

"You're alive. Alexa is dead. And we have no drive."

"Does that make my sacrifice any less valid? The ashes of the dead are strewn all over Arizar. Does that make my life less valuable? Do you have me locked up here because I breathe and she doesn't? Do you intend for me to die, so that you feel avenged?"

"You sicken me." Thomas whirled about and left. His assistant hesitated a moment, flung Rand a look which he could not read, then hurried after her employer.

He stayed very quiet in his chair, the wreckage of his meal strewn about him, as though it were the wreckage of his life, and listened to the footsteps fade. Of all the ambitious and contentious races of the Compact which he feared, he knew that it was his own he feared the most. If only he could get word to Rindalan. If only he still possessed the *bahdur* to attempt a cry which only those with six senses could hear. If only.

She found herself not believing in the charges of sedition as she ordered up a janitorial drone, and then began disconnecting the recording equipment. The medico had been dismissed as soon as Rand had gained more than random consciousness. Thomas had ordered the medico out, wanting nothing living around the prisoner. The tapes and files would remain, like the prisoner, in his highly secured underground vault. As she laid them in the steel drawer and slid it into place, locking it, she was never so much reminded of a morgue as now. The ambassador inserted his key in the second lock.

"I think perhaps," she said slowly, "we'll get farther with the deposition if you don't attend."

John Taylor Thomas drew himself up. "I'm too emotionally involved?"

"Something like that. Also, your visits to this secured area could draw attention you don't want."

"He's dangerous, Maeva. He has no scruples."

She gave a tiny smile. "As an attorney, I'm not supposed to, either." She stowed away her key. "But it remains that you have other work to do, and your time is already divided in too many directions. Let me get the deposition, and then we'll build the case together." She met Thomas' examination steadily, trying not to think of the tall, somewhat inelegant young man down below, with eyes of clear, earnest turquoise. She could not abandon her own sense of judicial fair play and the writ of habeas corpus. She repeated evenly, "Let me handle this."

John Taylor Thomas looked at Maeva. "I don't care what we have to do. He's never to leave the holding center. Never."

Chapter 16

Maeva reentered the holding cell to see that the prisoner had cleaned up himself, everything in a neat pile waiting for the medico. He was in the process of cupping up a last bit of scrambled egg, back to her, when he heard her step.

She lowered her terminal board which she had been carrying clasped across her chest as if it could shield her from the other, and said, "I can order some more for you."

"I'm not hungry," he answered shortly. He righted the chair. "I thought Thomas was done with me."

"He is. I'm not." She drew up a stool from outside the barriers and sat down.

"I don't think I have anything further to say."

She turned off her audio equipment. "Then perhaps you'd like some company. Or information. I can give you a little, if you wish."

Those light turquoise eyes looked at her. His voice was deeper than she had thought it would be—mature, crisp, and clean. "Should I sit down?"

"Only if you want to be more comfortable." Maeva felt the corner of her mouth twitch a little in dry amusement. Between them, the invisible barriers let out a warning pulse of light. Its faint reflection deepened the blue in the other's eyes, overriding the faint greenish tone.

He sat down with a fluid grace most humankind could not imitate. She wondered if he'd gotten it from the years he'd spent among the Choyan who, with their double-elbowed arms and other physiological differences, were among the most graceful of the alien races she'd seen in the Compact. He could be a dancer or an athlete; he was that much in control of his body and unconscious of it at the same time.

Rand sat. He rubbed his hands together and she could see

the burn wounds scarring across his palms. He followed her line of sight. "I found out about the barriers the hard way."

"Do you need medical attention?"

"No. They seem to be healing quickly. Or . . ." He paused. "I'm sleeping longer than I think."

They'd had him in reduction most of his conscious time, waiting for him to return to rational behavior. That was one of the things she could tell him. She dropped her chin slightly. "If you're asking, yes, you've been in suspension most of the time you've been here."

Rand rubbed his hands across his knees, as if drying them. "Passive exercise?"

"I beg your pardon?"

"I haven't lost much muscle tone. Have you had me rigged up?"

"Oh. Well, that's not really my expertise. You got whatever was needed to keep you healthy."

The turquoise stare regarded her. "Freedom," he said. "would help."

"I can't—" Maeva began, then stopped, slightly unnerved. "I have no control over that," she told him. "At least, not yet."

"At least give me my call."

"We're talking IG law here, not your basic Bill of Rights."

"Which is your way of telling me I have no rights." He sucked in a breath. "What is your area of expertise?"

"I'm a trial lawyer."

"Prosecution or defense?"

Maeva could feel herself rise to the edge in the other's voice. She curbed it and said, "Whoever needs me most."

Rand gave a dry laugh. "Right now I think I'd have better luck throwing myself on Abdrelikan mercy."

Her jaw clenched and her throat tightened. They stared at one another for a very long moment, before she cleared her throat to ask, "How can you say that? You know nothing about me."

He answered steadily, "You're with the ones who conspire to keep me here. I think I know all I need to." But he blinked, just before he looked away.

Maeva watched him, thinking of all that he was supposed to have done: brought down a firestorm attack on Arizar, a world which should have stayed off limits to all of them, according to the technology level of the Zarites; participated in an illegal invasion and colonization of the same world; then gone on to Cho where he had incited civil unrest and been part of an attempt to usurp the throne. Not to mention the attempted destruction of the order of pilots which all of the Compact worlds depended upon—and that he'd been present when Alexa Thomas met her death, details of which were sparse and unavailable at the moment. Did he really think he was innocent of all those actions?

Maeva felt her hand tighten on her terminal. She had become who she was because of her need to know, to understand, so that she could act upon the truth. Part of her job lay here, shuttered behind that face which had turned away from her.

Technically, she was part of the team which would present him with a defense when he went before the Compact. Realistically, she knew that the ambassador wanted to hang this young man out to dry.

"Like it or not, I may be the only chance you have," she told him.

Rand looked back. For that instant, she saw the echo of the Choyan in him, of the grace and gravity with which they carried themselves, particularly the burden of the horn crown they wore upon their heads. Did he know how he mirrored his association with them? He remained silent.

"It's your choice," Maeva persisted. She got to her feet. "It may be the only one you'll be offered."

"Things change," Rand answered.

She was not quite sure what he meant by that, so she decided to take it as an opening. "I'll be back," she told him. As she left, a little servo janitor unit came wheeling in to clean up the debris. She punched in a new order for breakfast, without knowing exactly why she did.

Rand listened to the fading footsteps. He stood up and moved away when the janitor came in, watching carefully how it pierced the barrier. There was no cessation in the fields. The robotic unit merely appeared immune. He did not take his eyes away from the unit as it cleaned up the mess, stored it within its canister body, wheeled about, and left. If he thought to leave with it, taking his chances, he changed his mind as he saw the shimmer of the laser field off the janitor's metallic shell. If there was a weakness, he could not perceive it.

And even if he could escape, where could he go? This was Sorrow. In all its teeming population, he could think of only one who might be his ally—and there was no way to let Rindalan know he was being held here. There was no one else he could trust, and thousands who were his outright enemies. He might be imprisoned, but he was also being protected.

Ironic, he thought, as he moved back to his bunk. On Cho, alone, he would have given anything to be among his own people. Now he would give anything to be allowed to return to Cho.

* * * *

Gathon answered the door of the suite with some irritation. Though Pan had told him that he would receive the contingent from the House of Tezars, he thought privately that the emperor was too weak to be dealing with enemies. But he also understood Panshinea's reasoning. Vihtirne and Qativar would spread the truth of his refusal if he had, well seasoned with rumors. The emperor had decided that he must meet with them to quell thoughts that he was on his way to his demise. *Show no weakness, no flank, no fear.*

Pan sat propped on his divan, the lighting set slightly lower to flatter his features. His convalescence had been long and difficult, the *bahdur* stubbornly refusing to rejuvenate rapidly, and he was lucky to be conscious. He had managed, by sheer dint of his will, which was considerable, to look as if merely resting after a mild illness and not as if the war he had waged against Palaton had nearly killed him as well.

Gathon stood back to allow Vihtirne and Qativar to enter. Vihtirne had shed her affection for blue and wore fuchsia, its rose hues flattering the artificial blush upon her face. The neckline was higher than usual, imparting a regal quality to her carriage. Her raven-wing hair had been knotted up and pinned with quartz jewelry and lay twinkling among her scalloped crown.

Qativar followed her, dressed in caramels, somber, but not at all reminiscent of the priestly robes he used to wear. Gathon had not thought much of Qativar as a priest. It was no shock to see he had shed his offices as a snake did its skin. Privately, the minister still held the opinion that Qativar had tried to kill the elderly Rindalan during the commons riots which had racked the city weeks ago. He was not pleased to be letting these two close to Panshinea now.

He announced them. Pan raised his face from the book he had been reading—Shakespeare again, Gathon had fetched it up from the music room library—and said nothing.

Vihtirne swept across the suite and came to a deep curtsy across from the divan. "My dear Panshinea. Let us be the first House to bring our wishes for your speedy recovery to you in person. Thank you for allowing us the inconvenience of seeing you this afternoon."

Bluntly. "What do you want?"

Qativar had caught up with Vihtirne, sketched a bow, and now stood at her side. He gave the appearance of one looking over the imperial suite as though he might one day desire to be an occupant. "We wish you well, nothing more."

Gathon closed the door and took up sentry duty, though if anything were to happen, he would have to call the guard. He could not protect Pan's personage alone, not any more.

Pan smiled thinly. "Everything is something more. If I recognize you as the first House to visit me personally, then the least of what I do is recognize the House of Tezars."

Qativar inclined his head. "A side effect, a ripple, of our visit, perhaps, but not our intention."

"Then what is your intention?"

"Your recuperation," Vihtirne answered lightly. She sat down on the long couch opposite, without invitation. The smallish fire in the fireplace reflected itself in the glowing hues of her dress.

"I do not look well enough to you?"

She smoothed a sleeve. "The whole city suffers, dear Pan, from the drain of imperial *bahdur.* You, of all Choyan, could scarcely do better."

The atmosphere of the room crackled and the fine, red-gold hair on Panshinea's head seemed to rise in a gentle aura, blue sparks contrailing through the air after each strand. Vihtirne swallowed tightly and moved back on the sofa, as if hoping to pull herself out of striking range. Qativar stood, looking thoughtful.

The power went out abruptly. Gathon moved two or three steps closer, knowing what that expenditure had just cost his charge.

"I take your well-wishes," Pan said dryly, "and thank you for them."

Qativar appeared unmoved. "No one of us is a *tezar*," he remarked. "Yet we understand that each of us burns as a torch, and when the fuel is consumed, it is gone, never to return. Do you not wonder, Panshinea, what it is we offer our pilots that their own Houses could not? He leaned forward intently. "Limitless power," he said, and his voices hissed with the seduction of it. "Never to falter again. Never to face the void of emptiness inside when the power is gone. Neuropathy defeated. We have a House because we can cure what no one else has been able to."

"You have a cure for burnout?" Pan's green eyes fixed on Qativar, a predator's stare which Qativar either did not care about or did not notice.

"As close to a cure as is ever likely to be found. We have a drug that will boost the recovery time ten—no, a hundred—times faster. It won't restore *bahdur* to those who have totally gutted themselves, and it won't help the God-blind, but it *will* rejuvenate you. Or any *tezar* who choses to take it."

Vihtirne leaned forward. "Isn't it about time?"

Pan's glance flicked to her, then back to her companion. "And what to you propose to do with this . . . miracle?"

"Extend a supply to you, to aid you in your convalescence. Make it available to those in the city who are currently struggling through difficulties of their own."

"And you would do this out of the goodness of your own hearts?"

"No." Vihtirne and Qativar exchanged glances. "No," she repeated firmly. "We do it to prove to you that we *are* a House, a House which will stand."

"I was not aware," Pan murmured, "that anyone had been working on such a drug." He still watched Qativar's face closely. "Although I had heard word of Rindalan's long, difficult, comatose recovery after the rioting. There was some talk of his being *bahdur*-impaired. You were, as I recall, banned from his quarters, were you not, Qativar?"

Qativar's face warmed. But he gave a nod. "Your intelligence is, as always, impeccable."

"That must have been difficult for you to accept and work around, as you were his closest aide." Pan slid aside the ivory-colored throw and stood. He wore gold and blue, and the gold seemed to hold the heat of the fireplace within it.

"The facts of Rindy's injuries and recovery are no secret, Your Highness. My difficulties with the office are unimportant. Rindalan is now your ambassador to Sorrow. And I," Qativar smiled, "I am one of the founding heads of a new House."

"Be that as it may." Pan put a hand down lightly on the back of his divan as he walked around behind it. Gathon knew instinctively that he was leaning on it without giving that appearance, propping himself up before his enemies. "My understanding is that you have already been overly generous with your drug."

"We have supplied those Choyan who seemed in dire need. How could we do less? There is an illness. We have the means to cure it." Qativar produced a small, ornately jeweled box from his jacket pocket. He laid it on the divan. "As you may see for yourself."

"Take it and get out. See that your charity on the streets is completed as well."

"Our people need this."

"You have no license to distribute it. I want it off the streets."

"You are defeating yourself. We've invested much in seeing Charolon recover—"

"I'm sure you'll be recouped by the black market."

Qativar bowed to Vihtirne and offered her his arm. She swept up her skirts and stood.

"Very well. We will withdraw boost from open availability. But you will not cut us off. I will remind you again of the water patent I hold, and this time, the upper hand is mine. This is a House which will stand. Make a move against us, and you will live to regret it." Vihtirne inclined her head slightly, adding, "May you be fully recovered next time we meet, Panshinea."

"I will be. Have no doubt."

She let Qativar escort her from the imperial suite.

Gathon slammed the door on their heels after ordering the guard to see them from the palace. He crossed the room briskly, reaching for the jeweled box. "I'll dispose of this."

"Leave it," Pan ordered.

"Surely you don't intend to—"

"No. I don't intend to do as they suggest." Pan reached out and caught up the box. "But neither will I be in the dark about what it is they are doing."

"But you don't intend to take it."

Pan's eyes held a smoldering in their depth. "No," he repeated. "Now leave me, Gathon. I think I'd better lie down again." He tottered slightly as he turned his back and wove across the suite toward the bedroom.

Gathon watched him go, thinking that he was probably the only Choya in the world upon whom Pan would turn his back.

Pan needed *bahdur.* Now, more than ever. Something twisted knifelike in his guts as he pondered what the emperor would do to retrieve it.

rrRusk brought the hard copy of the intelligence report in with him when he went to disturb GNask. The ambassador's muscular bulk soaked in the inner suite's spa, the temperature reflecting the heat and humidity of their home world. For a moment, rrRusk basked in it, before GNask's eyelids went up and the ambassador regarded him.

"The Ronins owe me a pilot."

rrRusk swallowed hard. Their uneasy alliance with the quilled assassins had brought them little satisfaction. The Ronins had reported traces of the Choyan colony fled from Arizar, but they had been in error. The rogue colony had gone to ground somewhere, untraceable. GNask had hoped to pick up specimens for observation and experimentation much as they had done with Alexa and Nedar. rrRusk did not condone it, himself. He had given his *tursh* up to be able to stay in deep space for long periods of time. The sluglike symbiont was a valuable commodity, possessing all of the wisdom and shrewdness of his line, as GNask's *tursh* did for his own. But unlike GNask, rrRusk was unwilling to segment his symbiont for implantation in an alien, no matter how intriguing the outcome might be.

While it was true that Alexa had been a successful outcome, the effect on the Choyan had been dubious. rrRusk could not see jeopardizing his symbiont further in experimentation. But then, the war general surmised, GNask had different ambitions than he did. It was not for him, ultimately, to question GNask's actions.

"There may be more reliable ways of suborning a pilot than the Ronins," he suggested.

"Yes?" GNask's eyes narrowed.

"You supported a vote to accept no contracts from the House of Tezars, but that was in your official capacity. Unofficially. . . ."

Water sloughed about the ambassador. "Mmmm. You suggest that it would be wise to establish clandestine diplomatic ties with the new House, to conduct an investigation of my own into the availability and reliability of the piloting? There could be an accident. One of the new pilots could be . . . lost. They would have no standing to protest. That is perhaps a viable option, rrRusk. Yes. Very viable. Thank you, General." Deep in thought, GNask sank to the bottom of his tank, buried up to his eyes in turgid liquid. After a moment, he noticed that the other had not moved.

"What is it?"

"I thought you might be interested. Ambassador Thomas was observed making a visit to his consulate's holding cells."

"And we, of course, could not get a recording."

"No. They are too well shielded. But our observations do not show that they, at the present time, have any prisoners."

GNask, who had been mopping at his tusk, stopped. "Visiting an empty cell? Not likely. Our old ally is much too busy." He half-reared his form from the water. "I wonder what he is hiding from us."

"I knew you would be interested," said rrRusk confidently.

The ambassador's *tursh* had been resting on GNask's flank, just below the waterline. It stirred now, as though awakened, and its two tiny pseudo-stalk eyes poked out curiously. "We will make every effort to discover what Thomas has down there, will we not?"

"I already have intelligence working on it."

"Good." GNask reached for a rough towel and began to dry himself vigorously. "You look dry, rrRusk. Why don't you come in for a soak?"

"Why—why, thank you, Your Honor." A blush of pleasure warmed rrRusk further. GNask took the report from him as he began to shed his suspender straps and short pants.

GNask moved to a sedan chair and sat back. He tapped a finger talon against his teeth as he read. "Yes, indeed," he said thoughtfully. "I very much want to know what he's hiding down there."

Chapter 17

On a half-moonlit night, Palaton paused on the brink of entering a bar which was darker inside than out, its atmosphere oozing out onto the street, murky and muddled. His gaze swept the neighborhood. Streets, littered and dirty. Buildings, some half-built, some half-burnt, others shadowed with disrepute, a slum. The sight tugged eerily at him, not unfamiliar in his travelings but nothing he ever thought to see on his home world. Not on Cho, never on the life-giver itself. The recognition left a bitter taste in his throat, which he swallowed down.

They had come back to Charolon to announce his rebirth. The danger was inherent, but he intended to send Pan an unmistakable message. It had been a scant four weeks since their meeting. It had taken him that long to regain his strength and to acquire the jet sleds, and to decide where to hit.

Palaton shrugged into the collar of his jacket, uneasy out of pilot's clothes, his horn crown throbbing with intuition. He prepared himself to step inward when the shadows boiled. A figure stirred at his feet, a youngster, thin and hunched over as though in pain.

He jolted to a stop and looked the beggar over soundlessly, his voices trapped in his throat by outrage and compassion. The streets and doorways of the capital had never held beggars before.

A hand wavered in his direction, fingers as thin as sticks waggling. "Can you help?" asked the Choya'i. "I'm hungry."

Angry and helpless, he looked down at the young one, saw horns thinned by malnutrition, rags about the slender figure. That one of his own should be found begging—*Emperor, that you could see this as well as I*—Palaton began to press money into her hand, enough money to carry her for several weeks.

He froze as they touched, and the distance between them could have spanned Chaos itself. He could fathom galaxies, he could cut between the curtain which separated time and space, but he could not see this poor one's destiny.

"No drugs," the pilot said finally, curtly as if he could dictate the other's future. Then he pushed his hand into hers.

Their fingers met, curled tightly for a moment, then the youngster wrestled the money away. She stowed it within the layering of her rags and got up, whispering, "*She* says to come to her. She says that she is not truly blind."

Palaton stiffened. "Who?"

The Choya'i looked into his face, her eyes the only thing about her not starved and wasted. They were deep, luminous pools of knowledge one so young should never have had. "She says you'll know how to find her. As for me—the guard's about. They'll have your horns." With that, the beggar bolted into the night.

He looked after her, rags flapping in the night air, her flickering of talent setting off the streetlights sporadically, highlighting her as she fled among them. She was not used to *bahdur,* he thought, for she was doing the opposite of what she wished: illuminating rather than shadowing her flight.

And yet the irony was that for most of the last century, few Choya could have lit any of those bulbs simply by thought, despite their design. This was one Rand must have Changed. How far they had come, and fallen, and yet reached again.

He waited a heartbeat while his eyes readjusted to the darkness. The threshold, sluggishly sensing his presence, opened and let him in. He entered and moved to the right with the grace of one trained for gravity-less flight.

There were no guards inside the bar, but that did not make the warning any less potent. His own senses traced icy fingers of alarm across his nerves. The crude *bahdur*-laced illusion which disguised him would not fool any who really knew him. The bar was rife with power.

As accustomed as he was to *bahdur,* he could not grow used to scenes such as this where the atmosphere fairly crackled with psi power ill-gotten and ill-used, a symptom of the epidemic raging across Cho. The hairs at the back of his neck rose in response. This, even for Choyan, was not normal. He stood amidst power undisciplined, unwarranted, untrained.

He was a *tezar. Bahdur* was his legacy. Bound into his genes, it made him master and reader of the nether world between navigable real space and time, and unnavigable Chaos. He was what he was because of his abundance of talent, yet he was perhaps more aware than any of his race of what it meant to have not been gifted . . . or to have had the talent burned out, seared from his very being.

Unlimited *bahdur,* once a dream, was now a nightmare mesh which bound them together. Palaton could smell the faint odor of the drug in the air, an off-worldly perfume which clung to every user, sweated off through every pore. The bar reeked of it.

They could not live with the power the drug gave them, and they could not live without boost once addicted. Yet the surge of *bahdur* left many rocketing out of control, living on a fiery edge of uncontrollable psi abilities. Drugs to boost them, drugs to bring them down again, the only control users had. In a few short weeks, his world had become nearly unrecognizable to him. Addicts, beggars, traitors. This was a Chaos he could not master. His world had changed so quickly that none of them could cope with it. It was still changing, like a river in floodtide.

He did not know for sure what he could hope to do—stemming the tide seemed impossible—he only knew he had to be there. Had to do something. He was a *tezar,* once elite, once proud, from a time before any fool who could swallow boost could pilot a starship.

Palaton moved again, unwilling to attract attention by standing too long in any one place. He found a table and ordered a drink from the servo. His contact either had not seen him or had not entered the bar yet. Palaton forced himself to lean back into his chair, lounging, disinterested in the muddied whispers in other parts of the room. As he relaxed, his hand brushed the end of his jacket, confirming that the enforcer, charged and ready, was still in its holster.

The drink came. Palaton took the chilled bottle, twisted the cap off, and poured it into a none too clean glass. Wary of ambush, he wouldn't have drunk it at all if the container had come already opened.

He felt a brush against his thoughts as he took a sip. He'd taken care to shield himself before entering the bar; now all the intruder would feel was a slight eddy of weariness and satisfaction, emotions rather than defined thought. The rebuff would be barely noticeable rather than if Palaton had suddenly flung up his barriers. The difference in reaction could mean his life.

"Tezar?"

Palaton looked over his shoulder as the speaker sidled up from behind, coming around and finally stopping, the table between them. "I'm Lescal." The Choya stood, hunched over to speak to him, his frame emaciated, his mane wild and uncombed, his cheeks gaunt hollows in his face. His horn crown looked as though it had begun to thin and curl. Most of all, Palaton hated the look in the eyes, the whites too gray-blue, too visible under the irises, intelligence fled, replaced by desperation: the look of a Choya addicted to boost.

Palaton smoothed over the revulsion he felt. Dealing with pilots addicted to boost was becoming a facet of life he'd never thought to face. But pilots who'd been through the proud flight schools of Blue Ridge, the Salt Tower, or the Commons were professional, highly trained, and, if such a thing could be said, they used boost in moderation. They sought after nothing that was not already theirs.

This Choya was nothing more than a street user, who, after having tasted boost could not endure living without it, no matter what the drug did to his system. He wore the patch of the House of Tezars, meaning he piloted because he'd suddenly been thrust into the powers which enabled him to do so—but though he could now perceive the Patterns of Chaos, Palaton knew this Choya could never master them. One day soon, under boost or not, he would lose himself and a flight.

Lescal would be dangerous, Palaton told himself, and forced a thin-lipped smile in response. "I am," he confirmed the other's inquiry. "Have a seat. A drink."

The Choya wiped his dry lips on the back of his hand, looked about, then sat quickly. "All right."

Palaton ordered another bottle. He sat, watching his guest, wondering where Rufeen was, if there should be trouble. He hadn't seen her in the bar, but he knew she'd entered before he had. His companion would be there, somewhere, backing him up from the depths. He could search for her with his *bahdur,* but didn't dare. The room was already too charged with power.

"What do you want?" The Choya perched at his chair's edge, one foot tapping the floor in a frantic, rhythmless beat.

"Information. And boost."

"The boost I've got." The other gave him full attention. "It's only been cut twice."

"Twice? You told me once yesterday."

Lescal licked his lips nervously. "I had to go to a different supplier. Twice is still good. Very good."

As indeed it was, Palaton reflected. The average supply was usually diluted three to four times. "I'm not happy, but I'll take it."

Lescal's eyes narrowed. His lip curled and even the intrusion of the servo with his drink did not stop his reaction. "You're all alike. You want it, but you act like you're too good for it." His gaze lasered up and down Palaton. "You're probably Housed, but can't burn enough *bahdur* to get anywhere, right? So use a little boost and make everyone take notice. We're not that much different."

Palaton felt his muscles tense, but he forced himself to stay in his chair, relaxing his body nonchalantly. "Maybe not," he agreed. "Price the same?"

"Yes."

"Done, then. Give me your deposit code and I'll have the money transferred."

Lescal showed his teeth. "Credit in hand, or no deal."

"All right. Show me the boost."

Lescal slipped a hand inside the jacket, showed him the corner of a tightly sealed packet. Palaton could see the fuchsia powder. He took out his money disks and slid them across the tabletop to the Choya. With barely a movement of hands, the exchange was made.

Palaton secured the packet inside his jacket.

"We're done," Lescal said.

Palaton struck, moving from his chair so quickly he had the other pinned to his seat before the streetrunner even knew he was moving. "Not quite," he said quietly, through his teeth. "I also need some information."

Lescal's eyes rolled. No one else in the bar paid any attention. If he were to let out a death scream, no one would even turn or raise an eyebrow. "What?"

"Your supplier."

"Trevon the Black. But you won't find him. He doesn't need boost. He can stay clear of you or anyone else." The Choya's jaws chattered in fear as he ran out of words.

"Then Trevon doesn't need to worry that you told about him, does he?"

"No—o," answered Lescal, unconvinced. "What else?"

"A stranger, an alien."

"Off-worlder?" Lescal blinked. "Hiding?"

"Possibly." Palaton watched the other think, knowing that there had only been one off-worlder at large on Cho in the last generation, and Palaton had lost him. He'd brought Rand to Cho to keep him safe from the stewpot politics of the Compact, and lost him to a traitor among his own people. If this boost-laced Choya could think, he'd put Palaton and Rand together. If not. . . . Would the query unmask him?

Lescal licked his lips. Most common Choyan were xenophobic. The reaction now showed in Lescal's eyes. He shook it off briskly. "I haven't seen anyone like that."

"But if you do. You know who's looking for him."

"Tezar."

"Palaton. Remember the name."

"But you're—dead."

"You're sure? Look at me closely. Look and remember. Panshinea will pay for that memory. Sell it wisely."

His captive pulled away.

Palaton let go and Lescal bolted, chair overturning in his haste. He fled the bar, never looking back.

Business done, Palaton finished his drink, dissatisfied. How could one humankind be wrenched from his guardianship and hidden away so thoroughly? And for what ransom? That was a failure he could not stare in the face, not yet.

Peripherally, he saw a shadow detach itself and drift his way. She took a chair and their eyes met.

Rufeen was frowning. "You take too many chances, boss."

"He was a burned-out boost addict." Palaton could feel his nostrils flare slightly with the disgust he felt. He could still smell the stink of it on him, the ooze from the other's pores, the chemical wrongness.

Rufeen faced him. She opened her mouth to say something more, then snapped it shut, and opened it again to warn, "If Jorana were here, she'd have your hide. The little street rat couldn't wait to get out of here. That ought to tell you something."

"But she isn't," Palaton said sharply. Rand had been taken from him, but the sting of Jorana's fleeing was just as sharp. She'd abandoned him, left him to face the wrath of the returning emperor alone. He'd failed as guardian to Rand. As heir to Panshinea's throne. But how had he failed Jorana?

What Rufeen said returned to niggle at him. Lescal couldn't have escaped quickly enough. He wondered if he'd stepped into a trap and stirred, agreeing with the Choya'i.

"No, he couldn't." If he knew imperial guards, his informant wouldn't get far. Aloud, he observed of Lescal, "He won't get far enough to spend his money."

Rufeen snorted. "If he's colluding, Panshinea will have his liver for breakfast."

Palaton did a quick psychic sweep of the table, altering the aura of his presence and hers as carefully as he could without attracting attention. As he finished, Lescal's attitude and the beggar's warning came together. Palaton stood. "I'm done here."

They got no farther. A hand of imperial guards broke in the door, awash in light from their helmets and belt lanterns, eyes coldly sweeping the bar. Rufeen melted away into the shadows with a muttered curse, heading toward the back. Palaton continued with a soft step toward the front as though the guards had not alarmed him, knowing that they would be night-blinded as he had been upon entering.

Another Choya did not take the invasion so calmly. He came to his feet with a shout, and the guards swung around in a united front, enforcers in their hands. Palaton hit the deck at the first discharge, heard tables and chairs avalanche about him. Footsteps ran past. He saw regulation issue boots as they went by. He rolled over onto his flank and peered cautiously over a tabletop. The guards had their target surrounded and were, none too gently, searching their prisoner. The downed Choya got a beam in the face and a boot shoved in his ribs.

Palaton shot a glance toward the rear, saw Rufeen waiting

near the archway, thumb hooked nonchalantly in her belt. She had the exit secure, for the moment.

He got to one knee, catching her eye, and signaled her to go on out and free their transport. As she moved out cautiously, the guards watched her go but did nothing to detain her.

Palaton doubted he would be that lucky. *Bahdur* tingled under his skin like a fiery network of energy and he drew on it, crafting the illusion of himself standing, readying to fight, staring them down. When he'd finished, he threw the aura at them, knowing it would hold long enough to get him through the back doorway. After that, he was in trouble.

As the illusion went up, he scrambled across the barroom floor on hands and knees, pitching upward at the back door. The guards were engaged in firing at the illusion, crying out in disbelief as their target failed to go down.

He caught his hip on the corner of the serving bar. It swung him around, a physical blow that brought a gasp of pain to his lips. As he moved, he saw a Choya'i react, a beautiful face to the rear of the bar, a familiar face swinging past. . . .

He went to one knee in pain, sucked his lip to stay quiet, and craned his neck to look, to see if it *was* her, drinking alone, Jorana, her bronze mane tied back from her crown and her exquisite face. . . . The blinding white arc of light thrown out by the guards had sent the room into shocking light and dark patterns, and he could not see her well, but he knew the way she moved. He could feel that burned into his mind, moving to him, with him . . . was it her? The Choya'i turned sharply away, and he lost her entirely to the shadow.

Then the guards started across the floor, their boot stamps drumming and he knew he was out of time.

Palaton drew a soft breath, focused, and threw one last illusion at the barroom's front counter. It would last far longer than the other, orange flames, gushing upward, engulfing the counter, guaranteed to send the remaining clientele bursting for the exits, a cold fire which would dwindle down to a single blue flame, burning icily from the ashes of its casting. He wrote his name within the flame. He felt the *bahdur* leaving him, an icy hole into which nothingness plunged, a weak, giddy feeling of expenditure that made him reel. Palaton caught himself, pivoted, put a shoulder to the back door,

rolling through and onto his feet in one fluid move even as
screams and shouts exploded behind him.

Quickly, he moved around the building to find Rufeen at
the jet sleds, firing them up. He panted too hard for the simple exertion, but with his *bahdur* nothing was as simple as it
had been, once. He put his chin down to catch his breath and
saw the forms at Rufeen's boots. Two guards littered the
backstreet. Her nose wrinkled.

"They'll sleep a while," she said. Her knuckles were split
and bloodied. She swung a leg over her sled, and added, "But
I suggest we get out of here anyway."

He put his transport into full throttle, and she followed in
his wake. Palaton signaled to Rufeen when they'd moved up-
hill, decently out of range, past a burned-out shell of a building, and they brought the jet sleds down to idle hover. He
brought scopes out of the tool bag, keyed in the night filter,
and put them to his eyes to watch. Night shadows hid them as
imperial guards stormed outside the bar. He did not like having to leave his psychic fingerprint behind, but he'd been left
no choice. He would rather have come and gone without
Panshinea's finest knowing he'd even been there. But he saw
no sign of Jorana. He trained the scopes on all the exits,
watching those who carefully and not so carefully fled the
scene. He tarried too long, watching, but he could not tear
himself away.

Rufeen brought up the idle on her jet sled. "Boss, we've
got to get out of here."

"I know." He watched the building, saw a few more occupants slither out and disappear. "I don't like to leave unfin-
ished business behind."

"You're going to leave your behind behind if we don't get
out of here." Rufeen glared at him, her face large and square
and homely, but honest, and boost had never dimmed the truth
in her eyes. "Let's go."

Nodding, Palaton reluctantly turned his sled about and followed her lead out of the ruins. A Choya more wanted than
any boost dealer, a prize the emperor would stop at nothing to
acquire, the former heir to the throne stole away in the night.

The emperor sat bowed at his *lindar,* his hands curved over
the keyboard as though prepared to play . . . or perhaps to

throttle. He turned his head slightly, bringing his green gaze to rest on the nervous captain of the imperial guard. The captain was new to his post, promoted when the former head, Jorana, had abruptly disappeared. That did not make Namen any more secure in his position. He set his jaw as Panshinea stared at him.

"He's alive."

"We got a handful of gutter rats leaving the bar. They've all reported the same thing." Namen felt his knees grow weak.

"What about the dealer? Have you found him?"

"He's in custody, awaiting questioning."

"I will," stated the emperor, "be there when you take your deposition."

"Yes, Your Highness." Namen could feel the burn in front, and back, as his own guards stared at him from behind.

Panshinea took his hands from the keyboard. He massaged one lightly. He was not old for a Choyan, but his hands had begun to show his age. The veins stood out in ropy lines, his knuckles had begun to knot. His luxuriant mane of reddish-gold, however, remained undiminished. "What good can you tell me, Namen?"

"Little. The bar was so rife with boost users we could not pick up an accurate aura reading. If this was Palaton, why here? No descriptions, and this facility has made a policy of not making visuals. There was only the fire illusion. . . ."

Panshinea finally looked away, and Namen suffocated the sigh of relief in his throat. The emperor gazed down the length of the room to the garden beyond the arched doorway. "Do what you can," he said, finally, his voices fading.

Namen dared not take it as a sign of weakness. He knew that Panshinea's fury toward his heir was unabated. He saluted and turned away.

"Namen."

The captain stopped in his tracks. He spun about as if twirled by an inexorable force.

Panshinea looked upon him again. "You will find him, won't you? Because I have no choice but to believe he's alive." *Alive and flaunting the House of Flame in my face. Alive and unpredictable. Alive and out there somewhere.*

"If he's on Cho, Your Highness, I will find him."

Panshinea launched himself to his feet. "He's a *tezar,* burn your hide, Captain! He has the universes to hide himself in."

"He's Choyan," Namen replied evenly. "And I have reason to believe he would not abandon his home."

"Do you, Captain?"

Namen felt his chin go up. "I have my convictions, Highness."

"I used to, once." The fire left Panshinea's eyes. He sagged into his chair. "Get out of here."

Namen left swiftly.

Panshinea listened to the rapid fade of the footsteps of his guard. Jorana, gone. Had she fled before Palaton's fall from grace to save her own hide, or had her pilot lover sent her away? None of Panshinea's intelligence within the palace could give him the answer. She had come to him young and beautiful, and matured into an experienced, intelligent Choya'i. The beauty had only strengthened. But once he had brought Palaton to the palace, she had never looked at him again in the same way. Panshinea knew then that Palaton had taken her from him.

As for the throne, Panshinea had given it to him, knowing the burden would destroy him. Instead, Cho itself had split asunder and the rival factions were tearing at its flesh like ravenous carrion eaters. Panshinea had destroyed the very thing he had hoped most to save.

The emperor swallowed his emotions, bitter bile in his throat, swearing to himself.

Palaton would pay for that with his life, and any and all who dealt with him, no matter who they were, would fall also.

No matter who.

Chapter 18

It was like keeping the carrion hounds at bay, Panshinea thought, and wearily put a cold glass to his temple, to ease the pounding.

Palaton alive, and harrying the black market for boost. The broadcasters had caught word of him and now he was some heroic phantom, fighting to reestablish himself and the lost House. They were making an icon of him. He was waging the war against boost that Panshinea ought to be waging, and could not.

The news of the water patent reversion had been the subject of the last three Congressional sessions, and though Vihtirne had apparently done nothing, the possibility of the privatization of the public utility held all the representatives in tension. But overshadowing all was the threat she had left with him. *Cut off boost, and I'll cut off the water.* Pan felt powerless.

The guard had sent out a detail, reasonably sure that they had finally netted Palaton, but their unconscious bodies had been found in the common quarter of the city, and nothing they said upon recovery made much sense. The doctor examiner had told Pan privately that he doubted full memory could ever be restored. The emperor was not certain that the Choya they had encountered had been Palaton. He did not think the *tezar* had it in him to treat even an enemy that way.

Rindalan's latest reports from Sorrow were not much more encouraging. The demand for open contracting with pilots was building and if it came to a full Compact vote, there would be no way to keep any of the space-going races from treating separately with the House of Tezars.

Even the comfort of his garden library did not bring him the ease he'd hoped for. He had given up his post on Sorrow to return, but his presence had done no good. He no longer held the control from the throne he once had, and his own people knew it, the Abdreliks guessed it, the Ronins lusted for it. The Great Wheel of God was rotating slowly about, his House was on the descendant, and when the Wheel rose again, another House would be uplifted. An emperor in descendant could ruin all that Cho had striven for these last few hundred years.

Panshinea looked at his reflection in the gleaming wood panels of his desk. Blessed by prelates after the God-blind had carved it, this desk had stood in the palace for, what, most of the three or four hundred years he thought of? The core that underlay all their *bahdur* was the acknowledgment of things organic, of the once living, of all which reflected the spark of God. He could not sit here and not know that this living thing had been sacrificed to make an object for his use. It would not live again, except in the essence of the God-in-all which lost nothing that had ever been created—except for those lost crossing Chaos. They were irretrievable.

Still ... Panshinea put his dewy-sided goblet down and drew across the heavily polished wood with a fingertip. Why him? Why was it he who had been doomed to be emperor at a time when the Wheel turned to its downside? Had he not worked as hard as anyone, no, harder, to keep the carrion hounds at bay, both upon Cho and in the Compact? Had he not sacrificed his youth and his prime? What more could he have done?

Anger flared in him. He curled a fist and slammed it into the pattern he'd traced upon the desktop. Who were any of them to judge him the dregs of his House! It would not be over until it was over, and not until then could any presume to judge him. And when the dust had settled over his coffin, his descendants would look at one another and say, "The House of Star never had a more brilliant emperor."

He would not quit. They would have to defeat him. And, by so doing, they would bring their own doom upon Cho.

Panshinea glared at his reflection in the desktop. The burls lent new lines to his face, new heaviness to his eyes. He lifted his chin and downed his drink, then put his head back and bellowed for Gathon.

* * *

The prime minister must have been napping, for when he came in, there were lines on his face which the bed linens had imprinted there, and his yellowing mane of hair lay uncombed upon his forehead. His jacket looked as though it had been pulled hastily upon his wiry frame.

"What is it?" Gathon asked softly, as though he had not been interrupted.

"I need you to make a little journey for me." Panshinea studied his minister. He saw the tiny signs of distaste he had been looking for.

"It is late."

"So much the better." Pan cleared his throat. "I would have Jorana do this for me, but . . ."

"Your Highness, is it necessary?"

Pan drew himself up. "Look into my eyes, Gathon. You tell me what burns there, and you tell me if this is necessary."

The prime minister stole the briefest of glances, and turned away, as if he did not like what he saw. Speaking almost in an entirely different direction, Gathon said reluctantly, "I do not like doing this."

"We haven't any choice. Would you rather I started using boost? What a field day the broadcasters would have with that, would they not? They would love to bring me down and let Congress and the commons dance on my bones. The emperor must absorb *bahdur* from the defenseless to maintain his throne and his powers. The fall of the House of Star, at last." Panshinea thrust himself to his feet. "Well, they can't have the throne yet. I'm not done with it. And I'll do whatever I have to do to keep it within my grasp."

"You risk much," Gathon answered him.

"I know." Panshinea's voices leveled. He paced across the room, away from the elderly Sky. "Your loyalty is remarkable."

Gathon's dry voices followed after him. "I try."

Panshinea turned quickly. "I only need one tonight, Gathon. But I do need him. I can't face tomorrow without him."

Gathon swallowed tightly, then said, "I don't . . . I'm not sure if I can find a suitable candidate. Finding unsullied talent is getting more and more difficult."

Panshinea looked out the garden room windows at the velvet blackness of his atrium. "I know," he answered finally. "Perhaps the alternative is preferable."

"Never!" The strength of Gathon's response surprised them both, and Panshinea faced him. Color had risen high in the prime minister's face. "The drug is off-world, we know that much. If you came to depend on it, and that dependency were known—"

"The throne of Cho would be a puppet on a string for anyone to manipulate," Panshinea finished. "So, disagreeable as tonight is, we're agreed it's necessary."

Gathon dropped his chin down in silence.

Pan took a deep breath. He crossed his hands behind his back. "Take the back ways," he said. "I'll be here waiting."

The faint sound of shuffling steps told him when Gathon left.

He had decanted a bottle of the wine known as Imperial Gold. It was rare now, Imperial Gold, the vineyards in an area forced to become fallow, the vines stored for that future when the land could again be used, the wine prized beyond value for its like would probably never be fermented again. That was the tragedy, and the success, of Relocation. The lands, all of them, and fishing lanes, and cities as well, were forced to cease and desist so that the land and water itself could take a breather, lie wild, rest, without occupation or disturbance. The vines which had produced Imperial Gold might be replanted successfully in the future. Or they might not. Grape vines, as Panshinea recalled, could be difficult and stubborn.

He had glasses waiting. The inside basin of one had been discreetly rubbed with *ruhl*, the aphrodisiac which quite disabled *bahdur*. It did not take much of the illicit drug to confuse and fog the mind. The glasses were placed so that he knew which was which, for the obvious reasons. He had retired to his chair and was reading a translated volume of Shakespeare, marveling at the richness of thought and emotion, telling himself that the humankind race proved the theory that all races, whether space-going or not, had the ability to reach spiritual maturity when he heard the voices and steps outside his study.

Gathon came in, face grayed with the cold, hunched under his jacket and hood, with a bracing young Choya on each arm. Pan set aside his book and stood. They were wilders, off the street, their hair roached, shining with the luster of newly fallen raindrops, the brown of newly turned earth, rich and virgin. They did not have facial jewelry as was the custom of the Housed, but they wore open-throated vests rather than jackets or cloaks to display their pectoral jewelry. They shook off the rain, scattering it like diamonds across the carpets of his solarium, and turned their green-gold eyes on him and waited.

He could feel the charge of their sexual energy, and felt the corner of his mouth twist a little in response. Gathon bowed his head without introduction and left, closing the doors firmly behind them.

They both had *bahdur,* borderline, and from the swagger of their walk, they used it, whether consciously or unconsciously, to enhance their appeal. The knowledge of their virility rippled beneath their musculature, and flashed in their eyes. Pan looked at the whites, could see little of the bloodshot appearance of those addicted to boost, and decided that Gathon had brought him appropriate subjects, after all. It only gave him a momentary pause to wonder how and where Gathon had known to look for Choya like these.

"I'm Farren," said the bigger of the two, and hiked a thumb back at his shadow. "And this is Syman."

Panshinea took down a third glass as he stepped to the liquor cabinet, dashed a drop of *ruhl* in it as his back was turned, and then filled all three of the stemware with Imperial Gold. He said, dryly, "No need to give you my name, is there?"

"No, sir," echoed the two commons.

Panshinea turned about, and handed around the glasses. "This should take the chill off." He drank deeply and watched as, nervously, they took the delicate glasses in their work-callused hands, and sipped at the wine. They were probably used to coarser brews, but an immediate appreciation of the wine bloomed over their faces.

Nice, he thought, to have both the brashness and the innocence of the young. He leaned his hips against the corner of the bar. "Now, then. What did you have in mind?"

Syman kept his nose buried in his glass, but Farren answered, "Nothing, sir. But we met your Choya on the downside, and we got to arguing, and then he told us he could get us this opportunity to meet with you ourselves. Said you like to keep in touch with the commons."

"I have been known to, from time to time." Pan swirled his wine and finished it. He held the bottle out and topped off Syman's glass.

The youth gave him a look, from gold-green eyes, and Pan gave him a level look back, from eyes which he knew were cold jade green. The other shrank back into Farren's shadow a bit, as if suddenly realizing that, despite their fitness and brawn, Panshinea stood over them by a good shoulder and crown.

Farren flexed inside his ebony leather vest. "So we're here."

"Indeed you are." Panshinea refilled Farren's glass as well. The wine flowed inside him like a river of sun. He let that wealth pour outside of himself as well, fueled with the last, flickering vestiges of his own *bahdur*. He could feel it cascading about the two youths, drawing them closer, intimate, warming, calming. He looked into their eyes and smiled. He had seduced far more important and intelligent Choyan than they with that smile; indeed, the impact of that gesture had been felt oceans of starlight away. He knew its power.

It did not startle him when Farren flushed, then put his hand to the throat of his vest, opening it, as if suddenly too warm. Syman cleared his throat huskily, responding to the charge in the air. Then Farren went to his knees, and Syman made an odd little noise and toppled, crashing headfirst among the shards of his glass. Farren looked up at Panshinea, terror striking across his face.

"Wha—" He did not finish before falling backward across the torso of his companion. His eyelids fluttered closed.

Panshinea stood over them a moment, waiting until their frightened breathing subsided into puffs barely sufficient to keep them alive. "There are many ways to serve your emperor," he told them, before kneeling next to their unconscious bodies and draining them of the soulfire which fueled them.

Rand jerked awake in his cell, gasping and choking, eyes staring starkly into the darkness of downtime, heart beating so wildly in his chest he thought it might burst. He put his hand to it, as if he could somehow quiet it that way, like he had once petted a dog, and felt his chest heaving under his palm.

He hadn't dreamed of vampires since leaving his father and Earth, but now he had. The terror had invaded a peaceful dream of Rindy discussing philosophy with him, a tract of peace and help and friendship, when something dark had pierced their togetherness. That darkness had grabbed him, ripping him away, had thrown him down, and with a cold, wet kiss, had begun to devour his soul. It had sucked him inside out, until his blood had grown cold and tired in his body, and his heart barely flickered. Down, down, it had reached inside of him and peeled him away from—what?

His *bahdur*.

But he had none. His only gift had been lent him by Palaton to be cleansed and taken back when Palaton's need was greatest. He had nothing.

Rand leaned back against the wall of the sleeping cubicle. His hair was slick and wet down his neck. He put a hand back to try and wipe it dry, without luck. His heart quit drumming, but his pulse still hummed loudly in his ears.

Nightmares. Or memories?

Subconscious memories. Did he think of Palaton as some subliminal rapist?

But the presence which had attacked his dreams had not felt like Palaton. Or even dead Nedar.

Vampires. Bogeymen. Rand forced a laugh as he pulled his knees up and hugged them, staring across the cell and wondering when uptime would lighten the corridors. He wondered if Maeva would come that day, even as he told himself the chances were that she could not.

In his fear, the rest of his dream, the part of the dream telling him of friendship and aid and peace and comfort fled completely.

Chapter 19

"He saw me. I know he did." The Choya'i paced the room of the tiny warren, her stride swift and sure despite the growing bulk of her body. Her distress was written all over, from the pallor of her expression to the sweep of her steps.

"And how could he recognize you? If indeed it was him. He was under attack at the time. He might have been busy trying to survive." The immense, sable-haired Choya who watched her sat at a table which he dwarfed, his work-worn hands in front of him, playing at a child's game of beads and sticks. He played at divination, and bright flashes of *bahdur* power struck sparks now and then. A game it was, but a game meant to measure the talent of the young and untested. He played it as though it were new to him, as indeed it was, for he had been born a Godless, a commons, until the Change came over him. Malahki watched the game patterns fall before him, as if he could not believe the fortune which had struck him. "And if it was him, then you are twice the fool for not turning him over to us when you should have. He gains nothing by taunting Panshinea now. The Prophet has things to tell him, but he refuses to go to Bayalak to see her. He is playing with fire, Jorana, and you won't be able to save him from himself a second time."

Jorana paused, put a hand to her stomach reflectively, noting the rounding of pregnancy, and said, "I couldn't have given him to you, you know that. He would never have forgiven me."

"I understand. That doesn't mean she would, which is why I'm holed up here with you." Malahki gave a wry smile. "We're both in trouble."

She combed her fingers nervously through her hair, loosening the forelock from its ribboned braid, colored like river clay, far from the natural luster of her gold-fire mane.

Malahki intoned, "It would be stupidity beyond measure to come back to the capital, well within Pan's grasp. Our *tezar* is many things, but I did not count stupidity among his faults."

"The guards were looking for someone."

"A boost dealer, no doubt. Panshinea hesitates to take a stand about the traffic, but whether he intends to shut it down or control it himself, I haven't been able to figure out. And I won't find the answer here!" Malahki shoved himself back in the chair, taking his eyes off the game and looking squarely at Jorana. "Perhaps Palaton would behave differently if he knew he was to be a father."

Jorana took a deep breath. "Malahki," she said softly. "I stole a child from him. If he knew then, or if he knows now, do you think he would forgive me that? Do you?"

"The only thing he knows is that you abandoned the palace before Panshinea returned. As far as he knows, you left so as not to be a pawn between the two of them." Malahki tapped a finger upon the tabletop. "What do you fear?"

"His hatred. His disgust and pity. You did this to me, Malahki, with your insistence that I take a child from him. . . ."

Malahki continued to level his gaze at her, until finally it was she who turned away. He said, "We each have our own destiny. Would you deny it?"

"I wish that you'd left me orphaned and destitute. I wish that you'd never raised me or sponsored me to be Housed. That you'd never educated me. Bullied me. Driven me to be that which I can't be anymore!"

"Or loved you?"

His voices were like a gentle hand under her chin, lifting her face back up so that she could look him in the eyes again.

"Yes!" Jorana gasped out.

"You are not worthy of love?"

"No." She looked askance again. "Not from anyone." A single, dewy tear escaped her right eye and began to slide down her cheek.

Malahki tilted his chair back on its legs. He put his hands behind his head. "You remind me of my Dara, rest her soul, when she carried my own children. This is not you talking, it's hormones running amok, preparing a nest for your young. You're an educated Choya'i—you should know this. It brings tears to the surface, like the quickening of a heartbeat. It stirs up storms. Yes," and he gave a rueful grin. "I remember Dara storming."

"I might know it, but I've never experienced it." Jorana collapsed onto a chair opposite Malahki. "I can't even be myself!"

"Of course you can. But you're tired, and worried, and you've been drinking. What do you think your system can do under an overload like that?" The immense, burly Choya reached across the tabletop now, his wrist brushing over the game pattern of beads and sticks. "I should get you a midwife. Let her tell you what you won't believe from me."

Jorana took another deep, shuddery breath, and realized she had been on the brink of sobbing. "I've months yet."

"Yes. But the life within you is brimming over. It may be unborn, but it has the same potent *bahdur* you do, that its father has. It's spilling out, affecting you, along with everything else. If only Dara were alive to talk with you ... you're isolated here. I think we should move you. Cross continent, if we can. You need to be out, among other Choya'i, and working. You've a fine mind, Jorana. You were the captain of the guard! Why do you think you were out, unwisely, tonight?"

She made a tiny sound which might have been ironic, or a hiccup. "I was restless."

"You see?"

"I see." Her voices sounded a little blurred, weary. She pulled a handkerchief from her pocket and blew her nose. "How long does this insanity last?"

Malahki shrugged "Motherhood goes on as long as the mother does, from the way my Dara behaved."

"Oh, God-in-all!" Jorana leaned forward and let her head drop to the table. "How could I do this to myself?"

Malahki cupped his hand over her hair. The color, which had been so beautiful once, was now as common as the river clay it mimicked. She had changed it to hide herself. But the texture of the hair had remained, and despite its drab appearance, it filled his hand with soft, luxurious waves. "We could not let that spark which made Palaton what he was go out. The genetic heritage—"

"I know!" Muffled, yet emphatic. Softer. "I know, I know."

"Yet do you?"

Jorana rested her chin on the table's edge, still hunching her body over, and put a finger out, where she stirred the pieces of beads and sticks. As if repelled by a magnet, the game pieces fled ahead of her touch, though she left a pathway behind of ordered patterns. *Bahdur,* if it was used, did not glow at all, so powerful was she, that she made her passage silently. Genetic heritage was so crucial to the Choyan way of life, yet its crossing and bastardization was blasphemy, so that she hesitated but a second before saying, "And I suspect that you've known it all along, too." And she canted her glance upward slightly, watching Malahki for his reaction.

The Choya sat back, shock on his broad, yet handsome face. After a long pause, he answered, "I was never certain."

"And what heritage is it, do you think, that I'm bringing into this world?"

He mumbled slightly. "I'm not sure. Whatever it is, it will be powerful."

"Powerful enough that it might be handy to have a mother who was formerly head of the imperial guards to protect it." Jorana sat up then. "Oh, Malahki. We don't know what will come of this mix. My DNA traces back to some long ago bastardization of a Star Householding, but this child . . . what can a Flame do? Why was the House set upon by the other Houses and destroyed? What happened—what will it do to me and my baby?"

"I don't know." He looked down at the table, and read fully the patterns which Jorana had stirred into existence. It showed the Great Wheel, its turning and destruction and reformation. He hoped that it was not prophetic. "But whatever the talents, they managed to elude complete genocide. They managed to *survive,* Jorana, and so must you." He swept aside the beads and sticks. "We need to do some planning. I can't stay here with you for long. Father Chirek is starting another campaign. The Prophet will forget her ire at both of us, and I'll once again be of use to her."

"Others need you," she echoed faintly. Then she drew her chair closer to the burly Choya. "All right. Let's make some decisions. I overheard something else, and I'm not sure what it means."

"Tell me."

"Palaton was asking for word of an alien. I think he was looking for Rand."

Malahki rocked back in his chair. "Rand has left him?"

He rubbed a thick finger between his eyes. "They would have to burn Blue Ridge down to get Rand away from him. That could explain much. Although why Dorea didn't tell me this—surely she *saw* it—"

"She's a Prophet, not a God," interrupted Jorana.

Malahki halted, then shrugged. "Then we have to wonder if Palaton does what he does because he's been directed, or because that's the course of action he's chosen."

"If he were being directed, his supposed death in the crash would have allowed him to go underground and stay there. He didn't choose to stay dead. It also means Pan doesn't have Rand, or the meeting on Emperor's Walk would have gone far differently." Her eyes widened. "It has to be Qativar and Vihtirne. They initiated the fight at Blue Ridge, then came in to pick up the pieces."

"Possibly. The House of Tezars remains relatively secure, at the moment. Of course, that might only be because Palaton has limited resources." He dipped a fingernail into the divination game in front of him, and a spark flew up. "He might have his hands tied, but I do not. Rand is as important to me as he is to Palaton."

"We do not play at games, Malahki," Jorana said softly.

He looked up at her. "I know, foster daughter. Believe me, I know." He frowned heavily, concentrating on his palms. "If Palaton is of the House of Flame, then I choose to become a Flame, newly empowered as I am. He won't have me, I know, because of our past enmity and my ties to the Prophet, but that doesn't matter. I will follow him, and all those linked to me will do as I do. Wherever Palaton takes a stand against boost or the emperor, a dozen others will do likewise. He will be mirrored wherever he goes, whatever he does. For his, and our sake, I pray that the good of Cho goes with him." As Malahki moved his hands apart, the illusion of a blue flame burned on the table in front of him, as like to the signature

Palaton had left burning for Jorana to see as if she had copied it herself.

Malahki stood up and shook himself, sable mane ruffling. "I have work to do."

Chapter 20

"You take chances," Rufeen said, her face pulled into a morose expression, her hand curled about a mug of steaming hot *bren*. "Chances that you shouldn't."

"A *tezar* not take chances?" Palaton injected humor into his reply, though weariness had settled into his bones as he sat down opposite her. The tiny room seemed bursting with them, though they were only three. The silent third went about filling two more mugs and sliding one of them in front of Palaton.

Rufeen rolled her eyes, looking at the Earthan for support. "You know what I mean. *He* knows what I mean, but he won't allow it to sink in."

Hathord sweetened his drink and then sat down heavily, both elbows and nearly his chin, too, on the tabletop. "*I* know what you mean but I'm not so sure *he* does."

Palaton put his fingers into his topknot, combing it away from his forehead. Even as he did so, he wondered if the forehead had gotten higher . . . the topknot thinner. He could tell without looking that the lines across his brow had gotten deeper. God-in-all knew that his horn crown felt like a ton of rock settled upon his head and shoulders. He flexed his neck slightly at the thought. This last recovery had taken him longer and had been difficult, though when the power came back, it always seemed stronger than ever.

Rufeen said, with satisfaction, "We're not talking about navigation, and you know it. We're talking about here and now. Your hide is too valuable to waste. And if you haven't noticed lately, we have imitators."

"I've noticed." Palaton thought of Jorana. Was she shadowing his deeds, giving a resonance to his campaign against Panshinea's seeming indifference, or was someone else hiding in the echo of his defiance? "We all need to be a bit more circumspect. No more kidnapping of broadcasters, though I will admit that was a stroke of genius."

"Thank you," Rufeen acknowledged modestly. "You needed to get that ugly mug of yours on the air. You will be pleased to know we put him back just where we found him, too." She took a cautious sip of her drink, pronounced it good, which by pilot's standards meant that a spoon could stand upright in it, and added, "You have a duty to remember what you are to Cho."

"I remember only too well," Palaton told her. "But you can't go in alone, and Hat's not good at it."

"No," Hat agreed, unabashedly. "Not at that." He blinked. "Not that I wouldn't cheerfully kill anyone pushing boost."

"There is that, but you don't need to be chasing down the black market while you're doing it."

"It seemed opportune." Palaton cleared his throat. "From what I saw in that quarter, boost has already eroded deeply into Charolon. I can't hesitate any longer. You didn't see what I saw."

Rufeen put her mug down thoughtfully. "I think the problem goes deeper. I've been talking among the few I can who will keep my confidence, boost or no, and there's a phenomenon we haven't heard much about. The broadcasters have been keeping silent under duress. Panshinea has a blackout on the media."

Palaton's gaze riveted on her. "What?" He wondered how much more damage could be done to his people.

Rufeen shook her head. "Pan's use of imperial *bahdur* has evidently created a drain through all of Charolon. Maybe even planetwide, though his effect is less farther out from the Emperor's Walk. The House of Tezars came in, offering the drug freely, which explains why the capital fell into it so easily."

"And Panshinea let them?"

"My intelligence says that Pan made them pull out after a week or so, but by then the damage was done. The need was created."

Hat said, "That doesn't explain *us*."

Palaton looked at Rufeen, then remarked gently to the Earthan, "You haven't flown the schedules we have, Hat. You don't know what it's like to have a few hours, or days, of downtime and then be needed elsewhere, and to always have to be master, in control."

"Maybe I don't, but—"

Rufeen put her hand on his wrist. "You don't. It's that simple. No one of us wants to be the one who burns out and loses a shipment in Chaos. But it happens."

"Boost is no guarantee it won't," said Hat stubbornly.

"It's as close as we can get."

Rufeen lifted a shoulder and let it drop. "There's something else. Pilots aren't allowed to fly regular schedules. They're using a second medication with the boost. I don't have a name for it . . . but my friends told me that, in order to pilot, they're forced to use it in conjunction. And," she paused, her eyes thoughtful, "it doesn't increase *bahdur.* It wipes it out. They say it's necessary to use both, to avoid the rather undesirable side effects of boost alone."

Palaton's mug slipped from his grip, crashing to the table. Hat reached out to steady it as Palaton's expression grew very grim. "Vihtirne's got the House of Tezars wired like a damn circuit switch. What's the coercion?"

"The coercion is that those who've resisted boost are fed the other stuff first." Rufeen looked at him levelly. "You know what we're like without *bahdur.* They're creating the same need in us that Charolon had after Panshinea's drainage."

Cold fingers traced down his spine. Oh, he knew very well indeed what it was like to have the power stripped away or burned out. Stronger Choyan than he had been broken over the very prospect. Under different circumstances, even Palaton could not swear that he would not eventually reach for boost himself.

Hat commented, "*Ruhl* can do that."

Despite her tough pilot's demeanor, Rufeen blushed. "It's an aphrodisiac, and outlawed at that. We're not talking inhibition in bed."

"Stronger doses."

Palaton shook his head. "Stronger doses are invariably fatal."

"Somebody's concocted something." Hat pulled his keyboard and terminal over. "And more likely than not, that somebody is Trevon the Black. He seems to have the pipeline into Charolon and it's probable he's supplying Qativar and Vihtirne as well." He brought up files they'd been gathering and named the most common cross-reference.

"Not a Housed name that I recognize," Palaton told him.

"Or I," chimed in Rufeen. The blush was fading slowly from her craggy features.

Hat did not take his eyes from the flat screen monitor. Tonelessly, he said as if it were something they'd discussed and turned down many times already, "We're going to have to network. Malahki or someone else."

"No," answered Palaton firmly.

"Malahki has the resources."

"He doesn't know where we are, and I want to keep it that way. If he gets his hooks into me, he'll set me up to directly oppose Panshinea. I won't do it." Palaton had always known Malahki had his own agenda and now that there was bad blood between them, Palaton would be another expendable pawn in his plans. The famed rebel leader of the common forces would never forgive him for taking Rand away. As far as Malahki knew, Palaton had the humankind secreted somewhere, out of Choyan sight and politics.

Palaton swallowed down a throat that suddenly felt lined with thistle. But no matter how driven, how desperate he was, he would not turn to Malahki, to be used in a plot to further plunge Cho into turmoil.

"That's your final word?" asked Hat.

"I've learned better than to say never. For now, while he has the advantage, that's my final word."

"What about Chirek?" Rufeen ventured.

"Too close to Malahki. And Chirek's religion is even more explosive than Malahki's politics. No," and Palaton paused to rub his eyes thoughtfully. "No, I'm afraid we're in this alone."

"We can't stay alone long," Hat responded. "I'm running out of resources, and we're running out of places to hide."

"On-world, yes. But off . . ." Rufeen let her voices trail off as she felt the other two look at her. She shrugged.

"That way we'd lose everything," Palaton told her.

"Our cause isn't much good if we're found by Panshinea." The pilot narrowed her eyes and looked into her mug. "Retreat can be a good tactical maneuver."

"I won't do it. You two can leave, but I'm staying."

"What if," Hat said softly, "what you're looking for can't be found here?"

Palaton pushed his chair away from the table. "When I've looked everywhere, when I've exhausted everything, then I'll go. Not before." He stood. "Why don't you two get some sleep? I'll take first watch." His *bahdur* flared into use, its aura about him like a faint, bluish flame, so powerful it was to those near him who were sensitive to the power. Hat had to turn his face away, as Rufeen squinted against the brilliance. Its presence flickered behind him even as he left the room.

Rufeen kicked back in her chair as the door closed. She looked at Hat. "He won't leave," she said.

"I know." He shut down his computer and locked it away. "But I thought we'd all decided we're in for the duration, however long it is."

"Oh, I'm in," Rufeen told the flightmaster. "But all I can do is navigate space. These political waters are much too murky for me, and I would like to see some allies. I don't know how much the three of us can achieve, even if we have shadows."

Hat answered, "Don't think he doesn't know that. But he won't give up easily, and he won't retreat until that or death is the only option."

"Sometimes death doesn't give you that much notice." Rufeen moodily poured herself another cup of *bren* and frowned into its depths.

Chapter 21

Maeva keyed in her entrance code and stood, weight shifted to the ball of one foot, the only sign of the nervousness she felt, waiting for the security door to open. She told herself there was no reason Ambassador Thomas would have her locked out, but there was no particular reason she should still have a valid access code, either. If he were with her, there'd be no problem. But if he were with her, there would *be* a problem, because she couldn't be doing what she intended to do now.

She told herself, while the electronic interface on the door blinked at her, that she was doing what she had to do for her client. Seeing Rand again was necessary. He had refused to be deposed, but she could bring him in as a hostile witness. Her dealings should be over and done with. But she was convinced that whatever he had to say would be so much more valuable if it were open, unforced, genuine. Both Rand and her client would benefit from that course, if she could only persuade him to cooperate.

Are you for the prosecution or the defense, counselor?

Maeva felt her eyes begin to water slightly as the retinal scan slid past. Good question, she answered herself. No answer. Not yet. That's why I want in. In! And she slapped her palm upon the grid as it lit up in soft inquiry.

Who, besides himself, could Rand be trying to protect by being uncooperative? If his actions, as he'd claimed, had been unintentional and undirected, then who would he harm? Could he be trying to protect the very Choyan he had been working against?

He was like a very complicated knot which could only be worked on a hitch at a time, she thought, and bit her lip slightly as the door gave her an affirmative entry and let her in.

Next time, she would have to erase the log entry. She could afford no more attention. *Next time!* she chided herself, as she pushed past the threshold and entered the myriad corridors of the underground facility. Just in, and already she was planning to come back again.

Strand by strand, both she and Rand were coming undone.

Maeva paused just inside the gates. She could turn back now, it was not too late; whatever might happen would not happen if she turned around right now and asked for egress.

She felt her spine stiffen even before her mind rejected that option. She had never turned back from a challenge in her life, and it was challenge she'd read in those turquoise eyes. Challenge and honesty and desperation. He did not believe that there would be any justice here on Sorrow. She feared that, if Ambassador Thomas got his way, Rand could be right.

Could she live with that?

No. Not without knowing as much of the truth as she could obtain. She would never know all of it. Truth was not black or white, it was gray and subjective and it faded with time, despite what she occasionally told jurors. But now, from one of the major participants, she could grasp a vivid enough accounting to make a judgment. And perhaps she could help him as well.

Counselor for the defense. Maeva felt her lips thin in an ironic smile. She'd made her choice without even knowing it. Having made that choice, she knew she would have to inform the ambassador as soon as she could. He might even deny her access altogether. What was she doing here? Trying to jettison a career which had brought her across *space,* for God's sake, a career whose student loans she was still paying off—and, if she stood frozen in hesitation in the corridor much longer, security-authorized access or not, she would bring the system alert on-line.

She put one foot in the front of the other, picking out the corridor which would take her to the elevators, to the lowest and most secure levels of the facility, walking as though she knew the cameras were taping her. She felt as though she had jumped a chasm. Her heart sped up a little. She could feel her pulse throbbing slightly at the base of her throat.

What was the worst which could possibly happen? Thomas firing her? She could go to the Compact and demand satisfaction on her contract or apply for a grant to work directly for the Halls. Something would be negotiated. One-way tickets home were expensive to come by, given the scarcity of pilots for the runs.

Plus there was pressure she could bring to bear. The ambassador would not do much overtly, she knew, rather than risk the revelation that he had Rand secreted away. That either made her very safe, or very much at risk. There were steps to avoid that, as well, and as soon as she left the interview, she would begin to take them.

For the defense.

Vihtirne slowed her pacing along the marbled flooring to throw yet another epitaph at her companion, then pivoted and began another circuit. Qativar leaned indolently against a column in the spacious room, watching the blues of her dress washing up and down her body, rather like watching rain blend into a stormy ocean.

He did not muster an answer until she halted again. Then he said quietly, "If I had not given over the alien to his consulate, we could bait Palaton and draw him out. Panshinea has his price. We can meet it."

Vihtirne of Sky slowly faced him. Qativar pushed away from the column, standing straight. He was at least as well dressed as she, in black and silver, forgoing the somber style of his true office of priest. "You might as well have dropped the manling in a black hole. There's been no word of him from Sorrow. The humankind has disappeared. I've not been able to find out what plans Thomas has for him."

Qativar waved a hand. "It doesn't matter. We can't afford to press Thomas. We can't afford an interruption in our supply yet, we don't have it synthesized successfully. But," and he met her icy glance, a smile growing, "we have Charolon in the palm of our hand. Panshinea is sure to follow. Palaton will operate as though we do still have our hostage."

Vihtirne smoothed a hand across her neckline. "Don't play at bluffing him. He's too powerful for that."

"Ummmm." Qativar rolled his voices deep in his throat. "I may not have to. There might be other bait to draw Palaton out. I shall have to do some research, my dear Choya'i." He leaned close to her. "Will you miss me?"

Her glance flickered but a second, downcast in false modesty which, somehow, suited her anyway. "You will take care, won't you, Qativar?"

"Oh, I'll be very careful. We have a House to build, you and I." Qativar trailed a fingertip across the very hollow she had just touched, brushing the caress across territory which he knew she could have him killed for trespassing.

A light kindled in her eyes, one which he had hoped for. Qativar's smile grew wider. "It's unfortunate plans won't allow me to stay." He straightened. "I'll contact you in a few days." He moved past her briskly, and was out of the room before she could protest.

But she wouldn't. She had the pride of her House, as well as her sex, and her ambition. Qativar wouldn't have worked with her as a partner if she did not. He needed a Choya'i with a heart and mind as chill as his own, who would not crumble under the pressure Panshinea was sure to bring as he saw his empire torn apart. If she were the type who would run faintheartedly after him, he would not stop, and would never return.

He had not put most of his adult years into subterfuge to be turned aside by an elegant face. If truth be told, she was a little too mature for him, but her strengths were too great not to let her play the role she'd fought for. The financial and intelligence resources of her Householding alone made her invaluable to many of his plans.

Plans could be changed if she became inconvenient or weakened. However, he could not discount that she was correct. He'd erred in giving the humankind over to John Taylor Thomas so quickly. He'd thought to force an open trial, revealing the peccadilloes of the Abdreliks, the Ronins, and those Choyan who were supporting a coverup of the incidents on Arizar as well as on Cho. He'd thought it would have been even more to Thomas' advantage than to his own; he had been mistaken. He had not gotten where he was by making mistakes. Not killing Rindalan during the commons riots in the capital was one. Handing the alien over was obviously another. He would not succeed in supplanting Panshinea if he continued to err.

He had a stake in Thomas and the ambassador's actions. Heretofore, he had not interfered with the other. But now, perhaps, a nudge in the right direction might force the ambassador into motion. He passed Asten in the corridors. His blue-black hair combed back, revealing the strongly masculine cut of his horn crown, Asten's eyes barely met Qativar's. The tall, handsome Choya scarcely acknowledged his presence as he strode to Vihtirne's chambers.

The corner of Qativar's mouth pulled tight. Hardly gone long enough for his aura to have left her rooms and she had summoned her lover to join her. It is well, he thought, that we have no illusions about our real importance to one another.

"You don't need to be here," Rand said flatly as she pulled up a chair outside the barrier. "Whatever you have to do, you don't need me to do it."

Maeva tucked her ankles in, staring at the young man Thomas intended to bury from sight forever. Was Thomas so bent on vengeance that he dared not trust justice in a trial? Did he think he could circumvent habeas corpus here on Sorrow? Looking at Rand, she could not see the menace to the Compact and national security that the ambassador had described. She did not see the manipulator and fabricator who had cold-bloodedly murdered Thomas' daughter.

She did not know who she saw.

Maeva leaned forward. "Tell me how Alexa died."

Rand flinched slightly. His hair waved forward as he did, threatening to drop into his eyes, hiding them from her scrutiny, but almost in the same movement, he brushed his forehead impatiently. Emotion, she thought. Real, not manufactured. *Give me more.*

"Are you recording?"

"I'm not. I cannot guarantee security isn't. In fact, it probably is." She slipped a small handheld white noise generator from her pocket, put it on her knee, and switched it on. "This should help."

"What is that?" A fleeting expression of both pain and surprise crossed his face so quickly she wasn't sure she'd seen it.

"It's making white noise."

"Ah." He rubbed his jawline, just in front of his right ear once, then shifted in his chair. "Why should I talk to you?"

"Because I'm here, now, and I'm listening."

"The Choyan have no ears," Rand told her. "But they heard everything I said, and more."

"More?"

"What I meant. Barring cultural differences. They're older . . . different."

"Alien."

"Not as alien as many of the races." Rand leaned forward on his elbows. "I still have no reason to answer you."

"How about your life? Gaining your freedom isn't important?"

His lips thinned slightly. "You work with Thomas. He isn't about to let me go. I know it, you should, too, if he hasn't already told you. If he weren't who he was, he would probably already have killed me with his bare hands."

"And what if I told you that, regardless of his plans for you, I think the law should come first."

Something in the depths of his eyes adjusted. Rand smiled slightly as he said, "Sounds like you have a conflict of interest, counselor."

Maeva could feel the heat rising in her cheeks. She turned away slightly, not wanting him to see her face. Her glance fell on his hands . . . hands which had healed remarkably over the last several weeks, even when he had been in reduction. The barest tracing of the burn scarring remained.

"What are you looking at?"

"Your hands. How did you do that?"

The young man followed her line of vision and held his hands and wrists up. "Oh. I'm . . . not sure."

Even with medical care, he couldn't possibly have healed like that. Maeva looked at his pale skin. He wouldn't even have a permanent marking. She remembered seeing the process begin and thinking of the outcome, but even then, she hadn't really thought it possible. She made a note. She looked up. "Did they teach you to do that?"

"No." He folded his hands across his arms and leaned on them again. "I wouldn't even know how to do something like this and neither would they."

"The Ivrians—"

"Are not Choyan," he interrupted.

Maeva sat back in a flash of her own irritation. Why should the mention of healing augmentation by thought control close him off like that? She opened her mouth to argue with him, then closed it without saying a word. Perhaps what offended him was that he'd been imprisoned and injured in the first place, as well as abandoned.

"I can't do this, if you don't want me to," she said, softly, finally.

"Do what?"

"Help you."

"And why would you want to help me?"

"Because I don't understand what's happening, and I'm a terribly curious person."

"Maeva," he said gently. "You won't get far in the Compact being overly curious."

The advice sounded as though it came from a terribly old, terribly weary personage. Maeva straightened her spine, felt her muscles move in a kind of knotted tension, and eyed the barriers which separated them. She took the sound generator and pitched it neatly through the bars. It thunked onto the table in front of him as she got up.

"What is this for?"

"That," she answered over her shoulder, preparing to leave, "is in case you want to talk to anyone else. Ever. You might need it, if you can find someone else interested in your story. It's got a twenty year warranty."

"Not that it'll do me much good if it breaks," he said.

"No. So I'd take good care of it if I were you. It's innocuous enough they'll probably let you keep it."

He got to his feet, still holding the generator. "I'll keep it for the next time then."

Maeva was in the hallway. She paused. "There won't be a next time, Rand. You've misjudged me. I am interested, and I would like to help you, but neither of us have the time to win each other's trust. Either you do, or you don't, and you've chosen not to. So I won't be back. I can't take the risk if it's not going to do any good, because every second here is stolen, every word precious, and you don't want to participate."

He took a step around his small table, terribly close to the barriers of his cell. The warning colors came on, notifying him of the placements and danger, but he ignored them. He was already all too familiar with the deterrents, she thought.

"If you want to help me, get word to Ambassador Rindalan."

"I won't do that without your talking to me first." She swung about. She could feel that tiny tic in her throat which started up when she was intensely involved. It throbbed with every heartbeat. She waited while he stared at her, as if committing every line of her body to memory. She'd been given licentious looks before, but there was nothing sexual in this. It was as though he could see *through* her, or into her.

He backed away from the barrier and sat down, placing the generator in front of him. "All right," he conceded. "How Alexa Thomas died." Then he waited for her to return to her chair.

Maeva was so stunned she could not move for a second, then, flustered, she moved too quickly and the chair clattered loudly as she took it. Rand seemed not to notice, though, as if gathering himself. He licked his lips and cleared his throat.

"I killed her," he said, "but it wasn't murder. There was . . . it's very complicated." He rubbed his hands together. "There was a *tezar* . . ."

"Did this have anything to do with the destruction of the Choyan flight school known as Blue Ridge and the founding of the House of Tezars?"

"House?" Rand looked at her, almost numbly, as if watching two realities at once. "Is that what they did? Try to raise a House of pilots?"

"Tried and accomplished, as far as we can tell. The Compact had been doing most of its contracting with them, although that's been temporarily halted."

Rand nodded as if he understood. "We were trying to save Blue Ridge. There was a dogfight—"

"Dogfight? You mean, with airplanes? Like the videos?"

"Something like that." Rand looked at her clearly then, a light in his eyes. "You can't imagine how they fly. They're absolute masters at what they do."

"And two of the best met?"

"Yes. Nedar attacked. Our plane was crippled, but Palaton managed to pull it out of a spin and retaliate. They took a direct hit. We didn't know he had Alexa on board . . . we didn't know that Alexa was even involved. I thought I was the only human on Cho. . . ." he stopped again, dry-voiced, and she caught a sense of the terrible isolation he must have felt.

"I'm still listening," she coaxed softly.

"Yes." He swallowed. "We went down, too, but their craft was all but annihilated when it hit. I was thrown clear. Palaton bailed out of the cockpit and ran to see if he could bring anybody out alive. Nedar was critically injured. I don't even know how he could have lived, but he did. His remains spilled out of the wreckage. He asked Palaton to finish him off. He did not want to live a cripple. Palaton did what he wished. But she was in the plane, too. She survived. She saw what Palaton had done. She came out of this hole in the twisted metal, her hair burning with sparks and smoking, and she didn't even know it, didn't even care, all she wanted to do was kill Palaton. He didn't . . . he couldn't defend himself against her. I had a . . ." Rand looked at his right hand as if he could see it still. "I had a piece of metal in my hand. Sharp, like a knife. I screamed at her to stop, and threw it. She took it in the shoulder. It stopped her. She staggered back with the pain, back into the fuselage—there was an explosion almost immediately, and there was nothing left of either of them but ash."

"Self-defense," said Maeva. "And the wound did not kill her, the explosion did."

"Yes. But I don't think it would matter to Ambassador Thomas."

"No." Maeva stood up again. "But it matters to me." She found her eyes very moist and resisted the impulse to dab at them. "I'll contact Ambassador Rindalan as soon as I can. I don't know what good it will do."

"Neither do I." Rand's voice remained quiet, halting, as if the effort to speak had taken a great deal out of him. He held the sound generator and stroked its plastic body. Then looked up. "You'll be back?"

"Yes."

Rand closed his eyes. "Good," he said.

Chapter 22

He slept more than he was used to. Rand knew that he was being kept in reduction, a lighter form of cryonics, because it was the only thing which could account for the gaps in time. It was part of the imprisonment to be without the anchor of time and place. He accepted it, for the moment. He accepted as much as he could, knowing that there would be a time when he would be unable to accept. Unable to bear what they had done to him. The solitude, the timelessness, these were things he could deal with. He did not know if he would see the edge of his sanity growing thin. He did not know if he would be aware when it crumbled away altogether.

When he dreamed, he dreamed mostly of Cho. It was a verdant world, kept that way by hard work and a delicate balancing act. The Choyan built mainly of metal, stone, and rock, those things which either endured or could be recycled over and over again. The cities were peppered with technology which was meant to be triggered by psionic powers, and which few now could activate. Beyond that, power used tended to be as clean as possible, and regenerative.

Most civilizations would have chosen to colonize other planets, lifting the strain from their native world while expanding elsewhere. The Choyan were adamantly against that. He did not understand it when Palaton first brought him, but he'd grown into it, just as he had come to understand the various esper systems which functioned only sporadically. Expansion of a race beyond its native boundaries invariably brought in genetic mutation, adaptation to new surroundings. No world could ever be found which would exactly duplicate the home world, so this change was taken for granted.

But not by the Choyan, into whose very genetic fiber was woven their power, their legacy, the ability which gave them the stars. They had no tolerance for any variation in their abilities. Perhaps that was why they had destroyed one of their own Houses. They feared that by leaving their home world they would lose all that they had been, so afraid that they dared not embrace all that they could become.

A few had splintered off, unknown to the rest, perhaps remnants of the lost House, perhaps visionaries, perhaps renegades. Rand doubted they numbered more than thirty or forty, given the air strike on Arizar which destroyed their experimental work. Somewhere in time, a Choya had discovered that, when paired with a human, his powers of *bahdur* could be cleansed. Instead of burning out, they could be renewed. It wasn't a permanent solution, like an oil filter for machinery, it would have to be used periodically, but the results—ah, the results.

The results had been enlightening. Rand dreamed of being filled with Palaton's power once more, so strange and yet so wonderful. The Zarite college had not been entirely successful. They had stolen humankind to perfect the transferal method, but even then, had not wanted the subjects to know or understand what was happening. Humans filled with *bahdur* often could not hold or contain it. They were chemically blinded in order to physically restrain their abilities, to make them dependent upon their Choyan companion, the same companion who had given them their powers and who would take them back.

More often than not, it was ultimately fatal for the human subject. He and dear, dead, strange Bevan and Alexa—of them all, only he had escaped unscathed, if this imprisonment could be called untouched. If the sinkhole which seemed to have swallowed his heart and was now working on his guts and his sanity could be called unscathed.

He had been lucky in that the treatments to chemically blind and mute him had not been completed, and the *bahdur* which flowed through him had defeated them. He had been lucky that Palaton was who he was, and had chosen to have Rand alert and aware, a true partner, a *durah*, as the Choya would have explained it. A soulmate.

But in the long run, even Palaton had been blinded by his fear, afraid of the possibility of living permanently with his power burning inside Rand, afraid of the use to which Rand had evolved it. They had parted, quarreling. He wondered if he would ever see Palaton again, could ever convince his *durah* that the soulfire they had shared should be used to transform any who desired it, even if it changed Palaton's world forever.

As he mused within his dreamtime, he saw Dorea, the reluctant Prophet, her blindfolded face turning toward him as if she sought the warmth of his memory. She sat upon the crude rocking chair as she had in Bayalak, her dress new and unstained by the fires and riots she had passed through, her hands working on a kind of knitting in her lap.

He felt as though he stood on the threshold, watching her. The weathered wood of an old seaside shanty framed him. It was daytime, a clear morning, the air still humid from the tropical weather earlier. He could hear the cries of the kites as they hung in the air over the harbor. It still smelled of fire, riot-burned as Charolon had been. *Did the burning follow him wherever he went?*

But there was peace in here, within and without, on the streets. Bayalak had settled down again and perhaps it had been due to her influence.

She must have been pretty once, before the Change. He was no judge of Choyan beauty, they were all an elegant, graceful race to him, even the square and stocky Earthan branches, but he thought she had been before the eyes had been torn weeping blood from her face, and the power she embraced had worn her thin. Her cheekbone structure dominated her visible expression. She turned her face, thick hair stirring as if blown by a sea breeze off Bayalak Harbor. Dorea reached up slowly, hand moving as if by some cause other than her own willpower. The fingers plucked at the blindfold, digging into the edge of the cloth.

And then ripping it down. "I see you," she said. The shadowed depths of her scars looked blankly at him.

He recoiled in shock and surprise and it was as if a vacuum had inhaled him. Wind rushed past his ears. He fell backward, fell and fell and fell.

What if she had seen him? *What if she had?*

Had she summoned him, or had he called for her? And if she had seen him, could she tell others? Was he truly alone and abandoned, or could he—somehow—make contact?

Recoiling ever faster, he found himself in chill darkness, hurtling through time and space at such a rate that the stars and suns became narrow pinpricks and then, suddenly, he found himself beyond the speed of light itself, and Chaos yawned around him.

The sensation of speed disappeared. So did the feeling of being torn backward. He floated about, ungainly and awkward, swimming through the swirl of color and darkness.

Palaton had told him there were patterns in the Chaos, patterns which his psionic powers could discern and use as landmarks. But those patterns were never the same, and migrated as constantly as space evolved, and every *tezar* viewed Chaos from his own reference point.

There *were* no Patterns of Chaos. That was the whole concept of the random activity of objects pushed beyond the speed of light. The Choyan only perceived that there were, foreseeing events and arrivals before they occurred, and arranging them to happen as seen. Rand swirled from one whirlpool to another, tossed back and forth, swallowed down and spit up, a miasma without center, beginning, or end. As he grasped for some sense of what was happening to him, he righted himself and found an edge of awareness that he was not alone.

Rand managed a turn and saw a cruiser, its slim lines blurred by the arc of reality where real-time met Chaos. The vessel lost its integrity; it was as though he stared inward through transparent walls, and saw the proud Choya standing at its helm.

He knew, albeit briefly, what it was to helm a starship. Knowing what he knew about *bahdur,* he also realized he would likely never pilot again. The power to navigate Chaos could not be grafted onto ship or man. It was not a computer-driven black box that plotted and shifted rudders, accelerated or decelerated engines.

It was flesh and blood. Heir to all the errors and promises thereof.

The Choya he watched had been born in the House of Sky. His dark hair was roped back off his shoulders, and the epaulets of his flight suit delineated his campaigns, contracts, and awards. His silvery-light eyes scoured the Chaos before him, never seeing Rand, never sensing him, though they stared nearly face-to-face. He wore only minimal onyx facial jewelry under his cheekbones and he might have been of an age with Palaton, young, but old enough to be experienced, to be in his prime. Worry furrowed his brow unnaturally, shadows of fatigue clouded his expression.

And there was fear in his eyes.

He can't see me, thought Rand, *and he can't see the Patterns of Chaos. He is lost, lost and without hope.* Rand was just outside the skin of the ship now, balancing beyond the transparent skin of the con, and he reached out, his hand going through the skin, stretching the membrane, as if he were pushing outward from an egg without breaking the molecular surface. Fingers wiggling, he stretched closer, closer, closer.

"This is my third run on boost," the *tezar* said. Rand jumped, startled, realized that he was not being spoken to, that the pilot was recording. "I'm experiencing a complete and total breakdown and failure of pattern recognition. I cannot *see* where I am going. I'm jettisoning the cargo, in hopes that an eddy might carry it back to the mainstream and it will someday be salvaged. If anyone finds this recorder, I am Jilaro of the Householding of Abran, of the House of Sky, of the House of Tezars."

He paused, licking dry lips. His hands roamed the control board and the vessel shuddered. Rand could feel it as the cargo hold broke loose, jettisoned away as Jilaro had said he would do.

He watched as the square compartment, gutted from the center of the cruiser, floated clear. It dropped quickly into the nebulous swirls of Chaos. He looked back to the Choya who broke open a packet of crushed powder and tipped it into a cylinder of water. It turned the water a brilliant color before Jilaro gulped it down.

The Choya shuddered as if he had swallowed a bitter potion. He spoke to the recorder again. "Forgive me, my House, for my failure. The boost is potent, my desire for it unslackable. But it no longer fills the emptiness within me."

Rand tried once again to touch the pilot, but although the membrane stretched so thinly as to be nonexistent, he could not break through.

The cruiser shuddered.

Jilaro looked ahead and pain etched his face. "The Web. It

expands for me, like a flower blooming in Chaos. I am lost."
He set his jaw grimly and piloted to his fate.

Rand bumped off the hull of the cruiser, pushed aside by
forces he could feel but not see or control, as the ship swept
past him. He'd heard of the Web. All *tezars* dreaded it. It was
either a hole in Chaos that swallowed matter, like a black
hole, or death itself. It had come for Jilaro.

The ship veered away from him, speeding farther and farther away, distorting—and then it was gone.

He fell.

The fall accelerated, faster, faster, until he was snapping
back into himself, heart pounding, as if he'd been pushed off
a cliff and knew that death awaited him as he hit—

and he sank into himself, found everything cold, colder
than ice, still and frozen. But he, himself, was not frozen, his
heart still thundering hotly, his pulse ringing like a hammer
on an anvil, his breath smoking from his mouth.

Without substance, he was yet trapped, spirit bound into the
flesh by a connection he had never understood, but as his
spirit heart slowed, he could yet hear, see, touch. Shapes, all
around him. Not the boundaries of himself, which contained
his journeying soul after its return, but other shapes. Jagged.
Rounded. Familiar. Strange.

He knew he should be alone. He sensed that his soul had
taken him, all of him, someplace where he should not be.
Someplace deadly.

Someplace still. Lifeless.

Among the dead.

He lay among the crystalline bodies of Sorrow. He could
sense them all around him, harder than his cold flesh, far
more dead than alive. His cell was not near them, but his current state had brought him among them. Rand took a slight,
shuddering gasp. He fought for calmness. He was trapped in
the quartz, his own molecules slipped in among the others and
soon he would cease to exist, and although he did not actually
breathe, it was the most conscious part of the process of his
life, next to his tripping heart, that he did breathe. He had to.

He felt himself sliding away, gliding among the dead. He
recoiled from the touch, yet it was not unpleasant. They
bumped back as if they pushed him, no, guided him, among
them, out of the quartz into the more familiar stone and sand

of Sorrow, and then into the air, and then into the cell which held him.

At the realization that he had joined his body proper, his heart began to slowly descend into the rhythms of reduced metabolic function, not cold sleep, but the next thing to it. Alone, losing all sense of himself, he thought vaguely that, frightening as it had been, the dead of Sorrow offered more comfort than his cell.

In the subterranean holding cells, the computer noted a variance in the reading of the limbic activity of the subject in reduction. It made a note and medicated to counter the unusual activity, and produced a printout to confirm its action. After long moments, the subject's readings fell back into normal columns again. The crèche computer noted that also, humming slightly as it performed its watchful calculations.

Chapter 23

"I want to try dosing the Eastern continent," Qativar said. His voices reflected his mood, indolent, casual, truculent. "That damned Palaton keeps showing up everywhere and going back underground. With any luck, we'll catch him long enough to put him out of commission. That should dampen his blue flame!"

"His actions are aimed at Pan. They shouldn't worry you much."

"They don't. But he is like a splinter in my hand." Qativar looked at his hand, at the long, elegant fingers, and flexed it, then made a fist as if crushing the object of their conversation. "*Ruhl* would knock the wind out of his sails, don't you think?"

"I think he's done half our job, harrying the emperor." Pages rustled as Vihtirne worked.

"And I could finish the other half if we dosed the outlying areas. The Eastern continent, Bayalak, the outer portions of the South."

Vihtirne paused in her study of the pilots' roster. "I think we've done enough."

"Don't forget we've created the impression of a ripple effect from Panshinea. That cloaks everything we've done, but suspicion will be roused if the pattern breaks. We'll lose that if we don't pursue it." He had been leaning on the doorjamb, watching her, but she refused to meet his glare.

"We're causing panic in the streets. We haven't enough boost for the market we've created . . . there is a point at which we're doing ourselves more damage than we are good. And what about your production of *ruhl?* We may need it for a concentrated attack later."

Qativar waved off her objection. "Don't worry about me. I

have what it takes to do what we want." Not all at the correct concentration, but she needn't know that. He had been laying his plans for years before the sudden advent of boost and his alliance with her. "We need to make a point."

She laid aside the printout, and lifted her eyes to his. "I think we've done that. The demand for boost is growing by leaps and bounds. Ambassador Thomas is protesting the production shipments he's making to us. Sooner or later, the traffic at Galern is going to raise eyebrows among the Ronins and Abdreliks. We don't have a Compact-sanctioned trade agreement with Earth. My mining operation won't be able to withstand much scrutiny. And . . . there is always the possibility that Thomas could change his mind."

"We'll have it synthesized by then."

"There are one or two elements giving my biochemists a considerable amount of trouble," she pointed out. "Until that time when we can stabilize supply, I think we should be more conservative. The demand within our own House is greater than we had planned for, and while we're on this discussion, there is something which has been troubling me . . ." Vihtirne paused as Qativar responded with an immense grin.

"I amuse you?"

"No. No," and he shook his head at her icy expression as he crossed the room. "Our House. The thought delights me. Does it not you?"

"Not if there are problems within our walls. They're too newly erected to take much strain."

He perched on an antique chair, not noticing the strength of her disapproval as it creaked under his weight. "You see trouble in everything. That's why we complement one another. I am the risk taker, you are the worrier. What bothers you?"

Vihtirne pushed her chair a little away from her desk. She crossed her legs with a rustle of the long, silken panels of her dress. "Too much boost. Our pilots are using a greater quantity and more frequently than we estimated."

His lip curled. "Pilots are spoiled. They expect to always operate at optimum ability."

"They're addicted, Qativar. The drug addicts quickly and thoroughly."

"All the better. We need to keep them bound to us—"

"I'm serious."

"So am I." He flashed another smile. "Vihtirne, they can't be so dependent. It's only been weeks."

"I have pilots here refusing to fly without an increase in their rations. Pilots who can't fly without boost. And we lost a *tezar* last week at a bay station, overdosed. The autopsy came back clean, so I suppose I can thank the incompetence of the Compact doctors for not detecting it, but I read the report from the others who were on layover. She'd been taking boost heavily without detoxing first by taking the *ruhl*. It's not the first death, it won't be the last. What if something happens on contract? We've got an alien substance here which bonds itself to our neural systems and we're pushing it as though it were honey candy."

"It built us a House. It's given us the finances to withstand almost anything Panshinea can hope to throw at us—"

"Unless he decides to outlaw the drug."

"He won't."

"Won't? Or can't?"

Qativar shoved himself away from his chair. "He won't touch us! Even the Abdreliks are picking up contracts the Compact isn't monitoring. As for the Compact, there is enough pressure now to bring a general vote, and you and I both know the ban against our pilots will be lifted. They can't afford not to."

Vihtirne repeated flatly, "If Panshinea is forced to take a stand against boost—"

"He won't. He'll fall first."

"I have *tezars* missing."

He shrugged. "It happens. Even with boost. The hazards of Chaos are eternal. The Commons still hesitates to join the House and we're working with some pilots who are substandard. Bring the Commons in, gather up the remnants from Blue Ridge. You do your work, mistress from the House of Sky. Let me do mine." He stalked to the doorway of the room and paused at the threshold with controlled fury.

Vihtirne's gaze fell away from his face. She resumed her interest in the paperwork before her. "Just so you understand," she said, "that I have concerns."

"Understand then, that I will take care of them," he answered tightly, before leaving.

* * * *

Maeva decided to apply for body armor, and found, to her surprise, that the Compact permits to obtain it were relatively simple. They did not even require her office's signature or proof of need. Her word was enough. Armor was, after all, she reflected, strictly defensive. What they did require, and this surprised her more, was that she make an appointment to be outfitted in person rather than send her holographic measures over and take delivery later. She scowled as the message came up on her terminal screen and said to herself, "So that's the catch. They don't say 'no,' they'll just intimidate the hell out of you when you show up." She keyed in her positive response, plugged in her signatory thread, and signed off as soon as an appointment time was assigned.

Maeva checked her watch. She had time to kill, with no place to go. She could try, for the fourth time in three days, to get an appointment with Ambassador Rindalan. Earth's status as a Class Zed planet did not give her any rank at all, and the Choyan at the embassy had been very uncooperative. At the moment, she did not understand what Rand found so enchanting about the race. They were stuffy, overly formal, and without compassion.

And she was not about to give up without a fight. Maeva signed out of the office complex and left the building.

The weather in the complex was brisk. The air, a little thinner than she'd grown up in, giving it the feel of high mountains, was clean from a recent pounding rain. The demisphere of peaks which crowned the complex grounds wore an icing of white, which would not stay, as winter was not yet here in full. Grass edging the walkways crunched under her steps, the stalks growing brittle with the approach of frost.

No matter what the season, there would always be the frozen crystalline lakes and streams of the main continent. Suicide or genocide, it scarcely mattered—an alien race inhabited the waterways of ruined cities, encased, inert, a warning against the ultimate enemy, whoever it might be. Maeva did not often have the courage to look in the canals or the lake which ran under half the Compact grounds. She could not bear the distorted, ethereal, haunting looks of a vaguely humanoid people caught in the deadly crystal embrace.

Like her own people, caught in Pompeian smoke and ash, these people had not died in private. But unlike the excavations of volcanic disaster, there was no knowing what had happened here. How had the crystal been created? Who had done it to them, and what had they done to deserve it? There were no overt scars of war on the planet's face, yet genocide on such a scale could hardly be the result of anything less.

Sorrow had been found that way, and taken by both the Choyan and the Abdreliks, space-faring and quarreling civilizations that the planet could be taken as nothing less than a warning against the ultimate fate. The ending which faced them all. The power of an unknown enemy which could strike at any of them unless they found a way to cooperate among themselves, and so the Compact had been formed.

The quartz had been analyzed. It could be broken down, if they wished, but that would destroy its occupants, and there was an unspoken agreement among all the races who joined the Compact and walked its Halls that the dead would lie unsullied. Scientific knowledge would be put aside for respect and monument. Without knowing for sure, it would be assumed that these who had died should not have done so in vain, that those who lived after would work never to see its like happen again.

She did not view the canals now, catching only a blurred glimpse of them in her peripheral vision, the ghostlike figures of the aliens caught in their depths unrecognizable, not even visible, perhaps, except in her imagination. Maeva found the afternoon teeming with other Compact members striding to the more major consulates, as well as the massive complex of Halls and wings which made up the main buildings. Many wore body armor, their outlines shimmering as they moved, but vastly more did not. Was she a coward?

No, she did not think so. What she was about to involve herself in could bring risk from the Abdrelik contingent, the Ronins, the Choyan, and perhaps even her own government. She told herself she was giving herself the freedom to act as her conscience dictated.

At the Choyan embassy, she barely got in the door. The

screen lit up, and a personage said, "Pilot requests are made through contract."

"I'm not here for a *tezar.*" Like the French, the Choyan were fussy about their language and she made certain to pronounce the word as authentically as possible.

The on-screen personage frowned slightly. "What do you wish?" The Choya's Trade was faintly accented, and she could not tell if the disapproval was inherent with the accent—or typically arrogant Choyan.

"I need to make an appointment with Ambassador Rindalan."

"I am sorry, but what you would like to do is not possible at this moment." Bored, the secretarial image began to turn away from her.

Maeva slapped a hand on the screen, setting off a buzz of static. "I did not say *like to,* I said, *need to.*" She could not get much stronger in the public lobby without attracting attention she did not want. "It is vital," she insisted, leaning forward, looking into the image now frowning heavily at her. "I have already been refused several times."

"And you will not take 'no' for an answer," the Choyan observed dryly.

"I cannot," she corrected him.

There was a very long pause. She did not know if the screen had been freeze-framed, with the image in place while the real-life secretary withdrew and made inquiries, but after a long moment, the screen thawed, and the Choya said, "I will take your request under advisement."

Maeva let out her breath. Not permission, but no longer a flat-out denial. "You know where to reach me," she answered and keyed in her comline. "Thank you."

Outside, it was later than she had expected and she wondered if a privacy shield had been thrown up about her while she stood motionless in the lobby. If so, she had not even realized it. Long, long moments had gone by with no recollection other than a vague awareness. If she didn't hurry, she would miss her armor fitting, and she knew that would not bode well if she had to reapply.

Indigo shadows stretched out as she cut across the grounds, eschewing the normal security gates and slidewalks. Foot traffic had thinned considerably as dusk began to settle its cloak over the Halls of the Compact, and globe lights had begun to warm. Maeva trotted briskly to keep warm, as a keening autumn wind began to rise.

Someone just a little behind her also began to hurry. She could hear their footfalls as the L-shaped wing of permits lay ahead, its black obsidian walls in sharp contrast to the surrounding greenery. It cast the deepest, longest shadow yet across her path.

Maeva was within earshot of the building when she was caught by the arm and spun around. A Ronin crouched in her path. Its grin was accented by its rodent-sharp teeth. Its quills lay flat along its sloping head and shoulders, but it rattled them warningly as she prepared to defend herself.

"You will come with me," the Ronin said. "Your appearance is requested."

For a wild moment, she thought perhaps the Choyan ambassador had sent the Ronin after her, to bring her back, but then she realized how stupid that was. There was no love lost between these aliens.

"And if I refuse to accompany you?"

The Ronin gave a shiver of delight. Its quills made another tintinnabulation of noise. "I can tell you that I have never been devenomed," it said. "Any one of my barbs will paralyze, perhaps even kill you, most excruciatingly. More than one will certainly bring death."

Ronins weren't allowed off-planet until they'd been devenomed. Their quills were never supposed to be lethal. Was she to believe that here, on Sorrow, an assassin dared to walk freely?

On the other hand, could she afford not to believe?

Maeva sighed and took an obedient step forward. It was already too late for body armor.

Chapter 24

The Ronin glided forward to put a hand on her sleeve, when the rich, rolling voice of a Choya spoke out of the shadows, startling both of them.

"Your appointment," the Choya said apologetically, and bowed into the faint light of a nearby globe. "I beg your pardon, but the ambassador will see you now." The deep shadows of the architectural garden had all but hidden him until he'd revealed himself. Unlike the Ronin, his eyes were large, expressive, inquisitive, and quite benign.

The Ronin snatched his hand back, his quill headdress chiming slightly as he did so, his coal black eyes squinted up the height of the Choya, who waited, as if to see what both their reactions might be.

The Choyan voice, she'd been told several times, came from the richness of a double larynx and two voices, one underlying the other. She could not separate them, just as she was tone-deaf and could not produce a decent rendition of a song if she had to, but now she could almost hear the irony layering the politeness.

Maeva turned her flank to the Ronin, though it made nearly every hair on her body stand on end to do so, exposing her blind side to the alien. However, the pivot took her from between the Choya and the Ronin, as well as presenting her face to the embassy secretary. "My apologies," she got out smoothly, despite the sudden dryness of her throat. "I didn't mean to keep His Eminence waiting."

"There is no problem," the secretary said. "He had a cancellation and thought this would be an opportune time, if a bit earlier than we had scheduled."

"We must hurry, then," she told him. She left the Ronin behind, saying, "I'm so sorry to be leaving you this abruptly."

The Ronin made a deep sound at the back of his throat for answer as Maeva swept past the Choya, down the walk, back toward the ambassadorial wings. She did not breathe easier until she had the Choya's graceful and athletic frame between them.

Within the bright glow of the building, she opened her mouth to speak, but the Choya said dryly in warning, "Say nothing. Tell it to the ambassador. I am unimportant in this matter."

"Unimportant? You have no idea what you just saved me from."

The Choya gave a slight bow as he opened the lobby door for her. "Actually, neither do you. It would be wise to remember, in the future, when walking alone or doing business in the outlying sectors, to request an escort. That could save you many anxious moments."

Maeva came to a halt. She tried not to grind her teeth at the other's mocking tone. "Do I have an appointment?"

"Not yet, but you will. The ambassador requested that I follow you, as he was a bit curious about your insistence on seeing him. He will make time for you, I think, once I've reported to him."

"Good." Maeva looked around, saw a basalt bench planter and sat down. "I'll wait."

The secretary bowed and left. No less physically imposing than the pilots she was used to, he was dressed considerably more humbly. He wore somber robes of gray and white, but his hair was that glorious yellow-gold with red highlights, an echo of Emperor Panshinea's color, which she had been told was a prime genetic characteristic of the House he belonged to. If she understood right, the secretary's dress was that of their religious order, for Rindalan was not only the ambassador, he was the High Prelate. She wondered if the Choyan equivalent of the Pope had as dry a sense of humor as his younger priest did.

She found out moments later as his voices boomed across the lobby, stopping traffic dead, as other embassy staff and visitors quickly bowed to the ambassador. Rindalan swept through them, a tall, gaunt alien who dismissed them all with a wave of his hands.

He had the most grand horn crown she'd ever seen on a

Choya, but the mane of hair tumbling through it and cascading down his back was considerably thinned and graying, and had more red to it than blond. He reached for her hand with a sweep of his double-elbowed arm, saying, "Madam Attorney Polonia. I am so pleased you could accommodate me."

The jewel-blue eyes fairly twinkled at her as he pressed, then released, her fingers. Of all the alien races she had met, none had eyes like she did, even the Choyan, though they were the closest. Their eyes were larger, more liquid, with very little whites. Typical of the Choyan, she thought, to be abundantly gifted in every way. She let herself smile. "I take it that perseverance is also a virtue on Cho."

"My dear. Everything about you would be a virtue on Cho. Come up where we can be a bit more private." The ambassador bent a little to offer his arm. "Prelate Timero here told me that meeting you would be an experience."

"I know that meeting him was one for me."

Rindalan let out a laugh, totally unpretentious and free. "I shall have to tell him. He does not appreciate the small errands he runs for me, you know." The intense eyes looked down on her as they entered a lift. "You must call me Rindalan. None of this Eminence nonsense."

"It isn't nonsense, and you know it. You earned every bit of it."

"Ah. I see. No sympathy for me, Timero has already been at you." Randalan let out a sigh.

Despite the levity of his words, she could feel the tension in the arm she still held. She looked up at him, and immediately understood that she had to keep up the pretense. She made herself laugh then. "Your secretary is extremely efficient, Mister Ambassador. I would let him chide you, if I were you. It will probably save time in the long run."

"Ah, efficiency. If Timero has indeed discovered that elusive virtue, he could bottle it and make a fortune here on Sorrow." Rindalan patted the back of her hand as if comforting her.

She could tell that he had measurably altered his stride to accommodate hers, and made an effort to keep up. The lift took them high into the building and then disgorged them on a floor which appeared almost deserted. Young and somber Timero, however, awaited them in front of a doorway.

Rindalan steered her into it, saying, "You know, my dear, I had not meant to put you off so long, but business always comes before pleasure."

The heavily paneled door closed almost on his words.

Maeva found herself ankle-deep in a plush cream-and-blue-patterned carpet. A wall fireplace crackled cheerfully in illusion, putting out homeyness instead of heat. A sedan chair was littered with hard copy, and a coffee table held the remnants of a modest fruit plate. She was in the ambassador's private quarters rather than in one of the embassy conference rooms. She blinked.

"Timero tells me he saved you from what could have been an unpleasant situation." As the door sealed, Rindalan's tone changed from jovial to serious.

Maeva shivered. "I don't think I was a target," she said, thinking about it in retrospect. "But I don't think I wanted to go with him, either. I can't thank you enough for seeing me."

The ambassador waved his hands to the chair opposite the sedan. "We can talk here, in complete confidence, unlike most of the rooms in the building. I have had the apartment secured."

"Good." Maeva let her bones melt. She waited until Rindalan perched opposite her. She could see the imprint of his bony knees through his robes as he sat.

"Now then. What is it you want from me?"

She was not used to blunt talk, especially not from the formal, almost flowery Choyan. It startled the words from her until Rindalan said, almost impatiently, "The appointment I canceled to see you was actually a late dinner. But I do have appointments waiting. . . ."

"I'm sorry." She looked around. She wished desperately for her white noise generator, in spite of the elder's assurances. She licked dry lips. "This could mean my contract," she began.

"Serious." Rindalan sat back on the divan. "You must have grave problems to risk a confidence with someone you've no idea whether you can trust. Who are you, madame attorney?"

"I'm on Ambassador Thomas' legal staff."

"Not with the business contracts wing or lobby?"

"No. Although the staff does lend us out, once in a while. My main work is with treaty and protocol."

"I see," said Rindalan, and she thought almost that he might. "And we do not need to step on any toes here, do we?" He smiled, and like the laugh, it was so fresh, so genuine that it could not help but evoke a smile in return from her. "How can I help?"

"I bring word from someone who—" Maeva plowed to a halt. There seemed to be no proper way to say this, although Rand had warned her that what she would say might be shocking to the aged ambassador. "Your Eminence, there's no easy way to say this, and I can't give you all the information you might want because of my position, but Rand asked me to get word to you. He's being held in security detention at my embassy."

Her words hit the Choya like a physical blow. She could see the translucent complexion go dead pale, and then gray, and the air leave his gaunt frame like a stuffing, as he sagged on the couch.

Then, Rindalan managed, "Alive?"

"Well, yes." There wasn't much point in holding a corpse, but she decided perhaps the Choya knew more about galactic diplomacy than she did.

Rindalan had been resting an elbow on the arm of the divan, and now he put his hand under the curve of his jaw as though the weight of his head had suddenly become too momentous for him to hold without help. "Will Thomas bring him to trial?"

"No. He intends that Rand never see the light of day again, although he will use whatever information he can get from him to consolidate his position between you and the Abdreliks."

Rindalan took a deep breath, muttering, "Would that Pan was here. He likes these games. Even Gathon. But no, they would send me, an honest Choya, here." He looked back at her intently. "Did he ask you to carry other messages?"

"No. He's putting his whole faith and trust in you."

"Is he?" Rindalan sounded faintly pleased, and the color had begun to seep back into his face again. "I shall have to see it hasn't been misplaced. He is too young to be thoroughly disillusioned by circumstances." The Choya rubbed his jaw thoughtfully, massaging the knifelike wrinkles along its jutting length. He looked then, to Maeva. "And what about you? What is your stake in all of this?"

She had thought about it, but had no resolution. She answered faintly, "I don't know. I may lose my contract."

"Have no worry about that. I'll see our embassy picks it up if necessary. That is, if you would not mind working for us."

She looked into the large Choyan eyes, so clear, so pure of color. "No. If it comes to that."

He gave a dry laugh. "We're the last resort, eh?"

She felt her face warming and shook her head quickly. "It's just that—I have other projects—my people—"

He reached over and patted her hand. "After being around Rand, I think I can truthfully say, I understand. Emotion often outweighs logic among you, eh?"

"Well ..." Maeva took a deep breath. "It did this time, anyway." She stood. "I don't know what you can do for him, or even if I can get back in to see him, to let him know that I've reached you—"

"That won't be necessary," Rindalan answered. "He'll know if I have any success at all. What you need to do now is determine what course Thomas intends to follow, and how you'll react to it. Leave the dear boy to me."

She searched his face, saw none of the machinations, the facades, she'd become used to since graduating from school and beginning her practice. Becoming an adult, she thought, had been more of an education than getting her degree. But here was a being who either had transcended that, or had stayed within simple childhood confines of honesty and loyalty. Either way, could she trust him? She decided, emphatically, that she had no choice. "Thank you," she said, and knew the bargain was struck as Rindalan settled back on his divan, nodding vigorously.

"I'll have Timero escort you. You were on your way to a previous engagement." Rindalan crossed his hands as the apartment doors opened almost simultaneously with his words, and the secretarial Prelate entered. She had seen nothing rung or signaled, but Timero took her by the elbow after saying good evening to the ambassador, and steered her out of the apartments.

"You were," the Choya said to her as they entered the downward lift, "en route to the armor shop, I believe."

"Yes, but—"

He continued smoothly, saying, "I took the liberty of informing them you would be delayed. They're awaiting you, at your convenience."

Maeva felt herself blink. "I didn't know," she said slowly, "that the Choyan were so devastatingly efficient."

Prelate Timero did not answer, but he could not hide the wide grin of amusement which bloomed across his face. She reflected that there was a great deal none of them knew about the Choyan, not the least of which was how they navigated across Chaos.

* * * *

Jorana stole into the rain, while Malahki slept, exhausted from implementing the planned move of his headquarters. As new as he was to the awakening of his power, he did not have their rooms warded, nor did he sense in his dreams that she rose from a light nap, packed the few things she owned, and left as silently as the misting drizzle which had begun to gray the late afternoon.

He would be furious when he awoke, and as unable to stop the flight he had put into motion as a piece of driftwood to move against a floodtide. He himself had ordered the evacuation, and now he would be borne away with it. It would be days before Malahki could pull out, return, and search for her.

Even if he did find her, she hoped that she would be able to accomplish what she wished before then.

Jorana shouldered her pack and cloak against the weather and narrowed her eyes at the broken horizon of Charolon. Lights had begun to come on, fitfully, as the mild storm darkened the capital. The Change had not come to the city. Choyan with unawakened power still slept. And as much as she had wanted to be by Malahki's side when the Change was brought to all her people, she knew that the catalyst, the Bringer of Change, had been torn from them and would not be coming back. Malahki knew it, too, having seen it himself. Father Chirek, the underground priest who ministered to a flock of millions, knew it as well.

She did not know whether or not to believe Malahki's assertion that Rand had been that Bringer. She knew only that when Palaton had taken guardianship of the humankind and brought him to Cho, circumstances had begun to evolve at an astronomical rate, and none of them could predict the future. It had all become too momentous.

So, while she was skeptical that Rand's touch could open closed pathways of *bahdur* inside the commons, she knew that he had done something to all of them. She also knew that Palaton had taken Rand from Malahki and Father Chirek, and even Dorea, the blind Prophet, could not see where his pathway led. If Malahki could use her to force Palaton to return Rand, he would do so, for even as he protected her, he would use her.

Jorana stood at the corner, under the eaves, listening to rain patter upon the broken concrete. This part of the city decayed. It had been left to the poor, the broken in spirit, those who had had the *bahdur* burned out of them and now reeked of *boost* in their attempts to restore it, and those who had never had power, and reeked of honest sweat, in hard-laboring jobs the more skilled threw them like scraps to a carrion eater. Here the drain of imperial *bahdur* had not been too devastating, for there were few here who could have been affected. Life itself had been the enemy here, eroding, destroying. She would be scared, but she could not afford to be, not for the life she carried inside of her.

Three million Choyan populated Charolon. She could not hope, even with her abilities, to single out a particular one so quickly. But she did hope, and it was not with her ability alone. Pregnancy affected her talent, making it ebb and flow as the tides did, but the child within her glowed as brightly as a small sun. She could feel it pulsing through her with every tiny beat of its still forming heart. It fed her as much as she nurtured it. She dropped a hand over the swell of her stomach. *I have to find your father,* she thought, and as though it answered her, she could feel a rising glow of warmth.

Supported by its acknowledgment, she pushed away from the corner and into the growing rain. Thoughts trickled through her head, unformed, bare, wispy things which tugged her this way and that, against the direction of the growing tide of Choyan who were heading home from work sites or bars. They shouldered past one another, horn crowns open to the elements, hair growing wet and running into strings down their heads and backs. If they lifted their heads long enough to look into her eyes as they passed, they would pause, and then smile gruffly, unknowingly, as warmed by their touch with her as she was by the child she carried. And they would pause to let her pass unmolested.

Jorana strode into the traffic of the late afternoon unaware of their responses, every sense tuned to that within her and to what she sought. With a precognition she had never had before, she knew that soon she would meet Rufeen on a corner, somewhere in this city. And where there was Rufeen, there could very well be Palaton.

But when? Where?

The drizzle stopped, gray clouds hung low and leaden, threatening, as she crisscrossed the city streets. She left the quarter and passed into another, even worse, burned out by the street riots of last year, the sickening smell of its ashes and fire scars rising as rain puddled among the ruins. It would take a monsoon to wash the smell clear of the carnage left behind. When she left there, however, she entered a crowded section of the capital, where the commons had built and lived and worked, crowded, busy, vibrant, a massive portion of the new city which had grown up around the ancient fortress which Charolon had been in almost prehistoric times.

Here, briefly, the rain had cleaned the streets. Window canopies had been lowered over storefronts, and Choyan shared the shelter as the rain began again, and she was not only stepped aside for, but often found a helping hand to bring her up over the curbs of the streets as she crossed them. As she passed from neighborhood to neighborhood, she met Choyan who were the backbone of Malahki's movement. Not downtrodden, but industrious, not powerful but seeking empowerment. The ordinary, the good-hearted and open-spirited. Yet as she moved among them, she could sense the depression, the furtiveness, the burden of recent upheaval bowing them down. It was as if Panshinea stood on their backs—had, all these years, but now this burden was too much and threatened to break them.

As captain of the guard, she'd had little to do with these citizens. They were neither prey nor predators, except by accident if one of them should stray. They were the foundation of the capital, and she barely knew any of them at all.

Someone caught her as her boot heel skidded on a wet patch, and righted her. She got out a, "Thank you," then froze, looking diagonally across a square of small shops. The Choya'i who'd helped her let go and continued past, leaving her looking at a corner, heavily shadowed by the clouds and rain and time of day, and it was from there she knew she would see Rufeen.

Chapter 25

She rented a small room across from the square, its windows facing down on the corner. The landlady asked her little, even when Jorana told her that she was a composer, though oddly lacking in instruments, recording equipment, or even luggage of any consequence. The Choya'i merely told her in a flat voice, as she coded the palm lock on the apartment that there were several artists' lofts and co-op studios for musicians a block or two away. Jorana had chosen her occupation because she had already done a spiral recon of the area and the fact that the landlady treated her in such an unremarkable way meant that she'd done her research well.

Jorana recoded the lock as soon as the Choya'i left, then went in and lay down on the stiff bed. The room was chill, but she did not feel like getting up and adjusting the warmer. Somewhen, somehow, she would be on that corner she could see from that bed, that window, and when she was, seeing in real-time that which she'd foreseen, she knew that Rufeen would lead her to Palaton.

What she did not know, what she could not summon up from within her, was what would happen then. Would she follow, and if she did . . . ?

The child stirred within her. It was not a kick against confinement, nor the first barely felt quickening of life she had felt a month or so ago, but it was like . . . a stroke, the stroke a swimmer gives when beginning to leisurely cross over an expanse of water. The child was not yet big enough to be cramped and hampered by the limitations of the Choya'i who bore it though formed enough to swim the environment of her womb.

Jorana regretted that she had never listened to the tales of other mothers and mothers-to-be. The folklore of motherhood had never interested her before. There had never been time for that, and even if there had been time, she wouldn't have taken it. She rested both hands gently on the curve of her stomach. Her talent for foresight had never been very measurable. If it had been, she would have trained as a *tezar*, regardless of any other career she'd had in mind, for Malahki would never have let the opportunity to have a pilot under his influence slip past. Beyond that, she had never let any limitations in her *bahdur* slow her down as she'd found her niche and risen in it. But she did have her regrets now which had nothing to do with her usage of her power, but her misuse, or her neglect, of her own sexual identity. To be a Choya'i inherently meant to have a capacity to bear life, to nurture it, and she had never had that realization until now.

When it was almost too late.

This child might well be the only child she could have. She was not past her prime by any means, but neither was she as young as she had once been. Time had fled while she had thought she was in command of it, and all the options it had opened to her. Foolish me, she thought, to think I could reorder even Time.

Was it as foolish to think she could change Prophecy?

Jorana rolled onto her side, propped her head up on her hand, and looked out the window. The rain had stopped momentarily, and the air smelled of its dampness, of the air it had swept clean, and the wind it had captured within its storm clouds. The challenge of foresight was not in the doing of it, though that was difficult enough. It was in the interpretation and, also, in the strength of it. Easy enough to *see* what one might do in the next five minutes or half an hour. Difficult to *see* beyond that, as the skeins of other Choyan became entwined and entangled, wrapped and unwrapped, impossible to separate all the choices which might be made and unmade. Unless one's path through life were so blazingly clear that it was impossible to turn from it, to make other decisions, to have others impact upon it, forecasting was nearly impossible.

She had heard of only one Prophet in her lifetime, and that was a newly risen one. Despite the rarity, she had not doubted Dorea once she met her. From still raw eye sockets from which the Choya'i had torn her own orbs out, because she could neither comprehend nor contain the *bahdur* sight within her, to the anguished words of confusion and self-contempt at their last meeting, the Prophet had been real. More genuine than any Choya Jorana had ever met in her life, with the possible exceptions of Rindalan and Palaton. The Choya'i did not know what she said until she said it, and professed no great understanding or portent of it—but foreseen she had.

Cho must not have two emperors—and you must choose.

With that, Dorea had placed upon Jorana a burden unthought of, and unthinkable. How could she make such a choice, and to what dire crossroads must she come that she would face that decision?

Despite the Prophet's assurance that ruin would come to Cho if she did not, that Abdrelik and Ronin hounds would harry the planet, that nothing of the world in which they had grown up would remain, Jorana had turned aside from the burden. It was inconceivable that such a choice should be in her hands. Who was she that it would come to that? How could she, if it came to Panshinea and Palaton, turn her face from one to the other and say, this one lives, that one dies— for the good of Cho. She had fled, rather than face that which was prophesied for her.

Yet, in her heart, she knew she had already made the decision, and that also was what had driven her from the palace. Palaton was no emperor. He was a *tezar*, his soulfire burned most fiercely there, and he had never wished the throne, though Panshinea had thrust it upon him.

If only Dorea had given her other options, but she had not. *One must live, and one must die.* To save Cho, Jorana knew that she had to condemn Palaton to death.

But she would not stand flat-footed in the palace and have that fate pushed upon them both. If she could run, if she could somehow change the turning of the Wheel of the Houses, if she could prove the Prophet wrong. . . .

And if not, then at least Palaton's child lived within her.

So what was she doing here and now, waiting for Rufeen? Would it lead her to that which she'd tried so desperately to avoid? She did not think so, but she did not know. All she knew was that love for Palaton burned inside her as fiercely as *bahdur,* and she wished to see him one last time. She would tell him what she had done, and then, whatever fate he walked into, he would do so with full knowledge.

Perhaps it would save him. Perhaps it would drive him deeper into the web of his destiny.

She could only hope.

Jorana sat up. The child within her made another tiny stroking movement, as if reminding her that she was hungry, and hadn't eaten yet that afternoon. There was a tiny bakery just beyond the corner. Afternoon *bren* and fresh fry bread with honey sounded delicious after all her dark thoughts of fate and prophecy.

One moment at a time. She would settle for that.

Jorana picked up her wet cloak, shook it out, listening to the drops patter to the wooden floor, and wrapped herself up. The inner layer of the cloak was dry and warm, and she shrugged into it as she left her room and hurried downstairs.

The fry bread buns were sandwiched around a filling of soft cream, into which honey and fruit juice had been whipped. She bought a bag of them, more than she intended to, unwilling to stay and be limited to only one or two. The store owner filled a jug with freshly brewed drink, capped it, and handed it to her with an understanding look which Jorana ducked away from, not wanting to be seen well enough to be recognized later. The rain had stopped, leaving the sidewalk tables and chairs dotted with drops, too bespeckled to be sat at, so she headed across the square to return to her room.

Instinct halted her at the arched hallway to the building. After standing still a moment, she could hear the timbre of other voices, voices which shivered through the old building, and, although she could not hear words distinctly, she knew from the pitch that questions were being posed, and the landlady was answering them unsteadily.

Cautiously, Jorana came inside and looked up the landings. Guard, it had to be the guard, although how they had found her so quickly, or even at all, she had no idea.

She put the sack of buns inside her cloak to muffle their scent from drifting out onto the air, as good a giveaway as any noise she might make, and stood indecisively. Go or stay? Bluff or run?

What little she had taken into the world with her lay in that room upstairs. God-in-all knew it wasn't much, but it was all she had. Jorana sucked in her breath and held it, thinking and listening.

Then the sound of boots on the landing drew her attention, and she realized that the guard was not outside her room, but on the fifth and top floor above . . . nor were they searching any particular apartment, but going door-to-door. The landlady trailed unhappily in their wake.

Jorana shrank back into a corner of the archway. They were not looking for her, then; they were making a general search.

She stepped back out onto the street. There would be no reason to go door-to-door unless they were fairly certain that their prey was somewhere in the vicinity.

Rufeen. Palaton.

Rumors. Thorough work would turn up the quarry if rumors were accurate enough. She knew the drill. Sometimes she thought she'd invented it.

She slipped a hand into her bag, now warm against her chest, and withdrew a bun. Retreating back across the street, to the fated corner, where she could safely watch the guard searching her building, she stood under the eaves and nibbled on a food which, though her stomach still craved it, her mind no longer savored.

The sweet, cheesy filling spilled onto her tongue as she watched the windows, saw shadows moving, saw the search go from floor to floor, saw an intruder pause even at her own window to look out briefly and move on. She leaned against the storefront with a nonchalance her pounding heart did not echo, as a light sprinkle began again, and then she saw Rufeen.

Jorana dropped the sweet to the ground, took a step forward, preparing to call out, to warn, but the rangy pilot did not see her, intent on her own sweep of the square. However, framed in Jorana's own room window, one of the guards watched.

Jorana moved back into the shadows, knowing Rufeen was out of earshot unless she yelled loudly, and that would alert the guardsman for certain. She swallowed hard, a little surprised at the taste of the fry bread and honey in her throat. Rufeen looked at her, directly at her, unseeing, the glance slid away, and then the pilot was going, down the alleyway, past the large artists' co-ops, and toward a dingy underground station.

She checked the line destinations. Outlying towns she was unfamiliar with, industrial sectors where many of the apartments were as much belowground as above. Jorana herself had canvased the area earlier and dismissed it as too borderline for her to feel comfortable as a Choya'i alone, though she had not felt unsafe there.

Jorana turned a shoulder and sat down at a bakery table, even though it was still dewed with rain, as the guardsmen came clattering out of the building and gathered in the square.

She could feel the flare of *bahdur* as they began to conduct an aura search, and she knew from his body posture and then sudden spin-around, to talk to the commanding officer, that the hound had picked up on Rufeen. In formation, they fell into a dogtrot toward the transport station. If she hurried, she would not be far behind them, as they were not far behind Rufeen.

There was nothing Jorana could do now but follow. She dropped the sack of buns on the table, put a hand inside her cloak to the small of her back, and undid the safety on her enforcer.

As soon as the square cleared, she bolted across the street and up the landing to her apartment. Inside the one bag lay something she'd thought never to use again. She put on the armored vest, found it difficult to secure over the curve of her stomach and left the side lacings loose. It was better than no protection at all. She found a heat knife and slid it into the shank of her boot. That was all the armory she could afford at the moment.

Jorana hurried back downstairs and, using her own tracking sense, picked up the hot trail of the guard, who had made no effort to disperse their aura. The dark and sooty-smelling tunnel transport swallowed her. She occupied a single car, no grand linkage of commuters at this hour, though later it would be another matter. She sat down as the car rocked into motion. Flashing lights told her of her progress. Where would she need to stop: Semola? Trivan? D'albalen?

She watched the begrimed and nearly burned-out screen showing her car's progress through the system, and the tiny, winking lights of cars preceding her. One of them was

Rufeen's. Another held a handful of the guard elite, intent on killing when they reached their destination.

"I've got him," Hat said triumphantly, shouldering his way through the narrow door, cloth bags of supplies swinging from his elbows.

Palaton looked up from the graphs he and Rufeen had overlaid on the wall and frowned, refocusing both his vision and his thoughts. "Who?"

"Trevon the Black."

The smell of Rufeen's cheap beer permeated their living quarters as she picked up her mug and took a deep drink. She put the back of her hand to her mouth, to dab away the mustache of foam. "We were just trying to pinpoint the most logical base of operations." The grids of the projection reflected oddly across her fair skin. She frowned and told Palaton how to manipulate the program when a glitch disrupted the grid.

"When'd you pick that up?"

"I made a scavenging trip into Charolon today."

"Oh?" Hat grinned slightly. "Brought back some beer, too."

"Naturally." Rufeen added, "there's a concentration of Sky Householdings here. It's something to consider."

Hat dropped the groceries down into the storage bin, obviously bursting with his news, and Palaton kept his attention away from the projection, waiting for the revelation.

Hat straightened, his face aglow with triumph. "But you're wrong if you're looking for a Sky."

"Trevon the Black," Palaton observed, "would most likely be from that House."

Hat shook himself all over. A winter drizzle had dampened his jacket and his bare head, his hair hanging limply. "But we've known that for weeks, and without much success. The info you got the other night was no more specific."

"No," Rufeen answered for Palaton. "But the contaminant they used to cut the boost is."

"Well, this is even better." Hat drew up a chair without shedding his jacket. "When I was a child, we had an uncle in my Householding, a dour Choya, as dark of temperament as any Earthan could be. I got to thinking—what if Trevon the Black referred not to his coloring, but his manner. We're not looking for a Sky here, we're looking for an Earthan. So I started asking around—and I found him!"

"Where?" asked Palaton.

"East on the continent, near the fallow lands of S'laneen, a minor industrial and agricultural area called Bitron."

Palaton shifted uneasily. He looked to Rufeen. "That's too easy. Better backtrack him a bit. See what you can pick up."

"Will do, boss." The pilot got up and shouldered Hathord out of her way as she went out the door into the wind and rain, heedless of the weather, intent on picking up auras.

Hat pivoted in bewilderment. "What—you think my information is no good?"

Palaton lifted a finger to silence him, saying only, "We'll discuss it when she gets back."

Hat clamped his mouth shut and resumed throwing groceries into the bins, his good humor gone, his frustration venting itself on their goods. When Rufeen shoved her way back in a few minutes later, he had his bags folded across the counter.

"Not a thing." Rufeen looked to Palaton. "And I've been thinking . . . if we haven't been set up, that fits the profile of the cutting agent. Since this is consumed, dried milk is not an uncommon extender. We're talking dairylands here, pasturing is common around the fallow lands in the east. It could be processed on the edge of the S'laneen well enough. Cheap enough, too." She sat down and retrieved her mug, eyeing Hathord.

Hat took a deep breath, as if trying to settle himself down. He said defensively, "The Earthan I've found manages a large penning and storage area there. More than one or two Earths I've talked to describe him as Trevon the Black."

"A stockyards manager?"

"More or less."

Palaton scratched his chin. If any of the Choyan could be called the salt of the planet, it was the Earthans, a House well suited to agricultural careers. Their empathy with the land, its ecosystems, and its animals was the mainstay of the House. He and Rufeen had just come to the conclusion that the cutting agent used in the boost, powdered lactose, had been rather low-tech, harmless, and elemental—almost echoing the description of the House of Earth itself.

Although, he reminded himself, they had spearheaded three

assassination attempts on him in the past, not nearly so harmless as they might appear. And it had been the Earthans who
had gleaned Flames from the ashes of the destruction of the
lost House, intending to "beef up" their own genetic pool.
They had done it so slyly that the other two remaining Houses
had not even guessed at their duplicity.

He decided that Hat's prospect deserved some attention after all. "He might have something." Rufeen's thick lips
pursed in thought as he said to her, "Can we get there?" Jet
sleds wouldn't manage the amount of territory they needed to
cover.

"Everything big is monitored. You know that."

"I also know we can't jet sled across an entire continent.
What about going off-world, to the mines, and then coming
back in? Would that be easier?"

The heavyset pilot rubbed at her eyes. "Don't know," she
mumbled for an answer. She shied a glance at the Earthan before clamming up.

The pleasure bled completely out of Hat's face. He stood
up abruptly, and went to the storage bins and began to shuffle
through them again, as if to make sure the groceries were
stored correctly. The damp back of his jacket, presented to
them, seemed stiff and hurt.

"I'm not afraid to talk in front of Hat," Palaton told
Rufeen.

She gave a shrug. It rippled through her abundant shoulder
muscles. Then, in voices light for her frame and looks, she
said, "I didn't mean anything by it, Hat."

He separated the packaged goods from the perishables.
Without turning around, he answered, "Of course you did.
You don't trust me. Because of Nedar. . . ."

"I trust you." Palaton's voices cut across the silence of the
cramped housing.

"Maybe you shouldn't. Nedar made a fool of me. I was
ready to turn the school over to him, the cadets, the trainers,
everything. I listened to him."

"There was enough truth in what he said that you would
have listened. As for giving the school over, who among us
hasn't thought that we deserved our own House, that we are
what vitalizes Cho. We *tezars* have two major traits: we're pilots, and we're arrogant. Our abilities give us that. Our hard-

ships earn us the right to keep it. I think," and Palaton leaned forward to retrieve his ever-present cup of *bren*, "you heard what you wanted to. You thought with your heart instead of your mind, and which one of us hasn't done that?"

Rufeen heeded the conversation closely, her glance going from Palaton's face to Hat's and back.

"I'm a flightmaster," Hat protested. "I had students to protect." He swung about, and his emotional agony was clearly imprinted across his normally stoic face. Lines of character had been etched deeply into him and Palaton realized suddenly that the years they had spent as cadets together were far behind them. As good a pilot as Hat had been, he was one of the few who had not minded leaving space before his time. Becoming master at the school had been his dream, and he had excelled at it—and the war of vengeance between Palaton and Nedar had destroyed that.

He could not bear Hathord's agony. "Which you thought you were doing. And if you had not listened, Nedar would have taken you out. Nothing was gong to stand between him and what he wanted. You were able to temper his plans and judgment. You are probably the only proud asset in Nedar's life. I'm the one who feels guilt here. Because of me, Blue Ridge was destroyed. I'm the one who needs to ask forgiveness, and trust. And so I do now, old friend. Will you forgive me for losing sight of what it is to be a *tezar*? For letting myself get embroiled in the machinations of the emperor and others, and jeopardizing the lives of *tezars* to come?"

Hat's face contorted, his mouth opened to interrupt or accept the apology, but closed again without uttering a word.

Palaton added gently, "As the God-in-all is my witness, I'll rebuild Blue Ridge for you. Panshinea told me more lies than Nedar could have ever hoped to utter if he'd lived a hundred more years. And my listening was just as discriminating as yours. Sometimes I think all I've been doing is some fancy dancing to Pan's *lindar* playing."

Rufeen muttered, "We should all dance so well."

Palaton gave her a quick glance, then turned his face back to Hat's, searching it earnestly. "We need this settled. Am I forgiven?"

Hat made a movement that shrugged throughout his entire body, averting his face. "If you forgive me."

"Done, then." Palaton swung his chair around. "Where on this damn map are these stockyards and our elusive Trevon the Black?"

Rufeen had gotten to her feet and was headed to the storage bins, trading places with Hat at the graphics projection, when she froze. Her hand went to her thick waist, where her enforcer was always holstered. Her hiss cut through the air as Palaton and Hat began to wrangle over the map.

"Ssssht." She tilted her head. "It can't be. I backtracked. Either of you hear anything?"

Hat lifted a shoulder. "I don't think so."

Palaton began to clear the table. "Both of you have been out. Either one of you could have attracted attention." The map faded off the wall as he downloaded the projector and locked the keyboard. He threw a bag to Hat. "Pack everything you can."

"But—"

"No time! Rufi?"

"I'm not quite sure." Her face unfocused slightly, as she sent her *bahdur* in quest of the unknown.

Neither Choya waited for a definitive answer, gathering up what they could get their hands on quickly. Before she straightened and frowned, saying, "A hand or more, coming down the alleyway," Hat and Palaton were ready to go. Hat had never even had a chance to take his jacket off and Palaton tossed Rufeen hers.

They almost made it clear, but the door blew open, and the uniforms of imperial guards filled the shattered threshold to bursting.

Chapter 26

"Put your weapons down by order of the emperor," the Choya in front shouted, to which Rufeen responded by going to her stomach, and dropping him with a single, clean shot. She rolled out of range immediately.

Palaton shoved Hat aside and dove in the other direction as beams split the air. The burly Earthan went down behind an overturned table with a grunt and sat up, blinking, clutching a bag of groceries to his chest.

Rufeen spat back, her voices gravelly but level, "Next one moves gets his head sliced from his shoulders."

Seeing that they had not been able to wound or immobilize any of the quarry, and that they now stood in a cross fire, the guard paused to assess the situation. Their commander writhed in front of them, grasping his thigh and attempting to stop the flow of blood from a none too neat and bulging wound. The sound of ripping fabric filled the air as he tore his tunic and tried to fasten it about the wound.

Rufeen slid across the flooring and behind the table barrier where Hat sat, muttering something about the lack of manners and ancestry of the imperial guard, as well as proper search and seizure notification, when the second in command snapped out, "You have no rights."

"You have a Choya bleeding to death," Palaton observed dryly. "I will give you the right to withdraw expediently and take care of your wounded."

Rufeen took Hat's enforcer from its holster, primed it, and put it into Hat's palm. "I think," she said calmly, "you might need this."

Hat swallowed hard and took it, still clutching his bag of supplies as if it were a shield. His hand shook a little. They both watched the guardsman, as if divining his thoughts by the look in his eyes.

The guard stayed between them and freedom, but Palaton knew that they had been sent to capture, not kill. Panshinea wanted him brought in alive, tortured exquisitely, and then executed. Nothing less would suit the emperor. He was not certain that the order would cover Rufeen's and Hat's lives, but the opportunity to gain information from them would probably protect them as well. So the only fear here was how much damage they would do before being taken in, or getting out.

He did not want any more on his head than he already had. He took his voices and *pushed,* feeling the *bahdur* leap to ready use, saying, "Take your Choya and get him clear. Then deal with us."

To his surprise, the guardsmen responded. The nearest one bent and grabbed his superior's arm and began to drag him back out onto the street. Surely, they would have been shielded against *bahdur,* surely they would have their defenses up—but he had either punched through, or they had not. Another guardsman wavered as if he would help the first drag out their comrade, but the second in command barked, "Stand your ground!" and he stayed, a look of torn loyalties across his face.

One less body blocking the doorway. One less between them and the street. Still, there would be no getting out without further bloodshed. He could try his influence again, but from the tightly set jaw of the second in command, and the way his bronze mane fairly bristled above his horn crown, it would not work.

Hat broke the stalemate. At Rufeen's sudden nudging, his burly form staggered upward and he broke into a shambling run toward the rear of the rooms. Palaton let out a coarse yell, feeling it rip at his throat, even as the guard fired.

The enforcer beam seared its way across the room. Rufeen shoved the table in its path, shearing it astray, as Hat went down and rolled to safety behind a bedstead, and suddenly there were three less guards in the doorway.

Palaton got up, moving quickly, and grabbed the second by his neck, pulling him in and holding him to his chest. Looking out on the street, he saw three guardsmen down, one of them still holding that messy thigh wound, and a fourth on his knees, arms about his head. Someone had come to their aid, and taken advantage of being at the backs of the imperial guard.

In a swirl of midnight cloak, the Choya turned, and Palaton caught a full face glimpse of his, no, *her,* features.

"Jorana," he breathed, even as he shoved the Choya he held out the door. He called back, "Rufeen, get Hat and whatever the two of you can carry."

The doubt that he had seen her before was replaced by the wonder of seeing her now, so that he could not think, but only feel. She looked, against the gray foggy drizzle of the day, like the edge of night, or perhaps the glory of the storm itself, come to rest and create havoc in this alleyway.

"Don't just stand there," she said, and her voices were clipped and dry. "You've got to get out of here."

"How did you—"

"Find you? I saw Rufeen." Jorana flashed a look at the rangy pilot. "What you don't know, Choya'i, about back-tracking, nearly got all of you killed. You left an aura trail a burned-out hound could follow all the way from Charolon."

Rufeen had the grace to flush in embarrassment, before she leaned down and stripped the guards of their weapons. Jorana turned slightly to watch her movements, and Palaton saw the slight roundedness of her outline. More than that, a spike of *bahdur* touched him, not hers, but from within.

With child. The realization stuck in his throat, along with the thought that it could not have been his. Whose, then, and why? She looked up, as if in response to a gasp, and their eyes met.

Jorana closed her eyes softly a moment as if to gather herself, then looked back at him.

"Jorana—"

"There's no time. I came to see you, to explain, but now there's no time!" Anger flashed like lightning through her words. "You've got to get out of here, and I've got work to do."

Their names, other details, would be leached from the minds of the fallen. It would take time and effort. Her role would be betrayed. He could not leave her behind. Not now, with so much unknown and at stake.

"Come with us."

Jorana shook her head. "Not now. Later. Where—"

He did not know how well she worked. He did not want to leave a trail. "After Trevon the Black," he said, finally, knowing that if anyone could trace the dealer, she could.

Jorana gave a curt nod. She pulled the second guard from Palaton's hold and clubbed him behind the cusp of the neck and crown. The Choya went to his knees with a soft grunt, then collapsed onto the bodies of his fellows. Jorana went to one knee, putting her hand across his forehead, already beginning to narrow her thoughts into what must be done.

Palaton had to touch her, to stroke the softness of her skin, to lightly trace the gold chain and onyx pattern upon her cheeks. His question surged wordlessly through him. Jorana caught his hand and held onto it for dear life, squeezing his fingers tightly enough to drive away the blood and bring pain.

"It's your child," she said softly, breathlessly. "Dear God-in-all, I don't know what it does to you to tell this, but I can't let you go without knowing."

"My child . . ." It could not be. Never with her or anyone else, had he prepared to conceive a child. The enormity of her words left him speechless.

"Believe me," Jorana begged. "Now go. I can't keep you safe much longer."

"You—"

"I'll be all right. I'll follow. Somehow." She released his hand. Blood sprang back to life with a stinging pain, an echo of the stabbing she had just wrought in his heart.

A child. Cursed with the blood of the Flames, as he was. Damned to unknown possibilities.

A child. To live beyond his own death, to carry on, to have a legacy. . . .

Did she know what she had done to him?

It had begun raining again, softly, upon Jorana's upraised face. She dashed the drops away and said roughly, "Get out of here."

He turned abruptly, shoved Hat into motion, and grabbed Rufeen by the elbow. They ran down the alley to the garage where the pilots had stowed their jet sleds. He did not look back, though he could feel Jorana's eyes on him still, smell the faint perfume of her hair, see the rain upon her face, and the well of her body beneath the cloak.

He could not leave her!

Palaton turned at the garage, preparing to go back down the alley and get her, but she was gone, the bodies of the downed guard left in her wake, and there was nothing to show she had ever been there.

Rufeen joggled his elbow. "Come on, Boss. She gave us a chance, let's not waste it."

"I can't—did you see her?"

"I saw her," answered Rufeen gruffly. "But she didn't want you to drag her along, and you have to let her go. Now let's get out of here before backup arrives."

"I can't. Even with talent, she can't possible wipe their minds enough to keep herself in the clear. At least one is bound to recognize her, later."

"She can do it if she has *ruhl*," Rufeen bit off impatiently.

Palaton gave a slight shudder, an involuntary response to the use of the drug which muddled those with *bahdur* almost beyond the point of sanity, depending on its dosage. Despite the fact that death was not uncommon, its popularity as an aphrodisiac among the God-blind was legendary. And if she had it to use.... His thoughts roiled in his mind, paralyzing him. "You two go on. I have to go back. I have to talk to her."

"I'm not going anywhere without you," Rufeen argued.

Hat added faintly, "I think I was hit." He stood, hunched over, face growing rapidly more pale.

The pain echoed in his voices. Palaton looked down, and saw the blood tracing on the hand Hat held clutched to his flank. The splotch was thin and pink, a flesh wound in the squat Choya's side, no doubt, but nothing to be trifled with. He took Hat gently by the arm. "Can you drive?"

Hat gave a convulsive nod.

"All right." Palaton mounted his jet sled. "Where to?"

Rufeen bared her teeth. "After Trevon."

"I can make it," Hat said tightly, before being asked.

Rufeen kicked open the unloading door to the garage, saying, "This isn't my idea of fun. I never thought I'd draw down on one of my own. A Drooler's my idea of a target."

She grabbed Hat's sled by the handlebars and slung it past

her, opening up the doorway for Palaton to leave. They exchanged glances, and then Rufeen ducked away, unable to meet his eyes.

"It'll be all right," she muttered, and kicked her vehicle into tandem with Hat's, guiding him through the alleyway.

Rain came down in sheeting curtains. Palaton, caught without a jacket or coat, shrugged his shoulders against the downpour. The weather was all the better for washing away their presence and hiding their escape.

But it did not keep him from thinking that the sky wept for him.

* * * *

The night was late when she returned to the legal wing of the embassy, having missed dinner and late tea. She would have to order something up to her rooms, which were little more than a hole in the wall, nothing more than could be expected to be provided by contract. She had a kitchenette, a bed, a bathroom, and an office/study. No window, of course, though she did have an imaging wall to keep her from feeling claustrophobic.

Maeva clutched her package tightly under her elbow despite its bulk, trying to free herself of the idea that anyone who looked her way would know what it was she carried. It was not as though the armor was unwrapped or marked conspicuously, but she could not shake the feeling as she made her way through the security lobby and into the general lobby, that anyone who looked could identify the package.

The traffic was light, due to the hour, and she squinted her eyes against the white-flood of illumination, after her walk in the gently lit night. She knew no one she saw as she hurried into the scanner. Maeva felt her chin go up defensively—how many scanners had she been through in her life, starting from her earliest school days until now—how many security portals, many of which were no promise of protection at all, but simply there to keep the masses quiet? She stepped out, feeling it was ironic that having crossed oceans of star systems, she was not that far from home, after all.

As she passed through the portal, a dark mass of a being

rose to greet her, a being of vast bulk and yet infinite grace, and she plunged to a startled halt as it met her.

"Good evening, madame attorney," the Abdrelik said. "As you would say in your language, if Muhammad will not go to the mountain, then the mountain must come to Muhammad." GNask smiled greatly, and drops of saliva cascaded from one ivory tusk.

Chapter 27

"What do you think you're doing?" Maeva retreated nervously as the Abdrelik drew close to her, a Ronin in his shadow. *The* Ronin, unless she was very much mistaken. Maeva swiveled on one heel, looking about wildly for assistance. The lobby had become deserted, and she quelled her initial reaction, realizing that this was a senior member of the Compact who could not possibly act so publicly, nor should she, not wanting to cause an incident to embarrass herself. She chewed on her lip, before turning back slowly to face GNask.

"I have a pass," the ambassador said mildly. "And if I were you, madame attorney, I would compose myself and listen to what is being said. Attracting undue attention at this time and place may not be in your best interests. Authorities such as myself, with passes, are not looked upon unfavorably in the Compact. I have a right to be here, and so I am." He lowered his rumbling voice even more. "And it might even be said later that I was never here at all."

Maeva hugged her package close. Though she could feel herself shaking (with fear? or anger?), she managed her next words with the calm the Abdrelik suggested. "I'm honored by your presence, Ambassador GNask, but one of my status can hardly be of any assistance to you."

GNask smiled warmly. He returned to the massive couch which had been his chair and beckoned for her to sit down next to him. Maeva perched on the cushion's edge, balancing the packaged armor on her knee. "How may I help you?"

"You are one of the legal counsel on staff here, are you not?"

She nodded hesitantly, wondering where he was leading, and what he wanted, and thought that if assassination were on their minds, she would now be dead and her body hidden in one of the phone cubicles off the lobby's main entrance. With a privacy shield down, it would take days to find her. An Ivrian pilot had been killed like that in his own consulate. Maeva felt her mouth getting dry.

The Ronin stayed in her peripheral vision. It occurred to Maeva that he might be doing that on purpose—or he might be unaware she had as much side vision as she did. Without giving away that she could see him, Maeva kept her attention directed toward the huge alien close to her. "My status on the staff could hardly be less junior. I doubt if I can be of any value to you." She paused, and added, "And I couldn't divulge anything to you without permission of the head of the staff, even if there were something I did know."

GNask put up a hand to stroke the sluglike creature at his throat. Maeva had not seen it there before, so perfectly did the fleshy purplish color match. She had thought it the wattle of his neck, and now saw the creature pulsate wetly. Its stalk eyes came out and flicked a look at her. She knew that the thing's main purpose seemed to be as a pet, and as a skin-fungus-and-bacteria feeder, although there were rumors the symbiont also leached blood from time to time to complete its diet. Revulsion rose at the back of her throat and Maeva felt her glance flicker away. She forced herself to look back.

One of the ambassador's thick fingers stroked the creature as he spoke. "You underestimate yourself. My allies and I have observed you in the company of your ambassador, John Taylor Thomas, a great deal lately. Therefore, you must be capable of some standards of hard work as well as loyalty. My old friend can be very demanding. And it is not likely he would prefer the company of a junior employee unless her abilities were superior."

Or unless the threat of having your contract sold out from under you made you very pliable. Maeva closed her lips tightly on her thoughts. Feigning disinterest, she eyed her watch and said, "Ambassador GNask, with all due respect, the hour is growing late, and I have some work to prepare for tomorrow."

GNask smiled again, the grimace exposing his gums as well as his teeth. "And a cumbersome burden to put away as well, I see."

"Yes," she replied evenly. The Ronin moved slightly on her flank, as if closing in on her. He halted as she turned her head involuntarily in response. He *was* trying to circle her. Her grip on her package tightened, despite her effort to look relaxed. What did these two have in common?

"I will try to be brief," GNask said expansively. He spread his thick hands. "What I need from you is information which will not compromise you at all. My associate here tells me you had a meeting with Ambassador Rindalan of Cho."

She could hardly claim confidentiality there. Besides, Timero had not kept the meeting a secret out there on the pathways. Maeva nodded smoothly. "Yes, the ambassador was gracious enough to set aside some time for me."

"And you will tell me why."

She eyed the Abdrelik closely before saying, in her best clipped tones, "I think not."

"Do you claim that to do so would betray your secrecy and loyalty oath to your embassy?"

She had not fenced with an Abdrelik before, and had not given them much credit for subtlety, and GNask was pointing toward something, something oblique that she instantly felt would be very dangerous for her to be cornered into. "What would you have me claim?" she countered quickly.

That took GNask back a moment, as his lips came down over his tusks, and his jowls sagged again. The beady eyes blinked once or twice.

"May I remind you," he said, "of my position."

"But you see," Maeva pressed, "that's what I can't understand. Why an ambassador of your position would be the slightest bit interested in a counsel of my position."

"Perhaps I am curious as to why such a junior member of the staff was recently assigned the embassy's highest security rating and clearance. Perhaps I am curious as to what you intend to do with it. Or are already engaged in."

Maeva let out a short laugh. "And you would expect me to tell you?"

"Yes."

She stared into the Abdrelik's broad, purplish face for a long moment. The alien did not flinch from her examination, although the symbiont had begun to ripple its way up the throat and onto GNask's jawline. It became clear to her that GNask honestly did think she would confide in him.

The Ronin moved. This time Maeva shifted her weight and looked directly at the creature. "Ask once nicely, and then torture?" she said lightly, although her throat had begun to tighten, and she knew her next words would be difficult to force out.

"Something like that." GNask smoothed his jowls with the back of his hand, patting away the ever-present moisture. "I am well acquainted with your ambassador. We have had, from time to time, some informal dealings. I do not think you too terribly naive about the internal workings of the Compact."

"Not terribly," Maeva echoed.

"I do not expect you to confide in me tonight, here, and now. But I have come to make you an offer. I know Thomas. His moods, his expectations—his shortfalls. There may well come a time when you need a safety net, madame attorney, when you find that your home world does not provide what you need to stay alive. May I make my own humble offering of assistance when that time comes?"

"Assistance? Provided I tell you everything I know."

GNask lowered his head slightly.

"And if I don't accept your generous offer?"

The ambassador said nothing, but he raised his head and stared at the Ronin who skinned his lips back from his teeth and rattled his quills. GNask then added, "Perhaps you will allow me to convince you. We will talk again." With speed belied by his bulk, the ambassador beckoned to the Ronin, got to his feet, and made his way to the security portal.

The archway lit up and let him exit without any deterrence whatsoever. The recording sensor stayed dim, and Maeva realized that what GNask had told her was true. There would be no record of his presence tonight, except those who saw him, and those few would probably not bear witness.

The package of body armor slid from her knee, and she let it drop to the floor as she realized she had just been offered both the carrot and the stick. How had the Abdrelik known about her security clearance? And if he knew that, did he in truth have the slightest suspicion of what she might be doing for Thomas?

To hell with the ambassador. Did the alien know about *Rand?*

She had begun to shake again as delayed adrenaline began to flood her body. She leaned over to pick up the package. It took three tries to coordinate her reach with her grasp, and another two tries to stand up holding the armor.

About one thing GNask had been correct. If Thomas ever found out what she had done, what she yet planned to do, he would cut her loose from the embassy. She would have no place to go for safety. She would be at the mercy of the reassignment courts of the Compact, and GNask no doubt had a great deal of influence there, as well.

Although the Choyan had been gracious, she doubted she would find refuge there. She would be outcast, just as Rand had been, and along the tide of adrenaline came a new emotion, one deeper than the compassion she had felt earlier. She knew now the despair and disillusionment he had tried to convey to her. She was alone among her own people.

Maeva walked to the lifts for her apartment tower. The halls were strangely quiet, abandoned, and her footfalls echoed loudly. She thought she could hear her heartbeat pounding.

The body armor didn't have a chance in hell of saving her.

The midnight hours brought little rest to Rindalan. He lay on his divan, rather than his bed, head elevated on the crown pillow, taking the weight off his aching neck and shoulders, and thought behind the blackness of his eyelids. He would rather have slept whatever hours he could, for he had reached that elderly portion of his life where even sleep could be a rare commodity. He could sleep in chambers where the arguments droned on and on, but he could not find rest in his own bed, during his own time.

Rindy sighed gustily and opened his eyes. He did not mind his age. With it had come a certain amount of wisdom, he hoped, and a great many memories of which he was excessively fond. But memory would not serve him now. Rand was with his own people, and though Rindy could not comprehend the logic of his treatment, the elder prelate was entirely uncertain of how to deal with it. He could no more delicately dislodge Rand from that imprisonment than he could wake the frozen race of Sorrow. Not without creating a great deal of turmoil, anyway.

Rindy shifted his weight on the divan. One hip was a little tender with arthritis. He moved off it slightly to assuage the pain and pressure. If Panshinea were not so avid a xenophobe, the emperor would be able to deal with the problem. Pan, though his *bahdur* burned erratically, affecting his entire temperament, was nonetheless shrewd and capable with these problems. Rindy couldn't hold a candle to him. But he could not ask Panshinea. The emperor would manipulate Rand to his doom.

As for Palaton, Rindy had no idea where he had gone into hiding, although there was that spark within the elder which told him the pilot still lived. If the *tezar* continued to wish to live, he would remain just as elusive. No, he could not reach Palaton though that was Rand's best hope of rescue.

No, no matter how he worried at the knot of problems and troubles, he kept coming back to the same conclusion. Rindy had no allies for this undertaking, and the burden was his and his alone. He sighed again, not liking the odds.

There was the humankind, of course, who'd come to him. Pretty little thing, if knowing Rand had taught him anything about that race. He thought them all rather awkward, though their eyes gave him pause, wide-eyed innocents like his own people's children. If eyes were indeed the windows to the soul, humankind was a deep well of psyches, and the Abdreliks an absolute drought. Maeva had risked much in coming to him.

Well, then, perhaps he did not stand alone in this enterprise. Maeva could be counted upon for something, surely, if not for more information. Unless he could read little of them, she had an interest in Rand. He had touched her. Though whether deeply enough so she was as willing as Rindy to risk all, the elder Choya could not tell.

Two, then, against the clever Halls and entrapments of the Compact. Rindy shook his head slightly. He still did not like the odds. He closed his eyes again. The problem with solving conundrums at night was that the possibilities, like the sky, tended to be dark. He decided to drift determinedly into sleep, and work on solutions in the morning.

Knowing that Rand was not possessed of psychic ability, he

sidestepped the embassy shielding, and sent him a thought anyway, of hope, of help coming, of comfort. Perhaps the boy had been around Palaton long enough to have absorbed something of the *tezar's* soulfire. If not, no harm done.

As he sank deeper into the rhythms of his mind, his thoughts went coiling out, visualized as a rope of smoke, curling through nothingness until it might find its recipient. It sank, through the warmth of his being, down, down, until it was seized and a shocking chill shot back into Rindalan.

He sat up on the divan, clutching at the upholstered back of it, feeling as if he had been doused in icy water. Dropped into a wintery pond, the surface had given under him, dunking him under its treacherous lid. He could not quite catch his breath, and his limbs reacted to the mental cold by thrashing about in violent shudders, throwing off the blanket he had tucked about his legs. Rindy gasped and his aged heart did a stutter step which frightened him almost more than the cold.

But worse, he found Rand in the center of it, frozen among lifelessness, like an anchor. The other's consciousness caught onto his, a drowning man reaching for a lifeline, pulling him under as well, immersing him in the chill aftermath. *Fool!* thought Rindy. *He's in cold sleep or reduction.* But this was more, less than cold sleep, but worse.

He lay among Sorrow's dead. Rindy could feel them as well, a realization which startled as well as frightened him. With all his psychic acumen he had never sensed their crystalline being before. The God-in-all had gifted him with the ability to sense the vibrancy of life in everything, even stone, but here on Sorrow those vibrations had never been felt. Shielded, perhaps? He caught an echo of intense sadness, and longing, and reluctance to let him go, to let him take Rand up with him.

As if rescuing a foundering diver, Rindy wrapped his thoughts about the lad and brought him up, kicking hard to reach a surface which existed only in his mind, his lungs laboring, his heart thudding. Rand lay in his embrace as if one of the dead, and stirred only when Rindalan finally broke clear.

They touched thoughts briefly, a faint brush against one another, and then Rand left him. Rindy felt him float away sluggishly, knew that wherever he was, he was indeed in near-cryonic suspension.

He opened his eyes to the familiarity of the diplomatic suite. The needlepoint upholstery of the divan which he had clutched until his knuckles turned white. The dim lighting of the room, the burlwood table, the Ivrian watercolor on the far wall, a light and feathery subject amid the tailored striped wallpaper. His chest heaved with the effort he had just expended.

He did not understand what had just happened. He only knew that if he had not been searching for Rand, the boy might have died imprisoned there among the mysterious people of Sorrow.

He could not wait to free him. There were things here which Rindy did not understand, and which might prove fatal if left ignored.

Chapter 28

"Did you dump the bodies?" The question came from the depths of the massive chair pulled up to face the fireplace. Its reflected heat did much to chase the chill from the wintry atrium room, but Gathon did not feel warm.

He hugged his spindly ribs with hands nearly blue beyond the cuffs of his robe. "I did," he answered, and he did not bother to filter from his voices the self-anger and repulsion filling him. The youths were alive but, with their soulfire drained, they were little more than warm hulks. The chore repulsed him, and there was the niggling feeling that this time, he'd been sighted. This time, his efforts had been watched. This time, the emperor had been found out. He shivered, trying to dispel his unfortunate thoughts.

Panshinea swung the chair around. Despite being at ease within the upholstery, he did not look rested. He appeared coiled, ready to spring, overflowing with energy as he had not been in weeks. Color blazed in his face and it was as if the fire itself danced in his glorious golden hair. It was the stolen *bahdur*, Gathon knew, and though he had the knowledge of where the emperor's well-being had come from, he felt no better for the knowing.

"That extra dose," Gathon added, "might very well kill them." He detested *ruhl*, with all its possible misuses.

"Perhaps they would think it better if I had." Panshinea curled his fingers about his wineglass, cradling it to his chest. "I tell myself it would be no great loss, that if I had only found those Flame bastards and treated them the same way, I would not be facing what I'm facing now." He let out a sigh, which was more a hiss. "But I agree with you, Gathon. I do that which no Choya should do to another, and I cannot help myself. There's no other way for me to continue." He drained the glass of Imperial Gold.

"You could step down," Gathon responded mildly.

Panshinea, who had begun to look down into the depths of his drink with a melancholy expression, snapped his glance back at the prime minister. "That is never a consideration."

Gathon could feel drops of sweat beading on his forehead, yet his arms and hands and feet remained icy, and shivers rippled up and down his aged body. He said, recklessly, "Perhaps it should be."

"And have you anyone in mind to replace me?"

The internal heat which had flared began to cool rapidly. "No."

"You're certain?"

"Do you doubt me as well as yourself?" His recklessness gave one final spurt.

Panshinea looked as though he had something to reply, but he closed his mouth on it, and his lips thinned as if he reconsidered. His gaze did drop to the glass he held close. "How could I expect to treat you better, dear Gathon, than I treat myself?" he murmured, barely audibly. He drained the wine. "Any word on our quarry?"

"None." Gathon took his hands from under his arms and chafed them together lightly, as pins and needles began to warm them. "If you do not mind, Pan, it has been a long night for me. I need to retire."

Pan said abruptly, "You do not like pimping for me."

"No. No more than did Jorana. But you are Cho, and Cho ails if you ail, and so I would wish for you to be well."

"I'm a parasite."

Gathon thought of the bodies he had disposed of in the outer slums of Charolon, the fourth such group in the weeks since Pan's attack on Palaton. "Yes," he agreed.

"But a necessary one."

Gathon did not answer.

"Perhaps not so necessary."

"Your Highness. The hour is late, and my duties are many in the morning. May I go?"

Wordlessly, the emperor of Cho nodded, but Gathon did not wait for dismissal. He simply turned and left.

Panshinea watched the door close, then put his finger into

the wineglass and stirred the tip of it around the bowl's bottom where a faint residue had been left. He licked the fingertip clean of the gritty powder, with misgivings. Vihtirne and Qativar had been right. This, *this,* was the wellspring from which renewed power could flow. With this, he no longer needed to do what he'd done that night, and every week since he'd failed to destroy Palaton. With this, he could rule as surely God had intended him to. With this, nothing was impossible.

He would never have tried it, without catching the taste of it in the youths he was draining. Their *bahdur,* weak and fragile as it was, had left him more hungry than sated, aching with the need to be filled. But their power had had an edge to it, a promise, and he had gone to the drug in search of that promise. And, Pan told himself, he had found it. This evening he fairly burned with potential, having found his prey inadequate, and trying the drug in Gathon's disapproving absence. What the old Choya did not know would not hurt him.

Gathon had sensed nothing, or if he had sensed how full of *bahdur* Panshinea had become, he would attribute it to the callow youths he'd just disposed of. It was just as well. He already felt condemnation from the elderly Choya. If Gathon discovered he'd used boost it would only have added to his disapproval, and Pan had no intention of letting the minister persuade him to leave the course he'd just begun. This was power, and this was his!

He had only to make sure of an uninterrupted supply.

Pan refilled his wineglass and sipped at it slowly and pensively.

Walking the streets, Jorana cautiously continued the perimeter search, fulfilling her need to know if her newly chosen quarters were safe. She had taken the guard and their hound by transport to Trivan and dumped them there, but she wanted to backtrack their aura as much as possible, confusing the trail when the hound awoke, so she had returned. She had found a new bolt-hole in outer Charolon, far from the musicians' quarters, and although it was seedy, at least no one had asked any questions when she had checked in.

The rain threatened to turn to sleet, so she kept her head somewhat bowed as the cold of it iced her face. She had not returned to the little apartment across from the bakery, could not, and mourned what few items she had left there. She could go back to Malahki, but knew the wrath she would face. No. She had taken this road, and did not wish to retrace her steps upon it.

She skirted a dark alleyway, then heard the faint moans issuing from it, and paused. This time of night, few traversed the city but burned-out boost addicts and beggars with nowhere to go and no prospects but another's misfortune. No one of any good intent might be hovering in the alleyways. Hard times, in Charolon.

She heard the moan again. Intuition prickled at the base of her neck, but she turned anyway, and stood in the alley's mouth until her vision narrowed to the velvet depths. She saw two tumbled heaps, and stepped closer.

The auras had been dispersed, but it did not matter. Two forms lay sprawled in the back of the street, dumped like offal, left to live or die as they would. She could smell the drugs on them, and the even rarer, more distinctive smell of Imperial Gold, and Jorana knew what had happened here.

She used to bring the emperor his victims herself.

She bent over them and felt for the pulses throbbing sluggishly in their necks. She stood for a long time, measuring the strength of the life ebbing through them.

They would make it, she decided, and straightened, drawing her cloak about her. They were young and vigorous, and even a night in a slush-filled alley would not harm them permanently.

But as to whether or not they would survive what Panshinea had done to them, that she could not predict. Those commons who had some *bahdur* but not enough to pass testing to be brought into Houses did not always even know what it was they had. They often thought it luck. Those who did, who used it and depended on it, erratic though it might be, were the ones most affected by the method the emperor had used to drain them. He did what he did not only to temporarily recharge himself but also to destroy the neurals within the victims. They would know the yawning hole within themselves which would never be filled again. They were not dissimilar to *tezars* of much greater power, who suffered neurological damage and burned out over the years from the usage of their soulfire. Those *tezars* who died in the line of duty were far luckier than those who had to face the depths of their scarred souls, and could not.

She could not know if these unlucky youths faced a mirroring reaction to what had happened to them tonight, and even if she were to know, there was nothing she could do to assist them. Even boost would not help. It could not spur what no longer existed. She wondered who was disposing of the bodies for Panshinea now.

Jorana tucked the cloaks in tightly about them and left them in the alley.

This quarter of Charolon was not safe for her if the emperor hunted here. She pulled her hood about her face, and walked off into the stinging wind.

A solid darkness arose from the corner before her, blocking the street.

"The emperor leaves his spore in the oddest places, don't you agree, Jorana?"

She looked up into the winter-cold eyes of Qativar. He added, "You know, of course, that many of us have been looking for you. I think it would be best if you came with me."

* * * *

The jet sleds carried them into the storm front, bucking against the aboveground thermals, and sleet-filled wind. Palaton kept an anxious eye on Hat, curled painfully over the handlebar grips, feet braced on the floorboards, but the Earthan kept his sled steady, so there was little Palaton could do but watch.

Rufeen tried to cut a path for them, attempting to draft Hat's vehicle in her wake. Her thick form was barely visible in the night despite the yellow beams from the sleds. Her mane flew loose from her coat collar, but it did not banner in the wind, for it soon frosted in icicle patterns. Palaton would have worried for them all, but his sense told him that the storm front only covered a few hundred miles and they would soon be out of it, even if it traveled with them a ways. They could not turn out of its path, and it covered their leaving far better than they could have hoped. Only someone as desperate as they were would fly in the face of the wind, sleet, and rain.

The front fell apart just as dawn began to creep through the sky, and Palaton saw Rufeen shear aside, taking the sled so close to the ground as to nearly plow it, searching for a lee. She turned about, he saw her face, frosted and pale, and knew she needed a fire and rest, even as she beckoned.

Hat did not respond, but he followed, and when Palaton brought up the rear, braking the sled to a halt where the other two had come to a stop, he saw Rufeen dismount stiffly. Hat stayed crouched on his sled, frozen to his grip on the handlebars. Palaton reached the Earthan before the pilot did.

He ran his hands over Hat's and gently pried the fingers loose. "Come on," he coaxed. "Rufi's getting a fire going. Let's take a look at that bleeding."

Hat turned a tortured face to him. "I brought them."

"No. I won't even blame Rufi for that. They were searching for us." Popping open the vehicle's tool compartment, he found the aid kit and slung it over one shoulder. He took Hat's arm gently and put his other shoulder in under, taking the other's weight carefully and lifting him from the vehicle's saddle.

"If it hadn't been for Jorana—" Rufeen was there, suddenly, helping him from the other side. They walked Hathord to the fire she'd already laid and had banked. Its sputtering warmth was taking hold amongst the rocks.

Hat tried to take a deep breath, coughed in discomfort, and let his weight sag upon their shoulders. Rufeen said nothing, but shot Palaton a worried look over the top of their comrade's head. He felt himself frowning. Hat felt terribly cold in their embrace.

Rufeen went to one knee so that Palaton could lay Hat down on the ground. Their companion fell back, his face so gray that he would have been camouflaged among the stone. She put his feet close to the bed of rocks which had begun to warm under the wood-fed fire, as Palaton stripped off his jacket, rolled it inside out, and put it under Hat's head and shoulders. He let the aid kit drop to the ground beside them.

Then his fingers went to the bloodstained coat front to peel it back.

Hat put his hand over Palaton's. "Don't," he pleaded.

"We have to take a look at it."

"I don't want to know."

Palaton kept his hand still. As a cadet, Hat had never been very bold. He had not taken risks. He had never liked surprises, and Palaton knew what frightened him now.

Rufeen rubbed her hands briskly and hunched over the fire, feeding more substantial deadwood into it. She'd found a copse among the broken rock field, and though the wind still howled steadily, the gray of the dawn had given way to a faintly blue light, and the chill of the storm could not be felt here. They'd come enough miles to be outside even the capital's agri district ... perhaps even to the fallow parklands. The trees rattled thinly, much of their foliage lost to the fall, their branches as dark as *bren* against the sky. In the lee of an immense marble-streaked boulder, its mates broken about it into stones and pebbles, there was a kind of beauty to the place.

Hat had followed his line of sight. He said weakly, "This would not be a bad place to die."

Rufeen snorted and then said, "Now that's what I need to hear."

Hat's face had been gaining some color. Now he flushed darkly, though the anger paled almost as quickly as it came. His fingers curled tightly about Palaton's hand. Before Palaton could say something to comfort Hat, Rufeen added, "We really need to be digging graves now, Boss. See if you can get a plug in him, okay? I'm gong to look for lightfoot, see if I can make some stew." She got up and sauntered away, her thick hips swinging.

"Lightfoot," Hat whined. "I'll be spitting out fur for a week."

Palaton looked back at him, and realized what Rufeen had been doing. He felt the corner of his mouth draw back in mild irritation even as he put Hat's hand aside and skinned back the bloodstained cloth.

Jorana's initial assessment back in the alleyway had been correct. The wound, though it seeped gently, had all but seared itself shut, and had done little damage, having cut into that portion of Hat's waistline settling over his hips, which the commons called love handles. He needn't worry about the fat roll on this flank for a while. It would be sore, and it still wept, but it looked clean, for all the slice it had taken out of him, and it wasn't even close to being life threatening.

Palaton told him as much in clipped, unsympathetic tones. Hat's face settled into a sulky, yet relieved expression as Palaton left his side. He found moss among the stones which had tumbled close to the edge of a tiny freshet at the edge of the copse, scraped it loose, brought it back, and bound it to the wound. Hat let out a quavering hiss as the cool lichen began to draw the heat from the puckered tissue. Palaton rocked back on his heels and waited for his friend to finish.

Hat touched the compress with tentative fingers and tried to look at the work Palaton had done. He let out a short laugh. "I was never very brave, was I?"

"The one reason you didn't make an excellent pilot. You've always been a little hesitant about the unknown." Palaton wrapped a bandage about the Earthan's waistline to anchor the compress and clipped it off.

"But I was a *good* pilot, wasn't I?"

He finished the bandaging with an antibiotic radiation spray, capped the flare to return it to the kit, and answered, "Of course you were. And you're one of the best flightmasters we've ever had."

"Without a school," Hat said mournfully as Palaton wedged him upright. He tested the position a little gingerly, then gave a relieved grin. "I can't go anywhere, or you'll build me a memorial instead of a school. And you did promise me a new school."

"That I did." Palaton repackaged the aid kit. There were no oral antibiotics to give Hat, but if he needed that kind of medical care, they'd have to find it for him. Another day or two on the jet sled to find Rufeen's bolt-hole, and he thought Hat would be all right.

"Rufeen knows," Hat continued.

"What?"

"That I haven't got the nerve."

"It's not that you haven't got nerve," Palaton said, sitting down beside the wounded Earthan, and stretching his legs out. "It's a different kind of nerve. Rufeen wouldn't have the courage to run a school, coordinating the fragile egos of incoming cadets with half-burned-out pilots and cocky wing leaders. Balancing budgets. Going among the God-blind and testing for *bahdur*—it hasn't happened recently, but there've been terrible riots over the tests. You have courage all right, Hathord. It's just a different kind."

Hat settled his back to the smooth side of the immense, fractured boulder. He blinked as he patted the bandage once as if to ensure it stayed in place, and answered, "I hadn't thought of it that way."

"Maybe it's time you should," Rufeen said gruffly, as she came around the granite- and marble-streaked structure. She threw two half-skinned lightfoot rodents onto the dirt by the fire. "We don't have time to keep mending falling egos."

"Well," Hat returned slowly, "if we have time to hunt for enough supplies to fill your dinner plate, we should have some time to set aside for me."

Rufeen shot him a look, then lapsed into a chagrined expression as Palaton began to laugh. Then she pointed at him.

"Laugh all you want, but these morsels aren't fully skinned yet. You want to eat, I need some help."

Palaton shifted away from Hat, took up a lightfoot and began to apply his heat knife to it. Tufts of fur swirled around the fire, *pfffting* as the heat destroyed them. Rufeen squatted beside him and finished the second. She pushed her chin at Hat.

"He's going to live, eh?"

"Looks like it."

Hat wrinkled his nose. "If your cooking doesn't kill me first." He wiggled around until he got his back to a boulder and sat up straighter. "Where do we go from here?"

Rufeen spitted her carcass. "I think I have the answer to that, too. There's a Relocation depot not far from here. It's got transports being fueled. Place looks fairly empty. I'd say it's probably under minimum maintenance."

"It would have to be." Relocation was a traumatic process of uprooting whole communities from their geographic location and transplanting them. In this way, the country itself was being recycled, bit by bit, territory by territory. There had been talk for years that Charolon was overdue for Relocation, but because of its position as capital, it was thought Panshinea had been fighting Relocation off successfully. This depot must have been built for the eventuality, which had never come. Palaton added, "We'll have to take a look at it in the morning. I think you may have found a way to get us to Trevon the Black."

Chapter 29

He summoned Vihtirne from her nocturnal chambers. It was so late at night as to be early the next morning, he thought, as he waited for her to come down. Her humor would not be good, but Qativar cared little about that. When she did appear on the stairs, she was wrapped in a purple robe of deep color, its silken folds whispering as she came down the stairs, its high collar hiding her neck but not her face. He realized with shock, when he saw her, that she must use a firming net, applied electrically, before she saw anyone for the day. She was awake, but not made up, and the sagging of her cheeks and jawline surprised him. As she neared the bottom step, seeing Qativar and what he had hidden in his shadow, her eyes widened. The faint smell of sex, of sex and lovemaking, came with her, perfuming her skin and robe. Qativar did not particularly care for the odor, but that dislike said a lot more about himself than it did about Vihtirne, he thought.

"What have you brought her here for?" demanded Vihtirne, the unexpected awakening not having dulled her wits at all. Or her tongue.

To keep you busy and out of my way, Qativar thought, as he bowed slightly toward Jorana, who stood, cold and sulking, in the foyer. "We needed leverage."

"She's more trouble than she's worth."

"Thank you. I try." Jorana smiled thinly. Her own beauty, though pale and wan, was fresh and dewy compared to the artifices of Vihtirne. Qativar wondered if that accounted for the incredible amount of tension which had built in the air.

"You won't do anything to harm her," he said.

Vihtirne had paused on the next to last step. Now she descended one more step, and stopped, drawing herself up, pulling her robe about her. She stood above both of them. "I would not presume. It's a raw night out. Wherever did you find her?"

"Doing the emperor's dirty work."

Jorana chafed her wrists lightly inside her shackles. Vihtirne glanced down at the bonds with distrust.

"It will be difficult to hold her here for long."

Qativar lifted a shoulder, let it drop. "I doubt that we will need long."

"You will consult with me, will you not, as to our plans?"

He looked up at Vihtirne. "Naturally. When both the hour and the weather are more hospitable. In the meantime . . ." he waved at Jorana.

"Put her in downstairs storage. It's dry and warm enough. Throw her a blanket and some cushions from the salon. Keep her shackled. I'll be down later to check on her." Vihtirne twisted about on the step to return upstairs, then paused. She tilted her head toward Jorana. "You are pregnant."

Her accomplice started, but Jorana did nothing. Her jaw moved as though she clenched her teeth, and there was defiance in the set of her face. Vihtirne gave a knowing smile.

"Poor timing, Jorana. It gives us an advantage we'll not hesitate to use. That abomination would be well off ripped from your womb. Do not tempt us."

Qativar laughed. It was without humor and as icy as the night they'd come in out of, and he did not stop until after he'd locked the door behind Jorana.

* * * *

Thomas awoke from uneasy dreams of Alexa, her dark eyes shining with a brittle light that seemed to pierce him. He could not remember what she had been saying to him, and for that he gave rueful thanks, for her words to him had never been kind since that fateful day when he had turned her over to GNask's ungentle hands for imprinting. From the chubby, toddling child he had given over, he never saw his daughter again in Alexa, never saw anything of him or her mother in her eyes or words. She had always been a shadow of the Abdreliks, a predator, hiding behind a mask, and terribly aware that she was different.

Perhaps it was better that she was dead now.

Perhaps.

The readout of incoming messages told him that the embassy had had a lot of traffic during the evening. Most had been dispatched elsewhere, one or two items were slated for his eyes only, and there was an appointment for incoming. The alarm had not yet gone off for it. He checked the time, saw that he had risen early, and neutralized the alarm, acknowledging the appointment. He had just enough time for a shower and shave. His hands shook as he scraped his face clean, tiny drops of blood welling up where he nicked himself.

The president awaited him as he sat down at the view screen. "Good morning, John. I trust I have not inconvenienced your schedule this morning."

Thomas did not reply, he was not meant to, but this was a real-time transmission and as he held his remarks until the president indicated he could speak, he wondered what had occasioned the call.

Gerald Mitchell had come into his office long after Thomas had, but he wore the robes of his authority with an easy familiarity. "We have been informed that one of our cargo shipments has been lost by the contract pilot. The incident occurred under FTL conditions and it is not probable that we will be able to recover our goods. As is customary, we have sent the Choyan our deepest regrets for the loss of their *tezar*, and we have filed insurance claims for the shipment." The president paused. He was sitting in the high-backed chair of his office, the windows behind nearly obscured by the protective weaving of the glass. The chair was permeated with keflex. It would stop most bullets, even hollow-nosed atrocities, although it was more probable the bodyshielding of the president would make such precautions unnecessary. But the chair was an antique symbol of the office.

"He was not under attack, John, and from preliminary investigations, he suffered from burnout. Normally I don't get involved in these incidents, but because of the nature of the cargo and its destination, I was notified. I've been sitting in with the Economic Council most of the night." The president leaned forward, bringing his face into close-up focus in the view screen, the salt-and-pepper coloring of his bushy eyebrows suddenly clear, the gold flecks in his brown eyes, and the shine of his thinning pate.

"What in the hell are you doing sending pharmaceuticals to the Choyan?"

Thomas felt his eyes close in sudden fear. He forced them back open, smoothing his face into neutral lines. He was a diplomat, after all. Bland neutrality had been schooled, ingrained, into him. He spoke. "Mr. President. Please convey my assurances to the Economic Council that this transaction is all very aboveboard. We have begun a preliminary trade agreement with Cho as benefits our status upgrade from a Class Zed. I have worked diligently for decades to improve our status and to open trade channels with those who will most benefit us. The pharmaceuticals lost in shipment are for a restorative remedy which the Choyan themselves requested. It is but a foot in the door for us, but one which should prove invaluable."

He sat back in his own chair, waiting for the long, long moments between transmission, his thoughts racing wildly. Boost lost in transit. The demand had risen sharply in the past few weeks, he could not keep up with it, had shifted a whole Terran-leased bay station over to the production of the remedy and hidden the paper trail for it as well as he could. Ironic that a pilot in burnout should drop a whole cargo of the drug which would have cured him.

He split-screened the view screen and scanned backup traffic while waiting for the president to respond. Nothing else seemed to be of any import to him except that Maeva Polonia had made another visit to the holding cell. Thomas felt a twitch in his composed expression as he viewed the authorization record. He would have to set up an interview with her to check on the status of the deposition. His attention distracted, he missed the first words of the president's response.

". . . without proper testing on alien physiology or field samples, are you crazy? Thomas, we come from a planet which has struggled with self-destructive chemical dependencies for most of our race's history. Without conducting a survey, how can you know what it is we're exporting to the Choyan and how it will ultimately affect them? I have to protest your actions—"

Thomas put his hands on the console in front of him and

broke into the president's transmission. "I beg your pardon, sir, but we are now trading with the Choyan. We now have a currency to barter with, a leverage to get their attention. The *Choyan,* sir, without whom we cannot ship or transport anywhere."

His words had overridden the president's but now Mitchell's voice came back powerfully. "Without any knowledge of their biochemistry or long-term effects, you cannot convince me or anyone else, let alone the FDA, of the harmlessness of any drug you might be selling them. I can well understand your urgent desire to effect trade with any one of the major groups of the Compact, but as you're aware, under the Compact's own rulings, the trade of foodstuffs and pharmaceuticals are among the last to get officially sanctioned because of the ramifications. There will be no replacement cargo sent out. I have stopped any authorization on future shipments. John, I don't think even I can protect your ass on this one."

Thomas forced himself to remain within the lens' focus for the view screen, inwardly seething, outwardly calm, finding it impossible to argue with an ages' long interval between transmission and reception. He found himself blinking rapidly as if he could time the minutes flowing past. President Mitchell seemed to move in strobelike flashes, out of sync with what he was saying. When Mitchell's voice had halted, he sat quietly for another long moment.

"You don't need to protect my ass, Mr. President. It's been my job to convince the Compact that we are a developing, responsible, sentient race which deserves membership here and not just a stop on the galactic food chain. I have sat in my office, doing my job years before you even thought of running for your office. My ass, as you so elegantly put it, was on the line some thirty years ago. As far as replacing the shipment, I don't think you want to tell the Choyan that we don't want to deal with them any longer. We have finally established a foothold of value with them, and I won't let you stop that. If I have to, I'll go to the Compact to get authority. All I have to do is tell them that this drug is needed by the Choyan, that it's a restorative that will keep their pilots flying, and the Compact will crack you open like an egg. But I think," and Thomas leaned forward, lowering his voice a little, "you won't want that, because we'll lose whatever advantage we have now. The Choyan predicament will become public, and they're a very private people, Mitchell. Very private. What I have begun between us is a bond which will prove absolutely invaluable to us in the coming years, and I won't let you ruin that."

In the next lapse, Thomas could see Mitchell listening closely, and, at the same time, noticed his attention diverted off-screen. There, Thomas realized, must sit the head of the EC, or someone of like stature.

Mitchell finally replied, "Am I to understand that the Choyan have asked you for utmost confidentiality in this matter?"

"Yes."

An incredibly long wait for his one word answer. Then, Mitchell put his shoulders to the back of his antique, bullet-proof chair. "In making that request, the Choyan have assumed full responsibility for the consequences of this commerce. Under those conditions, providing we will be allowed to conduct field surveys and tests in the future to protect our own interests, we will allow you to continue to conduct business." Mitchell scratched an eyebrow. "Don't make us pimps, Thomas."

"I won't, sir." Thomas waited, out of courtesy, but he knew the president's last words had been both a warning and a signoff.

Mitchell's request had been pointed toward the future. From where Thomas sat, it was already too late.

* * * *

Panshinea woke just after dawn, his head aching, his dreams fading so quickly that he was not even sure if he had had any. His limbs responded woodenly as he got out of bed and he stood unsteadily, gathering strength to keep his balance. His tongue felt dry and heavy and he cleared his throat several times. Too much wine, he thought, though he had a head for wine and the fruits of the vine did not affect Choyan as it did many of the races of the galaxies. Still, there was no denying he throbbed and suffered, the sensation a most unpleasant one.

Too much Imperial Gold, he thought, and before the thought was spent, he knew he was wrong.

He stumbled out of the bedroom, to the communications console in the corner of the suite's living room. He kicked aside the small, wooden-framed ottoman irritably as he banged a shin on its corner. It skidded away from its companion chair and table and he skirted it a second time, weaving toward the console.

Gathon had the day's agenda already posted. Panshinea looked at it in despair. As full as he had been, he was that empty now, and as he eyed the meetings and negotiations awaiting him, fear pulsed through him. How could he face them, face them down, without those instincts and intuitions which would give him the key to his opponents, to the compromises they would accept and the ones they would not— which gave him the foresight to know the future to which Cho should be guided. How could he function? He had nothing on which to draw. It had seeped out of him in the darkest hours of the night, and he had not even felt it go.

He could cancel the majority of his appointments, postponing them for another day or two. But there were meetings here which had already been postponed past prudence, and he knew he must meet those obligations. One or two of those, he might be able to bluff out—after all, this was his career. There were things ingrained in him down to the very bone which even the loss of *bahdur* ought not to be able to negate.

Even as Pan leaned over the console, looking at the display of the agenda, he felt as though he were disconnected, unable to stand because he was nothing more than a shell of himself, and that shell had begun to collapse, to implode, from outside gravity and pressure.

He took a step back from the console and half-fell, half-sat, on the edge of his divan. His head suffered another lingering throb as he shouted for Gathon. The com came on at the sounds of his voices, and after a moment, he heard the blurred response.

"Attend me."

He heard no affirmative or denial as the com went quiet. It would be a few moments. Gathon had his private apartments several levels below and at this time of day, though the minister would normally be up and around, Pan did not doubt the elder Choya was probably napping late. Pan thrust himself to his feet and got himself cleaned and dressed, feeling as wobbly as a newborn, before a soft knock issued on the door to his suite. Gathon came in without further preamble.

"Sire. Is there a problem?"

Panshinea finished the lacings on the cuff of his shirt before looking up. He had braced one hip against the back of the divan to keep himself steady although the shower had refreshed him somewhat. He cleared his throat. "I've altered the agenda, you will want to go over it." He cast a look out his window. It was still so early the sky had barely lightened. Perhaps it would be a dull day throughout, as dull and leaden as he felt. "And I want you to find me another pair."

Gathon had paused by the desk console, his attention caught by the deletions on the appointment display, and he barely looked up. "Pair?"

"I'm spent already, I've done nothing! Go down to the tech schools in the Western quarter, you should find a handful or two of youths readying for classes. Coax them back with you."

"Panshinea," Gathon protested, scandalized. "It's impossible. What you ask is risky enough at night, but in broad daylight—"

"I don't ask. I order. I demand! I can't function like this."

Gathon drew himself up, all brittle strength and indignity, his yellowing dark hair combed hastily back from his forehead, his eyes watery from too little sleep. "I can't do this, Pan. You'll have to make do for today. I'll handle the cancellations—" He put his hand out to further adjust the schedule, and Pan grabbed him by the wrist, halting his movement in midair.

"There are some meetings I must take today, or they will sue for tacit agreement, citing the many cancellations. I won't be talked about, Gathon, as finished. I am not done, not yet." Pan flung the other's arm aside.

Gathon winced slightly. He put his chin out. "What do you wish me to do, that I am able to do?"

"You refuse to procure for me?"

"Under these circumstances, yes." Gathon looked as if he might shatter under Panshinea's glare, but he would not bend.

Pan's mouth had stayed dry, now it felt as if his lips were

cracking. The momentary flare of strength had gone, leaving him feeling weaker than ever. He softened his voices. "Gathon, I can't do this without you."

"I am afraid, sire, that you will have to. If you will ignore my advice and counsel, all I can do is stand aside."

"I don't want you to stand aside! I need you with me. I need to . . ." Pan swung around. "Cho takes all I have. There has to be a way—"

Gathon said nothing, his eyes wary as he watched.

"Don't stare at me so." Panshinea found a chair and perched on it, rather than fall to the floor in front of the minister. "What would you have me do?"

"I would have you straighten your jacket, put on your boots, go downstairs and get a breakfast down your gullet, then go to the throne room and take your appointments. Do you think they're thinking of you, Pan? No, by God-in-all, they're standing down there in the waiting room, after a body search, knees knocking, wondering if their story is good enough, their evidence compelling enough, wondering about *themselves*. It's the way of the world, Emperor. We're all egocentric."

"And not one of them wonders about me."

"Perhaps one or two, but you are more than *bahdur*, we all are. Use your mind, your training, your vast experience. This is your throne. Assert yourself."

Every word drummed hollowly somewhere inside of him. Pan rubbed his brow. "Is that what you would do?"

There was a moment's pause. Gathon answered slowly, "I don't know what I would do. I thank God I don't have to."

Even breakfast sounded like a challenge Panshinea did not wish to face. There would be his staff, reports from the guard, other informal meetings that were not on the agenda, and he would have to handle them all. His stomach, however, rumbled and clenched slightly, reminding him that his body had needs he would do well to meet. He looked up and saw the bureau against the farthest wall of his suite, a drawer slightly ajar.

He remembered the boost.

He licked his chapped mouth, remembering the gritty taste of it in his wine. Even as he spoke, the intensity of his attention drew Gathon's stare to the far end of the room, to the drawer. "Perhaps all this is for nothing, Gathon. Perhaps I have an answer." He got up, bounded to the drawer, and pulled out the container Qativar had left.

"Pan, don't."

He pulled a clean wineglass out of its rack and tapped a packet into the bottom of it. "We have all the evidence that this is the restorative the House of Tezar says it is."

"We have evidence that it is addictive enough to wreck a city, a civilization! Where has your mind been the past weeks? Palaton taunts you from boost dens, daring you to act, to help your people, to outlaw boost— Pan, you cannot do this."

Pan's anger, of which he never seemed emptied, blazed. "Palaton is a bug which, once he stops scampering around long enough, I will squash."

"Palaton is *right*."

Gathon stood next to him, reaching for the ever-present decanter of Imperial Gold even as Pan grabbed for it. Their hands collided and Panshinea reacted with the fury that had been building out of his empty center. The back of his hand cracked across Gathon's face.

The elder flew back as if hit by a cannonball. Going down, the divan's ottoman acted as if it might stop the fall, carved legs meeting the back of Gathon's head with a sickening smack.

The room went deadly quiet.

Panshinea did not move for a long moment. When he did, it was to pour the wine into the goblet, swirl it around, and drain it, then pour again to catch the dregs of the powder which had not dissolved. He set the glass down and crossed to Gathon, who had not stirred.

There was very little blood, as if his aged and wiry body could not have spared anything. No breath. No blush of life or anger or betrayal in his face except for the bruise where Pan had hit him. The eyes stared, wide and sightless, at him.

Panshinea lifted the body off the small ottoman. Its wooden frame had sharp corners, had nicked his shins more than once, the cushioned center the only thing soft or comforting about it . . . and that cushioned center was now soaked with blood.

Choyan were dreadfully hard to kill by hitting them on the head. The horn crown which protected their brow and their

dual brainpan ran down the back of their skull. Gathon's had
grown thin and brittle with his advanced age. It had done
nothing to protect him from this blow. Pan couldn't have
killed him more surely if he'd picked up the furniture and
purposely caved his head in. He sucked in his breath and laid
Gathon gently on the floor.

He was alone now.

The warmth of the wine began to course through his stomach and his feeling. He ought to have a tear or two for
Gathon. He ought to be able to find that.

Nothing answered him.

Finally, he walked away, backward, until he reached the
bureau, one hip bumping its solid surface. The wineglass
rocked. Pan reached out to retrieve it, and swallowed the liquid down automatically. When he could look away from the
stillness that had been Gathon, he saw the empty container.

He ought to do something about that. He would need more
boost until he could find someone he could trust to help him
as he'd trusted Jorana, and Gathon.

The com came on, startling him.

"Sire, Qativar is here, requesting a moment of your time
before official audiences start. He does not have an
appointment—"

"Allow him up. I'll see him privately." Panshinea began to
burn with power, felt the confidence start to surge through his
veins. There was a fated convenience to this visit. He would
use it. Gathon was right in that he held it in his power to outlaw boost. He had the House of Tezar in the palm of his hand.
Of course, a secondary market would spring up; that was inevitable if he banned the drug, but if Vihtirne and Qativar
wished to build a legitimate House, they would need a solid
foundation.

They would be wise to curry his favor.

He had them just where he wanted them.

Chapter 30

A thump jolted Jorana out of her cold-laced sleep. She sat up, blinking her eyes in the dim surroundings of the storeroom, saw the door shut like a beacon closing down, and realized it had been open. She cursed herself for sleep-dulled reflexes, knowing she had just missed an opportunity to escape. Her eyes adjusted to the minimal light and saw a rolled-up rug settling not far from her makeshift bed. She recognized the color and weave. It had been one of many area rugs in Panshinea's private suite. With dismay she saw a black dampness seeping from it, darker than the other shadows pooling in the room.

Worse, though, was the aura of death which rose from it like a fog. Hesitantly, Jorana crawled over on her hands and knees and peeled back a corner of the rug. She sat back with a stifled cry, as both the sight and the feel of a painful, shocking, unexpected death hit her.

"Gathon. Poor Gathon. Who did this to you?" A warm river of feeling cascaded down her face. Jorana scrubbed the tears away awkwardly. She cried too easily now, flooded with hormones she was too often at odds with. He did not need her tears now. It was too late for him.

Had it been Qativar who'd killed him? Why, when Gathon could have been removed so many other ways?

She knew she was dealing with ambitious Choyan, ruthless and driven, but this— No. Even as she thought it, she knew she was wrong. Gathon would never have left his post voluntarily. The throne of Cho had been his life, though few not intimate with the workings of the palace would have targeted him in order to usurp that throne. His death could not have been purposeful.

No. Not unless Qativar had gone to get Panshinea and dealt

with Gathon instead. This rug was from Pan's quarters, after all. Hesitantly she ran her palm over Gathon's face, not touching the cooling skin, but attempting to read the aura more closely. The bruising along the jawline had not been enough to have killed him, but had driven him back, perhaps into another blow or a fall. She had seen enough postmortem wounds to recognize the bleeding pattern of the contusion. Her hand skimmed the surface of his face.

Jorana touched another's signature and snatched her fingers back, folding her hand up quickly, denying what she had felt, jolted into her consciousness. She would not have believed it if she had been told by Gathon himself.

Her training, to protect the throne at all costs, rose in her now. She could disperse the signature aura, but doubted it was necessary. Weak, it was already thinning, and even the most competent hound would have difficulty recognizing it an hour from now. Jorana worried at a tooth, then moved Gathon's face ever so gently to look at his damp and matted hair.

The deathblow had come from the rear, where the rug was most sodden, though bleeding had long since stopped, when the heart itself had stopped. She did not need more than a probing touch or two to identify bone fragments shifting, the dome crushed. She flipped the rug back into place, hiding her old friend's face.

She looked at the locked door, and crept back to the cushioned bedding where she had fashioned a nest of sorts, warmth of a kind, on the hard floor. She had thought perhaps they'd let her live; now she knew better. She would be hostage to a purpose, but when that purpose was gone, she would be disposed of, just as Qativar had decided to dispose of another of Panshinea's kills. Her life would be of no more value to anybody and, like Gathon's body, perhaps more valuable as a corpse.

She wondered if Panshinea knew of the destructive spiral he'd begun, and how far into it he'd fallen . . . and where the bottom was likely to be. He must have plunged farther than she thought, to have been so careless as to have left Gathon's body where Qativar might find it. As for Qativar's plans for herself and the emperor, she had no illusions. Perhaps they'd die together, but she realized that she was little more than a

. pawn in his ultimate destruction and that she would be used where Qativar needed her the most.

She tucked a corner of a blanket under her chin to stave off the chill which crept inexorably toward her, spread by the cooling body.

Poor Gathon. Poor her.

"You did *what?*" Vihtirne said, points of color high on her face. It was the first real color he'd seen appear on it.

"Stowed Gathon's body down below with Jorana, but we'll have to move him soon, get him into cryo as soon as possible. I want that body saved. Pan thinks—" and Qativar paused dramatically, "he actually thinks that this puts us in collusion with him. He threatened to have boost outlawed, to have the House of Tezars shut down, as if he still had enough power to do such a thing." Qativar put a finger to his mouth, smiling. "He discounts us—"

"And Congress," Vihtirne said coolly.

"Not to mention Congress." He paced the rooms which had been turned into their offices, skirting consoles and readouts, reversing direction before the storage closets and filing cabinets, their racks empty of the diskettes which would be laid to rest there.

"Someone will miss Gathon soon."

"Pan plans to have him be sick in his rooms for a few days, then, like Jorana, gone, abandoning his emperor. His disappearance will cause a great deal of public speculation, but there will be no real proof by then of any wrongdoing. No one would suspect Panshinea of killing Gathon. The old Choya has been his minister and father figure for decades. If anyone believes the defection story, it simply weakens Pan that much more for us to take down. As for the boost . . ." He mused, half-aware of her.

"We have a problem there."

Now Vihtirne had Qativar's full attention. "That cargo jettisoned in Chaos happened to have been our shipment. Thomas has sent word that he's pressing production but there will be a delay. We don't have adequate supplies, Q, to enslave the world."

He ignored her ironic tone. "But he does expect to make shipment."

"Shortly. It's to our advantage to synthesize this as soon as possible. Our labs are having little success with identifying it as yet. Perhaps we could persuade Ambassador Thomas to be a little more cooperative."

Qativar answered, "I haven't the time. Use your charms on him, Vih. Remind him that we know he has Rand and that hiding a criminal from trial and prosecution is a Compact offense."

"He won't like that."

"I don't care if he likes it or not! He's a drug runner in Compact eyes if they find out what he's doing here. I'll get what I want from him, when I want it from him, or he will regret it."

Vihtirne smiled briefly. "Perhaps you had better explain that to him."

Qativar paused, composing himself. He ran a hand over his brow, brushing his thick hair back into place. He looked at her. "Is this something you think you cannot handle?"

"Why, no, but—"

"Then I suggest you handle it. I will be busy with other affairs. I have to cover half a continent this morning. Leave our guests alone, I'll have arrangements made for both of them shortly."

He took some small satisfaction in her look of surprise as he left.

* * * *

Palaton woke on cold, damp ground, his mind still fogged with dreams that he had had which were not dreams, but insistent sendings from the Prophet. She hounded him now on a nightly basis and he continued to resist though he did not know how much longer he could do so, if it only meant a full night's sleep.

Rufeen leaned over him, a mug in her hand. Its steam smelled familiar and inviting. She pushed it into his hand. "You looked like you could use a cup."

"Thanks." He struggled to sit up, *bren* to his lips and washing down his throat with a bitter, scalding welcome. "How's Hathord?"

"Up and about. We let you sleep in. You were thrashing around."

"Thanks. I needed the rest." Which he did not get, but would not admit to Rufeen. Palaton stretched. The cloud cover overhead looked thicker and denser toward Charolon, but hung thick enough even here to disguise their movements. He would have been disappointed in them if they had let him sleep the morning away. He tossed down his drink and stood, feeling its flavor infuse him with well-being.

They had decided to hit the depot in the early morning. Night would have been more favorable if they had had weapons, been sound, and had time to scope the place out, but they had not. Therefore, the gray light of dawn seemed preferable for an attack that would require coordination and wit.

Hat strolled into view, his jacket wet and nearly devoid of bloodstains, a bag full of fresh greens in his hand. "Breakfast," he announced as he shrugged out of his jacket, laying it over a rock for whatever drying it could do.

"Make it quickly."

"A simmering would be nice, but your wish is my command." Hat stooped over a pot of boiling water and dropped in the newly washed vegetables. "We're at the leading edge of another storm. It should be overcast enough for your liking before we're done eating."

"Good." Palaton eyed the overhead sky. "We're due for a break."

That wish, too, seemed to be at his command. The depot was not carrying personnel. Rufeen had a tricky moment at the gate, but then they were in. One hangar held a four-seat skimmer, reminiscent of a flight school's trainer craft. There was no runway, but that did not stop the three *tezars*. A long flat meadow or wind-cut plateau would do just as well. They were in the air, cruising in under the network of security any Choyan city held, long before the skim craft would be missed.

Palaton let Rufeen pilot. Hat was still a little sore around the flank and as for himself, he was too uneasy at the stick. His restlessness would have translated itself as the light craft rode the winds and thermal ridges of the countryside. This was just such a plane as Traskar had flown, and thinking of it worried Palaton.

He did not know how Traskar had died. He wished that he did, for then the burden of the Choya's death would not gnaw at him. He knew now that the bitter tang to the *bahdur* which had bled so furiously out of the disabled pilot was the taste of boost, that Traskar had not trusted his own abilities. Whether his attempt to cauterize the flood of power had saved Traskar, who then gave his life to shield Palaton he would never know. Had he been successful? Had Traskar died because it had been his choice, or because the power bleed had brought him down, or because the boost had sent him into convulsions as it had the Blue Ridge cadet? There were no answers to his questions, and riding in the skimmer now only made him that much more aware of it.

He missed Rand, more than he liked to admit, and likened himself to Traskar. Rand was his missing arm, his shield arm, that which made him complete. When he used the *bahdur* they had shared, he fought the feeling that he, too, was bleeding to death, that the soulfire roared out of him like a flash flood seeking . . . Rand? On his good days, he thought perhaps it was seeking. On his bad days, he thought only that it was leaving, burning out, and he would face that ultimate day all *tezars* faced and feared.

"Deep thoughts," said Rufeen, looking back over her shoulder at him.

"How do you know?"

"You've been quiet all morning. When I missed catching that last thermal and we dropped twenty feet, you didn't twitch."

He hadn't even felt it. Palaton shook himself and moved into the front seat, next to Rufeen. Hat pulled himself in tightly to let Palaton pass, then stretched back out with a noise that was more snore than sigh.

"How much farther?"

Rufeen put a thumb down. Palaton looked out the cockpit window at the patchwork countryside. He could see the grazing samdrens, their spotted coats like shadowy clouds below. They were over the dairylands.

"Find a place to put it down."

"And hike for two days? I thought I'd wait for signs of civilization first."

They traded looks. Palaton shrugged. "If you can stay off the nets."

"Aye, sir," she responded.

He sat back in the copilot's seat and watched their shadow race along the ground below them. They had outrun the storm's edge hours ago, and the sun gave them the outlines of a bird skimming the earth. After a marked length of time, the instrument panel began to respond, and he could see a township on the horizon.

"Rufeen," he warned, but she'd already reacted, pulling the skimmer about and under the security network, so low to the ground he worried about sudden hillocks and too tall trees. It was from a pilot's instinct—he wouldn't have been worried if he'd been at the controls. He made a poor passenger, he reflected. Their instrumentation told them what they needed to know, locating a center of unusual activity and another landing strip where there shouldn't have been one. It also held a huge cradle berth, and that had to be a launch for a shuttle.

She brought them down in another meadow, taxiing to the edge of a grove where even overhead surveillance would have trouble spotting them. When they got out, Rufeen looked the craft over.

"Wish I had a cover."

A screen would have been convenient, but they hadn't had time to procure one. Palaton said, "By the time they know to look, we won't be here."

Hat had pulled their jet sleds out of the craft's slim belly. "Fuel cells are still holding a good charge," he announced. He fired them up and left them idling while Palaton told them what he expected of them.

Rufeen listened gravely, but wordlessly. Action suited her methodology. It was Hat he expected to protest, but although his friend stood, chin down and listening, he did not say a word. When they had made their plan and agreed on it, they each claimed their jet sled and made themselves comfortable. It was then Hat spoke.

"For Blue Ridge," he said.

"For Blue Ridge," they echoed.

The outbuildings of the manufacturing center were old, well-maintained but not extraordinary. If the need to produce more lactose powder to cut boost had pumped new life into the facility, it was not readily apparent. The outlying security fences relied on sonics, more for animals than Choyan, and they got through it with minimum discomfort. Once in the lee of the outbuildings, they stowed their jet sleds and circled the perimeter of the main labs.

Rufeen gave a nod to the berth, across the quad but fairly visible from where they stood. "They're preparing for incoming."

"This is no port," Palaton argued, thinking of the need for clearance.

"None needed if it's from one of the bay stations or Galern."

The bay stations in permanent orbit were for repairs of the deep space cruisers, weather monitoring, and early warning. But as for Galern . . . Palaton knew that the House of Sky had extensive mining rights on the outer moon. He did not answer Rufeen and from the grim look on her face, he knew that she thought as he did. The mining venture would successfully hide any smuggling unless investigation were called for. Even then, it was probable Vihtirne had a smoke screen set up that would make tracing the off-world pipeline difficult.

"We need to take out the berth, if nothing else."

They eyed the concrete cradle. Not only did they have an extensive amount of open space to cross to get to it, but its configuration alone made the operation formidable.

Hat offered, "I have a grenade."

"You have a what?"

He blinked at Palaton. "A grenade. I bought one last week."

"Along with tubers and greens, I suppose," remarked Rufeen dryly.

"It doesn't matter. Placed properly . . ." Palaton leaned around the corner of the building, taking in the layout of the berthing cradle. He put his hand out. "Give it to me."

Hat hesitated. "You know how to activate it?"

Rufeen frowned and opened her mouth, but Palaton interrupted her gently, saying, "I was a combat pilot, Hat. Although I prefer strafing, I have been known to lob a grenade or two under duress." Actually, truth be told, he preferred to stay in orbit and drop war planes out of the cargo hatch of a mother ship, but he could handle what he'd told Hat he could.

Hat took a carefully wrapped bundle out of his knapsack and passed it over.

"Holy mother," said Rufeen as Palaton unwrapped it. "You've been carrying that around?"

Hat looked innocently at her. "I was told it was perfectly safe until activated."

Safe was a relative term, but since Rufeen looked shocked practically wordless, Palaton decided not to argue the matter with Hat. He had wondered whether the grenade would be powerful enough if placed strategically. Now he merely wondered if he'd have time enough to get out of the way before it blew. He looked at the timer. "Actually, Hat, this is more of a bomb with a fairly unsophisticated timing device. You're lucky you didn't blow our heads off carrying it around."

Hat's look of innocence became distressed. "I didn't know—"

"That's the trouble with picking something off the street," Rufeen said. "You never know where it's been. Give it here, Boss, and I'll be back in a nanosecond."

"No. I want the two of you here and there," he pointed, "to cover me."

Her good-natured face froze. "I think you're missing the point. I'm placing that."

"No."

"I'm expendable. You're not."

"This is my flight. You're along for the ride."

They stood toe-to-toe. "This," Rufeen drawled, "is for all of Cho. Do you think I'd risk my worthless hide just because you wanted to get even with Pan?"

A thick arm moved like a wedge between them. "It's my bomb. I'll do what I want to with it."

They both looked down at him, his Earthan height less than theirs. "You're wounded," Palaton noted.

"And you haven't a clue about the timer," Rufeen added.

Hat took a step back. "All right, then. I'm with Rufeen. She should go."

"This is not up for discussion. But if it is, I'd say I should go because I've got the bomb in hand."

Rufeen looked down as his fingers wrapped white-knuckle tight around the oblong object. She met his eyes. "Okay. We stand around much longer, and we'll draw attention." She elbowed Hat. "You stay here, I'll take up the angle over there. And, Palaton—"

"Ummm?"

"You better be able to run a hell of a lot faster than you look like you can." With that parting shot, she motivated her muscular form across the quad to take up her position.

Palaton said quietly to Hat, "If anything happens, I want you to get out. Understand?"

"But—"

"No buts. You have the capability to survive all this, better than the two of us. You're valuable to Cho's future. You're a teacher, a maestro. You remember that. And see if you can help Rindalan and Jorana if they should ever need it."

Hat swallowed tightly. "All right."

"I'm going to place the bomb, but I'm also going to start a distraction when I enter staging. They'll be boiling out of there like ants out of a hill, if they have any kind of staff there at all. Keep them pinned down. I'll be climbing."

"All right," Hat said again.

"See you in a few minutes." Palaton patted him gently on the shoulder and began to make his way across the quad.

He did not have a distraction in mind, but the walk would take him six or seven minutes, even without being circumspect. He should have something figured out by the time he reached the staging area of the berth.

There had been activity aplenty on the quad earlier. He could read mixed auras, nearly faded, nothing indentifiable or remarkable, crisscrossing the area. There were transports parked at the airstrip's edge. He wondered if he were catching Trevon the Black on a busy distribution day. So much the better. He planned to make his visit as inconvenient as possible.

The massive staging doors were open. He could hear muted voices beyond and knew that the elusive work force was busy inside, perhaps loading or unloading cargo bins. He paused inside the hangar doors, gauged his quickest approach to the cradle, and decided what he would have to do.

He threw a flame, a torch of blue heat, his signature, as big as a Choya standing on the shoulder of another, to the far wall of the hangar and let it burn. As the *bahdur* left him to fill the illusion, he made it hot, hot enough to set off any fire sensors in the building—which any decent berthing would definitely have, in case of fuel spill or bad ignition or any one of a dozen other problems he could think of.

He moved in the opposite direction, toward the cradle structure, as alarms went off almost instantaneously. His analogy to Hat had been correct. Like a churned-up hill of insects, workers began pouring out of the warehouse beyond staging, through and out of the building. No notice was taken of him. He made it up into the berth itself, climbing the armature, and toward the most vulnerable part of the placement equipment for the shuttle's cradle.

He placed the bomb, checking the timer setting. Unsophisticated had not been correct. Downright primitive. Analog numbers began to flash as soon as he activated it. Palaton slid, not climbed, his way down the concrete arch. He hit the ground running, shouting, "Fire!" along with the other workers who had decided to evacuate the building rather than put out the unquenchable flame.

He was a stride outside, when the remarkable tones of voices he knew well hit him. "Deactivate the sprinkler system! The bins are waterproof. Quit running you fools! That's no fire, that's a sending!"

Palaton turned despite his instincts. He came back a stride and halted on the threshold, his tall form parting the sea of fleeing workers, and looked to see if he had indeed recognized the speaker.

Their gazes met across staging. He was dressed in black, black with a silver piping, his conceit always in clothes, his jaw tight with contempt for the Flame facing him. No doubt they had called him Trevon the Black because of his suits.

Qativar fairly shook with rage. "Get him!"

Palaton smiled, then turned and ran with the tide of exodus. Halfway across the quad, the ground to the left of him exploded with enforcer fire. A worker stumbled with a howling cry and rolled. Palaton sprinted past him and angled toward Hat as Rufeen fired back. Her shot, however, intentionally went wide of its mark.

Like an echo of her shot that grew and grew until it swallowed the world immediately around it, the bomb blew. The force of the blast lifted Palaton off his feet. He could feel the heat, the intensity, his horn crown thundering with the sound of it as it flung his body carelessly across the open ground.

He thudded into Hat who grunted and fell back under him. For a moment they were tangled and then Palaton got up on one knee. He could see Qativar stagger back to his feet, away from staging and the berth, its face all black, billowing smoke and orange flame, debris still floating to earth about Qativar in smoldering meteorites. No shuttle would be received or launched from here in quite a while. Palaton unholstered his enforcer and put a discouraging beam into the staging doorway, adding to the confusion.

Qativar let out a hop of frustration and irritation, shouting, "Get in there and save the cargo!" He grabbed at the stunned workers near him, hauling them to their feet, shoving them back into the smoke. "Get in there! Get those bins out the back!" He turned, still howling with anger, shooting wildly across the quad.

Rufeen, seeing Palaton in the clear, had started back to join them. It caught her. She went down, arms flailing, enforcer falling from her limp hand.

Palaton watched her get back to her feet and run, but not toward them. Away from them, decoying, determined not to draw fire to them.

Hat started to bolt after her. Palaton caught him and held him tightly.

"Where's she going?"

"Away from us."

Hunched and cramped over in pain, she wove across the quad. Qativar fired twice more. The first shot clipped the ground at her booted feet. The second sheared off one of his own men, hitting her as well. One screamed, the other did not, before the momentum of their fall took them out of range.

Palaton wrestled Hat around the corner. "Go get the sleds!"

"Rufi—"

"I'll get Rufeen. You get the sleds." Patiently, as he would to a child, to Hathord who'd never been in combat, even though he was a *tezar.* "Now."

He did not wait to see if Hat comprehended. There was no way he was going to leave Rufeen for Qativar's untender mercies. Angling around the building, away from the quad, he ran, sore and bruised, as he'd run from the bomb blast. Halfway around the building, Palaton realized he still gripped his weapon in his hand.

The outbuilding must have been a storage shed. It was mercifully compact. He reached its lee side, its shadowed edge, breathing hard, and saw Rufeen's sprawled form. His pulse thundered in his neck, he knew his body was pumping *bahdur* like it was pumping adrenaline. He built an illusion of his friend, blood and all, and left it in the sunlight for Qativar to see. Then he went to her and managed to get his shoulder under her flank, pulling her up and over in a lift.

She moaned. "Don't. Be. Stupid."

"Save your breath." Palaton took a step, felt his knees wobble. He took a deep breath and filled his body with power, felt himself shimmer and burn with it. If anyone looked, they would see a blue flame striding with its burden.

He carried her the length of the building and then cut across to where they had secreted the transports. Every step was deliberate, every movement dampened by the warm blood trickling onto him. The shallow breath from her face tickled his temple, her moans nearly inaudible. She lived and died with every heartbeat, every step, he took.

Hat met them. His face went dead white as Palaton bent over and laid Rufeen upon a sled. The Earthan had hitched two together, figuring that Rufeen would be disabled. He bit his lip, hissing with shock. He looked up at Palaton.

"I don't know," Palaton answered his silent query.

"Where do we go?" Hat shuddered, put a hand to his shoulder, and brought his palm away bloody. He looked at it in surprise.

Then Palaton saw the two bodies slumped against the side of the building.

"They were here," Hat said. "I had to do something." He put a hand on his shoulder again, wincing in pain.

The *bahdur* left Palaton so suddenly it was as if everything in the world had come to a chill and crashing halt. He took a deep, quavering breath.

Rufeen was dying. Hat had been shot a second time. He'd just expended a lifetime's worth of power. He had no choice. He had to go where he knew they would be cared for, where they would be welcome and hidden. Sled to skimmer. They might make it in time.

He helped Hat onto a sled and strapped him in. "South," he answered. "To Bayalak."

"The Prophet?"

Palaton did not answer again as he mounted the jet sled and roared it into motion. Hat leaned against the steering wheel, following.

If she was any kind of prophet at all, she would know they were coming and be ready.

Chapter 31

Qativar climbed into the control tower by the emergency stairs, the main stairwell having been cracked open like an eggshell by the blast. The rest of the tower seemed operative as he pulled himself into instrumentation.

The Choya'i taking readings turned a pale face to him. "Sir?"

"Find them!" He stabbed a hand at the readings from her console.

"Who, sir?" Her head swiveled back and forth on her neck as she scanned the board, her hands moving uncertainly across.

"Pilots. They have to have an aircraft out there. They came in to sabotage us. I want them tracked!" Rage boiled through him.

She seized on his words. "I've had no incoming traffic since set-down yesterday—they must be in a skimmer." One hand went up to adjust her headset as she listened. The other hand danced over her panel now that she had some action to perform other than watching the base disintegrate into havoc around her.

"I don't care how you do it. I just want them found." His anger flowed out of him, a visible aura, but the controller, engrossed in her task, did not seem to notice.

Qativar looked out at what remained of the tower. This unit alone seemed intact. The berthing cradle and staging below smoldered in ruins, smashed open and laid bare. The shuttle had already been transported to its hangar, but it was useless without its launch. Crew scampered at the ground level, trying to put out the fire in the warehouses, but the main warehouse had gone up. Any cargo in there, binned or not, would be ruined. The last shipment from Galern had gone up in

smoke, and the last shipment from Thomas had been jettisoned in Chaos.

He only had what had already been pipelined into the various distribution centers.

He should have killed Palaton in the wreckage of Blue
Ridge when he'd had the chance, but Vihtirne had stayed his
hand. She had wanted the pilot to live with his humiliation
and defeat. She'd convinced Qativar that it was better than
death.

He should have killed him.

I'll kill him this time.

"Sir?" The controller looked up, the whites of her eyes
showing.

He had spoken aloud. Qativar shifted weight, to lean over
her shoulder. "What have you found?"

"I have a heat distortion one clic east—it could be a liftoff.
If it is, I won't find anything more. They're staying under the
net, too low for instrument reading. And they're gone."

"What do you mean gone?" His fist pounded the console.
"What do you mean you can't find them?"

"They're flying too low for the net to pick up readings."
The Choya'i's face, already pale, grayed with fear. He could
smell it on her, like a perfume. "It's risky, takes a lot of skill.
No one would do it unless it were absolutely necessary."

"And they had the skill to do it." He'd gotten one of them,
badly unless he missed his guess. But not Palaton. Not the
one he needed to demolish. Qativar straightened up, glaring
out the control tower windows as if he could see what her instruments could not read.

Vihtirne had talked him into making a grievous error. Now
he would have to expend time and cunning to correct it. He
dropped a hand on the controller's shoulder. She jumped, startled by the touch, and her breath quickened. "Keep looking.
Tell me if you track anything."

She gave a tremulous nod as he made his way back to the
emergency stairs. He had two choices now, two courses of action, and despite what Vihtirne might say to him this time, he
wouldn't be swayed. He had Jorana, and he had *ruhl*. He
would use both as ruthlessly as he had originally planned. Regardless of Vihtirne's objections, he would release the *ruhl* in
the water systems they had breached. The chaos, the panic,

the blame would fall on Panshinea. He, Qativar, would stand as a lone figure amid the havoc, the wreckage of all that they knew. Cho would turn to him for restoration. The world would be the way he longed for it, no longer subject to the erratic surges of *bahdur.* No one would have it, until he restored it, and then only for the length of time he allowed. It would be reliable as it had never been before, and it would no longer be allowed to stratify Choyan society.

He would do this, was doing it. Soulfire had not saved those he worked against, and could not save them now.

Jorana stared at the muzzle of the enforcer, calculating her chances, as Vihtirne faced her, and her aide struggled to move the rug-wrapped body of the dead minister. Although the storage room stayed winter chill, rigor mortis had set in, and the bundle was cumbersome. She could barely stand to watch the Choya struggle. The irony that Gathon's body would betray in his death all that he had worked to protect and uphold in his life left a harsh taste in her mouth. Asten finally got the stiffened rug over his shoulder and through the threshold. Vihtirne lingered a moment longer. She looked at Jorana.

"Whose child is it?"

"I have no intention of telling you."

Vihtirne gave a brittle smile. "Fool. That, in itself, tells me. Does Palaton know?"

"No." Jorana kept her gaze steady, her heartbeat rhythmic, wondering if Vihtirne's branch of the House of Sky were extremely empathic or not.

Vihtirne responded, "Perhaps." She tilted her head. "I could take it now, if I wanted, because of Nedar."

"Then do so." Jorana kept her chin up, letting the defiance gleam in her eyes.

"There are other purposes."

"Why are you doing this?"

"Again, fool. I had not thought of you as being so naive."

"You already had power as head of Sky. I cannot believe that Qativar's perversions would have anything to offer you." Jorana watched the enforcer.

"My House was useless." Vihtirne half-turned her face to the door, as if listening to Asten's progress with the body. "If Nedar had had half the ambition Qativar has, none of this would have come about. But he did not. All he cared for was the piloting, and bringing down Palaton. He should have been emperor! The throne was his for the taking. His weakness destroyed him."

"Qativar will destroy us all. You must know that."

"He is the means to the end."

Jorana shifted her weight. "Why don't you take the throne? We've had our share of Choya'i emperors."

A bitter shadow darkened Vihtirne's face. "I am too old now. If I had had the means, the confidence, when I was younger! But I didn't, and it all passed me by when I lost Nedar. All but Qativar. I had no choice but to take the opportunity he gave me."

"You think too little of yourself."

"As, perhaps, you do." Vihtirne stepped back swiftly, across the threshold of the imprisoning room. "I've made my choices, have my loyalties." The door began to seal, framing Vihtirne's face in a diamond for a brief moment. "We all make sacrifices."

Panshinea awoke a second time, a coppery taste in his mouth as though he had bitten his tongue in his sleep. If sleep it could be called, for though his body tired and ached, his mind had not found peace, thoughts racing endlessly about his dreams. The blankets of his bed twisted like cable, drenched with sweat. He disentangled himself and lay for a moment, assailed by crimson visions which could not be true. He got up, found himself fully dressed, and left the bedroom.

A rug was missing. He looked at the bare, tiled floor in some bewilderment. He'd dropped a wineglass on the floor, but it had not broken. It rolled about as his boot brushed it when he passed. Panshinea stooped to pick it up. For an uneasy moment, vertigo swayed him and his aura sense picked up violence and death. He stood, free hand palm down, reading the scene until his stomach sickened. He stood, fighting for balance.

The moment swept by him, unnerved and lost. Not enough sleep, too many dreams. He felt as if he had been searching for something taken out of his soul, ripped out and cast away. Listlessly, he dropped the glass onto the divan and went to the agenda, which had been left on display. Cancellations and deletions filled the screen as if an idiot had played here, decisions made senselessly.

He put in a call to Gathon's rooms. "Gathon! What is this mockery? Get up here as soon as you can."

His head swam again, and gooseflesh crawled across his arms and the back of his neck. Panshinea put a hand there and rubbed it reflectively. The touch of his fingers chilled him further. The taste in his mouth, he decided, had not been blood but the after dregs of boost. He recalled dropping the wineglass. Pan twirled about, the room swinging around him, none of it seemingly ground in reality, waiting.

Gathon did not answer the private line. He steadied himself and impatiently put out a call on the general palace lines. After long moments, Namen answered cautiously.

"Sire."

"Where is Gathon?"

"Sire, he—he resigned this morning. You passed his resignation along to me. He's gone."

"Gone?" Panshinea drew himself up beside the com, his fingers on the speaker button as if detached from him. His head spun and then throbbed.

"He left early this morning," the head of the guard repeated. "Can I be of any assistance?"

"No. I—" Pan looked across the room, images crowding his mind like a bizarre sending, of blood and murder. He closed his eyes and took his hand off the comline.

He could not have done what he remembered.

When he opened his eyes, he saw the bare tile where a rug normally lay facing him. There was a dissonance in the pattern of the other throw rugs. In the fireplace, ashes glowed where something had recently been burned. He did not remember lighting a fire, but the impression of Qativar throwing in a bloodstained ottoman and torching it filled his vision.

"No!" He scrubbed his hand over his face. "No."

Qativar rolling a rug tightly about a chill and shattered bundle.

No. He would never have turned to Qativar, never.

Pan put a hand out to the console to steady himself, thrust it wrist-deep in packets that rustled as he touched them. He turned to look down.

Boost.

Sparks of red-gold *bahdur* fire crackled throughout as he snatched his hand away. One or two of the packets clung to his hand, fastened there by the static energy of the soulfire. He shook them off, screaming.

The raw sound of his howling reached him, and Panshinea stood, desolate, his throat torn by his fear and grief. He bolted from his apartments and ran into the corridor, calling for Gathon, unable to believe. His voices echoed obscenely off the stone, broken and desperate, all trace of sanity gone.

* * * *

He brought the skimmer into Bayalak under full speed, winging over the swamps with a speed that boiled the water, bent the trees, sent lingering fogs swirling away. Rufeen had lapsed even from moaning, her face more pale than alabaster. Hat slouched against the fuselage wall near her, his eyes closed, his breathing harsh and shallow, but he moved from time to time, a most un-Hat-like curse issuing whenever he did.

Palaton looked for the security network over Bayalak, found it missing, and came in over the port city, the skimmer engines screaming as he unwound them, setting the plane down with brakes smoking, the light plane bouncing harshly—and then they were down. He popped the front canopy and threw himself out, catching himself feetfirst on the wing. He could swear he felt the metal skin's heat through his boot soles.

She was waiting. Conveyances pushed forward. She was on her feet, leaning on the arm of Father Chirek, the priest who had sent her unknowing into her Change. and had been at her side ever since. He brought her forward as med techs opened the side doors and clambered inside, shouting orders at one another.

The Prophet smiled. "It is enough," she said.

He clenched his teeth against warring emotions a moment, then looked at her, though she could not see him. "Do you know that?"

He had meant, do you *see* that.

Dorea's expression changed slightly and she gave a small

shrug. "It must be enough to have faith. I *see* very little, in the spectrum of all that has happened and will happen."

He jumped to the tarmac. "So help me God, I'll turn around and fly them out of here if you can't give me a straight answer."

Dorea reached out and touched him. "None of us has a surety on life, Palaton. None of us. But you've given her as good a chance as you could. Let that be enough."

Father Chirek added, "We've done what we can by being here, waiting."

They had, of course. Palaton looked toward the skimmer, watching the techs handing Hathord out the door and bringing a portable crèche in for Rufeen. He forced himself not to watch, knowing he could not help any more than he already had. To Chirek, he said, "The network's down."

"For you. It's already back up."

That meant that Chirek and his newly Changed were in total charge of the city now. Bayalak had metamorphosed into something they had all feared once, and now must embrace.

"No one knows."

"Not yet." Chirek made a mouth. He was a mousy Choya, common in every line of his body, dressed in modest colors as befit the clerk's position he'd held in the imperial palace.

The crèche rushed past, wheeled by med techs on the run, and disappeared into its conveyance. As Palaton blinked a suddenly misty view away, it surged forward and vanished across the tarmac. The second emergency vehicle followed. He caught a glimpse of Hat through the rear panel portal and raised a hand in salute. Just before it would have been impossible to see, Hat waved weakly back.

The Prophet turned her blind face to him, seeking him out. "You stand alone now."

"Not with you two here," he answered wryly.

"Good. It's time you realized that. We have a lot to talk about. Chirek."

He took her in charge again, leading the way back to the single conveyance waiting for them. As Palaton sat down, the tang of salt air reached him, accented sharply by the smell of the skimmer's engines. He sat back in the car.

"I wouldn't be here, if I hadn't been driven to it," he commented.

"We know that." Father Chirek took the wheel and steered them ably down the landing strip to the security gates.

"All that matters is that you are here." Dorea plucked at her blindfold, then dropped her hands into her lap, twisting her young and slender fingers. The light blue dress she wore looked like bird's wings. "I must talk to you about Rand."

It did not matter if she could see his face or not, he did not want to look at her. She wanted him to bring the manling back so that she could direct the *bahdur,* the Change, and Rand was no longer capable of that.

It was Palaton's power, and he knew he did not want to use it for that. He could not have, at that moment, even if he had wanted to, having spent it on saving Rufeen. But when it returned, and it would, he knew he did not believe in Changing the world the way she did. The way Father Chirek had sacrificed himself for. *Bahdur* belonged in those who had been trained for it, who could understand its dangers and its limitations. The God-blind had no concept of what would happen to them, of what they could do, and because of that, the Change was just as dangerous and insidious as boost.

The only good thing about boost, if there was one, was that it only aided those who had been ingrained with *bahdur* from birth, who had been guided and trained.

"I don't know where Rand is," Palaton said bitterly. "I don't dare move against Qativar openly as long as they have him."

"Qativar doesn't have Rand. He's on Sorrow," the Prophet told him. "And he's in deadly danger."

Chapter 32

Maeva was sleeping in the law library when the clerk of the librarian came to rouse her, disapproval wrinkling his already prunelike face.

"Attorney Polonia, you have a visitor waiting for you in the lobby."

She sat up at the table, dazed, her elbows sore from the books and printouts she'd been leaning on. Desktop screens blinked opalescence at her, the only light in a room that had dimmed into a downtime mode. She'd meant to sleep there, feeling it the only place safe enough, but she had not thought she'd actually escape into slumber. She cleared her throat and straightened her blouse.

"I'm sorry. What—what did you say?"

"You have a visitor in the outer lobby." The librarian's clerk stood shorter than she, lank brown hair thinly combed back behind his ears, and a bow tie bobbed up and down with his Adam's apple. "I believe it to be the Choyan ambassador."

"Rindalan?" She snatched her purse and stood up, the body armor pinched her tightly under one arm as she did so. "I'll be . . . I'll be right there."

The clerk sniffed. "He can wait."

"Don't touch anything," she ordered and bolted out of the private research niche.

She brushed past him, in a hurry for the restroom. Once inside, she laved and took care of her needs as quickly as possible, then straightened her clothes and her armor, trying to imagine how it was he had even found her. She'd left no word, no trace, of where she'd gone, hiding from even Thomas. The law library's research maze had seemed the only logical place to go.

Maeva looked into the bathroom mirror. Her eyes appeared

cloudy blue, red-rimmed with worry, and her hair seemed like lackluster straw. She'd aged in the past few weeks, but the character she'd hoped for in her face did not show, only faint lines of fatigue. She grimaced. So much for mirrors. She'd rather look at herself reflected in Rand's face, at what she saw in his eyes.

There she saw only beauty, and appreciation, and perhaps . . . perhaps a certain regard.

Maeva slung her purse and terminal pouch over her shoulder and made her way out of the lavatory, then downstairs several levels to the lobby. She could see Rindalan though he could not see her through the paneling, but then the tall, spindly Choya turned toward her unerringly.

She went through the door.

"Madame attorney."

"Ambassador." She reached out impulsively and took his wrist, drawing him to one side so he could sit on a bench.

"Is this area safe?"

"To talk? Yes. We're in legal. They take incredible precautions here."

"Good. I have a matter about which I need to speak with you." He inclined his head gravely. A sparse strand of chestnut hair fell loose from his massive horn crown. "I would like to claim attorney/client privilege."

"To do that, I'd have to—"

"Yes. I would like to employ you as my attorney."

Unheard of. Choyan did not need to contract the services of another species. This had to concern Rand. Perhaps he had finally found a way to free him. She swallowed. "I cannot take contract with you if it interferes with previous obligations." Warningly, in spite of the fact that the lobby should be secure against recording.

Rindalan looked at her, eyes large and warm. "I can assure you there will be no conflict."

"Tell me why you think you need an attorney."

"I am about to commit treason most grievous against the throne of my people."

Maeva rocked back on the bench. Rindalan looked at her gravely.

"Treason?" she stammered.

"Against my emperor. Does that pose a conflict with your other contracts?"

"N–no. But I have no familiarity with your civil laws—"

"It doesn't matter. If I am wrong and lose, my life is forfeit. If I am correct and win, I won't need an attorney." Rindalan gave her a tender smile. "Do we have a contract?"

His expression urged the answer out of her. "Yes." She fumbled with her back pouch, getting the terminal out, setting it on her lap and opening it up. "Let me register it. Just a basic representation contract, nothing fancy." She brought up the model contract, affixed her thumb, and asked the ambassador to do likewise.

Bemused, the ambassador took a few minutes to scan the screen before he depressed his print where indicated. He watched as Maeva sent the transmission and waited another second or two to make sure a clear sign came up, along with a registration number.

"Waiting for shock waves?"

She glanced up at Rindalan. "Well . . . I thought somebody might notice who you were." She closed her notebook, thinking that somebody somewhere might well notice later, when the day's entries were logged and reviewed.

"May we talk now?"

"May I suggest we move upstairs, to where I have a research room reserved? It's even more private and a little more comfortable." Not that she minded sitting on marble, but the lobby was chilly and her bottom had begun to feel like part of the stone.

"If I am allowed."

"As a client, you are. I can even request an interview room, if you wish. But those are recorded."

He inclined his head. "Not necessary. However, I would like you to know that time is of the essence."

Settled in the research room, she realized she thought of him as grandfatherly, his manner elegant, reserved, and yet teasing. His mane of hair even reminded her somewhat of her own grandfather, on the side of the family from which her name, Maeva, had come. Her other grandfather had been Italian, from Rhode Island, with a great nose and huge, expressive hands. Her own more delicate features and blonde coloring had come from the maternal side of the family.

He waved a hand over the disarray. "What, if I may ask, were you researching?"

"Habeas corpus," she answered, "mostly, although a lot of this is camouflage."

"Camouflage?"

"Disguise. I was hoping to find something to force Thomas to free Rand, but Thomas has him buried under protective custody, so I haven't been able to make an issue of it. And the rest . . ." Maeva felt her face warm a little in embarrassment. "I've been living and sleeping here. I wanted to make it look like I was busy."

Rindalan put his head back and began to laugh, a warm, hearty laugh. It was the kind of humor that spilled over and finally, she tucked her chin down and laughed, too, although she had been so desperately tired she hadn't thought any could be found in her.

"And now, if you could explain habeas corpus?"

"Oh. It simply means 'holding the body.' In other words, charge the prisoner and try him or free him. But Thomas has gotten around it this time by using the legal fiction of protective custody. Although," she mused, "it's not so much of a fiction."

"If by that you mean that he would be in considerable danger if wandering around, your ambassador is most correct. But that is why I am here. Madame Polonia—"

"Please," she interjected softly. "Call me Maeva."

"Maeva." Rindalan looked amenable at the interruption. "We have to free him as soon as possible."

"That's what I've been trying to do."

"I do not necessarily mean legally."

Maeva took a quick breath. "Ambassador—"

"If you would please. Call me Rindalan, or Rindy, if you like. That's what my friends call me."

"Rindalan. I realize our contract is mostly a screen, but what we're talking about is in direct conflict with my work for Thomas."

He waved about at the clutter a second time. "Yet you were already working on it."

"But not for you. For me. . . ." She paused. "And what does this have to do with a treasonous act?"

Rindalan frowned. The expression not only creased his brow heavily, it deepened his other wrinkles. "I received word this morning that Emperor Panshinea is roaming the halls of the palace in what can only be termed as a mentally depraved state. He is distraught, howling, disoriented, and he cannot be confined or sedated."

"Why not?"

"Because—" Rindalan stopped abruptly. "That is another matter. Trust me, he cannot. Neither can he be restored. Normally, in his lack of capacity, our minister would step in, but Gathon has either resigned or been removed. No sign of him can be found."

She was aware that the heir to the throne had been forced to abdicate, though his reported death had been in error. She knew Palaton was in hiding. "You've got no one running Cho."

"For the moment, yes."

"You're not thinking of putting Rand on the throne."

His face reflected abrupt horror. Then he rearranged his expression to something approximating neutrality. "No, Maeva, that would be unthinkable."

She'd already gathered that.

He shifted in the high-backed, most comfortable chair she could find for him. "Rand's return to Cho could accomplish two things: possible restoration of Panshinea, for reasons I cannot explain to you now, or convincing and enabling Palaton to take the throne; again, for reasons I cannot explain to you now."

"Attorney/client privilege only extends so far, eh."

He lifted a brow. "Even so."

"Thomas will never release Rand."

"So you communicated to me earlier, and I cannot request his release in official standing."

"So, then—"

"I need your help assisting in what your people euphemistically call a jailbreak."

Her chair shifted abruptly under her. Maeva caught herself on the table's edge. "Impossible."

"No, it's possible. To do it, I must exercise some abilities I have not used in many years, and I need your assistance."

"I don't see how I can possibly—" and she stopped, shaking her head. "We're talking the most secured levels of the embassy."

"Do you think, young one, that your embassy is the only one on Sorrow to have been built in such a way?" Rindalan smiled. "All of us here in the Compact are here, not because we love one another, but because we know that to continue hating one another and acting upon it will destroy us all. The enemy that imprisoned the race of Sorrow is the common enemy that bonded us. Trust is another matter altogether."

"We're talking solid rock!"

"Even so."

"What do you think you can do?"

"First, I would like you to tell me anything and everything you've observed about Rand since his imprisonment here. I will assume he was brought in under cryo and diplomatic pouch as my intelligence shows that is the only activity out of the ordinary in the last few months. I would like to know anything that has occurred in his waking hours."

She was not surprised that Thomas' actions had not gone unobserved. "He's only been awake off and on. The ambassador has him under reduction much of the time."

Rindalan nodded. "That would explain part of my experience. Anything else? Any . . . talents . . . you would consider unusual?"

She thought of Rand caught in the laser fencing, the wounds, and the remarkable healing after. She told the elder Choya of the incident, and he listened carefully, his head inclined, face grave, without interrupting. When she finished, he questioned her.

"A blue network of energy sparks and tracings, you say?"

"Yes. I thought it was the lasers, but I've never seen anything like it."

"Does he remember it?"

"No. And he doesn't seem to have any explanation for the healing either."

"Neither do I." Rindalan tilted his chair back a moment. When he brought it back to the ground, he said, "But I think I have some indication of what I'm looking for. I will have to proceed based on what we know. Can you access his cell any time you like?"

"So far. Thomas could unauthorize me, but he hasn't yet. He's been busy with some other projects, and I don't think he knows what I'm trying to do."

"Then we need to go now."

"Now?"

"Yes." The ambassador stood up. "I have a ground shuttle ready to lift off and once at the bay station, we can pick up any transport we need."

"Hijack a cruiser?"

He wrinkled his nose. "If necessary. Anything you need we can acquire later."

"I'm going with you?"

"Once this goes into motion, we cannot stop."

She stood, gathering her purse and her notepad. On second thought, she lowered her terminal to the library table. She took a deep breath. "Then I'm ready."

Standing in front of the cell, she was not so sure. Rindalan had gravely instructed her on what to say to Rand, making her pronounce a Choyan word again and again until he was satisfied she was saying it properly, then leaving her to make the journey alone. She did not understand why she had to think of Rindy as being with her, as imaging him standing there in the corridor next to her, but she knotted her brow tightly as she did so, waiting for Rand to leave the refresher and meet with her. On that, she'd been lucky. He was out of reduction and up for an exercise period.

She had no idea what the word she was to say to Rand meant, nor how Rindalan thought he could carry out a jail-break from outside the embassy. She had neither weapon nor plan to her name. Nothing but words . . . and a mental image. She frowned so tightly her head ached.

"You'll wrinkle," commented Rand softly.

She looked up. His hair was still slightly wet and slicked back from his face. He looked thinner and paler yet. He knew that she'd been able to meet with Rindalan, but not that GNask had accosted her, or that she'd eventually fled to the safety of the law library. For all he knew, their last meeting could have happened minutes ago, instead of days and days.

She massaged her forehead with her fingers. "Thanks. How are you feeling?"

"Well enough." His expression was strained, and she had the distinct feeling he was hiding something from her. She noticed he had the white noise generator. He placed it on the floor between them.

"We haven't much time," she told him. "I can't even explain to you why. Rindy says that it's urgent—"

"Rindy? You've seen him again? He's able to help?"

"I'm not sure help is the word for it. Please. You've got to listen."

His turquoise eyes mirrored her anxiety, but he closed his mouth firmly.

"Rindy says that it's urgent you believe what I'm going to tell you. He says you're exhibiting *bahdur*—"

"*What?*"

She repeated the word a second time: "*Bahdur*—God, I hope I said it right. You have *bahdur*, not Palaton's, but your own, and he's going to help you use it to escape. We can't get you out of here quickly any other way."

His mouth tightened. She could not tell whether he understood her or not. As Rindalan had instructed her, Maeva added, "Now, Rindy," and thought of him, a beam of thought, directed through the steel and stone, upward, toward the garden where he'd told her he would be waiting.

Her head ached, then her ears felt an unbearable pressure. Just before she thought she might explode, there was movement in the corridor, a sound like thunder booming, and Rindalan stood next to her. He shook off a faint dusting of blue motes.

He looked pleased. "I have not done that in a score of ages."

Maeva thought her heart would never start beating again. She stared aghast. "What?"

"Teleportation, my dear. A rare art, even among my people."

Rand protested, "Rindy, what are you doing? And in front of her?"

"It's all right, child. She's my attorney. We have privilege. She's got to keep her mouth shut." Rindalan flexed slightly. "She knows about *bahdur?*"

Rindalan's mouth twisted a little. "Not exactly. I taught her the word, but not the essence of it."

Rand looked about the cell as if searching for a scrap of sanity. When he looked at them again, it was with a face deeply saddened. "Get out of here while you can."

Rindy shook an age-knobbed finger at him. "We haven't time for arguments. I thought she explained that. It's belief we need. You have *bahdur,* and if you hadn't been so ingrained in self-pity since being locked up here, you'd have realized that on your own. But we have met in dreams, you and I, and I know what I know. What you shared with Palaton may have changed you, just as you are the I'falan—"

"How do you know?"

"Child," and Rindalan looked at him with infinite fondness. "I know as much about you as I possibly can."

Rand straightened. "All right. *Bahdur* does not necessarily mean teleportation."

Maeva felt as though everything were rushing past her. She fought to grasp it. "What is *bahdur?*"

Rand looked at her. "They're a psionic race, Maeva. In fact, their abilities are probably off the scale. It's how they navigate Chaos. It's what their entire society is built on, and the talent is called *bahdur.*" He squared off to Rindalan again. The laser fencing gleamed between them. "But there are different abilities with the talent, and just because you can teleport, doesn't mean I can."

"No. But you can augment me. I can get all three us out of here with a little help."

"Through solid rock."

Rindalan inclined his head.

Maeva said weakly, "That's how he got in."

Rand ignored her. "It's better than rotting here. What do I do?"

"Wait a minute—" Maeva began, but Rindalan grasped her hand.

"Sssh," he admonished. "And think only of my garden. Rand, you must think of our *bahdur,* two streams becoming one. Do not flow into me once you feel weakness, however. That would be going too far."

"I understand."

She wished she did. Maeva closed her eyes. *Oh, beam me up, Scotty,* she thought, and imagined the embassy garden.

Rand had wanted to protest, but when he saw Maeva hold onto Rindy's hand, as trusting and earnest as a child, he decided that he could not. There was something in what Rindy was hastily trying to convince him of—perhaps he had a remnant of power left in him, enough to aid in what might be his only chance to gain freedom. For that tiny hope alone, he would try.

"Think of me," Rindalan said softly to him, and as he did so, the Choya opened his mind to an image of a garden, nothing such as they had left behind in Charolon, but a small, spare unique area of its own. *Focus on that,* Rindy said to him, but there were no words. He could sense a blue stream bathing the other, cold and clear in power and purity. He reached out to join it.

There was a moment, an aching moment, when he could feel all of them mutating, lifting, changing, and he was with them. Then, like a flicker of vision where vision had gone blind, something distracted him. Something else called him. He mentally turned toward it, and was lost.

Darkness ripped. A chill like ice pierced him. He thought he heard Maeva's voiceless scream. His own heart stopped. They were gone and he was—

Imprisoned.

As in his dreams, many times over, he found himself embedded in the crystal grave of the dead of Sorrow.

Chapter 33

Open air hit Maeva in the face. She flung her eyes wide, found herself clinging to Rindalan in the midst of the tiny embassy garden. Rand was nowhere to be seen. Her throat ached. "He's gone! Oh, God, he's gone."

Rindalan hugged her closely. His two-elbowed arms made the embrace intimate and she had never felt so protected. "Hush," he said to her. "We are still between time and place. He may yet be with us."

But his voice was bleak, and she knew he did not believe it any more than she did.

Had he materialized in solid rock? She shook, despite Rindalan's hold on her, bit her lip, and waited.

rrRusk lurked in orbit around Sorrow. He had not been successful in separating a pilot from the watchful confines of his assignment, but he knew it was only a matter of time. He had left Sorrow's surface to ready the cruiser which GNask often frequented, knowing the ambassador might request flight on a moment's notice, when the salvage request came in.

Cargo, perhaps jettisoned from a recent Chaos loss, had been located. He'd given permission to attempt to recover it. They would, if it proved convenient, file a salvage request with Compact later. It might be garbage, for all rrRusk knew, and if it was, the general had no desire to wrestle Compact red tape in hauling it in. He would simply blast it and leave it where it was.

On the other hand, if it were valuable, rrRusk was of the opinion that what the Compact didn't know, it could not protest. Either way, he felt his actions justifiable.

He sat now on the bridge, eyeing the spy monitors on the various complexes dirtside. His were duplicates of what rested in the Abdrelikan embassy and he did not often take note of the various printouts, readings, and recordings.

This time he did. From within the Terran embassy came an esper reading that was like a lightning bolt, a surge of energy that set his machine to trembling. Then, as quickly, it was gone.

rrRusk sat forward in his chair, staring. He thrummed his barrellike chest with interest. What in muddy hell had that been?

He picked up a readout. Just moments before, the human-kind GNask had been most interested in surveying, Maeva Polonia, had entered the embassy wing. Terran humankind were absymally low in the esper scale. Such activity was highly unusual.

He leaned forward to the comline. "Get me Ambassador GNask," he growled.

He had been imprisoned with his eyes open, Rand thought. Like dreams which he remembered only vaguely, his body had slowed almost to a cryogenic pace. If not dead yet, he would be soon, his heart stilled, his lungs slowly eking out the last of their air, his molecular body irretrievably comingled with quartz.

Yet he did not feel dead or dying, and if he was between heartbeats, he felt as though an eternity could pass before the next, before he would begin to feel the failure. He felt expanded, the world about him as thin as a snowflake, a veil of icy coldness. He thought about putting a hand up to his face to see if he could feel his breath, and a wraithlike object moved, whisking by his chin.

Yesss, mooove. . . .

Many voices, whisper-thin, a wind of nearly inaudible tones, brushing past him. Rand tried to step forward, had the sensation of leaving or stretching out of his body, and the body shape catching up with him.

Yesss . . . come to usss. . . .

Breath as cold as death, a breeze of faint sounds, reaching him, caressing him, pulling him forward, the same attraction which had wrenched him away from Rindalan and Maeva.

What was it?

His unpumping heart leaden in his chest, his body not a

body that he had ever used before, he moved through caverns and walls of crystal. His mind continually pushed out ahead of him, his body catching up with an almost elastic snap, as though he were stretching the atomic bonds of his existence to the limit before they rebounded. He was drawn, inexorably, toward something embedded, like himself, in the quartz.

He found himself terribly afraid to go any closer. Was it his own death he was approaching? Was this his spirit self, torn free from his imprisoned body? What would happen when the two met? Would he then die, horribly, intermingled with cold earth, earth not even of his home world? Who called him? Did he summon himself?

Even as he thought that, he knew better, for the cajoling he answered was incredibly alien. If it was himself, or the *bahdur* remnant still within him, he knew he could not face it.

Feeearrr nooot . . . come to ussss. . . .

The pause between heartbeats passed, even as he moved forward, and his organ struggled horribly to contract and pump as it had been evolved to do. The pain in his chest began like a sharp prickle and grew to a heavy, hurting weight.

He was dying.

An icy veil hung before him. Beyond it he could sense his destination, a gathering of others, voices beckoning to him. He would take a deep breath and gather his strength to pass through it, but he had no breath, and his lungs had begun sharp stabbing pains, reminding him of the urgent need for air.

His chest hurt. His heart quivered as it attempted to beat. His temples began to throb.

He moved toward the veil. Into it, cold, colder than its misty substance. It passed through him, icy fingers touching every part of his being. Was it death itself?

Rand pushed.

He emerged.

The dead of Sorrow moved foward to touch him.

Maeva shuddered. She had been holding her breath, and it had seemed to stretch forever, but now she must breathe. She buried her face in Rindalan's arm.

"He's gone."

"Not yet." The alien moved, tilted his head as though lis-

tening, no ears to help him do it, but the attitude of his body
told her what he was doing. "Don't give up."

She wondered if it had been a horrible death or if Rand had
died instantaneously, trapped in the stone below the embassy.
Or perhaps he had made it out to the open air, gone, his molecules stretched out so thin that he was part of the wind?

Rindalan released all but her hand. "Come with me."

He steered her into a walk, then into a run, across the grav-
eled pathways of the embassy, through the barrier which gave
before them as though they did not even exist. Was it true—
were they somewhere between then and now? She struggled
to keep up with the long-striding ambassador as he raced
across the parklike grounds, between the trees, down to the
river of crystal.

"Here . . ." said Rindalan, then faced downstream. "No.
Down there." He fairly sprinted down the riverbank, carrying
Maeva with him, she could swear her feet never touched the
ground.

When he stopped, he looked down into the frozen waters.
She hesitated to look, the grotesqueries of the lost people of
Sorrow so distressing to her, but she did.

She gasped, lost her breath, heart thumping, went to her
knees beside the quartz.

Rand. Rand, embedded in the crystal with the long dead of
another world.

"Do something!" she cried to Rindalan.

The Choyan ambassador leaned forward. "I would," he answered gently. "If I only knew what."

Welcome. You hear us. You see us.

Their voices, so reedy as to be nonexistent, heard not in his
ears, but in his skull. Rand put a hand out, insubstantial, not
flesh, more feeling, and brushed a nearby cheek gently.

You feel us.

He faced only a grouping of dead. He knew they lay all
over Sorrow, in the rivers and lakes along the cities, as if they
had been herded into the water and then transformed into a
quartzite base which Compact science had not fully been able
to analyze. Their alien bodies were and were not a part of the
mineral, and only one had ever been allowed to be excavated,
but the findings on it had been undetermined.

"I feel you," he said.

We are dead.

"I am dying."

We know. You must listen. You are the first to hear us, though we have tried for . . . the words for time eluded him, but he had a sense of millennia, as only the dead could experience it.

"Who killed you?"

If anything could save him from the laws and dealings of the Compact, it would be that answer, the answer to the mystery of Sorrow. For himself, as well as for others, he felt he had to ask it.

We killed ourselves. Listen.

They filled his mind with images, mothers taking up their children and walking down to the water, fathers and sons, brothers, employers and employees, adversaries, young and old, wanted and unwanted. All. All into the water which bordered their immediate homes, into the chill water one early spring day.

And once there, a single unified flash of their minds changed the fabric of their world, killing and entombing them for eternity.

"Why? *Why?*" He was losing feeling in his own limbs, and his heart felt as though it would explode in his chest, and he reached out. They upheld him.

Listen.

They told him a story not unlike that of Cho, of a people with powers of the mind which could affect their physical world. Of intolerance of the differences of those minds. Wars. Suspicion. Regulation. Rejection. Of an enemy from without which had been repulsed, but which had shown them a mirror of what they had themselves become, and in horror, they knew they were destroying themselves. Would go on to destroy worlds about them if left unchecked.

Warned him of their mistakes.

He thought of Palaton's fear of *bahdur* spreading among the commons. It was not the *bahdur* which would kill Choyan, it was the fear and intolerance.

They patted his face, wiping away tears.

Yes.

He had to, had to remember, to tell. Had to live.

He could not move, all strength gone from him. They supported him. One of them, moving as slowly and yet surely as a glacier, uptilted his chin. Lifted his vision from the caverns of crystal toward the surface of the river and the sun.

He saw Rindalan's face looking down at him.

The aged Choya reached out.

Rand felt them extend his arm, his hand, thrust him upward. His body ached and groaned, heaved up through solids as it became inexorably solid itself. He must weigh more than whole planets.

How could dead people overcome such gravity?

Help us.

His heart gave one last, limp flutter. Rand kept his sight looking upward. What he knew would save Palaton. To save Palaton, he must save himself.

He reached up with one hand, and with his mind, reached down. Touched the *bahdur*. Felt it flare, a nova inside him, an explosion that sent him driving upward.

His hand touched flesh. Warm, living flesh. He clasped it tightly as Rindalan drew him forth from the crystal, birthing him.

Chapter 34

Bay stations surrounding Sorrow were, of necessity, neutral ground. They intercepted incoming deep space flights and ran cargoes and personnel through customs, transferring them to harmless freight shuttles, hopefully precluding open attacks on the Halls of the Compact. They succeeded, but probably only because any one species knew it would be genocide to open fire overtly on the Compact. Retribution would be swift and unrelenting. That did not mean, however, that scurrilous acts and renegades did not abound in the bay stations.

As they came into Bay 2, Rindalan explained to Rand that he hoped to find not only a willing pilot, but an available vessel to take them as quickly as possible to Cho. Rand understood what Maeva did not, that finding a pilot would not be difficult. The *tezars* understood all too keenly that their world hung in a critical balance. It should not be hard to find one who would abandon his or her current contract, House of Tezars or no, to bring them home.

Taking a vessel, on the other hand, would be a bit more difficult. Any deep space craft docked at the bay would already be under orders and unavailable. They would have to commandeer what they wanted, and that would surely draw notice from Compact authorities. They were likely to be pursued all the way to their jump-off into Chaos. And it would take a day or two to gain the acceleration needed. Like blood in the water, that would draw the attention of the Abdreliks and the Ronins. Therefore, it behooved them to be as circumspect as possible in locating a pilot. They did not want their descriptions or needs broadcast too soon after successfully commandeering a vessel.

"You keep saying commandeering," Maeva noted. "What we're doing is stealing."

"Yet another good reason for having my attorney with me," Rindy said cheerfully.

"Not if they arrest me as well."

"We'll have to make sure to stow you away before that happens," Rand told her. "Or we can throw you off with the crew when we take the ship."

"Inside or outside the air lock," she tossed back.

"Preferably inside." Rindy looked at the deck map bayside. "When you two children are done sparring, we need to make some serious plans."

"I thought you'd already made the plans." Maeva tossed her head, and a strand of her hair fell loose across her cheekbone. She stroked it back into place. "I thought you'd already made these arrangements."

Breezily, Rindy answered, "No time." He stabbed a fingernail at the deck map. "There's a way station on level three. We can find a room, get a meal, and make contacts there." He herded them into a lift, ordered "Level three," and shepherded them out.

Maeva lifted a slim eyebrow as the ambassador obtained rooms for them under a name she didn't recognize and paid in cash. Rand, if he noticed, did not react. He remained pale and drawn, and she wondered if the strain would be too much for him. He seemed to have something on his mind that he wished to discuss privately with Rindalan, and she knew as soon as they were given their rooms, she would be shunted aside. She debated with herself as to whether she would allow it, or give in to the chance to have a hot meal and a real rest without her head on a library table. Her feet ached, her shirt looked as though it had been slept in (it had), and she wondered if Rindalan had enough cash for her to buy grav boots and some sensible clothing.

Rand looked at her and said, "She needs some decent traveling gear."

Maeva started as if he'd read her mind. He gave her a slight smile, as if he had, and had known her last thought as well. He pointed at her shoes. "You walk like your feet hurt, and it won't be comfortable going through Chaos in that."

"Right."

Rindalan peeled off some plastisheet denominations. "There should be a shop here in the way station. Don't go far."

Maeva hesitated. Both males looked at her. She said, "I know you have something to talk about, and I don't know if I want to be here or not."

Rand said, "You don't want to be here," while Rindy cleared his throat, answering, "I don't know what you're referring to."

They traded looks. Rand's expression closed. Rindalan said, "In a conspiracy, it is not wise to keep your partners in the dark. She has as much to lose as we do. Perhaps, hmm, more. She has a reputation that is still intact."

"I am considering the security of Cho."

"In that case," Rindalan dropped a hand on each of their shoulders and squired them down the corridor toward the rooms they had rented, "I suggest we find a place more suitable to discuss this."

Rand opened the larger of the two rooms, which he would share with the elder Choya, and a whiff of fresh-scented air greeted them. He cast around the room like a dog sniffing for something, and Maeva realized as she sat down that he was searching for tangible and intangible means of surveillance.

He lifted and dropped a shoulder. "I can't find anything."

Rindalan stretched out on one of the beds. "That is sufficient for me. Now, what is it you wish to talk about that you do not wish Maeva to hear."

Rand, tired as he looked, would not sit. He said, "We don't need a pilot. I can do it."

"You?" Rindy's brow arched.

"You know I have the ability."

"Ability is not experience."

"I have some experience."

"Ahhh. That explains much."

"Not to me, it doesn't," interjected Maeva. "Are we talking FTL navigating here? Because I'm not too happy crossing Chaos as it is, but without a *tezar* at the helm . . ."

"You'll be sedated," answered Rand without looking at her. "You won't know anything anyway."

"I'll know it before I go under. And I've never been very good at sedation. It's hard for me to relax when I'm tense."

Rindy asked, disregarding Maeva completely, "Why would you offer to do such a thing?"

"The fewer who know what we're trying to accomplish, the

better. You need to get back. You need to tell Palaton what happened on Sorrow."

"You're not intending to go back?"

Rand looked at the floor. "No. I'll get you back, and see Maeva wherever she wants to go safely, but no. There's no place for me on Cho. The message, that's what's important. Not the messenger. I'm a *tezar* but not one which Cho will ever accept. I'll go find the experience I need, see if I can expand my training to help others."

"You are the I'falan. Would you abandon that?"

Rand wet his lips and answered slowly, raising his gaze once more to Rindy's face. "I think that part of me went with Palaton. And even if it did not, Cho rejects me for that as well."

"Not all of Cho."

"Enough. I don't want to be a part of anything which could destroy your society. There will be another, someday."

Rindy took in his words. Maeva sat, her mouth slightly open, as if listening but not comprehending a word which had been said.

"I cannot agree with you on this."

Rand put his shoulders back. "Which part?"

"The part where you want to pilot," Maeva countered. They looked at her. "Even if he could, he's in no condition to."

"That," said Rindalan gravely, "I agree with. We find a pilot."

"And increase our risks."

"This entire venture is a risk, but though I applaud your courage, you have a long way to go before you can master the Patterns of Chaos. *Bahdur* alone is not enough, or I would be a *tezar*." Rindy watched him from the pillow he had made of his hands. He lay on the bed as though tired, and Maeva suddenly said, "You should rest."

"I should," he agreed. "But we have some things to settle first. You, outfitting, and Rand and I, transportation."

"Word will spread fast enough, Rindy, without us looking for a pilot. I can do it."

This time, Rindalan raised his head and held it steady, learning on his upper elbow. "As you should be more than well aware, I can search without raising or risking a great deal of attention. If, that is, the two of you will leave me alone to rest and meditate. If you are so eager to wear down the anxieties of youth, I suggest you boot up the bay records of recent dockings and find us a likely candidate to borrow."

"You won't let me do it."

Rindalan lay back down and closed his eyes. "No."

Rand paced off three rapid, angry strides, then stopped. He rubbed the back of his neck.

"He's right."

He looked at Maeva. "I know. That's why the Choyan are so infuriating. They're invariably right."

"You should be resting, too."

He shook off a quiver, as if the thought of coming to a rest bothered him. He crossed to the small desk attached to the cubicle wall. "I'll check the dockings."

"Then I guess I'll do some shopping."

Rand sat down. He eyed her. "If you need any help—"

"I'll know," Rindy put in.

Maeva leaned back in the door. "I'll be right back." The door sealed after her.

Rand twisted in the chair as if to say something to Rindalan, but the elder's lips pursed and he let out a gentle, puffing snore. Rand opened his mouth, then closed it. Rindy looked more frail than he remembered, as if the last days had taken a heavy toll. He turned back around and gave his attention to the screen.

Something exceedingly interesting came up almost immediately.

* * * *

rrRusk watched his monitors, while responding to the patch-in, trying to mollify the agitation which rippled throughout GNask. "I don't know why your monitors didn't record the event. Analysis here shows that the increased activity and other functions are ninety-eight point two percent probability a real-time event."

"In other words, our central system has been masked."

"Ambassador, it happens. The question on my mind is not whether it happened or not, but why. To cloak the movements

of one humankind attorney? The effort, the expenditure of
the strategy—"

"I see," interrupted GNask, and rrRusk could tell from the
sudden narrowing of the other's eyes and the widening of the
pupils, that the ambassador did, indeed, see. The sluglike
symbiont riding his shoulder turned antenna stalk eyes toward
the screen as if equally focused. "What else have you observed that would interest me?"

"My records indicate that Rindalan and companions un-
named arrived by shuttle at Bay 2 just under an hour ago."

"Visuals?"

"No. But tracking from the shuttle confirms his identity."

"And we do not have further indication of movements of
the humankind attorney. Do we even know if she left the embassy?"

'No, we don't." General rrRusk held his temper. It was not
his systems' failure, and he knew that the rage GNask was attempting to master was not directed at him. "Her presence in
the embassy has not been unreasonable, only the effort expended to cloak her entrance."

"And possible exit. But why? What does Thomas hold that
he doesn't want me to know about? *What?*" GNask looked directly at rrRusk through the screen. "Check the masses on the
shuttle. If we can't ID his companions by screen, perhaps we
can by other means."

rrRusk nodded.

"Do we have a fix on Thomas?"

'He's off-world, Bay 4A, been there since yesterday, checking on cargo from what intelligence has been able to ascertain."

"What cargo?"

"We don't know."

"And the cargo your troops salvaged?"

"Being brought in. I don't know if we have anything of
worth or not. The shipment came from nowhere, is going to
nowhere."

"No dents?"

"No."

"Smuggling."

"That would be a logical assumption."

"Ummmm." GNask relaxed slightly, leaned back in his

chair, musing. "Ambassador Rindalan. There's a revote tomorrow on piloting contracts. He would not dare to miss it. rrRusk, you were correct to alert me. I don't know what's happening, but I don't intend to miss it. Order me a shuttle liftoff immediately."

"Done, Ambassador." rrRusk cut the transmission, dropping his thick hand back to the rim of the console. He had not made general by ignoring his gut intuitions, nor by following outmoded or incautious strategies. He hoped he had not damaged his career by his actions in this matter. The discovery that the Abdrelikan embassy monitors had been successfully blacked out for nearly a day, however, tended to back his judgment.

Something was stirring. He could not pinpoint the whys or wherefores of the humankind involvement, but it did not matter if Cho had been drawn in. The Choyan had been a canny adversary for far too long.

Sooner or later, they had to stumble.

He caught himself staring blankly at the monitoring screens when word came in that Ambassador GNask was boarding. rrRusk shoved himself to his feet, his mind still groggy—mud balls, how he wished he had his symbiont with him, but that was impossible, with the amount of deep space voyaging he did. A *tursh* did not take to the environs of space well; losing one would be worse than leaving it at home, to be with the family line. He missed its steadying influence, however, as well as the creature's ability to clean his hide of fungus and parasites which bothered Abdreliks, even in space.

Without a *tursh*, an Abdrelik was nothing but a hulking predator. With their intelligence and guidance, imprinted slowly after hatching and reimprinted periodically throughout adulthood, an Abdrelik could do anything. His potential was limited only by the boundaries set upon him by treaty with the Compact. He puffed his chest out as GNask entered the bridge.

"Anything new?"

"The statistics on the shuttle are indeterminate. Humanoids could have been with Rindalan. They could also have been of any one of a number of other like-massed species. Even Ronins."

GNask's eyebrows went up. He grinned hugely. "Now that would be an interesting situation, would it not? A kidnapping. I wonder if our Ronin allies have something planned which they have not shared with us?"

"They rarely stage anything without a warship within back-up distance. I have no reports of any Spiders nearby."

"Still . . ." GNask strolled past the bank of monitors, assessing what he saw. "It would spice up what is already an intriguing stew. Not that we need any more distractions. I will bow to your acumen, rrRusk. I doubt that the Ronins have made any drastic moves without us. So. What do you suggest?"

"We wait."

"Wait?"

"The Choyan ambassador is here for some reason. He will disembark or return to Sorrow."

"And we stand ready in either case."

rrRusk nodded.

"All right, then. We wait."

* * * *

Late night surrounded the palace. Qativar saw few signs of activity as he approached. A member of the guard let him in reluctantly. He was met by a minor clerk at the staircase. Strains of a *lindar* being played—no, played was not the word, pounded—drifted through the palace in a kind of frantic, desperate up-tempo. But the notes were a coherent melody, recognizable for all its fury. Qativar knew who was playing and stepped by the clerk to go in search of the player.

"Sir, Honored Qativar, the emperor is seeing no one."

"He'll see me." Qativar brushed by and the clerk scurried to catch up with him.

"I'm—I'm sorry, sir, but I cannot let you into the emperor's private quarters." The clerk's upper lip twitched frantically. He had invested in good, gold chain to layer under his derma, it twitched now with his expression.

"Who can?"

"M–m–minister Gathon, sir."

"Well, find him, wherever he is." Qativar stood in determined good humor, watching the clerk squirm.

"He's not about, sir."

"I know that. He's not been about for days. Panshinea will see *me,* and if you can't escort me, I'll find him myself. It shouldn't be difficult." Already, just by moving beyond the staircase, the music had grown more distinct.

"N–n–no one is allowed in the emperor's private downstairs quarters."

"Enough of this." Qativar swerved, stretched his longlegged stride past that of the trembling clerk, and began to search the vast lower halls of the palace. The clerk was winded and ashen pale when they both pulled up outside a door. The *lindar* music boomed loud enough to make the corridor echo.

"Let me in."

"You don't have access."

Qativar clenched a fist that he desired to wrap about the obstinate clerk's throat. "If he throws me out, he throws me out. But if you don't let me in, he may well have you ordered executed in the morning. Do you understand?"

Hand shaking so hard he could barely decode the threshold lock, the clerk let him in, then bolted.

Qativar stepped into the atrium music room, taking in the surroundings. He had indeed, never been there, nor he doubted had many others. The garden, visible through the arbor was a surprise in itself. The palace, for security reasons, had never been sounded or mapped, and overhead shots were strictly forbidden. Still, most Choyan had a rough idea of the layout. This garden, though, was something else. Qativar found himself quite surprised.

Panshinea sat, disheveled, at the *lindar*. His hands hammered the keyboard, flying in sleeves grown limp from the wearing. His hair was unbound and spread over his shoulders, red-gold sparks flying from it every now and then as if he smoldered while he played.

He looked up when the piece ended and rested his hands upon the top of the instrument. "They were supposed to keep you out."

"Me? Surely you don't mean that."

Panshinea turned his arms slightly, exposing his wrists, and looked at them as if he contemplated slitting them. His veins bulged from the vigorous activity he had just completed. "I cannot rest. I cannot sleep. They tell me I am not always sane."

"That, Emperor, I hear to my sorrow." Qativar dipped his fingers inside his inner pocket and pulled out a bundle of packets. He threw them onto the seat of the nearest chair. "I brought you some additional supplies. I worry that you are abusing them."

"What have you done to me?" Pan thrust himself to his feet, voices piercing, then abruptly collapsed back to the bench.

"I would ask, what have you done to yourself?"

"I took the boost."

Hearing it gave Qativar an enormous sense of satisfaction. He had no doubt, of course, never had had, but hearing the defeat in Panshinea's voices was sweet beyond compare. "It was the only thing you could do."

Pan put a hand over his face as if he could not bear to look at Qativar. "Was it? Was it? Tell me, no one else will, where is Gathon?"

"Do you not remember?"

"Sometimes . . ." Fingers screened his expression. "Sometimes I think I do."

"You killed him, Pan. In a fight over the boost, I expect, I don't know. You called for my help. I agreed to take the body and dispose of it. You agreed to continue to allow distribution of the drug." Qativar moved toward the massive desk which dominated his corner of the room. The wood felt alive and warm, though the room itself was chill. Pan obviously did not feel the cold, his shirt was untucked and opened practically to the waist, and sweat gleamed upon his chest. He had lost more weight and had begun to look emaciated, shrinking in on himself. Qativar perched a lean hip on the desk. "Ask me more."

Pan pushed his hand so it masked his forehead, as if checking for a fever, or brushing off unruly bangs . . . or holding the weight of his horn crown. "Where is Gathon?"

"I have his body well hidden. It will never be found unless I choose for it to be found."

The emperor closed jade green eyes a long moment. "What is it you want now?"

"I came to apologize, Emperor. To tell you that boost is,

sadly, not the miracle drug we thought it. Evidence suggests that it is severely addictive. In a few cases, it can cause death. In others, it is contraindicated because the *bahdur* cannot be contained or controlled. It burns, like wildfire, out of control." He smiled at Panshinea.

"You came for the throne."

"Emperor, you accuse me of treason. No. I am here only to advise you while Congress decides whether to replace you or not, while Palaton decides whether to reclaim his heirship or not, while you decide. . . ." Qativar paused dramatically. "Whether you will let him."

"Never."

"Then take my counsel."

"Never," repeated Pan, though his voices dropped to barely audible.

"I can stand by your side as Gathon did. Then, when you are prepared to move away, I will be ready to step in. Do you think I am so foolish as to believe I, or Vihtirne, or any of us could simply take your place? Perhaps, centuries ago, when all Cho needed was a warlord, but not today. The Abdreliks and the Ronins, even the two-faced Ivrians go all aflutter at the thought of our fall. I don't want to give it to them. I want Cho, you've not mistaken me or my intentions, but not until I'm set and you're ready to give it to me."

"Do you expect me to believe you?"

"I expect you to know that you must."

"And if I do not accept you?"

Qativar tilted his head and pointed his hand at the packets of boost. "You will run out, eventually. You can try to run Cho, empty. I'm sure it won't be the first time an emperor has kept the throne while past the ability to do so. You can even buy boost on the underground . . . but it'll be cut, there. Harmless, and sometimes not so harmless, fillers and additives will have been used to extend it. You will be even less sure of your *bahdur* than you are now. Or you could take what I'm offering you, because I am young, Panshinea, and I can afford to wait. I can even afford to spar with Congress, if that's what it takes, although Cho will suffer in the long run if I have to do so. Or we can deal, you and I, and both profit."

The stream of sparks which had been running from Panshinea's mane ceased. Without the shimmer, he looked spent, pale, as much a corpse as Qativar had left in cold storage. He looked into Qativar's eyes as if reading his thoughts and put his shoulders back.

"What do you suggest I do?"

"Coax Palaton back in and finish him this time."

"How would I do that? He's not only elusive, he must be in duplicates." Pan laughed shrilly.

"I have the bait which will bring him. I have Jorana. She carries his child."

"He would kill me if I tried to hurt Jorana."

"Indeed. That is the idea. First, we must let the people know that you are gathering imperial *bahdur*—"

"I haven't the strength."

"You know that, and I know that. But I want Palaton prepared to strike with everything he has, and the world will be expecting it. If all goes as I've planned, neither he nor Cho will be able to help themselves."

"I don't understand."

Qativar smiled again. "You will, my emperor. You will."

* * * *

John Taylor Thomas listened as the last bulkhead door clanged and locked into place. His eyes felt gritty with lack of sleep. Vihtirne had agreed to conference with him on Galern to seal contracts. He thought ruefully that perhaps the jettisoning of the last cargo had been fortunate. They were desperate enough for the pharmaceuticals that they would give him official status and channels for the trade. That gave him enough legitimacy to keep President Mitchell off his back, even if it did not give him surcease in other matters.

"Prepare for bay launch."

Thomas went to his hammock. The freighter shimmied as the berthing cradle put it into position. Its metal skin echoed every winching and angle-thrust. He thought of sleep, blessed rest once they went into Chaos, sleep even he could not avoid. Perhaps he would feel human again when they landed on Galern.

Something slammed up against the ship. It shuddered with

its whole being. Thomas slipped half out of the hammock, listening.

Everything went deadly silent.

He was headed for the door to his cabin when it burst open, his Choya pilot in the hands of another.

"Your Eminence, I am sorry, but we've been commandeered." Dilarabe did not sound particularly distressed.

Thomas shook himself free of the hammock. "What's going on here? Get out or I'll have the bay authorities on your tail."

He recognized Ambassador Rindalan as the tall, chestnut-and gray-haired being moved more fully into the light.

"What is the meaning of this?" He stopped and stared as the two Choyan moved into his cabin, Rand and Maeva in their wake.

Dilarabe looked at Thomas blandly. "I believe it is called a 'jailbreak.' "

"I beg your pardon, Ambassador," Rindalan said. "But we're taking your ship. It seems most provident."

* * * *

rrRusk caught the incoming alert. He was on his feet, and at the monitor, shouting over the com to ready the cruiser for departure.

"What is it?" GNask, still dripping with mud and ooze, climbed over the bulkhead from the spa which was kept for him.

"We have a launch from Bay 4A, sir." rrRusk stood, watching the telemetry readings and other information being transmitted. "We have Rindalan and two humanoids boarding a freight ship, a freighter bearing Ambassador Thomas, making an authorized, but very unorthodox and hasty launch."

"Do we?" GNask toweled his shoulder, gently avoiding his *tursh*. "I make that out to be a possible hijacking, general. If you ascertain that the boarding was forced."

"Initial readings indicate that an outer bulkhead was blown. It looks forced to me."

"Then Ambassador Thomas and Ambassador Rindalan appear to be in danger. I see it as my duty to go after the criminals. Get us launched as soon as possible. I'll inform the

Compact of our action." He paused in the doorway. "And rrRusk . . ."

"Yes?"

"Do whatever you must to catch up with them."

Chapter 35

Gilat had been a hard worker all his life. As a God-blind, he could expect nothing more as his lot. He believed in the teachings of a Change to come, and of a Bringer of that Change, the I'falan, but he did not hope to see it in his lifetime. Instead, he had learned a skill among the workings of the water filtration plants and he worked hard at what he did. He kept his mate and children happy, owned a small but sturdy house, drank *bren* for breakfast and wine on special occasions and, generally, led a good life.

He would have been content if not for his mate. Oh, Bretha had been a comely Choya'i when they were young. She'd been courted by many youths, including one brash Choya who claimed he was Housed, though they all knew he couldn't have been. No one sane would sully their genetic line with a commons if he came from a Householding. That she had chosen him had filled him with joy, and his small house with children.

But she had never quite loosened her hold on the idea that she might have married into a Householding. That her children's father might have been a Choya with the power, with *bahdur,* which could breathe far vaster possibilities into all their futures. She might even have birthed a *tezar.*

They were still young, for all their family and years together, and she still had a longing for children, but refused to have any more. Not any to be born as God-blind.

Gilat knew there was nothing he could do about it, but when she had begun going to the underground sermons, he let her go. True, the religion of the Change had been banned centuries before, and once emperors had executed those who ignored the ban, but that had been long ago. He let her go because it gave her hope, and kept her from carping at his

crown day in and day out. Could have done, could have
been. . . .

She had, instead, filled him with stories of Father Chirek
and Malahki, the latter a Choya who had been a luminary of
Danbe, until that region had been forcibly Relocated,
Malahki, a common Choya with enough charisma to become
emperor himself. He'd even listened when word came of a
Prophet. It made her happy. She still carped at him night and
day, but now it was with excitement, not complaint. It seemed
harmless enough.

Until she had professed that an alien had come, the I'falan.
That Gilat had rejected and it still remained the one harsh
note between them. When the I'falan had gone as quickly as
it had come, she had lapsed into silence.

He missed her enthusiasm, her cheerful gossip, her reports
of hopeful insurrection among the underground. The glint in
her eyes when she talked of being young enough to bear a
babe which would have been touched by the Change.

Although Gilat had taken a kind of personal delight in the
weakness spreading like wildfire among the Householdings
because of Panshinea's use of imperial *bahdur,* Bretha had
said little. She had retreated into a depression over which
Gilat was as powerless as he was over the other matter, and
it bothered him. As he took his battered conveyance to the
power plant, he reflected that she did not want Cho lowered
to her level. She wanted them all to be elevated.

He didn't much care as long as equal was equal and fair
was fair. Hard work and will were what counted.

As he drove, the edges of dawn cleared the mountain ridge.
Light spread across the basin of Charolon and its outer regions. He liked to watch the dawn, though his shift sometimes
began before and he came to work in the dark cloak of night.
Better than stormy weather.

The plant hunkered on the horizon, a dull, Choya-carved
mountain of its own. It would stay, even when (or if, Gilat
thought morosely) Charolon Relocated. He liked being beyond the outskirts of the townships, working outside the mill
of traffic and manufacturing strips. Bretha did not care for the
hours of his shift, but he took care not to wake her or the children when he left, and he was often home early enough to
help her with dinner or afternoon games with the children.

As his conveyance puttered toward his destination, a broadcaster came on with the current weather report and some speculation that Panshinea had once again fallen into a decline. The emperor had not been the same. Perhaps, thought Gilat, he never would be. Perhaps, in his lifetime, they would see the investiture of a new emperor. Now that would be something. Minister Gathon was not available for a statement, and rumors were rife that Gathon had left Charolon, abandoning his emperor. Rumor also said that Panshinea had gone mad.

Odd. It was not in his genetics, although if the *bahdur* had burned out of him, like it did in a *tezar*, insanity could be possible. Congress, with no legitimate heir named to the throne, was pondering its actions.

Gilat found himself chewing on the corner of his lip as he considered the broadcaster's report. It would make an interesting topic at lunch break. His mind thus mulling, he only half-noticed an unfamiliar shift crew pulling out of the water plant just before him.

He changed into his waders in the locker room and went to check on main filtration. He liked the cavernous room, with its thunder of water pouring through it, though the catwalks could be slippery now and then, and last year a coworker had fallen and been towed under to his death. He usually did not tell Bretha when this chore rotated into his shift. As much as he liked water, she feared it.

Although the inspection was supposed to be done in pairs, his coworker was late again. He thought privately that Latner probably drank too much. He could not seem to cope with the rhythms of the early day shift. Gilat decided to suggest to his supervisor that Latner be moved over.

He moved over onto the main catwalk, water spray dampening him despite his coveralls and waterproof jacket. Thousands of gallons rushed under the metal gridway, sending up a fine mist, thoroughly glistening and dampening the underground chamber. His waders gripped the surface well, and he had no fear.

In the churning, foaming water, something bobbed. It caught his eye immediately. Gilat peered closer. It did not appear to have been anything organic. Some sort of inanimate object where the water poured by in whitewater rapids. Something trapped in the pounding, artificial surf against the chamber walls. Finally, he got on his stomach and crawled to the edge of the catwalk for a better look.

A container of some kind. He needed to get that up and out, before it got caught in one of the turbines or drains. It would not bob forever. If he hooked one arm around the ladder, he should just be able to reach it. . . .

There was a moment, when the metal groaned, and the sleeve of his jacket slipped, when he thought of Bretha's fears and his drowned coworker and knew there was a possibility he might join him. He tightened his first elbow, felt his sinews stretch to their utmost, his joints groaning the way the catwalk sounded. His fingers wiggled and hooked like cunning creatures with minds of their own. Then . . . he had it!

His fingers caught the rim of the container, fishing it toward him. Gilat managed a better grip and pulled himself back to safety.

Once crouched on the catwalk, he looked the object over. Definitely a container, good-sized, out of the water, nearly as big as his torso. Once full, and now empty. Its air-filled insides had kept it afloat on the rapids. There was no sign whatsoever of the container's contents or its manufacturer. Gilat opened the lid and sniffed.

Oh, but he knew that smell. Every youth had talked about it once, just as they cherished pictures of naked Choya'i and boasted of their sexual prowess. He himself had once held a vial of it in his hand, though he had never used it, because he had Bretha's love and other Choya'i were like fish to him—so you might catch one, but what would you do with it when you had?

This was *ruhl,* a pungent and potent concentrate of the aphrodisiac. More than old wives' tales, this was genuine, though rare, the stuff of legend among the young. He straightened, container balanced between his palms.

Gilat stood on the catwalk, his heavy, thick common brow furrowed with his thoughts. Empty, but it had been full. *Ruhl* muddled the senses. Drove *bahdur* out of the Houseds, or so it was said, acted as more than an aphrodisiac, though no one would be so foolish as to want to drive the Houseds insane. What would Cho be without *bahdur?*

He remembered an unfamiliar work crew leaving as he was

driving in. They had been remoting a freight hover with them, though he did not recall what had been stacked on its surface. Had they left a container behind?

To what purpose would anyone wish to dose the water supply with *ruhl?*

He thought of the madness which had swept the city when it appeared that Panshinea had drained off most of the *bahdur* into himself.

Or had he?

Anyone drinking water with this great a concentration in it—

Gilat tucked the container under his arm. He did not know what had happened, and he felt almost sure his supervisor would scoff at him. Something had definitely happened here which should not go unnoticed, but he had no evidence of what, other than this empty container which stank of *ruhl*. He had no one to go to who would take him seriously and be able to ponder this quandary, to decide if there was a problem or connection here or not. He was questioning the very existence of imperial *bahdur* and Panshinea's actions, something a commons could not do lightly.

But there was always Bretha and her idol Malahki, and the underground.

They were great thinkers. Perhaps they might have an inkling as to what could be going on. Gilat, as much as he loved his work and his solitude, left his shift early.

* * * *

"She will live," Father Chirek told him, "but she'll need time to heal."

"That means," added Dorea softly, "that she will not be able to help you through what lies ahead."

"Prophesying?" asked Palaton wearily. He sat at the edge of Rufeen's crèche, watching his friend's still face, expression folded into one of unconscious pain. It had changed little after the hours of surgery and the nighttime he'd been waiting for her to wake. The Bayalak hospital had all the modern conveniences, and she was enfolded, entrusted into them, but still he did not trust.

"A little. And common sense." Dorea stood up briskly. "Nor will Hat be of any use."

Hat lay a room away, fighting to keep his shattered shoulder from being cut away forever, to keep his shoulder and arm whole, so that he could remain whole in body to be a flightmaster. In many ways, his fight was more crucial than Rufeen's. He had been lapsing in and out of consciousness, after two surgeries, and scarcely knew Palaton when he was at his side. Though Rufeen was hardly more conscious, Palaton had felt his presence more important to imprint on her.

As Father Chirek gave her his arm to guide her, Dorea turned her face back to Palaton, as if seeing him through her blindfold. "Coming?" she asked. "The battle will not be won within these walls."

She was young enough to be his daughter, but there was that in her voices which had become ageless, tones issuing from her gift rather than her experience. Palaton looked back at her, unable to deny the urgency she projected, unwilling to give his life and destiny over to her hands.

Softening, as if sensing his resolve, she added, "They will know you were here, and they will understand why you left."

Palaton looked back at Rufeen, who barely breathed within the crèche unit.

"Palaton, you burn like the Flame you are. They will know." Dorea repeated herself with patience.

He sighed and got to his feet. "And you have plans for me, I suppose."

"No, but we are ready for whatever plans you have for us." She held out her other arm to him, and walked steadily between the two of them through the hospital as if she needed no guidance at all, but had foreseen what her path would be in this moment.

As, indeed, she could have. He reflected, as the conveyance carried them from the hospital complex in the new, Housed high-rise section of Bayalak back toward the weather-beaten Common and old harbor city, that he wanted to rely on what she had seen, cling to it like a guideline as to what he should do. He wanted her to have it mapped out so clearly for him that he would not have to trust himself or make another decision. He wanted that. From the few words they had exchanged since he'd brought the skimmer in, he realized that she knew less than he did.

But they still had to talk about Rand. And, as isolated as he'd been in the critical care ward, he'd heard the rumors coming from Charolon. Panshinea ailing, Gathon gone. Soon, it would not matter whether the prophet knew his destiny or not, he would have to act.

The quarters Father Chirek had set up as the Prophet's base of operations were not terribly different from the weather-beaten, fish-bait-and-creosote-soaked wooden hovel that Palaton had first met Dorea in. As he walked in, he realized it had probably been a storage hangar, dry dock for boats, and huge racks for mending nets were folded up against the wall. It smelled of the sea. It was nothing like the many-roomed hall which he had dreamed of, though Palaton had not expected it to look the same. There were dorms, a galley, conference rooms, one communications center brimming with equipment that looked as out of place here as he would in an Abdrelik mud pond, and a small meditation room where Dorea received callers, her lithe frame resting in a hand-carved and very battered rocking chair.

She looked more at ease in the chair than Panshinea did on his throne, Palaton thought. He took a nearby divan that Father Chirek motioned him to. Chirek went to the corner and fixed them all an iced drink before he took a chair himself.

"Where is Malahki?" asked Dorea abruptly.

Palaton flinched, then realized she directed her inquiry at Chirek. The mouse-haired cleric shook his head, then said aloud, "I don't know. I thought he would be here before us. Something must have come up."

"No doubt." However, she looked unsettled as she knitted her fingers together in her lap.

The drink soothed his parched throat, but did little to quiet him. Palaton set it aside on a small table which was little more than a balanced stone, weathered by time and tide. "Tell me about Rand."

As was her usual habit, she plucked a second at her blindfold. "He is in great danger," she answered. "Although he has passed through part of it."

"On Sorrow? How did he get there? Qativar and Vihtirne

took him from me. I dared not move against them as long as he was hostage—if I had known, I would have—"

"What?" demanded Chirek. "What would you have done? Attacked them openly? With what means? Panshinea would have devoured you if you had divided your attention between them. Would you have left Cho to free Rand?"

"Possibly. Who has him? The Abdreliks?"

"He is being held by his own people. Ambassador Thomas does not ever intend for him to be free."

"There's no love lost between Thomas and Rand. I can't leave him there."

"And you cannot forsake us, either. You go, and Panshinea and Qativar will split the world between them. Nor," added Dorea gently, "can you do anything alone. You need us as well."

"I would have been stronger with Rand."

"Tell me why." Dorea lifted her chin, stared at him.

Palaton had never told anybody before of his bond with his friend. "I cannot explain it."

"I think you can."

Chirek leaned forward, one elbow on his brown-clothed knee. "You risked much bringing an alien among us. It could not have been easy for him or you."

"Would you have had me do otherwise?"

Chirek smiled ruefully. "And have lost the I'falan? You know better. But what about you? What have you lost?"

Before Palaton could say, the Prophet spoke.

"He was your *durah,* soulmate. He cleansed your *bahdur,* you shared it, he knows the heart of the Choyan empire. You were his destiny."

Her words fell into the silence of the tiny room like heart-beats.

Chirek said, "You told him of *bahdur.*"

"You knew that. You must have known it—what do you think made him the Bringer of Change? What do you think he carried?"

The priest said reflectively, "I did not think. I . . . experienced it."

"I met him on Arizar," Palaton recounted. He told them what they had only had hints of before: renegade Choyan colonists who had fled Cho and done what no others had done

before them. Their experiments with transferring their powers
to humankind for cleansing, the many failures as humankind
could not cope with *bahdur,* their successes. That the colony
had done what they did out of selfishness, that the humans
brought to Arizar had come hoping to become pilots, that
they had been blinded, muted, made passive receptacles for
tainted *bahdur.* That the humankind had come as scarcely
more than children, stolen from Earth, never to return. That
he, desperate to avoid burnout, had been seduced by the renegades to join their College of the Brethren, to be cleansed.

"I am not proud," Palaton added.

"You have a prodigious talent. It must have been difficult
to feel its first ebbings."

"You cannot possibly imagine."

Dorea prompted. "The Abdreliks attacked. You saved
Rand, brought him here."

"I had to. He carried my power. And . . . I was responsible
for him. Many died on Arizar, many more fled. He was all I
could salvage . . . my pride, my faith in myself, all was at
stake. What we did not know was that Alexa, one of his
friends, and Bevan, another, would be tangled in the Abdreliks efforts to secure the *tezarian* drive."

"Who is Bevan?"

"Bevan is the pilot who led the Abdrelik attack on us. He
carried Nedar's power. It drove him insane, destroyed him. As
for Alexa . . . I can only assume that she was an agent of the
Abdreliks to the very end, though she was with Nedar. She
perished with him at Blue Ridge."

Chirek lifted his chin from his hand. "Rand restored your
bahdur?"

"I took it from him," Palaton answered shortly. "When
Blue Ridge was attacked."

"Then," Father Chirek concluded, "it is you who are the
I'falan."

Palaton stared at Dorea. "Ask her. She knows why I would
not answer her summons."

"You cannot refuse to Change our people."

"I can, and I will. Giving you the power does not give you
the wisdom and the training to use it. Look at the mess I've
made of things."

"Most of our strife has come from the struggle to be equal."

Palaton got up, paced a step away from Dorea, thinking of his dreams in which he had run, to no avail. He would not run now, though he had an undeniable wish to. "Our strengths should come from accepting our differences."

"We can be diverse and still be equal." Dorea set aside the drink she had held. "*Bahdur* molds itself to each and every Choya who holds it. Like water, like air, it is always there, seen and unseen, yet always shaped differently. But to deny us the right to breathe, to drink, is wrong."

"I need your help! Don't you think I know that? But I cannot, will not, pay your price."

Malahki entered, his sable mane lying upon his shoulders like a cloak, his bulk filling the room. "You may feel differently when you hear what I have to tell you."

Chapter 36

Removing his jacket, shaking off a light dirt, Malahki added, "My pardon for the lateness, Dorea. I have been busy."

"I know."

Palaton took the look Malahki gave him and returned it, standing firm.

Chirek said, a touch of impatience in his voices, "What do you need to tell us?"

"I've been in contact with my network." Malahki's mouth twisted. To Palaton, he added, "You're a hard act to follow."

"I should have guessed it was you who spread the House of Flame all over Cho."

"It seemed a good thing to do. You must admit, it kept Pan off your heels."

"Not entirely. But it kept him thinking."

Dorea said, in a soft warning, "Malahki."

"Ah. Yes. I got some interesting information this morning by way of a water filtration plant worker outside Charolon. I've been verifying what he's told me. Our water is being dosed with *ruhl,* at some fairly incredible concentrations." Malahki scratched his temple. "We've not been able to stop it, but we've found a pattern of sabotage in a majority of the urban areas."

"*Ruhl?* By whom?"

Only Dorea did not seem surprised. "He plans to incapacitate as many of us as he can."

"Who? And why?"

"The why should be as obvious as the who. The myth of imperial *bahdur* and the toll it exacts on the people may be hiding the real problem. Pan is weak, he can only expect to dominate those who are weaker."

"Widespread loss of power creates a need for boost," Palaton remarked. "We can't be sure Pan is at the bottom of all the trouble. Qativar is capable of doing anything to further his plans."

"Or they could be working in conjunction."

"Pan knows they want the throne. I don't think he would give it to them just to forestall any threat he sees from me."

"There is more," Malahki said grimly. "Panshinea has Jorana. There's to be a public execution tomorrow."

"He means to draw me out." Palaton's expression creased in anger. "How does he justify her murder?"

"If the emperor needs any justification, she's carrying your child. The House of Flame is never to be rebuilt again."

"Palaton," Dorea murmured. "We are here with you."

"He's mad." Palaton sat down abruptly.

"She's my foster daughter," Malahki proclaimed. "I have no intention of letting him get away with it."

Father Chirek added, "Do we assume he's ordered *ruhl* into the systems with some hope of reaching Palaton? That he would annihilate the *bahdur* of an entire planet to reach one Choya?"

"Perhaps. We're secure here at Bayalak. I've left guards at the filtration plant. We can carry bottled water if we're going into Charolon for the day."

"We'll have to do more than that." Chirek rubbed the base of his horn crown, staving off a headache. "We know what it's like to be common. We're going to have to go in, try to keep the streets calm."

"No," argued Malahki. "I need every Choya I can get for backup."

"Our people will need whatever we can offer them."

"Palaton has to go in alone."

They all stopped talking, turning to look at the Choya'i. Dorea took a short breath.

"The trap is meant for him. He alone can spring it."

"I won't allow—"

Palaton cut Malahki off. "It's all right. I expected this."

Dorea put her hand up. "We will be there, Palaton. As Father Chirek wishes. Malahki will have a handful of agents he can trust to assist you. But it is you who must face Panshinea.

I tell you now, as I have spoken from the first: There cannot be two emperors on Cho."

To Palaton, she added urgently, "You must face Panshinea and his shadow, and you must be prepared to do whatever you have to."

"I am."

"Even loosing the House of Flame?"

He did not answer her immediately then, understanding the depth of her question. To the others, Dorea spoke. "The House of Flame was destroyed centuries ago for reasons we do not know. It was the tree which branched all of us, but even that did not save it in the end. We do not know why its lines were cut off, what the other Houses feared, but it must have been formidable. Are you strong enough, Palaton, to face what the rest of us could not?"

* * * *

"They're right on our tails."

"This is a freighter," Dilarabe pointed out patiently. "Not a cruiser. Not a warship. We can't hope to outrun them forever."

"I don't want forever," Rand answered. "I just want to hit Chaos ahead of them."

"I think," the *tezar* continued, his hands playing over his instrument board, "they will let us run until they're sure we're going to warp. Then they will hit us before we can make the final jump into Chaos. I am not a combat pilot. I have preferred, in my career, to be a chaperon. But they're arming. It seems logical they plan to attack us."

"Oh, God," Maeva squeaked faintly. She shut her eyes.

"Don't worry." Rand put a hand on her shoulder, squeezed it lightly. "They don't want to blast us out of space. What they really want to do is board us."

"Oh, God," she repeated.

Rindalan suggested, "Perhaps she should be sedated for the jump."

"It's a little early for that," Dilarabe told him.

"I think it might be best."

"I disagree," intoned Thomas from across the bridge,

where they had him bound to a chair. "You need everybody with their full faculties, particularly if the Abdreliks try to board."

"If we make the jump without their stopping us, we may not have time to medicate."

"There are only two of us here that the reality fugue in Chaos will bother, me and Maeva. But if the Abdreliks board us, we're all at risk."

Rand wanted to say, "Don't listen to him, he has the silver tongue of the devil," but he said nothing.

"And why," prompted Rindy, "would we want to deal with the Abdreliks?"

"You may not have a choice." Thomas turned away from them and looked at the wall.

A sudden intuition prickled at Rand. "What are we carrying, Ambassador, and what were your original flight plans?"

"We're following our original flight plans," Dilarabe answered instead of Thomas.

"You were headed to Cho anyway?"

"Yes."

"Why? This is a cargo ship. We don't have active trade treaties with Cho."

"Boost," said Rindalan faintly.

Rand's and Maeva's attention swiveled to him. The elder Choya got to his feet, despite the acceleration sway of the freighter. He stabbed a hand through the air. "You're bringing the drug in."

"Of course," answered the other wearily. "You knew it was off-world. Who did you think supplied it?"

"I have not had the time to contemplate the stupidity and greed of the species who are destroying my people."

"It was never meant to destroy you. It was never meant for you, period."

Rand put his hand on Rindalan. He could feel the agitation coursing through the Choya's body, the surge of the pulse. He feared losing Rindy. "Tell me about boost."

Rindalan returned to his chair uneasily. "It restores *bahdur.*"

"That can't be bad."

"It would not seem so. But it is highly addictive, occasionally toxic, and the *bahdur* which returns is often out of control. I am told that it creates a craving which even the restoration of *bahdur* cannot sate. Nothing good can come of it. Perhaps we should let the Abdreliks catch us and annihilate the ship."

Thomas shrugged within his bonds. "Before this flight is over, you may all wish you had a dose of it."

"What good would you ever expect of it!" Rindy's voices boomed in the control room.

Thomas paused a long moment before he turned fully to speak to them, and Rand was surprised to see a wetness upon the man's cheeks. "I had it developed to save my daughter."

Maeva got up to go to him, hesitated, and when she saw no visible protest from Rand, she crossed the bridge to stand by the ambassador. "Why?"

"I wanted to free her." He leaned his head back, let Maeva dab the tears from his face. "I never knew what GNask would do to her, how it would change her. She was my daughter! I loved her. But she was never mine after he took her."

"What did he do?"

Thomas stared at Rindalan. "You drove me to it. You Choyan. You took our children. They never returned. I could find no trace of them—not even any of you who would admit to it—"

"The renegades on Arizar took them."

"I know that now. I did not then. I went to the Abdreliks and offered to help them build a case against you."

Dilarabe said wryly, "They are ever looking for leverage."

"I needed them to promote us out of Class Zed status. GNask and I formed an alliance. I did nothing that I am ashamed of, except for Alexa."

Maeva smoothed his hair from his forehead. "What did they do to her?"

"It was decided she would become one of the lost children."

"Then it was Alexa who brought the Abdreliks down on Arizar." This, from Rand.

"Yes. It did not matter that she loved you, what little love

she had left in her. I gave her to GNask when she was hardly
more than a toddler. What he did took her away from me forever." Thomas swallowed harshly. "That symbiont they
wear—"

"The *turshes.*"

"Yes. It carries some of their genetic coding, from what I
gather. It segments. GNask took a section of the worm and
implanted it into my daughter. After that, she was his, totally.
It was as though I watched an Abdrelik wearing the skin of
my daughter. She tried to hide it, but I knew. The cruelty, the
darkness inside of her—"

"She never let either Bevan or me get really close to her,"
Rand murmured. "I thought it was because she preferred him.
He thought it was because she wanted me."

"She could not have lived with either of you. I know. I
caught her once when she was small. The family dog was
missing, a small pet . . . I found her devouring it. Like a
jackal, bathed in its warm blood, she'd hunted and killed it.
She fought me when I tried to take the carcass away. I don't
know if she remembered that, later, but I do know she became
very secretive and reserved as she grew. She knew that she
had monstrous tendencies which we wouldn't accept. I didn't
know what to do, how I was going to live with what I'd created, how she could live."

"How did boost come about?"

"We found neural bonding when we did extensive tests on
her. Nothing we'd ever seen before. I had a research doctor
who agreed to work with me. It took years. He found a way
to clear the nerve pathways of the contamination. There was
also something about gene tags, I'm not entirely sure—I only
know that, eventually, Dr. Maren found a drug which succeeded. By then, GNask had picked up her and Nedar."

Rindy jerked, startled. "He had Nedar?"

"Yes. And imprinted him as well. That, Ambassador, is
why we may all want those drugs before this is over. GNask
has learned how to infiltrate our very beings. It's the only
way to deny him access."

"It'll be a long, cold day in hell," Rand said, "before I
would believe anything this man says."

Thomas looked at him defiantly. "It doesn't matter if you

believe me or not. You'll have the proof before your eyes in hours."

As if to punctuate his words, the freighter rocked violently, and the dull echo of an explosion reached them.

Dilarabe cried, "We've been hit!"

Chapter 37

"Everything is in place," Malahki told Palaton. Evening had long since supplanted day, and even those dark hours were wearing away. He had a few to sleep, then he would be back in Charolon, weaving his way toward a public execution scheduled to take place at noon on the Emperor's Walk, in front of the steps of Congress. Malahki stood as he spoke, sweeping away a platter of crumbs and meat scraps. He moved carefully, so as not to wake Dorea, who sat at the other end of the table, her shoulders and head slumped in sleep.

"We have been at odds," Palaton began.

Malahki interrupted him. "I prefer to think of us as uneasy allies."

Palaton looked at him levelly. "I have never thought you had less than the concern of our people in your heart."

Malahki opened his mouth to respond in kind, then paused and grinned. "I wish I could say the same for you."

He muted it, but Malahki had drawn a laugh from him all the same. "I am a *tezar*. I am sorry, but that is all I have ever wanted to be."

"I know. Perhaps that is what Cho needs most on its throne, right now."

"What Cho needs on its throne now is someone like you." Palaton looked at Malahki, and his thoughts suddenly seemed crystal clear.

Malahki ducked away and would no longer meet his gaze. "It was not I who said that." He put a shoulder to the room's door and left, food platter in his hands, looking for all the world like a waiter.

Palaton sat back in his chair, muttering to himself. "No. It was I who said it." He felt weary again and rubbed his eyes.

Dorea stirred. Her mouth curved. "It appears I must wake up, so that I can be put to bed properly."

"Did you rest?"

"As much as I ever do, now. Sleeping dreams, waking dreams . . . I am always searching for portents." She gave a sigh, for once sounding like the young Choya'i she was.

"Do you wish you had never met him?"

"The I'falan? Yes. I had a handsome young Choya courting me then. Those first few hours after the Change, I frightened him away with my ranting and raving. I needed help and care. He had nothing for me."

"Chirek is devoted to you."

"Yes," and she smiled more fully, joy in it. "He is a good Choya. I only hope he realizes soon the possibilities we have together."

"Your being the Prophet blinds him, as well."

"I think so. And what about you?"

"Being blind? I would say I have my moments."

"Was Jorana one of them?"

"Is there any doubt? I only wish I could understand how my heart could be so divided. There is Jorana, and there is . . ." he hesitated.

"Rand?"

"Yes. An alien, yet my *durah*. He is the twin to my soul, the part of me which flies and hungers for truth and tries to understand the world around me. I always thought a soulmate would also be a sexual mate. This baffles me."

"Does Jorana understand?"

"I think so. I don't know for sure."

"And Rand?"

"Of course."

"Then you have nothing to worry about, except securing their safety."

He laughed again. "You make it sound so easy."

Her face clouded. "Nothing this next day will be easy."

"I owe you and Malahki much."

"He would ask only one thing of you: the same thing I would ask."

"I am not the I'falan." He shook his head, even though she could not see him.

"It was your *bahdur* Rand carried."

"I cannot do this for you."

She looked at him, longing aching in her face. "It is the only thing I ask."

Palaton pounded a fist on the table, muted, helpless. "Dorea . . ."

"We will take care of her. Shield her. But she has done so much for us, and she was not able to get to Rand before . . ."

"One Choya'i."

"Yes." Dorea whispered, but her voices cut into Palaton as if they had been knives.

Only one. Did that damage his resolve so much, to give in for only one?

It would be like a dam giving way. Do it for one, he would have to do it for others. It would be against everything which he had decided for himself.

The door creaked ajar. Malahki held it open and let the child slip in.

She had hair the color of winter wheat, and eyes of seafoam green, and she was so young, her horn crown had just begun to scallop its edges. The sun had not yet creased her eyelids or mouth, and she stood shyly just inside the room, watching Dorea, trying not to look at Palaton. That she was common seemed obvious, no Housed children had hair naturally her color.

"My future," said Dorea and held out her hand.

Another Prophet? Would he be doing her a favor to light the fire inside her? Or did Dorea realize that coming to the art of prophecy gently, guided, would be more of a blessing? Had she *seen* this child and brought her to the I'falan, only to be denied?

Palaton parted his lips to tell them both no, when the Choya'i looked at him with those guileless seafoam eyes.

"Please."

"Do you know what you ask of me?"

"I know it is both terrible and beautiful. It is like something you dream, and forget, and fear, and want to remember all day. I think it must be like eating fire and ice, in the same mouthful."

He sighed. Could not face that look on her face. Turned to Dorea. "What is it I should do?"

Triumph leaped in the Prophet's expression, something she curbed immediately. "Touch her with *bahdur.*"

"There has to be more than that." And less. If he touched her with all the fury of the *bahdur* at his command, he could knock her senseless. Even as he thought of the child, he thought of Panshinea. Suddenly, he knew what the Houses had feared of the House of Flame, what imperial *bahdur* really was, a mythic remnant of an ability which had actually existed at one time.

Two sides of the same coin. Power that healed, opened up nerves which had not been able to conduct their genetic potential for some reason, power that unsealed those conduits and allowed *bahdur* to flow. The other, lethal, side . . . *bahdur* that shut down systems as it flowed inward, killing as it touched.

Not all Flames would have had the ability to the same extent, but losing that House explained much. Explained why no Houses had healers in their lines . . . why *bahdur* was not generally lethal. Why commons existed.

He put his hand to his head, thoughts swimming.

"Palaton?"

He looked up. "I'm all right. Come here to me . . ."

"Nerala," supplied the Prophet.

"Nerala."

The Choya'i hesitated. She looked to the Prophet, studied her blindfolded face, put her hand shyly into Dorea's. "Will I have to tear my eyes out?"

"God-in-all willing, never," the Prophet said fervently.

Nerala stepped close.

Palaton summoned his power, felt it quicken in his veins, asked of it what he willed and reached out toward the child. The power leaped, arcing, blue flame without heat crossing from his hand to her forehead.

She had her eyes closed, mouth twisted tight, feet glued to the floor. She rocked back a little as he touched her, holding her breath. Palaton reined his power back as quickly as he had made contact.

After a long moment, she opened her eyes. Her lips turned down. "Nothing," she whispered fiercely. "Nothing happened!"

Dorea sprang to her feet. "It can't be." She groped toward the child with her hands.

Power speaks to power.

Palaton stretched his own hand out again. Nothing called to him. Nerala was as empty as she had been born. As much as he had never wanted to be the I'falan, disappointment racked him. "I could not do it."

Nerala let out a sob and ran from the room. The door banged in her wake. Dorea clung to the table's edge. "I can't be wrong. I can't."

"All this means is that I have to come back. As soon as Jorana is in the clear, you have to find Rand for me. We can't wait any longer."

"There may not be enough time." Dorea looked toward him, tugging uncomfortably on her blindfold. "I have not tried to keep things from you, but you must understand, the visions are not always perfect. Sometimes early, sometimes too late. . . ."

"What is it!"

"Chaos," she cried softly. "Lost forever. Oh, Palaton . . . I did not know."

* * * *

"Third hit," counted Rand grimly as the old freighter rocked again. Central lighting flickered, then came back on. "She can't take much more." Maeva, in her sling chair, looked at him in dismay.

"I can't get any more maneuvering speed out of her. The port retros are gone."

"How much longer before you hit FTL?"

"Not soon enough," Dilarabe grunted, his attention caught by the helm. The freighter shuddered again and there was a whine which carried throughout the framework, and they could all feel the sudden deceleration. The hours spent in flight had just ended.

"That's it," stated Thomas. "They'll have a tractor on us in minutes and we'll be pried open like an oyster shell."

Rindy looked across the bridge. "I am not familiar with your oysters, but I think I understand the analogy. Ambassador Thomas, I am going to release you. I trust you have the same self-interests we all do." He reached Thomas in two strides and struck open the bonds.

Thomas hissed softly through his lips as he massaged his wrists. He looked at Rand. "I would be lying if I said we did not have a score to settle, but I agree with Rindalan. Our mutual survival has a higher priority. We have a truce for now."

"A truce does not mean trust."

Thomas examined his hand. "You are right again." He started to get up, was rocked from his feet as the entire vessel shuddered violently.

Rand grabbed for Maeva's sling to steady himself. "It'll be all right."

"Sure. If they try to implant me, I'll sue 'em." Her voice sounded braver than she felt.

"That should stop them in their tracks."

Dilarabe secured the helm. He opened a cabinet under the console. A rack of enforcers dropped into place. "Weapons, anyone?"

The ship's engine cut out, and emergency power kicked in. Metal creaked, then let out a scream which thrilled the length of the freighter.

"They're in," said Rand.

Rindy looked at the weapons thoughtfully, then shook his head. "We don't want them to think we have something worth fighting over. We have two ambassadors here. Let's see if we can get by with a little diplomacy."

GNask rocked back in the massive chair which held him. The cavernous belly of the Abdrelik ship was but one of the small service docks inside the craft which had swallowed up their freighter so effortlessly. It smelled of the Abdreliks, dank, moist, predatory. GNask had had them escorted there with little ceremony, his war general remaining a wary distance from all of them. His small, round eyes examined them with beady interest. He had been listening and questioning for many minutes and now sat silent. Even his symbiont, which rested atop his skull like a humorous hat, appeared to watch them with stalk eyes. The Abdrelik wiped the corner of his mouth. "Now let me get this straight. You," and he looked to Rindalan, "left Sorrow of your own accord, with these two humankind."

Rindy nodded solemnly.

"And you did not have your vessel commandeered, but recognized the urgency of Ambassador Rindalan's request and agreed to carry him and his passengers to Cho."

Thomas lifted a shoulder, let it drop. "That sounds about right."

"And you," the Abdrelik frowned, coarse gashes in his thick, purplish brow. "Were not being held against your will in the Terran embassy."

"You got it," Rand answered.

"You realize that you alone would be held by my president's express command and returned to Sorrow for trial?"

"I think I would have to claim diplomatic immunity."

"Would you?" GNask gave a rasping laugh. "Which one of these diplomats would have you?"

"I would," both Rindalan and Thomas answered simultaneously.

The Abdrelik let out a roaring guffaw and even his tense general, rrRusk, chuckled a bit.

When GNask had composed himself, he said, "You are most humorous. Do you expect to stand here and have me believe a word of what you've told me? After chasing you from Bay 4A to the jump-off for Chaos?"

"It does not matter if you believe us or not," Rindalan answered. "It matters only if you can prove otherwise, and I doubt you can."

"Ignoring our hailing request to heave to and let us board might prove evidential."

"Do you have any record of what transpired on Sorrow or on Bay 4A or on this vessel?" Rindalan persisted. "If you haven't, I suggest you make repairs to our craft and return us to its decks."

"I doubt you expected this would be easy." GNask heaved himself onto his feet. "Recordings such as you request would be difficult to produce, given the articles of the Compact. However, whether they exist or not, I would be hard-pressed to ignore the fact that you left Bay 4A without authorization and in a tremendous hurry, carrying personnel which the Compact has long desired to question officially. I may not be able to prove what has transpired behind closed doors, but I do have records from the station and I have warrants from a Compact court for the young manling here. I did not know he was with you, but now that I have identified him, I can scarcely ignore the fact. I would be exceedingly remiss to let any of you slip through my fingers."

His eyes narrowed. "There are other possibilities. The freighter is old. You were in full flight. It could have disintegrated under the strain."

Maeva retorted, "You wouldn't dare. Two senior ambassadors and a full attorney!"

He looked at her, curled a lip off a tusk. "Oh, wouldn't I? You should have cooperated with me when you had the chance." He crooked a finger at rrRusk. "Separate the pilot from the others."

Dilarabe reached for Rindalan as if he were an anchor. Rand put himself between the approaching Abdrelik and the Choyan, heedless of the difference in height and bulk. rrRusk shook his head in disbelief.

"Move aside, little being."

"I don't think so."

rrRusk looked around the hold. "You cannot possibly think of evading me."

"I don't have to think about it, I just have to do it."

"Weapon, rrRusk," grumbled GNask.

"They are carrying nothing."

"Not true." Rand spread his hands. "I am all I need."

Maeva, who stood at his back, said, "Don't do this, Rand."

"Move toward the bulkhead," Rand told her without looking around. "Get everybody secured in the life pods in the freighter."

Thomas said suddenly to GNask, "Take me."

The Abdrelik's coal-dark eyes flicked toward him in contempt. "I no longer need you." He moved a hand, a shape filled his fingers, and fired.

Thomas went down with a cry, grabbing at his thigh where crimson blossomed. Rindy bent over and dragged him back to his feet. Blood leaked copiously from between Thomas' fingers.

"I suggest you all sit down. rrRusk, the pilot."

rrRusk moved once more toward Dilarabe.

"There are three of us," Rand suggested to Rindalan.

"We risk much."

Dilarabe stepped around Rand. "Too much. I will bear this burden."

Chapter 38

He let rrRusk grab him and haul him across the hold.

Rand held himself very still, but Maeva could see the tension in his body, the fury he fought to contain. GNask stepped out of the bay behind his general.

When the bulkhead had sealed behind the Abdreliks, he had only one word for Rindalan.

"Why?"

"Because," Rindy said, slowly and with great fatigue, "he offered. It is our way, Rand. It is part of being a *tezar.*" He bent, letting Thomas slump to the deck.

Maeva knelt beside the ambassador. "We've got to get the bleeding stopped." She put pressure just above the wound.

Thomas put his head back, his face pale and sweating. "Whatever happens to me, you've got to get boost down your pilot. After the implant. It's the only thing you can do for him. It'll counter whatever imprinting GNask manages."

Rand swung about almost casually, pointed his fingers at the wound, and blue fire leaped from him. Maeva flinched, but the flame bypassed her and sizzled into Thomas' leg, where the flesh gaped and blood oozed. An intense smell of burning skin filled the air and she gagged with the scent of it. She took her hand away, shaking. "It's—you've closed it."

The discharged flame dissipated, but a fine shimmering continued to envelop Rand. Thomas moaned once or twice, then grew silent. His head lolled back, and she let him sag to the floor.

"It will heal," Rand pronounced, almost absently, as if unaware of what he had done. He stared at the bulkhead beyond which GNask and rrRusk had taken Dilarabe.

Rindy sat, spindly legs suddenly uncertain, watching Rand closely. "What did you do?"

Rand did not answer, but Maeva did. "He's done it before. In the holding cell, he injured himself trying to cross the laser barrier. He was burned, to the bone. I never saw such injuries. His hands, his wrists. . . ."

"I see no scarring."

"Healing began before he was even conscious. Within days I could tell there would be no scars. I've never seen or heard of anything like it."

"Rand." This time Rindalan got his attention. "Did you know you could do such a thing?"

Rand turned and came over to Thomas' limp body. He looked down at the wound which, although it smelled as if it had been cauterized, had sealed as though invisibly stitched. Healing had already started. "I can't—" he stopped. "I had the power worked up to strike rrRusk. It had to go somewhere. I had to discharge it. That seemed the most logical thing to do with it." He spread his hands, looked at them. The aura of power remained about him.

"But did you know—?"

"No, I didn't." He peered more closely at the wound. "It's far from healed."

"And it's equally far from being fatal, which it could have been the way he was losing blood." Maeva wiped her hands on her trouser. The dark navy fabric absorbed the stain. "What do we do now?"

"We wait," answered Rindalan. He had his hand on his chest, and looked slightly pale himself.

"No. We take the chance Dilarabe gave us, and we get out of here." Rand grabbed Thomas by the shoulders. "Help me get him on his feet."

"Those bulkheads are locked," Maeva protested.

"Not to me."

She appealed to Rindy. "Can *bahdur* do this?"

"Not to my knowledge. But then, he is the I'falan. He brings a whole new dimension to the heritage of my planet." Rindy forced a wry smile as he got up, and helped Maeva with Thomas' weight.

The ambassador stirred. He said thickly, "I can walk."

"With help, maybe." Maeva got her shoulder under his.

Rand went to the bulkhead. The cloud of motes encircling

him spread out like a blanket, covering the locked exit. He put his hands and head to it, listening.

From far away came a muffled scream. It ululated throughout the craft like a primitive howl and carried with it unutterable pain and loss. Rindy, who had Thomas' other arm, stiffened. Maeva felt tears come to her eyes as he murmured, prayerfully, "Dilarabe. God-in-all have mercy on you."

Rand did not seem to notice, his eyes narrowing in concentration. Machinery hummed and the door inched open. The bulkhead widened, slowly, reluctantly, three-quarters of the way.

He turned, strain mirrored on his face. "Go on."

Rindy and Maeva got Thomas through. Maeva leaned back through the doorway. "Come on."

"No. I'm not leaving Dilarabe behind. You take the freighter. Jettison the cargo once you blast free. The bridge is a self-contained unit. Freed of the cargo, you should get max acceleration fairly quickly. We're inside, we can't feel the Abdrelikan cruiser moving, it's a smoother ship, but I'm willing to bet we're pretty close to jumping. GNask wants us near his home base, in his pocket. Get out, hit FTL. Rindy's no pilot, but I think he has what it takes to get you through. Get the hell out of here."

"What about you?"

"I'll be right there with you if I can. Give me fifteen minutes. If not—" He leaned toward her impulsively, and his lips brushed her face. "Sue me," he said. He pushed her gently away from the exit, took his hands from the heavy metal threshold, and let it snap shut.

GNask watched the *tezar* who had come with them so proudly writhe now in voiceless pain. He took his *tursh* up, speaking soothingly to it, gently licked the fluids off its body where it had surrendered a segment. He settled his symbiont on his shoulder. He had done the work himself, taking satisfaction in his skillful handling of the scalpel. The task had taken a blade, not a laser which might have cauterized fine cellular layers even as it cut.

As he watched Dilarabe flail, he realized what an exceptional individual Nedar had been. What discipline for that pilot to never show the agony he had felt, to never hint to

GNask that the procedure could work, had worked, upon his Choyan physiology.

He said to rrRusk, "We are making history here."

The general stood watchfully.

"Not today, perhaps, but tomorrow or the day after, all that the Choyan have hidden from us will be ours. I have done what cunning and torture have failed to do."

rrRusk lifted his eyes to GNask. "You will face Frnark."

"Eventually. Our president is still in his prime. It would be a shame to depose him now. What I hope to gain by this, my general, is to be his only competitor. To meet him one to one, and not have to claw my way up a heap first. To conserve my strength for the one and only opponent who counts. Delivering him the Choyan empire should give me that edge." He toed Dilarabe's distressed body. "Leave him. The others will try to make a run for it. I need to decide whether we will destroy them or let them destroy themselves."

Silence fell.

Dilarabe raised his head to ascertain if they had gone. His nakedness did not bother him, but he clawed his way along the floor to his discarded uniform, a long and treacherous journey on hands he had broken pounding out his agony on the deck. His blood made the journey slick. One of his elbows had dislocated. He crooned to it, trying to soothe the agony he felt.

The *thing* which was of and from the Abdreliks insinuated itself inside of him. It crawled under his skin with a ropy sliminess he could not avoid. It left a trail of black fire that made his head pound and devoured his *bahdur* until he knew all that was left of him would be emptiness and pain. And then that *thing* would take up residence, and every thought, every memory, all his heritage and all his teaching, would be given over to GNask as though they were precious gems.

As, indeed, they were.

Dilarabe stumbled on a broken tile. It poked into his rib cage, which was already raw and bruised, and if he crawled farther, he thought it would pierce him like a stake. He hugged the deck, put his face to the cold tile, to muffle the sound of his own crying. So easily defeated.

A footfall sounded next to his hand. Dilarabe looked up.

Rand hunched over his flight suit, searching the pockets. Thomas had made them all secrete packets of the drug in their clothes.

"Rand."

The manling pivoted. "Quiet. I'll have this stuff down you in a minute." He patted down the many pockets, finally found what he was looking for, what had drawn Dilarabe crawling across what had felt like a continent.

Dilarabe thought a great deal, but could only say, "Gone."

"Not without you. Here." Gently cradling his head, Rand tore open a packet and poured fuchsia powder into his mouth.

It tasted like bitter fruit, and exploded in his mouth with a static electricity. Dilarabe felt himself jerk once, twice, in reaction to it. His tongue went dry, but he tried to swallow, tried to gather enough spit to dissolve the drug in his mouth.

"They did this to you?"

Dilarabe could not answer. He tried to shake his head in the negative, because he had done it to himself, battering himself as the worm had entered his body, cleaving him from his power, bringing nothing but pain. He tried again to swallow.

A kind of relief pushed its way down his throat. He could feel it muting the black fire of the worm, the symbiont.

"Is it working?" Rand leaned over him anxiously. "I know you're hurt badly, but I've got to get you up. I can't carry you out of here."

"Working," Dilarabe managed. "It's . . . neutralizing."

The medical bay split open. GNask ranged in the gap. "Pity," he said. "I had hoped for a successful experiment. The initial results were so spectacular. Exactly what was it you did for him?"

Rand laid Dilarabe back on the deck. "I came back for him."

"Don't be as stupid as the Compact claims you are. I have the room wired. Did you think I would go and leave my subject unobserved? What did you feed him?"

rrRusk shadowed GNask. He passed the ambassador and kicked the flight suit out of their reach. A second, unopened packet went skidding across the floor toward them. The Abdrelik general picked it up.

"I would guess it was this." He handed it to GNask.

The ambassador turned it over several times with his stubby fingers. "A pharmaceutical. Herbal or synthetic?"

"I wouldn't know." Rand stood his ground. Behind him, noises suggested that Dilarabe was attempting to get up under his own power. "Thomas had it made up for Alexa."

"And how successful was he there?" GNask smiled. "Not very, I wager. She was always more my daughter than his." He looked at Dilarabe, and his cheer fled slightly. "Although there are degrees, I suppose." He opened the packet and took a cautious sniff. "It erases the neural imprinting."

"So I'm told." Rand held himself very still, watching the two Abdreliks, as though he knew instinctively that to run against predators would set off their instinct to pursue.

GNask gave the packet to rrRusk. "Take it."

The general stammered. "W–what?"

"Take it."

"It's off-world. It could be toxic. Your Eminence—"

"Take it!" GNask roared.

Rand braced himself as Dilarabe leaned against him from the rear. He could hear the Choya's labored breathing. But he could also feel the return of the power that had coursed in the *tezar's* body, for it called to his own. The boost had worked, as intended.

rrRusk hesitated another moment, then lifted the packet to his mouth and ate it whole. He chewed a moment and then gave a hard swallow. GNask took a step back, watching with interest.

Rand watched also. He had no experience with the drug other than what he'd just seen Dilarabe go through. The ingestion seemed to be rapid, the results dramatic. He whispered out of the corner of his mouth, "Be ready."

Dilarabe did not answer, but one of his broken hands tightened slightly on Rand's shoulder in answer.

The Abdrelik stretched his neck and flexed in his uniform jacket as if uncomfortable. He peeled it off. He wore the customary suspendered trousers under it, torso bare. His purplish skin held a sheen of sweat. He blinked rapidly several times. Then he tossed his head up and down. Rand thought of a large bull getting ready to attack.

GNask had taken another step backward. "Tell me, rrRusk, what is it you feel?"

The general shuddered, his skin flapping inordinately, an immense amphibious dog shaking off an unseen enemy. When he swung around to face Rand and Dilarabe, nothing of intelligence glittered in his piggish eyes.

"Shit," said Rand, and lunged to the side, carrying Dilarabe with him.

rrRusk bellowed, charging into the lab.

He lost the pilot as the Abdrelik barreled into him. rrRusk tore Dilarabe in two. The pilot went down with a soft cry as rrRusk launched himself into Rand. Their momentum carried them across the room and Rand slipped away a bare second before they crashed into the wall. The section shattered under the impact, buried Rand in preform shards as rrRusk bellowed again.

The Abdrelik hauled himself to his feet, searching, glaring at the debris. He began to claw it off Rand. In those seconds, Rand knew what it was to be hunted by an Abdrelik, how it must have been on their world in ancient times. The amphibian must have been a terrible king of their world, just as a T-Rex or velociraptor had been of Earth. Hot breath grazed off Rand as drool cascaded from rrRusk's panting mouth.

The Abdrelik lifted the last panel off Rand, grunting as he did so, eyes red with blood lust. He threw the partition to one side and reached to hook Rand for himself.

GNask's weapon popped. rrRusk staggered back. He clutched at his chest. The weapon popped two more times in rapid succession. The general continued to fall back, staring in amazement at the gaping holes which flowered in his chest, at the maroon blood which gushed out. Then he toppled to the floor in a massive crash.

Rand got shakily to his feet. GNask advanced halfway across the lab.

"Too bad. He was a valued employee. He knew too much though, to keep much longer. He had . . . secrets." The ambassador looked at Rand.

"Get out of here while you can."

"You'll destroy us in mid-space."

GNask gave a rumbling laugh. "I might. Might not. That's the chance you'll take. Now go."

Rand looked across at Dilarabe's body, and did not wait for a second invitation.

* * *

As the freighter neared jump-off speed, Maeva responded to an alarm on the console.

"Rand, you were right. He's targeting. What are you going to do?"

"Open the channels."

Rindy hailed the Abdrelikan vessel. GNask's unmistakable voice filled the comline.

"Should have run faster, manling, while you had the chance."

"We'll get the speed up when we jettison the cargo," Rand answered. "You don't want to hit us."

"Don't I?"

"No. We're carrying boost. That's the drug you poured down your general's gullet. Now, I think his reaction probably meant more to you than it did to me. I think that's why you killed him, to hide the evidence. But if you want that drug, you'll let us go."

"You're carrying it."

"Yes." Rand gave an indication to Thomas, who limped with a camera and panned a shot of the hold. They'd broken open several of the packaging bins.

"I see," said GNask. "And you will jettison that for me."

"I won't have much chance of making FTL without doing it."

"All right, then. Make your run, little one. I'll be seeing you around the galaxy."

Rand cut communications. He waved everyone back to their slings, and shut the bulkheads and hatches. "Okay. Prepare for jettison. When it goes, we're hitting Chaos almost immediately. Brace yourselves."

The freighter trembled and then the bridge responded with a leap as it broke free. Maeva brought visuals up. They could see the massive body of the cargo ship tumbling free.

Rand said, "NOW!" and jumped them into Chaos.

Maeva remarked, "I wonder what GNask is going to do when the cargo blows."

"He will," Rindy said, "plan a severe and devious revenge."

Rand stood at the helm, feeling the ship melt away, his body become the craft, his eyes the instruments which would pierce Chaos. There was a dizzying moment when he did not know if he were the master, or if the miasma would swallow him whole. His blood rushed through his veins, galaxies tumbled at his feet. Faintly, he could hear the voices of the others.

He knew with dismay that Rindy had been right. He could not get them home. He was not a master of these patterns, he had not the experience. Sweat beaded his forehead as he fought to navigate the ship safely through vicious eddies.

He caught a glimpse of a pattern, began to thread their way toward it. It was not Cho. He did not know where they were.

He had taken them, and lost them.

He could only pray they did not realize it. He could only pray that the webbing he sent them after would be a signpost toward a destination he could reach for them.

Or they would be lost forever.

Chapter 39

Vihtirne woke Jorana none too gently. She tried to swing her legs around, to rouse herself and stand, but her bones felt like jelly. Her head throbbed, and the child within her protested, feeling as if she had swallowed the sun itself.

"Drink this."

Meals had been scant, but water plentiful. Jorana drank it because her body craved filling, craved the drink and the food that it needed to build the babe's body, and because her throat felt like a desert. She grabbed at the glass to drain it dry, and Vihtirne twisted it away.

"Not too much!"

"Not enough."

The older Choya'i laughed. "If you only knew. Can you stand?" She tried to balance Jorana on her feet. The jellified bones gave way. Jorana sagged, feeling as helpless and foolish as some newborn herself.

Vulnerable. This was her enemy who held her. But her thoughts twirled, muddled, as if she'd drunk and been drunk, for days, now. She'd lost track of time, Jorana knew suddenly.

Vihtirne made a noise of disgust and let her drop back onto the pallet. It creaked under her as though it would collapse entirely. "You have to get dressed."

Jorana raised an arm limply, let it fall back to her side. "Am dressed."

"Oh, no. You have an appointment this afternoon, Choya'i. You must be dressed to keep it. And on your feet."

The pleasant muzziness which cocooned Jorana felt dangerous. Inside, deep, something tried to prod at her, to awaken her senses, to kindle her training and wariness. It got a sluggish response, which whirled around and around in her brain as Vihtirne left, slamming the door behind her.

She heard muffled voices, could not make sense of them. ". . . to much *ruhl!* I can't even keep her on her feet!"

"Follow the plan. Everything will work out. If we can't get her up, we'll give her a blast of boost. Now get in there and get her into these things!"

Jorana tried to listen, to concentrate, but nothing made any sense. Her head pounded and she could not hear through its knocking. She sat up on the pallet, balancing her back against the wall of the room. She could not think of anything but hunger.

Hunger and the child.

She folded her hands protectively across her stomach. Hardly showing yet. Just enough to curve her palm. Jorana closed her eyes, letting the whirlpool of confusion drag her down. If only they would feed her and let her sleep, everything would be all right. . . .

K-arack! The sting of a hand across her face jolted her across the pallet. Her teeth clicked and her head snapped on her neck. The blow flared across her skin like a firebrand. Jorana felt a stab of energy answer the attack. She sat up and shook her head, clearing her vision. Vihtirne stood over her.

"Can you dress yourself or shall I have to?"

Jorana looked dazedly at the clothes hanging from Vihtirne's outstretched arm, the moment of clarity already fading. Her captor sighed and bent down. "Never mind. If you feel sick, tell me. I don't want these soiled."

Her face rough and bruised from the blow, she complied listlessly as the other pulled garments one way and tugged them the other. Something about it struck her as funny halfway through the ordeal and she began to giggle and did not stop until Vihtirne finished with an exasperated grunt.

"Go back to sleep if you must, but sleep sitting up."

Sleep sounded like an excellent idea. The burst of laughter had exhausted her. There was only one other thing . . . "Hungry."

"Later. When you're up and on your feet. Then I'll feed you."

Jorana felt herself sag, started to roll over and curl up on the pallet, when she remembered that she must sit up. She righted herself and let her head lean back against the wall.

She must also remember something else. An appointment to keep. Somewhere to go. She never heard Vihtirne leave.

* * * *

Palaton walked the back streets toward the palace center, just as he had walked them before. This time, however, he was not alone. Far from it. Strung throughout the quarters were those who followed Malahki's orders and direction, an invisible network of Choyan who worked for a common purpose. He paused as Emperor's Walk became visible. Crowds filled the park below it, just as they had before, although more guardsmen than he had ever seen before restrained them. He started off again, but Dorea had dropped her hand onto his arm.

He turned to Chirek and the Prophet. She drew him into a hug. When she released him, she said, "Follow your heart, Palaton. When all else fails, follow your heart."

Father Chirek added, "We'll meet you when she is free."

He nodded. They left him, blending deftly into the flow of Choyan who gathered to see the death of an innocent Choya'i. He could hear them murmuring as they passed, then gathered him into their inexorable tide.

". . . plays the *lindar* all hours of the day and night. Howls at the moons."

". . . and no word of the minister. None, none at all! Some say he's gone to join the renegades from Arizar."

Now that, thought Palaton, was a possibility. He had been concerned about old Gathon. Could the minister have left while he still had a life of his own? He quickened his step to stay with the flow of the crowd, letting them carry him, be his barrier, his shield, their babble of thought hiding his. They were full of boost, he could smell it on them, high-priced boost, having given their *bahdur,* so they thought, to Panshinea's draw.

So full now, to be so empty and aching later.

He kept his jacket collar high. Dorea had braided his hair for him, twining her fingers deftly through the strands, pulling it back from his horns and his brow. It was a new look for him, one that might confuse the enemy, even if only for a moment.

A moment was all it would take. He would strike down Panshinea, once and for all, free Jorana, and be gone in the confusion which Malahki's throngs intended to create. He had only the guard to worry about, and he thought that Jorana would be able to quell them. If not, the crowd might overrun them. They would stampede, he knew, after the last incident, at the slightest sign that Pan's *bahdur* had gone amok again. He could contribute to that.

After Jorana was safe, he and Malahkhi would decide how to confront Vihtirne and Qativar. Congress might be persuaded to do the job they were supposed to, to create a government and stand firm.

"Stay back!"

Palaton stopped in surprise. Caught up in his thoughts, he had not realized that the tide had carried him to the end of the Emperor's Walk. A guard put a shield to his chest and pushed him back beyond an imaginary barrier. He went.

The sun rose high overhead, breaking through a scattering of clouds. Palaton resisted the desire to look at it, just as he did not allow his sight to wander to the area where Traskar had crashed. He kept his eyes on the walk.

Around him, various chronograms began to chime the hour, but he did not need to hear them. A figure wearing black, and wrapped in a black hood and cloak was brought out on the walk and pushed to her knees. Jorana, wearing the colors of the dead.

He could not see her face. She knelt, with her head bowed and the hood drawn over as if she could not stand to face the crowd. If he could not get to her, could not free her, he had hoped for at least one last glimpse of her face.

Perhaps it was better not so. Palaton began to make his way through the gathering, slipping sideways, moving into position. He was jostled a lot, but more than once he was guided, a voice whispering, "Malahki," at his collar, a password, and sending him closer to his destination.

"There he is!" A murmur went up as Panshinea came onto the walkway.

Palaton watched him, slow hatred simmering inside of him. The ravages of his disability showed. He had shrunken down beyond slimness, and his hair had been bound back and red and gold ribbons fastened it, making up for the glint of auburn among the gold it had once carried. He wore a hooded cloak as well, though it was translucent and Palaton could not see his face. His colors of crimson and gold seemed tawdry in the brilliant sunlight. He walked with an escort as if he needed assistance and Palaton felt bitterness burn the back of his throat that this Choya still clung to the throne. He would take them all down with him, all to the pits of the descendancy of a House in full collapse.

Palaton thought he caught a glimpse of Qativar in the escort as they stepped back. The face was gone too soon and he let it go, concentrating on saving Jorana.

A clerk was nudged onto the walk between kneeling Jorana, who had not moved, and Panshinea, who looked as though he had to balance himself to stay upright. Palaton remembered the nervous Choya. He stuttered when stressed.

"We are g–gathered here this day to w–w–witness the execution of J–jorana of Star, for crimes against the throne and s–s–sedition with the enemy, and for the execution of the child she carries, of the House of Flame, an outlawed H–House."

Someone cried out, "Innocent!" only to be shushed. The guard lowered their riot shields and looked out over the gathered Choyan, their faces solemn. Palaton wondered how many of them she had trained, handpicked for their assignments, served with night and day in the years she had been their captain. The clerk scampered out of range of any and all outrages.

He knew that this was the bait for his trap, that Panshinea had but one reason to parade her out here like this, and yet he hesitated to spring that trap. The *bahdur* burned in his gut, a firestorm roaring to be loose, and he thought of striking and killing Pan where he stood.

He could not do that. He sprang at the edge of the walk and somersaulted over, landing on his feet between Jorana and Pan. The guard scattered, dropped to their knees and drew bead on him, but they did not fire.

"You issue your own death warrant, Panshinea of Star," he cried, and his voices rolled out of him, carrying across the vast parkway. "For abusing the throne of Cho, and abandoning it. For dosing your people with *ruhl* and for pandering the

drug known as boost and for refusing to leave your office
when you were no longer capable of filling it."

The figure draped in red and gold looked wildly at him, but
did not step back.

"Meet me, Panshinea, for the good of Cho."

Pan did not answer, but raised a hand as if to strike the first
blow.

Palaton took a deep breath, preparing to free the power
which churned inside of him, the power of his newly risen
House. He thought of the emperor he had known, and ad-
mired, and served, a Choya who no longer existed and perhaps had never really existed as Palaton had perceived him.
At his back, the kneeling Jorana never said a word.

Upon the Emperor's Walk, he could look out over a sea of
Choyan who seemed to hold their breath as one. He could not
tell Malahki's people from Panshinea's supporters from the
merely curious.

Because we are all one. He readied himself to take
Panshinea's strike and send out one of his own, but he noted
that the guardsmen were doing nothing.

He wore bodyshielding, was prepared to take a hit or two
as they defended their emperor, but they seemed to have
dropped into the same wrinkle in time that he had, remaining
motionless. Jorana would not have liked that. She had trained
them to be loyal, regardless. They had protected him as heir,
Pan before that, and now Pan returned.

And they waited, hesitant, holding back.

Why?

He could feel a drawing of power about Panshinea, oddly
coalescing outside of him, an aura about the red and gold, and
knew that he must do what he must do.

Follow your heart, Palaton.

But his heart did not want him to strike at the figure who
stood, now swirling in crimson and gold, whose aura had begun to blaze as bright as the sun above it. And behind him,
why did not Jorana react, cry out, welcome him? Did they
have her drugged?

Palaton pivoted, and sent his *bahdur* striking into the figure
in black, the craven imposter who knelt on the Emperor's
Walk as he had been told to do, told that Palaton would strike
the emperor's colors. Pan let out a cry of pain and betrayal,

throwing off the ebony hood, rising up and lifting his *bahdur* against Palaton.

It stank of boost. Palaton could smell it clearly now, even as Pan staggered on the walk. Palaton struck again, with *bahdur* the like of which had not been seen or experienced on Cho for centuries, because it killed as well as healed.

Pan dropped and lay quite still.

Jorana managed to throw off her stifling cloak, and dropped to her own knees. Palaton saw a movement behind her, but did not get to her in time. He threw a curtain of power out, between her and the guard. His bodyshielding took a shot which rocked him, but did not pierce the armor.

Qativar drew his weapon. He did not waste time with *bahdur*. Enforcer fire blazed into the walkway, skimming past Jorana, missing on the first shot.

Instinctively, she rolled. The second shot caught a corner of a guard's shield, and was deflected. It sprayed into the screaming onlookers.

Then, as Palaton reached Jorana to defend her, he saw the big, sable-haired Choya rearing up behind Qativar.

Malahki caught him by the neck and twisted. The resulting snap cracked through the air. Qativar went limp in Malahki's arms. Malahki held him for but a second, then cried, "No more!" He threw the body over the walkway where the frightened crowd, running from enforcer fire, trampled it into ribbons in the ground.

Jorana began to sob. Palaton drew her up. He took the ribbons from her hair, releasing its bronze glory, wondering how he could have mistaken her for Panshinea.

Over her shoulder, he saw Vihtirne. She stepped back into a brace of guardsmen, ordering them briskly about her. She put her hands up, palms out, and then disappeared into the disorder.

"Palaton."

Her tears wet his neck. He did not think he had ever seen her cry before. He held her back a little, and touched her face.

"What is this?"

"Your damn baby," she sobbed. "I cry about everything." She put her head back on his shoulder. "Thank God for adrenaline. I can think for the first time in days."

"Nearly too late." Palaton held her tightly, thinking how

close he had come to doing what Qativar had wanted him to do . . . eliminating Jorana, thinking her to be Panshinea, and then destroying himself when faced with the truth. As for Pan . . . he would never have been allowed by Qativar to live much longer. Palaton did not want to think how close he had come to doing the unthinkable.

Malahki reached him. He put his hand on Jorana's hair, tilting her head back. "Daughter."

"I'm all right," she answered. "Finally."

He nodded.

Palaton and he traded looks. He started to say something, but Father Chirek and Dorea appeared at the side of the walk. Instead, he leaned down and gave them a hand up. Dorea held his hand a moment longer than necessary before dropping it.

"It is not over."

"No. Not until we have boost out of our system, and *ruhl* banned. And I must find Rand."

Dorea looked away from him. "I'm sorry. He is lost. My seeing. . . ."

Palaton stood, stunned, unwilling to accept any kind of defeat in that moment. "No."

"He took a ship into Chaos. He has the *bahdur,* Palaton . . . but he has no guide."

"No."

Jorana said, "You were always his guide."

He looked down at her. She smiled. "You are a Flame. Burn for him. Be the beacon that draws him home to Cho. He was meant to be here, to stand with us."

And Palaton knew what she was trying to tell him, what Rand had been trying to tell him. Here was a partnership which could cleanse *bahdur,* without drugs, without harm. Different perhaps than any partnership their ancestors could have imagined, but one which could withstand the House of Flame, could temper it.

He loosened his embrace on her and stood back. He spread his arms. He threw back his head, felt his hair come loose from the Prophet's bindings, wafting in a comet stream of energy motes. He *burned* as only he could, blue flame enveloping him. He was a *tezar,* a pilot, and no pathway of the heavens could elude him, not even this one, of the purest spirit, the hottest flame.

* * *

Rand stood at the helm, his eyes stinging, his heart pounding. Somehow his *bahdur* protected them all from the ills of flying through Chaos, yet now Rindalan and Thomas had lapsed into unconsciousness, the air in the tiny pod thinning, their time running out. It would scarcely matter if he knew where to go, for then he would still have had ample time to bring them to safety, but he had not been able to find their way. Maeva took his hand, her skin chilled in his, her fingers incredibly slender and delicate.

"After all this," she said, "I want you to know I could love you."

He dared not look at her, but something in his heart shifted a little. "I could, too," he whispered back, his throat hoarse. He had been talking, and she had been listening.

And then he *saw*. Arcing like a bridge through Chaos, built out of pure *bahdur*, calling to him. Calling him home. Bringing a voice out of Flame to him, a voice so alien he could never forget it, the twin of his spirit, Palaton, navigator and master of the Chaos of the soul. He stood, a blue star on the horizon, a blazing, unmistakable beacon.

Rand let out a shout of joy, and steered toward home.

Charles Ingrid

PATTERNS OF CHAOS

Only the Choyan could pilot faster-than-light starships—and the other Compact races would do anything to learn their secret!

☐ **RADIUS OF DOUBT: Book 1**   UE2491—$4.99
☐ **PATH OF FIRE: Book 2**   UE2522—$4.99
☐ **THE DOWNFALL MATRIX: Book 3**   UE2616—$4.99
☐ **SOULFIRE: Book 4**   UE2676—$5.50

THE MARKED MAN SERIES

In a devastated America, can the Lord Protector of a mutating human race find a way to preserve the future of the species?

☐ **THE MARKED MAN: Book 1**   UE2396—$3.95

☐ **THE LAST RECALL: Book 2**   UE2460—$3.95

THE SAND WARS

He was the last Dominion Knight and he would challenge a star empire to defeat the ancient enemies of man.

☐ **SOLAR KILL: Book 1**   UE2391—$3.95
☐ **LASERTOWN BLUES: Book 2**   UE2393—$3.95
☐ **CELESTIAL HIT LIST: Book 3**   UE2394—$3.95
☐ **ALIEN SALUTE: Book 4**   UE2329—$3.95
☐ **RETURN FIRE: Book 5**   UE2363—$3.95
☐ **CHALLENGE MET: Book 6**   UE2436—$3.95

Exciting Visions of the Future!

W. Michael Gear

☐ **THE ARTIFACT**   UE2406—$5.99
In a galaxy on the brink of civil war, where the Brotherhood seeks to keep the peace, news comes of the discovery of a piece of alien tech]nology—the Artifact. It could be the greatest boon to science, or the instrument that would destroy the entire human race.

☐ **STARSTRIKE**   UE2427—$5.99
They were Earth's finest soldiers, commandeered to fight together for an alien master in a war among distant stars. . . .

FORBIDDEN BORDERS
He was the most hated and feared power in human-controlled space—and only he could become the means of his own destruction. . . .

☐ **REQUIEM FOR THE CONQUEROR (#1)**   UE2477—$6.99
☐ **RELIC OF EMPIRE (#2)**   UE2492—$5.99
☐ **COUNTERMEASURES (#3)**   UE2564—$5.99

THE SPIDER TRILOGY
For centuries, the Directorate had ruled over countless star systems—but now, as rebellion fueled by advanced technology and a madman's dream spread across the galaxy, the warriors of Spider, descendants of humans stranded centuries ago on an untamed world, could prove the vital key to the survival of human civilization. . . .

☐ **THE WARRIORS OF SPIDER (#1)**   UE2287—$5.50
☐ **THE WAY OF SPIDER (#2)** 01   UE2438—$5.50
☐ **THE WEB OF SPIDER (#3)** 01   UE2356—$4.95

C.J. CHERRYH
THE ALLIANCE-UNION UNIVERSE

S. Andrew Swann

☐ **PROFITEER**   UE2647—$4.99
Book One of Hostile Takeover
In the 24th century, the Human race spans 84 worlds. All but
one accept the rule of the Terran Confederacy . . . Enter now
the world called Bakunin, where anarchy reigns and power
belongs to whoever can seize it. With no taxes, no anti-trust
laws, and no governing body, Bakunin is the perfect home
base for both super-corporations and ruthless criminals. But
now the Confederacy wants a piece of the action—and they're
planning a hostile takeover!

OTHER NOVELS
☐ **FORESTS OF THE NIGHT**   UE2565—$4.50
☐ **EMPERORS OF THE TWILIGHT**   UE2589—$4.50
☐ **SPECTERS OF THE DAWN**   UE2613—$4.50
